Dreams to Ashes

Dreams to Ashes

DORIS ENGLISH

Sweetwater Legacy Series
Dreams to Ashes
Copyright 2015 © Doris Staton English

Published by Maplewood Publishers
Atlanta, Georgia
Cover Art by Jimmy Manor
Photography by Dawn Bloye

ISBN: 978-0-9856132-2-8

First Edition: November 2015

Maplewood Publishers

Dedication

This book is dedicated to my loving family, both those born into it and wedded into it. I stand amazed that our Lord has so blessed one so undeserving as I with the gift of you.

Acknowledgement

Once again, I thank my daughters Dawn and Donna   for their   hours of arduous toil, without which the book would not be a reality. I thank Jen and Jim for their artistic ability and input. I thank my granddaughter, Cara, and my grandson, Jim, for donning civil war garb on a hot summer's day and becoming a perfect _Josh_ and _Laura_ for me.

...give unto them beauty for ashes, the oil of joy for mourning, the
garment of praise for the spirit of heaviness...

ISAIAH 61:3

Chapter One

Andrew stepped out onto the balcony with a steaming cup of coffee in his hand and looked toward ribbons of pink and gold streaking the eastern sky. In the dim light of morning he could see a light mist had rolled in from the river, blanketing the fields below him. He took a deep breath and reveled in the fragrance of fresh plowed earth.

Unwarranted anxiety tripped down his spine, and he shivered. How could he be so blessed? He turned toward the window and saw Rachel's auburn tresses covering his pillow. She must have reached for him in her sleep while he was downstairs getting coffee. Andrew smiled, uneasiness forgotten at the sight of her. It was all he could do not to intrude on her slumber, to awaken her, and to drown in those magnificent eyes.

His early morning ritual, here on the balcony surveying the acres before him while the love of his life slumbered behind him brought him more satisfaction than all the financial mergers and successes that he had ever accomplished.

He shook his head and chuckled quietly. "You're acting like a lovesick schoolboy, Meredith. No way for a man of your age to behave."

Yet how could he quell these emotions she stirred in him? All these years he had put aside the thought of marriage. He had been too busy building an empire, thinking he had discovered the sum total of life. With Daphne managing his household and Aunt Tilde and Laura his makeshift family, he considered himself fulfilled and happy. Until Rachel. Then Rachel standing on a hot Savannah dock invaded his life and turned it upside down. Could it have been only a year? It seemed rather like a lifetime, and then again like yesterday.

What a tumultuous year. He despaired he would ever win her and when he did, she threw his life into an upheaval. Who would have thought that he would walk away from all his success and influence in Savannah, divest himself of his lucrative northern business holdings, abandon Daphne, and settle on a small plantation in northern Georgia with an ill equipped, unprofitable textile mill thrown in for good measure?

Meredith pursed his lips in a moment of truth. Initially he had wanted Sweetwater plantation because Rachel wanted Sweetwater, but he'd have to admit, the old plantation had become important in its own right. The land, the surrounds captivated him. The thrill of restoration seemed to unleash new life in him. The fact that his wife shared that passion was icing on the cake.

A frown creased his forehead and reality crashed in, disturbing his tranquility. The past year had been one of upheaval not only for him personally, but for the entire country. Circumstances looked dim indeed for the South and time appeared short for the changes he needed to make.

Then there was the question of how Rachel would react when he told her his plans. She felt threatened if Sweetwater was threatened, but he could go on no longer with the heartfelt conviction that slavery was wrong and continue to hold slaves that profited him from their bondage.

He had put off telling her, not willing to disturb the idyllic life they had enjoyed these last weeks since finally he had claimed her for his own. He knew he could put it off no longer. Secession and, inevitably, war loomed on the horizon. Today he must tell her and set his plans in motion. He shuddered and turned toward the open doorway and Rachel, dreading for the first time in their married hours to face her. He had to prepare for her future in order to protect her from the disaster that was surely coming.

Moonlight gilded the Savannah waterfront with a mantle of silver, giving it a false ambience of peace and beauty. The city postured in her tarnished splendor that nothing had changed and life would continue on as before. But it was 1860, and in the political gatherings around the nation, the South was in the death throes of survival.

The moon retreated behind a shallow bank of clouds and shrouded the river and docks with a blanket of darkness. Only the gentle swells of the river nuzzling the hull of the Sea Sprite broke the midnight silence.

Agan Chero slipped from the shadows. His dark body stripped to the waist, remained invisible, swallowed by the night. His moccasins moved inaudibly on the cobblestones. A sharp stone pierced his foot, and he grimaced but remained silent and continued on, limping. Suddenly above him wings fluttered. A lonely pigeon, perched in the eave above his head, took flight, stopping him in his tracks.

With a glance behind him, he paused to listen for footsteps or, worse yet, the baying of hounds, but the pounding in his ears pushed out any other sounds. Finally his heart calmed, and he could hear only the slop, slop of the river. Then, in the distance, a dog barked and grew silent.

A breeze wafted in from the river laden with the smell of night and sea mingled with garbage. It felt good to his perspiring body. He continued down the waterfront as rapidly as his throbbing foot would allow. Now hugging closer to the buildings with one eye to the sky, he anxiously gauged his time before the moonlight returned to steal his cover. His fingers touched the tabby walls of an abandoned waterfront shack and relief spread through him. He had reached his destination at last.

A sliver of moon peeked out, casting a pale light beyond him. He pressed his body to the wall and crept toward the door. The rough wall tore at the skin on his hands and chest, but he dismissed the pain, his ears searching for any sound of danger. Finally, he felt the door beneath his outstretched hand and, with one last glimpse behind him, he lifted the reluctant latch. Its rusty, metallic complaints pierced the night and his heart thundered again. He paused to listen, but the night held no other sounds, and he slid into the dark haven of the dank and musty building.

Perspiration lined his brow and dripped rivulets down his face leaving a salty taste on his lips. He wiped the back of his hand and tasted grit. He spat, disgust contorting his face.

Agan's plans had not included participating in a fiasco like tonight. Nor did he relish hiding in a vermin infested waterfront ditch for hours. He shuddered as the stench of stagnant water clinging to his flesh filled his nostrils. It reminded him of his close call with disaster. He owed his escape to luck and nothing else. By all reasoning he should be manacled with those poor devils he had left behind. Luck or no luck, he did not intend to let it happen again. He had to think and plan.

A grim smile parted his face. Maybe he could salvage something of tonight, play it to his advantage. Tonight's episode showed poor planning and weak leadership. Not his. He had followed his instructions to the letter, but somebody somewhere had slipped up. They failed to get the facts straight, or they opened their mouth once too often. Either way it proved a grave error.

He was lucky the slave patrol had been so interested in the poor wretches on the ground that they never looked toward the ditch. He had waited beneath the thick foliage of an ancient live oak tree a few yards away scarcely breathing.

As a precaution, he had arrived early and hidden himself several yards from his assignment. Sheltered by the thick brush overhanging the gully and the shadows cast by the moss draped branches of the tree, he had waited impatiently for his contacts. He recalled tensing with every ripple of the puddled water; fear gripped him that some poisonous nocturnal reptile might slither in beside him.

Tonight's operation had been a catastrophe from the start. His assignment was to assist escapees to a boat hidden on the river and transport them under the cover of darkness to a barrier island where a ship would take them north. Finally, an hour late, two malnourished men and a scrawny teenage girl limped down the road toward his hiding place.

He had paused. Caution dictated that he make certain they had arrived undetected before he revealed himself. While Agan observed the trio with pity, the brush behind them exploded with lights and

11

shouting voices. The weak escapees proved no match for the slave patrol. Soon they were manacled, whimpering, their eyes wide with terror in the dancing lantern lights.

He grimaced as he remembered the patrol trying to beat information out of the escapees; information they didn't have. They only knew that a man they did not know had left them down the road, telling them another would meet them at the crossroads. This man would guide them on to the coast and freedom. As a precautionary measure, their information failed to include how or where.

The ruthless committee waited hours for a contact that they thought never came, but in truth was waiting just a stone's throw from them. Agan's biggest fear rested in the snarling pair of dogs tied tightly to two posts holding up a sagging fence. He grew thankful that the salty breeze filled his nostrils with the scent of unwashed bodies mingled with canine stench. He realized that at any moment the capricious breeze might change, and reveal his presence. His whole body ached from the tension.

After several hours the captors grew impatient and started quarreling among themselves. When they turned their backs toward him, he slithered on his belly from his hiding place and melted into the brush, relieved he was still downwind from the hounds. Even now he shivered at the thought of what might have happened.

The whole plan had seemed a simple procedure but not one that he had relished. To be honest he considered it beneath his dignity even though he had volunteered for the mission. He had hoped it would garner him acceptance and entry into the organization he planned to use to foster his own plans. Up to now the powers that be had looked on him with suspicion because of his enviable position at Balmara. Free to come and go as he pleased, he managed the largest tidewater plantation in the area with little or no supervision. This caused the leadership to question his loyalties. How could he possibly relate to the less fortunate? And worse, why would he risk what he had? Tonight should put all those doubts to rest.

A cunning light warmed the coldness in his eyes. Having participated in tonight's catastrophe and escaping would gain attention and the credibility he needed. When he told his story, all would see the shrewd wit it took to escape and the faulty plan that had led to the calamity in the first place. If he stepped in with another plan and dynamic leadership, he might attain overnight what he thought would take months to achieve.

His ambitions far exceeded smuggling a few renegade slaves to safety. Although that aspect did interest him, his plans embraced a far grander scale. It was not altruism that drove him nor even greed, but a passion born of a resentment burning toward one man. Agan held Andrew Meredith, wealthy entrepreneur and plantation owner, solely responsible for standing in the way of the one thing he had desired more than life itself.

He shook his head as topaz eyes sparking angry, amber lights invaded his thoughts. His face contorted in pain as he remembered their last meeting and her rejection of him. He could almost feel the warmth of her breath against his cheek as he held her against her will. His fingers had dug into her soft flesh resistant to his touch as he tried to force her to acknowledge the love she had once felt for him. It was then in the darkened passageway at Balmara that he vowed he would have his revenge and his plan was born.

His brain whirred in excitement as once again the lovely face and form with golden skin and topaz eyes teased his memory. Daphne was the missing key to his success. Would her fiery eyes look at him with longing again, instead of hostility? If she did, his plan would be impervious to failure. Smoldering embers ignited his eyes as he reveled in her beauty. The tragic events of the night receded momentarily in the rush of emotion she always stirred in him.

When he was in control, assisting poor wretched bodies to a better life would be just one small piece of the larger puzzle, the necessary stepping-stone to his power. He had no doubt that with Daphne at his side he would be in command, sooner than later. He believed with all his heart that the amber-eyed beauty was the key to a rapid success, tonight simply presented the opportunity for advancement. As soon as he achieved his goal, Andrew Meredith and his crowd would experience their due comeuppance.

He gloated silently, knowing that when she returned home she would no longer be under the watchful eye of her wealthy patron. Without his protection life as she had known it would be over, and then she would need Agan. Harsh reality alone would force her to come to him for whom else would she have? Then victory on two fronts would be his.

His tongue darted out licking his lips. To conquer Daphne would be a just recompense for all her years of hostile rejection to his advances. Tonight, like a ripe plum, fate had dropped her future and his into his hands, and he was eager to seize the moment.

Daphne stared out the window as the landscape whirled past the train's window. The train hurtled southward away from Andrew Meredith and his new bride. Daphne had done her due diligence. She had supervised the arrangements, and the wedding went smoothly.

Now Andrew had embarked on a new life, one away from her.

She watched the clay hills of northern Georgia give way to sandy plains. The lush hardwood forests had changed gradually to one of slash pines interspersed with broad fields of cotton plants nodding their yet tender heads in the brisk westerly breeze. Each strike of wheel against rail brought her closer to the moss draped live oaks of coastal Georgia and her uncertain future.

Unwillingly a sigh escaped, and the golden haired giant beside her stirred. He glanced at her and for an instant she noted her pain mirrored in his brilliant blue eyes. Then it was gone, his eyes dulled, his emotions curtained in a manufactured indifference. Only the husky timbre of his voice revealed the war of relinquishment going on within him as he asked, "What did you say, Daphne?"

She shook her head slightly, "I said nothing, Mr. Philip."

A strained silence had prevailed in the private car provided for their convenience by her employer, shipping magnate, Andrew Meredith. The painful emotions that buffeted both separated them. Then, bridging the self-imposed gap, Philip took Daphne's small hand between his two great paws, tenderness softening his gaze.

"I don't want you to be worrying child. As long as I'm around you'll come to no harm."

She pulled her hand from his and looked away, not willing that he should see the tears that threatened the cool, aloof Daphne.... "I'm not a child, and it is time for me to look after myself. Isn't that what you and Mr. Andrew have been preaching to me?"

"No, that is not what we've been telling you."

"You said my position with the Merediths had crippled me. Have you changed your mind?" Her lips curved slightly in an attempted smile that failed to reach her eyes.

15

"You've twisted my meaning."

"That's what you said-----!!!"

"Said to Andrew, not to you. Don't you know I was trying to wake the man up? His attachment to you was ruining both your lives. You have too much to offer the world in beauty and talent to stifle it in a sacrificial service to someone who doesn't need it." Philip's voice rose in exasperation.

The beautiful woman beside him flinched slightly, then raised her eyes to him, defiantly, "I chose the only course open to me."

"That's ridiculous, Daphne. You chose what seemed to be the safest course."

"Not safest, only."

"If that were true, my dear, then you would be adrift because Andrew Meredith is no longer available to look after you, and he has a wife to look after him."

"I'm well aware of those facts, Mr. Philip." Pain flickered in Daphne's eyes, but she continued to hold his eyes, never wavering.

"However painful the facts may prove to you, acceptance is your only solution. When you can face them, then you are ready to plan the rest of your life and I am eager to assist you."

"I still have Miz Maltilda and Miss Laura to think of."

"Only temporary responsibilities, Daphne. Soon they will move to Sweetwater to be with Andrew and Rachel, and then what will you do?" His gaze held hers, willing her to face the truth.

"I'll find work at another plantation. I'm sure someone could use my skills. Even you might find you need them." She retorted, lifting her chin with determination.

"Oh yes, I could use your skill and wisdom. You would make my life a thousand times easier as I assume new ownership of Balmara."

Philip agreed easily.

"Well, hire me. I've spent all my adult years managing the household affairs of the largest tidewater plantation in the area, which now happens to be yours. You will have your hands full managing the business affairs and unlike Mr. Andrew, you have no wife."

"Not only would it be self-serving to hire you, but to keep you from your destiny would be the gravest of offenses." Philip responded, his voice pleading.

"Destiny?" She questioned.

"Yes, the fulfillment of your hopes and dreams."

"My dream? I never dared to dream."

"No hopes, no dreams, my dear?"

"Hopes and dreams? That's a luxury that someone like me can ill afford. I learned early in life not to dream, then disappointment won't destroy you."

"How bitter you are for one so young."

"Not bitter, realistic. You refuse to take into account that this is the South, and I am a free woman of color set adrift."

"God- given talent is not determined by the color of one's skin."

"Opportunities are. Maybe it's different in England, but in the South, skin color dictates all of life. A black person is never 'free' in the way you are. We have to register our presence if we even go to another community. If they don't want us, we can only stay a specified time. We are no more than aliens in the only country most of us have ever known."

"Must you be so stubborn? You are a gifted artist."

"No, I am a black artist."

"I told you that won't matter."

"It does matter. My world will accept my being free only if I remain in my station. They will accept me as a seamstress, not an artist, a cook, not an entrepreneur. I can make them clothes to cover their nakedness and cook food for their bellies, but to step up into the arts and the finer things of life is forbidden to me. I'm willing to accept that and to do whatever it takes, no matter how menial, to carve out a life. I will do this for one reason alone, I would never want to stand in the way of Mr. Andrew's happiness."

"Andrew's happiness is a noble motivation, Daphne, but that is not enough. You must see your future through you own potential!"

"What potential? Do you think that white Savannah would be interested in anything I have to offer?" Cynicism tinged Daphne's soft tones.

"The world is broader than Savannah."

Suddenly, the bravado left Daphne and she dropped her head, her voice almost a whisper, "But my world is Savannah. It is here that I must make my life and I can see no future for me."

"Come on now, Daphne, you know Andrew provided you a lovely studio and apartment facing the river." Philip's voice rose, impatience sharpening his countenance.

"Most generous of him. But then what?"

"I will be your patron and protector. I'll open doors for you. I want to invest in your future."

"And what benefits do you expect from this investment, Mr. Philip?" Daphne's topaz eyes turned hard, suspicion a cold light in them.

Philip's azure blue eyes darkened, anger flared in them, "Not one thing but your happiness."

"Why are you interested in my happiness?"

"Because you have value as a person, Daphne, and beyond that you have an exquisite, God-given talent that I don't want to see wasted."

Daphne's eyes narrowed, still unbelieving. "Why would you give me your help without wanting anything in return?"

Philip's full laughing mouth tightened, impatience fired his eyes. "I feel the responsibility of discovery. When I happened on your paintings hidden away in that alcove at Balmara, I knew that I had found something created by someone with extraordinary talent."

"If you become my patron I will just trade my dependence on one man for another." She shook her head slightly,

"No, it won't be the same at all. I will assist you in establishing your life, not absorb you into my life."

"You mean like you accused Mr. Andrew of doing?" Her topaz eyes darkened, hostile.

"Not accused, confronted him with the truth. Why can't you see there was nothing malicious in my actions? I only had your interest and Andrew's at heart."

"And Miss Rachel?"

Philip paused and looked away from her, grieving the death of his own dream. The silence hung heavy between them, almost tangible. Then he sighed, a smile curling his lip upwards while not extinguishing the sad light in his eyes. "If you remember when I said those things, Rachel hadn't entered the picture."

"If she had, would you have been so quick to 'set Mr. Andrew free' from me?" Daphne responded, her voice tinged with bitterness.

Philip bit the corner of his lip before answering, his eyes pleaded, vulnerable to Daphne's probing "It would have been tempting not to, but I know that happiness is never found by sacrificing someone else's hopes and dreams."

Daphne shrugged and dropped her head, "For those who are allowed no dreams, sometimes it is enough to assist the privileged to attain theirs. Helping Mr. Andrew succeed was all that I ever wanted in life."

"But were you happy, fulfilled?"

"Happy? I was safe."

"Now you are free to have more than safety. You can fulfill your potential."

"What potential?"

"Your gifted ability to make life come alive with your paintings. With a gift comes a grave responsibility not to waste it. What's happened in your life is an opportunity not a tragedy."

"It's easy for you to say that, Mr. Philip. You have a whole new challenge for you. You are a British nobleman about to become a Southern plantation owner. It's not your life that has been ripped apart," Daphne fired back, then flinched when she encountered the raw pain in his eyes.

"Not my life, just my heart," Philip responded, fighting to bring his emotions under control.

"Then we both have Rachel Meredith to thank for our situations." Her soft voice took on a hard edge. "When I saw her that first day on the Savannah dock, I sensed life would never be the same."

"How's that?"

"Call it intuition or ----."

"Or what?" Philip probed.

"The way Mr. Andrew looked at her." Daphne closed her eyes as if to banish the scene.

"Love is a capricious element. Who can account for its choices? It may be that someday both of us will thank her for loving Andrew instead of me." Philip commented sadly, his guard down.

"And until then?" her eyes opened wide, questioning.

"Until then, let me help you pursue a dream."

Chapter Two

Laura Meredith shrieked from the landing, "Aunt Tilde, Aunt Tilde!" Then she bounded up the stairs as fast as her skirts would permit. Finally hoisting them up and revealing two shapely ankles, she took the steps two at a time.

Reaching Maltilda Burnsides' closed door, she slowed to a lady like stroll. She tried to smooth hair and dress before she knocked and modulated in a softer tone, "Aunt Tilde, are you up? I've just received a post from Uncle Andrew. He's making arrangements for our move and is expecting us to leave next week."

Excitement glowed in the young woman's eyes, her voice barely in control. Only silence greeted her and her blue eyes took on a puzzled look.

"Aunt Matilda, did you hear me? Uncle Drew wants us packed and ready to go by the first of next week."

Still she heard no response behind the closed door, Laura knocked and entered.

"Aunt Tilde!" Laura screamed as she saw the frail body of her aunt crumpled in the floor, her voluminous dressing gown covering her like a mantle.

Laura rushed toward her all the while shrieking for Daphne. Reaching her aunt's side, she fell to the floor and placed her arms beneath the shoulders of the only mother she had ever known. Lifting her, she caressed her aunt's face, tears streaming down her own. Then she tenderly grasped the small, cold hand, its skin like thin parchment and stared into the open, unseeing eyes.

The door opened, and Daphne swished in, efficient and questioning, her face showing distaste for Laura's usual emotional exuberance. Then she stopped short at the scene before her. Two dark faces peered in at the door behind her, their eyes wide, unwilling to enter the room.

Daphne knelt beside Laura, her strong fingers searching for a pulse in Maltilda's thin neck. Laura looked up expectantly, hoping for a miracle, then screamed when Daphne shook her head.

She pulled her aunt tightly to her bosom and sobbed out of control, "Aunt Tilde, Aunt Tilde, what am I to do? Don't leave me. I'll be alone. I'm sorry, I'm so sorry I caused you so much trouble. Don't leave me! I'll be good. I'll act like the lady you want me to be."

Finally, Daphne grasped Laura's shoulders, "Turn her loose, Miss Laura. Your crying won't bring her back. Nothing will. Get hold of yourself. You're the lady of the house and now you have decisions to make."

Laura turned toward the young woman, "What decisions? She's not dead, she's just sleeping."

"She's gone, Miss Laura. Her heart has stopped beating."

"And it's all my fault. I should have listened to her, not caused her so much trouble."

"It's not anyone's fault. Death is a fact of life. Miz Matilda was old and her heart was weak. All of us will face death one day."

Laura stared at Daphne, a sudden flash of anger exploding in her eyes, "Do you have ice water in your veins, Daphne? She was good to you and you don't even care that she is gone."

"On the contrary, Miss Laura, I cared a great deal for Miz Matilda, but that doesn't alter the fact. Death is certain and her health was very fragile."

"Oh, I can see that you really care. Don't you have any emotions, Daphne?"

"Showing my emotions is a luxury in life that I've never allowed myself. And I might add, it is time you learn to bring yours under control."

"What a mean thing to say to me!" Laura shouted.

"Sometimes the truth does seem rather cruel."

"What truth?"

"You are no longer a child, and you need to start acting like who you are."

"How dare you talk to me like that!"

"I dare because you have to assume certain responsibilities."

"Responsibilities? Not now. I've just lost my aunt. She was like a mother to me. Don't you have an ounce of compassion in you, Daphne?" Laura sobbed as she clutched the body of her aunt even more tightly.

"I have compassion, but you have a job to do, and, you will do it."

"I can't"

"You will. Now lay Miz Maltilda down and stand up."

"No, no, no." Laura buried her face in her aunt's hair, weeping.

"We have to get her back on the bed and prepare her body."

23

"For what?"

"For burial, what else?"

"I don't want to bury her. Maybe she isn't dead. Go get the doctor."

"Now you're thinking, Miss Laura. We have to get her on the bed, then send for the doctor."

"O.K. call Agan."

"No, Miss Laura, you and I will put her on the bed."

"Why can't someone else do that?" Laura shuddered as she surrendered the body of her aunt.

"Because it is your responsibility."

"And yours?"

"Yes, and mine." Their eyes met across the lifeless body between them and, in that moment, resolution dawned in Laura, initiating her transformation from child to woman.

After the doctor had left and the body prepared, Daphne went to Laura's room. "Miss Laura, you must plan the services for Miss Matilda."

"Won't you do that? I don't know how to begin."

"I'll plan the food for the wake and the guests, but you are responsible now. Until Miz Rachel comes, you are the lady of the house"

"Rachel? Coming here?" Laura dried her eyes and stood up.

"Of course, Mr. Andrew will bring his wife with him."

"How will we get in touch with him?"

"We'll send for Mr. Philip. He'll take care of everything."

"Oh, yes, Philip. What would we have done without him these past weeks?"

"I can't imagine."

"Will Uncle Andrew be able to get here before the funeral?"

"Yes, and you must be ready to return with them."

"But what of you, Daphne? Aren't you and Agan coming with us?"

"No. Agan will stay here to assist Mr. Philip in running Balmara."

"And you? Will you stay on here and assist Philip, also?"

"I'll be moving to town."

"But Philip will need you."

"Nevertheless, I shall leave when you do."

Impulsively Laura threw her arms around the aloof Daphne and exclaimed, "But whatever will I do without you?"

Daphne smiled, amusement lightening the sorrow in her eyes for a moment, "Very nicely, I'm sure. Miss Rachel will see to that."

"Is that good or bad?" Laura asked, her eyes, red from weeping, now wary.

Daphne paused, then chuckled mirthlessly, "You'll have to decide that for yourself."

"But Aunt Matilda loved her."

"Yes, Miss Matilda admired her."

"But Aunt Tilde loved everyone."

"That's right. Her approval was not difficult to win."

"And what about you, Daphne, do you like her?"

"To approve or disapprove of your uncle's new wife is not my privilege or responsibility," Daphne answered sharply, then added as she swished out the door, "but I think Miz Rachel is just what you need."

Laura paced the station's waiting room, giving an impatient glance down the tracks as if she could speed up the train's arrival. "Philip, are you sure the telegram said 2:00 p.m? What if they are delayed?"

A patient smile curved the generous mouth of the handsome

blond giant, affection igniting his azure eyes, "Laura, they won't be delayed. It is only 1:00 p.m. We came early in case they arrived early. Now settle down. You have done a herculean job this week and I am so proud of you. Come sit here beside me."

"You mean Daphne and I did."

"Yes, you and Daphne."

"Oh, Philip! What am I ever going to do without Daphne? I'll never be able to manage without her. What was Uncle Andrew thinking leaving her here?"

"You forget that you will have Rachel." A brief sadness dimmed the light in Philip's eyes.

"That's what frightens me."

Philip laughed, "You're afraid of Rachel?"

"Just that she won't like me or maybe with Aunt Tilde gone she would rather not have Uncle Andrew's niece to look after."

"She is not like that. You will be welcomed with open arms. In fact you both have some similar characteristics."

"Oh? Hope they are not conflicting characteristics."

"Hmm. Now that's a thought. You are both beautiful and have a zest for living."

"You know I was away in Virginia when she arrived in Savannah so I have never met her. I keep asking Daphne about her but she is so closed lipped about her. Will you tell me? Is she very beautiful?" Laura asked glancing in the waiting room looking glass, her thoughts turned in a different direction.

"Very beautiful," Philip answered, his voice husky.

Hearing his change in tone, Laura turned toward him just in time to see pain flicker in his eyes, "Philip, you love her!!"

"At one time, I did."

26

"Why did you stop loving her?"

"She became another man's wife."

"You mean you and Uncle Andrew both loved her?" Laura's eyes widened.

"That's correct. She chose Andrew and I will commit my affection for her to assuring she and my friend have a happy marriage."

"Oh, what a tragic romance. Surely you're not done with love and will find another." Laura sighed, her young mind suddenly intrigued with romantic possibilities.

"I wouldn't say I'm done. Maybe I'll wait for you to grow up. How would you like to live in England and be a duchess?"

"Me, a duchess?" Laura rolled her eyes. "Do they like to climb trees?"

"I hardly think you will always want to climb trees."

"Not if Uncle Andrew has anything to do with it. You know he is sending me to boarding school in the fall to see if they can turn me into a lady."

"That is a good idea as long as they don't suppress that spontaneity for life that makes you so delightful."

With an abrupt change of subject, Laura asked, "What is a duke? Is that what a duchess' husband is called?"

Philip chuckled at her exuberance and nodded, "A duchess is what a duke's wife is called."

"And you are a duke?"

"I will be one when my father dies."

"What does it all mean?"

"A title that is handed down along with estates and houses to look after." Philip shrugged.

"You don't look very happy about it. Don't you want to be a duke?"

"It is not a question of what I want to do, it is what I must do. I'm an only son and I have a role to fill. Many people's welfare will be dependent on me."

"Hmph. Nobody is going to force me to do anything when I'd rather do something else." Laura said tossing her head.

"That, little lady, is a dangerous thing to say and very childish." Philip challenged.

"But I'm not a child anymore." Laura objected pursing her lips.

Philip smiled, "Even adults make childish comments sometimes."

"Why do you think what I said was childish?"

"Because adulthood should mean making responsible choices and that means we sometimes have to do what we are supposed to do rather than what we want to do."

"Like this week?"

"Yes, like this week. You acted very responsibly in making very difficult plans when I know that's not what you wanted to do. Andrew will be very proud of you."

"You think so?"

"I know so. He may not tell you because his heart will be hurting, but later on he will think about it and be so proud. You couldn't have done a better job."

"It definitely wasn't something I wanted to do. In fact I really tried to make Daphne take care of it, but she wouldn't hear of it. So there, you see we are back to Daphne and how much I need her and how terrible I think Uncle Drew is for sending her away and you, too, for not keeping her on at Balmara. You really do need her."

"Daphne is a very gifted young woman; as long as she is looking after Drew or even me, her gifts would go unfulfilled."

"I know she can paint, but she told me she does that for fun. You just said that adult means doing what you are supposed to do rather than what you want to do. Shouldn't she continue to look after Uncle Drew and me?"

"How do you think Rachel would feel about that?"

"Aunt Maltilda was satisfied with that arrangement."

Philip laughed aloud at Laura's reasoning, "How would you feel if you were in Rachel's place?"

Laura wrinkled her nose and thought a moment, "I wouldn't want some beautiful woman looking after my husband and my home."

"Now you are beginning to understand."

"But Daphne must feel horrible to be tossed out after years of service at Balmara. She does a perfect job running the place, supervising the servants. Only she and Agan seem to clash sometimes." Laura's voice dropped to merely above a whisper, "I think Agan is in love with her."

Philip rubbed his chin, his eyes alert, "That's an interesting observation. I never noticed."

"Sure! That's just like a man. I wager Uncle Drew never noticed either."

"Do you think she returns his affection?"

"Absolutely not. Fact is she seems to dislike him."

"And why do you think that is?" Philip probed, his interest sparked.

"I'm not sure, but it seems to be something that happened between them that Daphne can't forgive him for. You know they grew up together. You'd think she would return his affection; they have so much in common. They are from the West Indies and Uncle Drew educated and gave both of them their freedom. But it is obvious to me that Agan lost his chance with her for some reason."

"And you don't have any idea of what happened?"

"No, and that's why I feel so sorry for her. She has no love in her life and now Uncle Drew is taking away her identity, you might say-- her reason for living."

"Don't you see, little one, that's why he had to do it?"

Laura shook her head.

"A person's identity and who they are can't be wrapped up in someone else. Daphne's whole personhood was bound up in what she did for your uncle. Although it was never right, it became most inappropriate when he took a wife. It presented an intolerable situation for her, Andrew and Rachel."

"Couldn't you remedy that by keeping her on at Balmara? You don't have a wife to object."

"No, but society would."

"Oh, poo! Are you talking about what people said behind Uncle Drew's back?"

Philip's brow wrinkled with surprise, "What do you know about that?"

"I overheard some silly women talking, and then my friend, or formerly my friend, said that she was more than a housekeeper, whatever that meant."

Philip's brow wrinkled. "And what else did they say?"

"Only that she was very beautiful and very well treated, but I understood that they were alluding to some kind of evil goings on. I didn't give Mary Jane a chance to go any further and that's when she stopped being my friend. Uncle Drew is a good man and he treats everyone well. He hardly does more for Daphne than he does for Agan."

"Laura, can you not understand that is one of the reasons I can't have her at Balmara as much as I would like to retain her services."

"Uncle Drew didn't give in to gossiping old women."

"Maybe I wouldn't be inclined to either, but I have a heartfelt conviction that Daphne needs to be a person in her own right, that she needs to recognize her own worth, to be her own person regardless of anyone else."

"And how can she do that?"

"By making her own way with her God-given gift."

"In the South?" Laura reminded, her comprehension surprising Philip.

"With my help."

"So then you are saying you are going to fill Uncle Drew's shoes, just in a different way."

"No, because she is a free woman of color, she needs a sponsor here in the south. I will be that sponsor. I have lined up potential customers for her art in Boston but she will not be living her life vicariously through me. Drew, along with you and Aunt Tilde, were her life. That has crippled her, I want to set her free."

Laura shook her head, "I know you have good intentions, Philip, but this is the South and things are looked at differently down here."

The twinkle in Philip's eyes dimmed in response to Laura's observation. He rose from the bench and turned toward the door facing the track, thus avoiding Laura's gaze. Walking to the door, he paused and stared down the track. In the distance a whistle blew, heralding the imminent arrival of Andrew and Rachel. His heart lurched at the thought of seeing her again as doubts bombarded his usually confident heart. Could he place his own feelings aside when the love for her burned every fiber of his being? He shook his head. No matter the cost to him emotionally, she was another man's wife, and he would be loyal to his friend, true to his own convictions.

And what about Daphne? Could he rescue her? Or were both Daphne and Laura correct in saying southern mores would prevent his success?

Philip squared his shoulders, a solemn look in his eyes. With a forced smile on his lips, he held his hand out toward Laura, bidding her to join him as the train pulled into the station.

Laura rushed forward as she spied Andrew step from the train. Suddenly she paused and drew back in awe as he turned to give his hand to the exquisite creature just behind him.

Philip reached out and resolutely took Laura's arm, gently moving her forward toward a defining moment for both. Then pausing, they watched as Andrew's loving gaze enveloped the woman. Tears welled up in Laura's eyes as she took in the tender scene before her. The transformation was undeniable...Uncle Drew was a different man. Was this beauty beside him responsible for this change?

Laura glanced up at Philip and her heart wrenched as she saw the unvarnished pain in his eyes fastened on the couple who seemed oblivious to the world around them. Philip dropped his head and his gaze met Laura's. Determination masked the pain and a half smile parted his face as he advanced toward the stunning couple. "Come on, Laura, it's time for you to meet the newest member of your family and me to greet my dearest friends."

Chapter Three

"Laura, I am so proud of you and all the work that you have done. This was a colossal job, a job which I was dreading. You handled the arrangements for Aunt Tilde perfectly. You left nothing for me to do."

"You forget that Daphne was a big part of it," Laura reminded.

"Daphne told me that you did the lion's share of all the planning."

"I could have never done it without her," Laura protested.

"Of course Daphne helped you, but you shouldered the responsibility like a trooper," Andrew sighed. "It's just hard for me to accept that you're growing up. But not away from me, I hope."

"That's up to you, Uncle Drew. Do I have a place in your new life?"

"Most assuredly. Rachel is eager to have you join us at Sweetwater, and you know how I feel about it."

"But only for a short while. Then you want to send me away to school."

"Rachel and I discussed that. She feels that you should make that decision. She remembers how she felt when her father packed her off to school."

Laura's eyes brightened at his words, then pursing her lips, she replied, "You know Uncle Drew, I've fought you all the way about going off to school."

"I know, and I told Rachel there will be no future school for Laura if she is allowed to decide for herself," Andrew chuckled.

"Well, guess what?"

"I can't imagine. You tell me."

"I have decided that although I don't want to go to school, I need the experience."

"You what-----?"

"You heard me correctly. I am going on to school as we planned before Aunt Tilde died."

"Now what brought about that change of heart?"

"Not a change of heart, but a change of mind."

"I am all ears."

"First of all, I think as a newly married couple, you need the time and space together without any outsiders… ."

"Now, that's not true, Laura," Andrew protested.

"No, it is true, Uncle Drew even though both you and Rachel have gone out of your way to let me know how much you would welcome me. But during these past days I've observed that beautiful wife of yours. If school will transform me into a lady like she is, one who knows all about correct behavior yet has her own mind and determination, I think it would benefit me greatly."

Andrew smiled and shook his head as he took one of Laura's hands and drew her into his embrace, "What a treasure you are, and how much you have matured. I am so proud of the woman you are becoming."

"I want so much to make you proud, Uncle Andrew. Aunt Tilde's death made me realize how really important family is and how much I had taken for granted her love and yours. I'm so glad that you found Rachel, and I look forward to the day that God will bring that special someone into my life to love as you love her."

Andrew's voice grew husky, "I never imagined what I was missing and my prayer is that you, too, will experience such a blessing."

"Meanwhile, I want to prepare myself for that day."

"You will come back with us?"

"Oh, yes, I'm already packed up and ready to go whenever you want to start back. I can't wait to see Sweetwater. Rachel has told me so much about it and how she grew up there. I want to explore every inch of it."

"School starts in a couple of months, and you won't have a lot of time to, you know."

Laura sighs, "I said I was going, and it was the right thing to do…I didn't say I was looking forward to it."

Andrew's face grew serious, "Laura, you know Aunte Tilde wanted you to go to that school in Virginia, the very same one that Rachel attended. That's a long way from home and the political situation doesn't look very encouraging."

"You think that will have any effect on me?"

"I greatly fear that everyone in our country will feel the effects of what's going on in the halls of Washington."

"So what are you thinking?"

"I'm planning for the worst and hoping for the best. If war comes, I will want you to come home. I can't protect you up in Virginia. If I go to war, I want you to stay with Rachel and assist her. Meanwhile, I am making plans for our survival after the war."

"War? Are you serious? You really think there will be a war?"

"If Lincoln is elected, the South will secede. When the states secede, war will come."

A sense of foreboding caused a chill to run down Laura's spine. "Oh, Uncle Drew!"

His lips curled in an unhappy smile. "We'll make it, sweetheart, but we must be prepared. Life as we have known it will be over."

***

Philip watched as the train pulled away, his heart heavy with loss but comforted by the knowledge that Rachel was happy and content. His next assignment would be difficult. As soon as Daphne had all Balmara's furnishings that were going to Sweetwater packed up and her own things ready to go, he had to settle her in her new surrounds. Her stoic composure denied the anguish that he knew was ripping her apart inside.

Andrew had provided well for her. Her townhouse on the river was spacious and well appointed. He had told her to take whatever furnishings from Balmara that she wanted and to decorate it however she saw fit, that money was no object.

Understated and lovely, the decor represented exquisite taste. There was a large studio with wide windows facing the river and bringing in plenty of light. Philip had seen to that. He was determined that she have everything that she needed to promote her new life.

Daphne had been diligent in every aspect of her new venture, but there lacked any enthusiasm in her endeavor. She followed orders, did what was expected of her, but her heart was not in it.

Philip remained convinced that she would adjust and thrive in her new environment once she settled in. Through it all, he could not help but question Andrew's largesse in providing for her. Was it guilt, guilt that he had shackled her to his life and convenience without considering her gifts and potential, or was it guilt about something else, some dark secret? He shook his head. He would not go there; he refused to entertain evil thoughts against his friend and Rachel's husband. Andrew Meredith was a man of honor, who acted honorably in all circumstances. He refused to believe the vicious gossip that was whispered in the finer homes of Savannah.

Daphne paused and looked out the broad windows. From her vantage she could see Meredith ships gently swaying as the oncoming tide rushed up the river. Soon those ships would be on their way back to Boston and in the hold would be a crate holding several of her paintings. Mr. Philip seemed to believe they would be a quick sale. In fact, the curator of the gallery assured him of it. But what about the artist, he had asked. He wanted to meet the woman who had such an exquisite gift.

She sighed. She should feel exuberance. Had she really suppressed a secret desire to be recognized for her art? If so, then her dream was about to be realized. Mr. Phillip had insisted but she had resisted, refusing to acknowledge it. And yet, something inside her yearned for that indefinable something. He had said that a God-given talent was a responsibility. She thought it was merely an outlet, an amusement. She believed that her real goal in life was taking care of Andrew Meredith.

Mr. Phillip was correct about one thing. Mr. Andrew didn't need her anymore, and she had to embrace a new life. So here she was surrounded by unimaginable luxury for a woman of color and it all was hers. Although the title was in her benefactor's name, he had told her it was hers, the furnishings given to her along with a monthly stipend that any wealthy white woman would envy. Except for the several hours of public service each month that the law required of her, she was free to paint to her heart's content. So where was the exhilaration?

Loneliness crept over her. Life was more than possessions, even more than accomplishment. What were achievements in life with no one with whom to share them? Andrew Meredith had discovered that on a hot river front dock little more than a year ago. She had been there to witness the experience.

He had found that a full life included a family of his own, a spouse to love, perhaps children to look forward to. But what about her? Where was her family? When she was mistress of Balmara, her world was there... they were her family. More to the point, Andrew Meredith was her world. Now, he was gone.

She had no friends. Her own people refused to accept her. Her skin was a shade too light for them and the advantages provided for her set her apart. They didn't trust her. As far as the white world, she received only scorn and ridicule except from the Meredith family and Mr. Philip .

It was time for her to reflect, to look at her life, her dreams and goals.

She had told Mr. Philip that she had none, but that wasn't quite true. From the time Andrew Meredith had rescued her and showered her with kindness, her goal in life was to repay him with devotion and service. Now, he didn't need her anymore.

She, too, had questioned the life he had given her. Only a teenager when he rescued her from the islands after her mother's death, he had freed her and treated her with the same care one would give a family member. He seemed devoted to her welfare without expecting anything in return. The question was, why?

Something from her past tugged at her memory. Suddenly a vision of her mother whispering to Andrew Meredith in a hut, the heat stifling, taunted her. A specter from that long-ago day lay trapped in her mind, buried in the anguish that had tortured her soul as her mother lay dying. What was it? What could her mother have said that could have garnered her daughter a life such as this? She shook her head. The answer refused to come. She had speculated but revelation remained just beyond her reach. Andrew Meredith was a good man, but good as he was why would he choose voluntarily to take on the responsibility of a young teenage girl?

As she grew older, she gradually assumed responsibilities in household duties. Finally when Miss Maltilda's health had failed, she had stepped seamlessly into the management role. The role fit her like a glove. She excelled at managing plantation affairs, both finances and staff. In so doing she had enjoyed a sense of fulfillment which was made all the sweeter knowing that she helped shoulder some of Andrew Meredith's burden. Now someone else was to fulfill that role, and she felt cut adrift. Time to move on. But to where? How?

Did the way she felt prove Philip right after all, that Andrew Meredith had set her free only to hold her captive in his world? She turned her head and her eyes surveyed her surroundings. Was all this an attempt to assuage his guilt?

She shook her head. Guilt for what? Rescuing a young girl from a future of unspeakable evil? Treating her with respect and honor? Giving her an education that was equal or better than any woman in

Savannah?

Daphne knew the ugly comments that all Savannah whispered. Yet they were all lies. He had never made any untoward demands of her. As for her feelings for him, as odd as it might seem, she had never felt anything but a deep affection and appreciation to her benefactor. He was handsome, no doubt about that, but he had never made her heart race as Agan had.

A frown furrowed her brow as the memories of the hours of tutoring in languages, math, and literature brought green eyes and his handsome face to mind. She remembered pleasant times of laughter and sharing with someone her own age. The one who, at one time, had set her heart to racing, now brought only chills of apprehension running up and down her spine.

Agan Chero came from the Islands along with her. Andrew Meredith had freed him and educated him along by her side. He, too, had assumed the responsibilities of plantation management. He managed the outside, while she managed the inside, relieving Andrew of the additional burdens of day-to-day operations. He trusted them both. He had proved equally giving to both, only Daphne responded in appreciation, Agan in resentment.

What had happened to her young fun loving companion? Searching her heart, she acknowledged the source of his resentment. It was she. He had loved her once, maybe still did but he fought against her devotion to Andrew. Then he began to believe the vicious lies told about their relationship. She tried to convince him that there was nothing evil in her relationship with their employer, but it proved fruitless.

As a result she turned away from him, shielding her heart and emotions. He had aborted what was the beginning of the love she had felt toward him. It gradually turned to disgust as she watched him hate his benefactor and began to seek ways to betray him.

Pain flickered in her eyes as regret for what might have been visited her heart. She and Agan would have made a handsome couple. They were well matched in intellect and ability. If circumstances had turned out differently, she would have her own family by now. And a home. Perhaps it would not be this luxurious, but it would not be a lonely palace of empty dreams.

But were they empty dreams? In that ship rested a promising tomorrow. Perhaps Mr. Philip was right in another area as well. Maybe there would be a future and someone with whom to share her dreams.

A knock interrupted her melancholy thoughts. She turned and made her way toward the expansive double doors that led to the street outside. In the waning light she could see the outline of a large man through the ornate leaded glass doors. Daphne opened the door and suddenly her pensive melancholy imagery became real.

"Hello, Daphne."

"What do you want, Agan?"

"Is that any way to greet a visitor? I wanted to be one of the first to welcome you to Savannah." He chuckled, knowing he would probably be the only one who would welcome her.

"So you've welcomed me."

"May I come in? I'd like to see this palatial abode that has all of Savannah talking." Agan taunted as he pushed his way in.

"Be my guest." Daphne stepped aside, her eyes downcast, her voice icy with sarcasm.

Agan looked at her with a half smile and grabbed her chin forcing her to meet his eyes, "You know I would like to be much more than a casual visitor."

"That opportunity has long passed."

"Maybe it is time we started anew." He released her chin, dropping his hand and walking into her studio, looked around.

Daphne braced herself for the caustic comments to follow. None came.

Agan nodded his head. "Quite impressive. I can see your understated touch. Just right. This is your studio, I presume?"

Daphne shrugged, "I suppose you could call it that."

"Where is your latest work?"

"Nothing yet."

"Where are your paintings?"

"I don't have them displayed." She demurred, not willing to let him know that most were on the ship to Boston.

"Your living quarters downstairs?"

"Yes, I reversed the usual so I could take better advantage of the light."

"That's a good idea. Can I see the rest?"

Memories of a dark passage and Agan's hands pinioning her arms behind her back as he whispered threats in her ear swept over Daphne. She shook her head, a cold smile tilted one side of her mouth, "I don't think so. Save that for another time."

Agan smiled warmly, "One I greatly anticipate."

"We'll see." Daphne commented, clearly ending the conversation and visit.

"I'll be going now. Just wanted to drop in and see how you are doing."

Agan turned toward the door, then paused and leaned in toward her, warm lights in his eyes, "Daphne, somewhere along the way we got off track. I want to find my way back. Do you think there is any chance?"

"You know where we got off track. It was your resentment and betrayal toward a man who had done you no harm, but only good."

"Betrayal? Perhaps resentment, but not betrayal. I worked hard for him." Agan defended. "Without my efforts his plantation would not have been so profitable."

"My question to you is did he receive all his profits?"

"All that he needed. He seemed satisfied."

"I don't doubt that you are an excellent manager. I know that he was pleased with his revenue, but how much went into your coffers? Only you know of the extent of your betrayal."

"I assure you there was no betrayal; only, I guess if what you have told me is true, it was misplaced resentment that drove me."

"I told you the truth." Daphne insisted.

Agan shrugged his shoulders, "Then we will leave it so. Only try to understand that when you love someone as I love you, anyone who gets in the way is a threat to be reckoned with."

"Loved. That's in the past."

"Not for me. Maybe for you, thanks to Andrew Meredith. "

"He didn't get in the way."

"Your devotion to him did."

"Can't you understand the obligation I felt toward him? He saved my life and cared for me."

"That's my point. His care for you and what that entailed."

"Entailed? What do you mean by that?"

"In exchange for his care, you surrendered to his demands and gave him what would have been mine."

"I gave him nothing that belonged to you."

"We had a promising beginning and I thought a promise for a future together, but he interfered."

"Only because we were too young."

"Because he wanted you for himself."

"Why can't you believe me? He never made demands of me."

"Nothing for all the privileges he provided?" Agan stepped closer.

"What do you mean? You experienced the same privileges I did; yet you feel no obligation to him. I cannot understand your attitude. He is a good man who has been good to both of us."

"I have repaid him many times over and what did I get for it? I lost you to him."

"You didn't lose me to him. It was your own attitude that destroyed what might have been."

"Perhaps we can change that to what might be?"

"What's any different now?"

"Andrew Meredith is gone. And you need me."

Despite her misgivings, Daphne's heart skipped a beat.

Chapter
Four

"Andrew, is it really necessary to take such drastic measures?"

"Rachel, we have been through this a thousand times. I can no longer continue to hold people in bondage."

"But whatever will happen to Sweetwater?"

"It will go on as before, but our people will be employees rather than slaves."

"Given the opportunity they will all run off."

"Some of them will, but I believe that with a good standard of living---a place to live and a share in profits, they will want to remain. Besides, it is only a period of time and they will be free anyway."

"Andrew Meredith, that's disloyal to our cause."

"What cause, Rachel?"

"The South's."

Andrew moved toward her, enveloping her in his arms, his voice tired, "Rachel, Rachel, we've been through this before."

"I know it, but I don't understand why you can feel as you do."

"Because I have a strong conviction that slavery is wrong and because I know if we go to war, we will not be victorious."

Rachel pulled away. "Why can't you love the South the way I do?"

"I do love the South, but I am not blind to her weaknesses. Her whole economy is based on a system that cannot be sustained. Most reasonable planters know this, and I believe that they will begin to emancipate their slaves, if the North would be patient. Of course the hostility against the North is more than the slavery issue. The tariffs they have imposed on us are onerous, leaving us at their mercy. Our economy is based on agriculture; ninety percent of our people are rural while only forty percent of the north live in the country. We need their manufactured goods and will until we industrialize. That's why we cannot win a war against the industrial north."

Rachel shrugged her shoulders in dismissal, "Back to my original point, why don't you opt for gradual emancipation? Sounds like a wiser plan to me, if you get Sweetwater used to it and the slaves accustomed to it, perhaps then maybe I could better accept the idea."

"I agree with you. That way would be less traumatic, but for some reason I feel a sense of urgency. With the current state of affairs, I don't feel that I can wait. But beyond that I have to follow my convictions."

Rachel stepped into his embrace and rested her head on his shoulder, surrendering. "I know, I know. That makes you the man you are and the man I love, but I can't understand how this will work or what you will do if we go to war. I don't even want to think about that."

Andrew lifted her chin, "I know you don't, my love, but you must. With the Democratic Party split between Douglas and Breckenridge there is no way Lincoln will lose. If he wins, the South will secede."

"You don't know that."

"You forget I was at the convention in April when they refused to nominate Douglas. I saw the mindset of those "fire-eaters" first hand. Even though Georgia is more moderate when it comes to secession... some of our leaders don't want to secede, they will support their sister states and we will secede. Lincoln will not let them go without a fight."

"Why can't they just let us be?"

"Because a nation divided cannot stand. In view of this, I want to make plans that will protect you whether or not I'm here."

"What do you mean, whether or not you are here? If you feel so strongly the South is wrong, then at least you won't have to fight."

His mouth turned up in a sad smile as he said, "Right or wrong, I will fight for the South. I love her no less than you, Rachel, I'm just not blind to her faults."

Rachel snuggled into his shoulder, "I don't want you to go, Andrew. I can't bear the thought of losing you."

"Nevertheless, we need to make plans."

"What kind of plans?"

"I've set up an account for you in England backed by gold. I am going to improve the mill. I will free the slaves and leave Roger in charge. I want to bring Laura home, and I need to do something about Daphne."

"Daphne?"

"Yes, Daphne. I don't know how safe she will be in Savannah. Emotions will be running high and she has never been accepted there."

"Can't Philip look after her?"

"Right now he is looking after her, but at some point he will return to England. I need a plan for her."

A frown marred Rachel's countenance. "I don't understand your attachment to this woman."

47

"I have a responsibility to see to her welfare."

"That's exactly what I mean. If I didn't know you better, I would think there was something inappropriate between the two of you."

Andrew stepped back and placed both hands on her shoulders and answered, an edge in his voice, "But you do know me, and I expect your wholehearted trust."

"Then explain your involvement in her welfare."

"I feel responsible for her."

"That's what I mean. Why do you feel this keen responsibility?"

"If you trust me, you don't need my explanation." Andrew answered curtly.

"Why won't you explain?"

"There are some things better left unsaid."

"I am your wife, Andrew."

"Exactly. So trust me."

Rachel sighs, "I do trust you, but I want an explanation so I can understand."

"Understand this, Rachel. A man expects unconditional trust and support from his wife, unless he has given her reason not to. I have not. There are some things that are painful to revisit. I'd rather just let it be."

Pain flickered for a brief second in Andrew's eyes before the mask came down, but Rachel saw it and wondered. Then changing her approach, "I don't like Daphne."

Andrew cocked a brow, "Don't like Daphne? What's there not to like about her?"

"Her attachment to you and resentment of me."

"Resents you? That's your imagination, my dear," Andrew dismissed.

"I can understand something of what she feels. She ran your home and I have displaced her, but if she comes here, then what? I want to be mistress of my own domain."

"And you shall be. Daphne was a vital help to me when I was single and Aunt Maltilda was ill, but there is no way she could equal what you do."

"I thought she was very efficient."

"Not anymore than you and then she had limitations that you don't have."

"And they are------?"

"She was an employee... you are my wife, the love of my life, the one who satisfies my deepest emotional needs."

A sly smile parted Rachel's lips, relieving the tension. "Your emotional needs?"

Andrew laughed, "My every need."

"How long do we have?" Rachel asked, all levity gone as reality sank in.

"We have until the election. I don't know how long we will have after that."

A shiver ran down Rachel's spine. "I wish Laura were here. Virginia seems a long way away."

A tender light brightened Andrew's eyes and he responded, "I'm so pleased with the way you two bonded."

"I never had a sister. I often thought it would have been easier after my mother died if I had had a sibling to share with. Papa was no help, he was grieving too hard to help me. When I met Laura at the train station, it was as if we had always known each other. I can't believe how she accepted me with no hesitation."

"She had been prepared."

"Prepared?"

"Philip."

Rachel dropped her head. "Yes, sweet Philip would do that."

Andrew reached out and placed his hand beneath her chin, lifting her eyes to meet his, "Any regrets?"

"Regrets? Only that I hurt him. My heart belonged to you from that day you rescued me on the dock."

"Oh, really? You surely kept it a secret."

"I resisted my heart, and I let bitterness keep me from seeing the truth."

"Truth?"

"That you were the finest man I had ever met and that my heart longed for you."

Andrew's voice grew husky, "I'm forever thankful that you let your heart rule and put the bitterness behind."

"Oh, I didn't. It was the Savior's sweet healing that did that for me, Drew. When I thought you were dead, I came face to face with who I was and what I had become. I threw myself on His mercy, realizing I needed the Savior about whom Roger had told me. Only then was I able to surrender to you."

"Roger truly proved a blessing to us in many ways."

"If you remember I thought he was anything but a blessing."

Andrew chuckled, "I do remember your determination not to have him around and all the strange reasons you gave me. I knew he was the one for the job of overseer. It was miracle that he ended up on the square in Marietta preaching at the particular time we were there. I had lost track of him."

"I thought that you were attached to him because he had been such a help to you when you were a young man."

"The greatest help. He led me to understand my need for salvation. He is a unique man. Roger has a passion for souls but is gifted with management and hands on skills in the secular world. He uses those skills to support himself and to connect with people so he can share his faith."

"You were so right, and I was so wrong about him. Not only did he lead me to the truth, he made all the difference in Sweetwater management. The workers would follow him to hell and back, I believe, and do it with a smile on their faces."

"I feel that is why emancipation of them here will work so well with Roger at the helm. He will know how to deal with their insecurities and point them in the right direction."

"He holds a church service every Sunday for them. Did you know that?"

"Yes, he got my permission before he did it. Looking back now can you give me a logical reason for your fierce objection to him."

"Not a logical one but an emotional one. His faith convicted me, his words haunted me until the day that I surrendered that pride and bitterness."

"What a glorious day that was! The sum total of all my dreams came true when you flung yourself into my arms beneath the 'old hanging tree.'"

"And we have Roger to thank for his quick thinking, or you and Samuel might have been hanging in that tree."

"It's a wonder that those horses we were on didn't bolt and finish us off when you came galloping right in the midst of those men." Andrew chuckled, "What a sight you were, hair flying, eyes sparking and fearless."

"I was terrified that they had killed you."

Rachel shuddered, "How relieved I was that God used Roger to rescue you from those men."

"You mean us. When you arrived they were going to take care of the both of us and make it look as if it were a lover's quarrel."

"I couldn't have survived if something had happened to you. It was my fault. If I hadn't let bitterness take hold of my life and blind me to the truth, none of that would have ever happened. I put you at risk and others by my own stubbornness."

"That's in the past, darling."

"But a learning experience that I hope I never forget."

"And what is that?"

"I came home from England with great expectations for Sweetwater and my future here. What I found was a plantation in shambles, the mill gone and myself penniless. Instead of accepting that life, as I knew it, was over and that I needed to let go of the past and move forward, I let bitterness take root. It blinded me to the truth. I blamed you for something that was not your fault and I refused to see the blessings and opportunities that God was offering me in your love. Roger called it a burr in my soul and so it was. He said the scripture says that bitterness can defile and that's exactly what happened. It blinded me, causing me to reject you and join forces with that evil Walter Banks. How could I have believed all his lies, except that I was blind to the truth which was right before me? In the end it almost cost me everything. I came so near losing you." Rachel shuddered.

"And Sweetwater?" Andrew questioned.

Rachel looked up into his eyes, seeing the pain there. "Yes, even Sweetwater. I can't deny that I still love Sweetwater. But it is no longer my god. I'm thankful that we have the plantation and that it is better than ever, but what I'm the most thankful for is that I have you, with or without Sweetwater. Truly you are a blessed gift from God and I thank Him every day for His mercy because I don't deserve you."

Andrew pulled her into his arms and buried his head in her hair, taking in the fragrance of her; unable to speak his emotions ran so deeply.

The cotton fields brought forth a bountiful harvest. By the last of September all the white cotton bolls had been picked, ginned and readied for the newly equipped mill. Andrew worked feverishly assuring that every precaution was taken to gather supplies that the family would need in the days to come.

He incorporated new crops of wheat and corn while adding livestock for food and milk production. His newly freed laborers worked harder than before with only a few opting to leave, thus proving that king cotton could be profitable without slavery. For those who were separated from their families Andrew offered to purchase family members and in many cases was able to do so. They enjoyed refurbished living quarters and music once again could be heard as they sang in the fields.

The community proved mixed in the acceptance of Andrew and his ideas. When he freed the Sweetwater slaves, many shunned them when they attended church, but the opposition was short lived, however, because Andrew Meredith was a man of wealth and they needed his business.

Rachel took to heart the warning Andrew had issued to her and supervised canning, drying and preserving the ample harvest. The root cellar was brimming with fruits and vegetables. As nearly as possible she felt prepared for whatever was to come. Only the thought of facing a future without Andrew by her side haunted her days and disturbed her nights. She then worked all the harder, pushing the troubling thoughts aside, until in a momentary lull they would crash in uninvited. Occasional thoughts of Daphne and what Andrew had said would intrude, but she refused to entertain visions of what Sweetwater would be like if the golden skin beauty arrived on her doorstep. That was something she would have to deal with if and when the time ever came. Meanwhile, nagging concerns about Laura and her safety caused her to question whether Andrew's decision to send her away was the right one.

Letters from Laura proved a delight. Andrew voiced his amazement at her progress. She constantly asked questions about the mill, the plantation and technical issues that seemed far removed from a young lady in finishing school. But it was evident that in all areas, Laura had traversed from young girl to young woman in a brief period of time. Andrew suspected it began when they lost Aunt Maltilda. Whatever the source he was thankful for it, because he felt the time approached when Laura would not only be safer at home but needed. It gave him comfort to know that Rachel would have Laura when he left. Now if he could only persuade her that Daphne was no threat and indeed could be of vast assistance to her, but time and God's spirit would have to work a miracle there.

His conscience told him that he could help by taking Rachel into his confidence, but some things were too painful and humiliating to share even with his wife.

October sped into November, and then the dreaded day arrived. On November 6 the country elected Abraham Lincoln the sixteenth president of the United States.

Quickly following the election Alabama, Mississippi and South Carolina called for state conventions. By December 20, South Carolina seceded from the union followed within two months by Mississippi, Florida, Alabama, Louisiana and Texas. Much to Andrew's dismay moderate voices like Alexander Stephens among the leadership in Georgia failed to prevail and Georgia seceded on January 19.

In February the seven states held a convention in Montgomery, Alabama and created a Confederate Constitution, which stressed the autonomy of each state. Because of Andrew's strong opposition to secession, he was left out of the loop and any connection with the future political direction of his state.

Andrew had a glimmer of hope that some sanity might prevail when at Lincoln's inauguration on March 4 the new president stated that he had no plans to end slavery in those states where it existed. However, when he added that he would not accept secession, the dye was cast.

Before the inauguration, President Buchanan had refused to surrender federal forts to the seceding states, and the states seized them. When a federal supply ship tried to supply Fort Sumter, South Carolina, state militia repulsed it and the fort went without supplies. The commander of the fort, Captain Anderson, refused to surrender until all his supplies were gone. When he did offer to surrender, South Carolina refused his offer. On April 12, 1861 the Civil War began when troops fired on Fort Sumter. After forty hours of continuous shelling the fort fell and the Southern commander let the Union troops leave safely as Confederate troops occupied the fort. The war took on a new reality when three days later Lincoln issued a proclamation calling for 75,000 militiamen.

Shortly after Andrew and Rachel received the news about Fort

Sumter, they heard that Virginia, Arkansas, Tennessee and North Carolina had seceded, bringing the total number of states making up the Confederacy to eleven. When Rachel told Andrew she thought the South had a better chance now, he objected. He pointed out that the eleven states had a population of nine million including four million slaves compared to the North's twenty million. Truly it was a tiny, ill-equipped warrior against a Goliath.

Rachel's spirits lifted with news of the victory at Bull Run twenty-five miles southwest of Washington. However, her jubilation turned to alarm when she and Andrew realized that Laura had been visiting a friend's home near the battle and that she had assisted with the wounded. Her letter described the battle, telling them that Washington citizens expecting a Confederate rout came out by the carriage full with picnic lunches to watch the battle. Pure panic erupted when they had to take their chairs and carriages, running and dodging artillery all the way back to Washington.

When Richmond was made capital of the Confederacy, Andrew felt it was time for Laura to come home to Sweetwater for he knew that the battles would be heated and plentiful in Virginia.

Laura refused his request reminding him that she was there to mature and become a young woman of value. Her role in the battle at Bull Run gave her a sense of worth that she had never experienced before, and she felt strongly that she could contribute more to the war effort where she was. In short, for the first time in her life she felt needed in a vital way.

Andrew growled when he read her letter, not accustomed to having his demands rejected. Staring at the letter Rachel had handed him, he pursed his lips and asked, "What am I going to do with that little miss?"

His wife got up from the table and put her arm around his shoulder, leaning over to read Laura's letter, then chuckled, "Sometimes when we get what we want, it proves not to be what we want at all! You wanted her to grow up, to experience something of the real world. Obviously she is growing up. Do you think she is in any real danger?"

"Not in the immediate future. Lincoln has to get his forces under a better command before the war starts moving in earnest. Still..."

"Still, what? Rejoice, Andrew, she is growing up and wanting to take on responsibility. When the war moves closer and more fierce, we'll bring her home."

"That's what I'm afraid of. I fear she won't be able to get home."

"Then you or Philip will have to go get her. Let her have this time of challenge with your blessing."

Andrew pulled Rachel down in his lap, "I never would have dreamed that you would become a mediator between Laura and me."

"Why are you surprised? I was young once and the constraints I felt when my aunt ruled my life is still vivid in my mind. Young people have to have a certain amount of freedom to learn and make decisions-----a breaking away of sorts."

" But within reason. Maybe I will consider letting her stay until I feel the danger is too great or I need her here with you."

"With me?" Rachel frowned. "Where will you be?"

"Eventually I'll have to go, Rachel."

"No, I won't have it." She cried into his shoulder.

"I don't think it will be anytime soon. I've got to finish my job here. Meanwhile we have to prepare to help our troops."

Chapter
Five

Daphne could scarcely believe her eyes. Philip brought her a small treasure of gold coins.

"Every one of your paintings sold and for far more than we anticipated. That's the good news. The bad news is that Lincoln has blockaded the Southern ports so we are going to have to find inventive ways to get your paintings to market or maybe open one up here"

"I told you, Mr. Philip, no one in Savannah is going to buy my work. On the contrary, I don't want anyone to know what I'm doing. I have to be very discreet in anything that I do or I might not be allowed to stay."

"Don't be ridiculous, Daphne, they will be lining up to buy your paintings when you become famous, and you will become famous."

"No, it would only cause them to drive me out. This is the South and they will never accept my art or me. If I were a seamstress or had a bakery and lived less sumptuously, then maybe they would leave me alone. Even now the terrible things they said about Mr. Andrew, they are saying about you. They just don't think a woman of color should be allowed this kind of luxury."

"Then what's to be done?"

"Proceed with utmost discretion. It is paramount that I don't stir up any more trouble than I already have."

"How many paintings have you done since I've been away?"

"About five. Would you like to see them?"

" Of course I do. We are in business together and I am a very interested partner."

Daphne cast him a puzzled glance, then shrugged and admitted, "I am finding a release in it that I hadn't expected. Gold coins make it all the sweeter."

Philip looked around the room. It contained no paintings. A new wall had been added at one end of the still spacious room and Philip gave Daphne a quizzical look.

"The studio was much too large, and I'd wanted a discreet place to store my paintings, out of view and away from curious eyes," she explained, nodding her head toward the wall and avoiding his eyes.

"Really? You are that selective as to whom you want to show them? That's interesting. I should think you would want them on display so you could enjoy them. Maybe a customer not from this area who would want one."

"In the first place, anyone who would visit me would not be prospective customers, they would be curiosity seekers or trouble makers. Anyway, you garner a much larger profit in Boston than I could ever get here, if anyone were interested."

"Is this new business woman the same Daphne who objected to my 'interfering' with her 'hobby'?"

Daphne smiled. "I suddenly like earning my own way. I don't

want to be dependent on Mr. Andrew. Maybe soon I can eliminate his stipend and pay him back for all of this."

"That's not out of the realm of possibility considering how much you got from the ones I just sold. By the way, I think we may be able to expand our market to New York. I've made some discreet inquiries and got some positive feedback."

Daphne walked across the room and slid back a hidden panel that looked as if it were just an extension of the wall. There in a line nestled her paintings, both landscape and portraits.

"Where did you get these models---?" Philip stopped as he gazed at a portrait of a small-undernourished boy with large, dark eyes. The sense of longing on his face brought tears to the blond giant's eyes. "So this explains the wall. It's not your reputation but your subject matter that dictates your need for discretion."

"That was an added incentive."

"Who is this, Daphne?"

"Just a small boy." She answered, dropping her head.

"No, not just a small boy. There is a story here."

"Yes, there is a story, but I can't share it with you."

"Why, not?"

"You're better off not to know."

"What are you involved in or should I say with whom are you involved?" He demanded as he looked around the room. His eyes fell on a handsome face, whose green eyes stared back at him, a cynical smile turning up one corner of his mouth.

"I see that Agan has found you."

"Yes. And as for his posing for me, I did it in exchange for some work he did for me."

"What work?" Philip demanded.

"Carpentry work."

"This panel?"

"Yes, in fact it was his idea."

Philip grabbed her arm, "What are you involved in that you need secret sliding panels?"

Pushing Philip's hand away, she ignored his question and commented, " I think it turned out quite well. Don't you?"

Philip sighed, "Quite well, but I'm surprised. I would think that he would be the last person you would paint."

"I guess you could call it a case of bartering. His skill for mine."

"Are the two of you on better terms?"

Her smile was mysterious. "You could say that."

"You two have known each other a long time?"

"Since we both came from the West Indies. We were young teenagers."

"What happened?"

"What happens in so many friendships, misunderstandings."

"Cleared up now?"

"He seems to understand better, but we'll have to see. One painting doesn't erase the past."

"I can sell these if I can get them out."

"I don't think Agan wants his sold."

"I'm sure he doesn't. The others will bring a good price, especially the one of the little boy. The abolitionist will bid high for that one. In fact, it will be inflaming. You sure you want to do that?"

"Had you asked me two months ago, I would have said 'no'."

"What has changed?"

"Seeing the abuses with my own eyes."

"Not all slave owners are abusive," Philip reminded.

"I know that. All I had ever considered was the way Mr. Andrew and now you treat your people. I didn't want to look any farther." Daphne shook her head, uncomfortable with the way the conversation had veered.

"What happened?"

"Someone opened my eyes."

"You mean forced them open."

"I guess you could say that."

"Who? Agan?"

"I'd rather not say."

"Both of you are on dangerous ground. If I find out that he is involving Balmara in this, he is gone. And as for you, you are risking everything that Andrew tried to provide for you." Philip warned.

"There are some things worth taking a risk for."

"So that's what the gold is for."

"I am making a life for myself like you asked me to."

"I didn't mean this kind of life."

"For once I am doing something that involves my heart. You saw that little boy. What would you have done? If I can make a difference in people's lives then don't you think it far out weighs simply painting for pleasure, mine and others?"

Philip shook his head, despair written on his face. "You've chosen a dangerous path and one from which Andrew nor I will be able to rescue you if you get caught. Are you sure you can trust Agan? Some of these organizations are self-serving and they have more malevolent goals than rescuing fugitive slaves and sending them north."

"Like what?"

"Like insurrection, murder and lining their own pockets."

"I wouldn't know about that. I only know that the people I've been in contact with come from a world I refused to admit existed. As you said Balmara and Andrew Meredith were my world, now I've spread my wings."

"Take care how far you spread them and be sure where your flight will lead you."

"Now to the business at hand. What about my paintings? Can you get them through the blockade?"

"Later on I may not be able to, but, right now, the North does not have enough ships to man the blockade so blockade running is a lucrative business. Eventually, we will have to change our market to England and Europe. There is a company out of Liverpool that ships between England, New York and Charleston. If they can, then I can. My Boston company has just finished two steamships that I am selling to them. We can get your paintings to Charleston and New Orleans, after a stop in Bermuda or Nassau, then on their way to Liverpool. I might even try it in one of my smaller steam vessels from Savannah."

"Sounds dangerous."

"So? It will be very lucrative, and I think my father would approve of bringing in a tidy sum to invest back in our properties in the old country." Philip's eyes alight with energy.

"Why, Mr. Philip, you are looking forward to the danger," Daphne exclaimed.

"No, little one, the excitement. I haven't had anything that has fired my imagination like this has."

Daphne shuddered. "I shall worry every minute about you. I don't think you will be just transporting paintings."

"Guns and supplies from England exchanging them for the cotton and goods grown on plantations---on my plantation."

"And you said what I was doing was dangerous. Is Balmara not enough of a challenge for you?"

"At first I thought so, but with Agan to run it, I'm practically a man of leisure."

"You trust Agan that much and yet you warned me."

"I didn't mean Agan, but whomever he is involved with. If Meredith trusted him, I guess I should."

Daphne wondered at the chill that ran down her backbone. But Agan had changed. He had, hadn't he?

"Do you bypass Boston?"

"I think I might be able to make one or two more trips there before the blockade tightens. Why?"

"I especially wanted to show a few of these in Boston and I wanted to take that trip to meet Mr. Carlton."

"I don't know about that, Daphne. It might prove too dangerous. I wouldn't want to risk anything happening to you. Meredith would have my head."

"You said yourself that most ships get through the blockade."

"But not all. About twenty percent are caught."

"What happens then?"

"Probably nothing to you, as for me, my guess is they would confiscate my property and probably send me back to England in disgrace."

"So I'm really not risking much?

"I'll think about it."

Daphne stood on the balcony outside her studio staring at the traffic on the river. She was tired...it had been a long day. She had finished the final painting that was to go out, and she was satisfied with it. Even at this hour the waterfront seemed unusually busy, especially in view of the blockade.

Since Philip's return she had worked feverishly trying to finish her one last painting of ships traversing the Savannah River. She no longer painted just for her pleasure, but for the money it would bring in. Turning back inside, she made her way into the room that housed her paintings, the ones that soon would be in crates and headed for Boston, that is, if Mr. Philip's people could maneuver around the blockade.

She paused in front of the painting of the little boy and a tear coursed down her cheek. He was what started it ... this new mission, this reason for the gold. His mother had died, and his father had been captured by the slave patrol. Somehow the little fellow escaped during the ruckus that followed, and Agan found him wandering just down the road from Balmara, abandoned and scared. Agan had brought the little fellow to her, and his plight had captured her heart. That started a series of unexpected guests in the middle of the night ... a brief stopping place on the way to what they hoped was a better world. Agan explained that her place would prove ideal. It was close to the river where a dingy could push off in the night to contact a larger vessel. From there it would travel to a barrier island and then, if lucky, on to Boston or someplace north, perhaps Canada.

She reflected on her conversation with Philip and the warnings he gave her. Her heart broke, though, when she saw the other side of slavery. Not all slaves were treated like those of Balmara. Of course, she had known that with her mind, but her heart had refused to consider it. Now she knew firsthand. She understood the risk she was taking, but her heart compelled her. And then there was the cost of freedom, not only in lives, but gold. Gold for transportation, gold for supplies and gold for keeping lips sealed. That's why she requested that Philip bring her gold.

A loud pounding interrupted her musings. She turned away from the paintings and slid the door in place, effectively concealing the room, the gold, and her work. Agan had suggested the need for such an arrangement and had designed and built the door that now secreted a large portion of her studio. She walked toward the door, her heart pounding. The gaslight illumined the outside of her entrance. Through the leaded glass door, she could see the outline of what appeared to be several men. She called through the door asking what they wanted.

"We have information that you are harboring fugitive slaves in your home and we demand to enter and search."

The slave patrol, her fear realized. Thank goodness she had no one hidden tonight, but her paintings were here and not in crates as yet. Would they notice the wall, find the hidden panel?

"There is no one but me here, and I have already retired for the night. How dare you disturb me in this fashion!" Daphne shouted through the door.

"We demand you open this door before we break this showy glass and give you what's coming to you, you fancy woman. Andrew Meredith ain't here to save yore pretty skin."

Pulling the robe around her more securely, she opened the door and stepped back. "See for yourself, there is no one here but me. I will just step outside while you search my house, but the authorities will hear of this!"

"You'll not step out and try to escape. You stay right where

66

you are and for good measure Charley is gonna guard you. This is serious business."

"You are correct. It is serious business to disturb a person's rest for no reason. You will pay for this!"

There was something familiar about the tall, thin man with the deep voice commanding her. She had encountered him some-where. His face, his mannerisms boiled up deep dread in her. But what, why? Her mind raced to and fro trying to remember some-thing lodged in her memory.

Suddenly, he grabbed her face, pinching it until she winced, "And who do you think will extract payment from us? You don't qualify for that kind of protection and yore fancy English boyfriend ain't got no say in Savannah, despite the way he runs around here like he's some-body. We'll do what we want and nobody will stop us. I wouldn't be a bit surprised if he ain't involved in this here underground railroad stuff. But don't you never mind. We gonna stop it and yore gonna pay. If'n we find what we're looking for, yore gonna pay big, but we might get a little enjoyment out'n it first. T'would be a pleasure to watch the likes of you squirming. You've had what's coming to you for a long time and now it's here. No Andrew Meredith to save you, what do you say about that, Missy"

"I told you there is no one here but me," she explained through clinched teeth, as the intruder dropped his hand from her cheeks, leaving ugly whelps.

Daphne stood just inside the door, guarded by a short, portly man who smelled of sweat and stale tobacco. He remained quiet, but shuffled uneasily. She sensed that he was not altogether comfortable with this forced search and the comments made by his accomplice. Even though he had denigrated Mr. Philip, she knew that the young Englishman did have a standing in this community. Perhaps not on the level of Andrew Meredith, but his influence was growing because he had money and with money came power. Also, he had the authority of the British government behind him. But Mr. Philip was at Balmara, and she was here beyond his immediate protection. She knew that it would be a matter of time before Savannah's outrage at her position would have consequences. Only payday came more quickly than she expected. She had hoped to bring in a tidy sum to finance her new mission and then perhaps ...well, who knew after that.

She flinched when she heard glass shatter and knew that it was one of her lovely crystal vases. Then around the corner out of view another crash, this time something heavy and she knew it was her easel and paints. But more important, it had her last painting on it. It was the one of the river traffic that she had just finished. It would be ruined, the paint still wet. Then, she heard something tear and feared they were slashing the canvas. Why were they so mean? Why this hate? She held her breath. Would they find the hidden panel? If so then all would be lost.

After searching the studio the trio made their way downstairs to her living quarters. An argument broke out between the leader and his two men. They were now searching every inch of her bedroom and sitting room. Snatches of their conversation drifted up. Relief soared through her. They had not found the secret room, and now the men were imploring the man, whom they called George, to leave.

The men shouted that they had found nothing incriminating, and this woman, though a woman of color, was under the protection of the English lord. If he were anything like Meredith, they pled, he'd have them hunted down and jailed for invasion of property. The two were unwilling to risk that just because George didn't like the uppity way this woman lived.

George shouted, "What's wrong with you, Amos? You yella or sumthin? We know this here woman is guilty and we're gonna prove it one way or 'tother'."

Amos observed that he was all for rounding up slaves but invading private property of somebody who might be innocent was going too far and he was leaving. He also added that he knew why George was so determined.

George lifted a wild eyebrow and commented, "Yeah? What do you know that makes you so smart?"

Relief turned to terror in the studio as Daphne heard Amos answer.

"We all know 'bout you. We heard about that bad blood between you and Andrew Meredith. It was all over town what happened down on the docks last year. You and some of yore buddies accosted one of his lady friends down there, and he didn't take kindly to it."

George sneered, "Ain't nuthin' wrong with killing two birds with one stone. This here little lady done ast fer it, with all her high falutin' ways and if old money bags gits his due meantime, so much better."

"That's what this is all about, now ain't it? Since he ain't no wheres around, you gonna get him back by harassing that little lady upstairs. I ain't agin some fun now and then, but you walking on mighty dangerous ground. I ain't gonna be a partner to yore plans for payback. I'm a duly appointed slave patrol, and there ain't nothing here that says this young woman is involved in harboring fugitives so I'm leaving."

His buddy must have concurred because both hurried up the stairs and out the door along with the man guarding Daphne.

George's shouts followed them up the stairs and out the door, accusing them of being cowards and not worthy to be part of the patrol. He was going to get the truth out of that woman and he was man enough to do it.

Daphne's heart raced as three of the men exited, leaving her alone with the tall, mean one. Memories of a warm Savannah dock and a disheveled Rachel Gregory Meredith rescued from three ruffians flooded her mind. She shuddered. It proved the day that had changed the direction of her life. Now history repeated itself but it was she, not Rachel, at this ruffian's mercy with no Andrew Meredith available to rescue her.

She backed up against the wall where a small, walnut smoking stand with a shallow drawer in it pressed against her back. Opening the drawer behind her, she felt a smooth metal blade. It was a slender dagger sharp as a razor. She used it as a letter opener, but that was not the purpose of the gift. Her fingers moved down to the carved ivory handle and clasped it. Would she dare use it? It would be prison or hanging for her to even wound this man, but more unthinkable was that she would allow him to violate her. She slowly removed the weapon just as her assailant entered the room. He saw her hand move from her back. The blade flashed in the light as she nestled it in the deep folds of her dressing gown.

The man's long gangly legs had him by her side in three steps. Twisting her arm behind her and pinning it to the table, the knife dropped to the floor where he swooped it up. He pushed her into the table and pinioned her head to the wall with his forearm forced against her throat.

He laughed, revealing a mouthful of broken tobacco stained teeth. Leaning in close to her face, he slid his arm sideways until his hand with the dagger stopped and pressed against her throat. Brandishing the weapon close to her face, he rested the point of it beneath her chin. "How would you like this little baby to take care of that pretty face of yorn? Then I bet Mr. Mighty Meredith or yore new English sweetheart wouldn't give you the time of day."

He moved the sharp tip just across her chin, drawing blood. He pressed his arm harder against her throat, and Daphne's eyes bulged as she gasped for breath. He laughed again as he released the pressure, and she gulped for air.

"Wouldn't want you to choke to death. That would ruin my enjoyment of this. I don't want you to miss a thing. Don't know as I'll kill you, although it would be all right seeing as you attacked me with this here knife. See?" He flicked the blade against his bony arm that was pinioning her shoulder and blood trickled out.

"Here, let me get some on that fancy gown you got on. There, that's evidence enough since this is yore knife and my blood is on yore clothes. Now let me see, where do we begin? First, yore gonna tell me the truth, or then it will be snip by snip until I get it all out of you."

Daphne shut her eyes. Her hand behind her back felt the smooth texture of the smoking stand. Irrationally she thought of the beauty of the piece. Book matched slabs of walnut hand rubbed until it left a rich warm patina. Often she had admired it at Balmara, and now it was hers. Mr. Andrew had insisted because he knew how much she admired it. Would this be her last pleasant sensation in this life...the texture of smooth wood against her fingertips?

She continued to stroke the tabletop with her free hand as if to remove herself from the vile man whose fetid breath of leeks and garlic warmed the cheek she tried to turn from him. He was now taunting in her ears, the atrocities he could bring down on her if she didn't tell all. He spoke of torture, pain, and violation. Death would be preferable. If she leaned in maybe somehow the knife would pierce her heart or cut her throat and it would be over. Philip warned her. She took it too lightly. She had never encountered evil like this. Flex her shoulder and bend just a little farther in and it would be over.

Her assailant felt her try to lean into the knife, and he shoved her harder against the table and wall behind. Pains wracked her back, but he never let up.

"I know what yore trying to do, Missy, and it ain't gonna work. I got you now and ain't nobody to help you. It's jest you and me and mostly it's me and whatever I want to do to you. You are helpless." He laughed a triumphant laugh. "Now come on. Tell George what he wants to know and save yourself a lot of grief."

She remained mute. Don't listen to him. Think, Daphne. Think about the table, its beauty, the pleasant sensation of its smooth texture. Think about Mr. Andrew, about Miss Laura and about Miss Matilda. Soon this will be over and you can join Miss Matilda where there is no sorrow or pain, no evil men. Think about the ones you have helped. Think about what you did for them.

She knew she was about to pass out so her free hand moved over the smooth surface of the table one last time. Just as her torturer whispered the vilest of threats in her ear, her hand encountered a heavy bronze statue gracing her table. She had forgotten about it. Her free hand grasped the base of it, and then swinging with all her might, she bashed the greasy black head bent toward hers. He crumpled to the floor as a gaping wound poured blood on her fine Persian rug, the dagger still clutched in his hand.

Daphne stared unbelieving. What had she done? What was she to do now?

Chapter
Six

Agan approached the townhome cautiously. He looked around to assure himself that no curious eyes had followed him. It was several hours before daybreak, but this was the time he usually came. When the sun was bright or even if there was a full moon, there were too many watchful eyes. Besides, he liked it early like this. He enjoyed seeing Daphne when sleep still clung to her, and she had yet to put on her cool façade. It was reminiscent of times past when they had enjoyed each other's company. Before they grew up and the world intruded, or more precisely, Andrew Meredith.

His feelings for Daphne were mixed. He had thought to conquer her would be just retribution for her past rejections, and she would prove the stepping-stone to all his dreams and plans. He thought his involving her in his plan would be payback for the pain and sorrow her rejection had wreaked on him. With her involved, his plan would be so much more expansive, and he could rise to the top more quickly. Bringing her into the fold proved a feather in his cap ... not to mention the gold she provided, gold with which he had expected to line his pockets. Yet when it had come down to it, he couldn't take it. He'd used what was needed and took none for himself.

Strange, it had been his plan from the start. A plan to bring him riches which he could take north, start his own business, ride in his own fine carriages and men would call him, "Mister." Ambition and jealousy had driven him. Envy of Andrew Meredith had been the fuel and Daphne had been the root of that jealousy.

Her place had offered the perfect setup. People knew that she cared nothing about the condition of some of her own people. She held herself aloof from white and black. By reputation she wouldn't be suspected, her location was ideal.

He had begun putting his plans in place, beginning with that little boy who had captured her heart. But suddenly his own heart had responded in a strange manner. Where there had been only cold calculations and the use of people for his own purposes, compassion intruded. Was it spending more time with Daphne? Had she unlocked something in his heart that he had sequestered? Lately, as they spent more time together, he found old feelings for her surfacing, then he would remember Andrew Meredith, and the familiar bitterness would engulf him. She said their relationship was harmless, but then she was so committed to the man, she would defend him at any cost. What was he to believe?

He frowned as he neared the door. It stood ajar. Why? He knew that Daphne wouldn't leave her door open. Hadn't he stressed that she was to keep it locked and bolted at all times. He paused as he entered and pulled the doors shut, then slipped further inside silently, moving close to the wall. A lamp glowed in the studio spilling light over mass destruction. He paused. The room remained silent as a tomb. Where was Daphne? Someone who meant her harm had been here. Walking over to the entrance, he lit a match and noticed stains on the rug. Bending closer, it looked like blood. Where had they taken her? Was she still alive? So what happened? Someone somewhere had spoken out of turn. Was it betrayal?

He slid down the wall to the floor, his head in his hands. Acknowledging the death of his dream, he moaned. Whoever had done this had finished his plan. Did they find out his involvement? If they found his picture they did. What had Daphne told them? He knew about some of their ways of extracting information. No one could keep silent in the face of that torture.

Many of their people hated Daphne because her privileged treatment had raised her above their station in life. Especially the ones who had their freedom. He, too, had received special treatment but he had never forgotten who he was, at least that's the line he gave his people. Agan was a master of disguise. His true purposes and emotions were always hidden. Until tonight

He forced himself to stand, his strong muscular legs still trembling. He walked across the room to the wall he had built for Daphne's protection and to facilitate his own plans. His thoughts turned to the beautiful form and face that haunted his fantasies. Suddenly his lost dreams and big plans meant little. A pain wracked his heart as he thought of her, what she must have endured. His own loss gripped him, the thought of never again reveling in those eyes with amber fire, excruciating.

Once more emotions buckled his knees, and he slid down the wall that he had so carefully crafted. The pain that wracked his soul was a loss so deep, so real that he could not deny it. He didn't want retribution. He wanted Daphne, and now she was gone. Tears filled the usually cold and calculating eyes and streamed down his cheeks as he mourned his loss. Agan wasn't aware of how long he sat in the shadows of the darkened room. But suddenly, he realized that morning would come soon, and he must get away. It would be a disaster to be associated with this place, with her now. Even earlier he had taken great care to come to her when no eyes would see him. It was vital that he depart before someone discovered him, but still he was reluctant to leave.

He looked around, and his heart ached as he took in the last place he had seen her. His mind resonated in the wonderful memories of her laughter as he posed for her, her compassion for the little fellow that was now on his way to Canada thanks to her protection and gold. And now she was gone, in a moment life had changed for him.

He shook himself and tried to stand up. Then behind him in the secret room, he heard a sound. Soft at first, then a whimpering like that of a wounded animal. What could it be? Had someone come in the night that he hadn't been told about, someone that Daphne had hidden in there. Could it be a dog, a child? Taking a lamp, he rushed to the panel and slid it to the side and there in the corner beneath her paintings, huddled a whimpering Daphne.

Agan ran to her. Enfolding her in his arms, he asked, "What happened?"

Sobs began in earnest. "I, I, killed a man. A horrible man."

Agan felt her in his arms. His joy was so acute; he could hardly take in what she was saying. Then reality sunk in. "When, where did you kill a man. Who was it?"

"S-S-Slave P-P-Patrol." She stammered between sobs. "N-Now they'll be looking for me and I-I-I have nowhere to go."

Agan touched her chin to raise her face to his. Blood oozing from her wound stained his hands, "You're hurt."

76

"No, no, I killed the wicked man."

"You're bleeding."

She shuddered. "He wanted to do terrible things to me. He cut me. Said he would disfigure me if I didn't tell him the truth and name names. I didn't tell him anything. But he knew, someone had to tell him. Was it you Agan? Do you hate me so that you would betray me?"

Pain dagger sharp pierced his insides. "No, of course not. Would I be here if I had? We had big plans, remember?"

"Not anymore. The gold is finished, this place is finished, and I am finished as soon as they realize George is missing. I heard his cohorts call him that."

"Where were they when you killed George?"

"They got scared and left. They didn't want to do anything to make Mr. Andrew mad."

Old resentment made him retort, "Well we are way beyond Mr. Andrew Meredith's help."

Daphne pulled away from him. "Must you resurrect that at a time like this?"

"Sorry. The truth hurts. We've got to think clearly. What did you do with the body? Maybe no one will miss him until we get away."

"WE? You don't have to involve yourself. I never told them anything and besides the ringleader is dead."

"You didn't answer my question. What did you do with the body?"

"I didn't do anything with it. Didn't you see him? He's lying in a puddle of blood at the front door."

"There's nobody there, Daphne. Are you sure you killed him?"

"I didn't check for a pulse but he was lying there still as death with blood pouring out his head. Do you suppose his friends came back to get him?"

"If so that gives us less time than ever. Get your clothes on, bring all your jewelry and all the gold that you have."

"What are we going to do?"

"I don't have a plan except to get you out of here before his friends come back and find you,"

"What about Balmara?"

"You can't involve Philip . For once your rich benefactors can't rescue you." Agan spat out. "The first place they will look is Balmara. I have a dingy down on the dock. We will use that to escape, but we will have to do it before light."

"You mean you will ship me north with the other fugitives?

"Can't. No vessels are planned for several weeks, and the dingy is too small to make it to the barrier islands. Our best course of action will be to get horses and go cross country, avoiding plantations and towns."

"Where to?"

"We'll have to decide that as we go. I've got to have time to think. But this one thing I know. We will have to get you out of here now. I will go back to Balmara as soon as I get you situated because they may come looking for me. I know they will question Lord Duval and he won't know a thing."

"He questioned me when he got back from his trip about what we were doing but I didn't tell him. Are you sure we can't go to Balmara?"

"Absolutely. First place they will look."

"What about my paintings?"

"I don't know what we can do about those. It's out of our control now."

"The destruction of your dream?"

A sad smile turned the corner of his mouth upward. "I guess you could say that. But maybe together we can dream anew. But dreams or not we've got to leave. We will go out the back, get into the river, and I will take you to a place that will be safe for today and maybe tomorrow. Then I will get us horses and go cross-country."

"But where will you get horses without arousing suspicions." Daphne asks, her mind calmer, thinking clearer.

"I will get Balmara horses. Tell Mr. Philip that Meredith has need of me and horses. He might question why he wasn't told first, but by then I'll think of some good reason to tell him. But first things first. We have to get you away from here and to a temporarily safe place."

"Why are you doing this, Agan, risking everything for me? You could walk away, hold on to your dreams, and no one would ever know of your involvement."

Agan looked at her for a long moment, his brow furrowed, "To tell you the truth, I don't know, Daphne. Sometimes our aspirations change in a moment or maybe suddenly we see them for what they are. Time will tell."

Daphne murmured, "Yes, time will tell."

"Now what 'cha gonna do, George?" Amos shouted to the tall gangly man, his head bandaged.

"Soon as I get over this here headache, I'm gonna make sumbody pay and pay big."

"We goin' to the authorities? What you gonna tell 'em as to why you wuz there"

79

"I don have to tell 'em nothing, jus that that lil gal tried to kilt me." George insisted.

"You gonna have to tell somebody sumethin 'cause you just destroyed Andrew Meredith's house and furnishings. He ain't gonna like that one bit and you know what that means. The people 'round here listen to him, even those people who don't like him 'cause of his politics."

"That don' matter. That woman struck me and that's agin the law."

"So is what we did."

"We wuz lookin' fer fugitives. That's our bizness."

"But we didn't find any fugitives or any evidence that there ever wuz any so she wuz just defending herself."

"No matter. It's agin the law what she done 'cause she ain't white, although she almost is according to her looks. I'll prosecute her and see her hung." George declared.

"I ain't in no mood to tangle with Andrew Meredith and that English duke or whatever he is. They's got influence an lawyers and although she's black, she'll be defended and as far as me and the other two, we wuz nowhere near that place so you is on yore own when it comes to placing charges agin her," Amos argued.

"You yellar livered scoundrels. I don't know why I ever included you in this here project."

"I don't know why we got involved 'cept you swore to us you knew she was hidin' slaves. I don know where you got yore information, but clearly you didn' know what you wuz talking about. We don' want nuthin to do with this anymore. Mr. Meredith is not one to cross. I done heard about what happened to you and yore buddies when you grabbed that little gal down on the docks last year." Amos shuddered. "Looks like that wud o' taught you sumthin."

"Well, he ain't here no longer."

"Where is he?"

"Don't rightly know. Probably gone up north sumwheres since he wuz one of them unionists. He may not even be around to see about his property."

"But that Philip is here and I don't want to tangle with him, neither." Amos whispered as if he feared someone would overhear them.

"Well, I jest may pay that fancy dude a visit."

"Count us out! We didn't destroy that place, you did and we ain't gonna take no blame for it." Amos turned to the other two men standing mute in the shadows. Nodding their heads in agreement, they motioned to their friend that they were leaving.

"Wait, don' ya'll go off'n and leave me here, injured and maybe dying." George commanded as he rubbed his throbbing head.

"We're goin and ain't nothing wrong with you that a good night's sleep won't take care of. Yo headache is more from all that rum you drunk last night than from what that lil gal did to ye." Amos chuckled " But I guess it is a good thang yore head is so hard or it might a kilt you.".

"It ain't funny."

"Yeah it is. Big ole mean George brought down by the likes of that little miss. I hate to say it, George, but you've had it comin' to you fer a long time. Me and the others are getting out afore you get us all in trouble."

"I'll tell them you wuz with me." George threatened.

"It will be yore word agin ours."

"An what about the little lady in question?"

"Be our word agin hers, but she knows we didn't tear up nuthin or bother her no way. It wuz all you, George. Yore the one that Meredith will be looking fer. Yore the one who tore up his stuff. She heard us telling you to quit and we left. Remember, George?"

"What kinda friends I got anyways?" George complained.

"We ain't yore friends. We wuz supposed to be on slave patrol. What we got into wuzn't nuthin like that. We is through with you."

"You wudn't be sayin that if I wuzn't injured."

"Injured or hung over? We ain't goin' to no authorities, and I'd advise you not to, on account of if we had to testify, we'd have to say yore injuries were brought on by yore own foolishness."

"Well, you may be skeert of the almighty Meredith, but I ain't. But you may have a good point 'bout goin' to the authorities, cause they'd jest put her in jail, maybe hang her, but since my buddies won't back me up, she might not hang. That gives me a better plan, and I'll have my revenge and a little sumthin' to line my pockets. Might be better to get my own, in my own way and get payment to boot."

"What you plannin', George? You better be keerful. Ain't you heard a thang I said?"

"Yeah, I heerd plenty. That's what got me to thanking. There may be more to harvest from this crop than revenge." George smiled and rubbed his head, a malevolent light brightening his dark eyes. "But I'll have to wait til this here headache gets better. Then I'll pay Mr. Philip a visit and ask him what he's gonna do about this here situation."

Daphne awoke with a start from her restless sleep. She heard the rustling of leaves and then through the brush, Agan appeared leading two fine Balmara geldings. Even in her distress, a slight smile tilted Daphne's full lips. The horses were lovely, some Mr. Philip had imported from Ireland. It was like him to send fine horseflesh if he thought Miss Rachel would have need of them. Was that what Agan had told him?

Suddenly, she was thankful anew for the hours she had spent in the saddle, the lessons that Andrew Meredith had insisted she take along with her education. A momentary bitterness boiled up in her throat, why would he insist on someone like her learning to ride? Another unanswered question to haunt her. But then perhaps it was like Miz Matilda had told her. God knows our future and prepares us for it in mysterious ways. She wanted to believe that. Wanted to believe that there was a God who cared and was concerned for her, who had her future in His control. What a comforting thought. If she could know Him in a personal way like Miz Maltilda did, then the terrible loneliness could be appeased. She had told her He was there just waiting for an invitation. She hadn't responded, she thought she didn't need His help, after all she had Andrew Meredith to take care of her. But now what? Was Miz Matilda right when she had warned her against making someone or something else her god? Had she done that? Is that why he was gone? Had God taken him away to get her attention? The questions unbidden tumbled through her mind as her heart raced, and her predicament threatened to overcome her.

"What time is it?" Daphne rubbed her arm, numb from lying on the hard ground.

"It will be dark soon. Then we can leave," Agan replied.

"Leave, where?"

"I don't have a plan yet. Just set out north across country."

"The slave patrols will be searching."

"I imagine so. We will just have to be careful."

"What did you tell Mr. Philip?"

"That Mr. Andrew had sent word by Mr. Clark, who had been to Marietta, that he would like to buy a couple of geldings, one for Miss Laura when she returns and one for a spare."

"You told him you had seen Mr. Clark?"

"Yeah, told him I ran into him at the Meredith offices."

"Doesn't it seem strange that he didn't require you to ship them by train?"

"No. I told him that Meredith wanted them thoroughly tested before they arrived at Sweetwater. They had only received them a few days ago, and he wasn't sure if they were trained well enough to be safe for Miss Laura. Since I trained and broke the horses at Balmara, I suggested I take them."

"He didn't object?"

"No, matter of fact he seemed relieved. Guess he thought he would have to take them, so I saved him a trip."

"What about your duties?"

"All taken care of, and gave me a pass in case we encounter a patrol."

"I don't have a pass."

"Quite true, so we will have to be extra careful. Come on, now. Sun's down, and we need to get out of this area where the patrols will be on alert for you."

Daphne shuddered and climbed on the horse as she began her journey into the unknown, her promising future in shambles.

Chapter
Seven

Laura ripped open the letter from home. It was the highlight of her week. She devoured these messages from home. She wanted to know about every little thing that occurred. Although some times the letters made her homesick, she determined to learn everything she could to be helpful when she returned home. She knew that she would, probably before long. Already Uncle Drew had called for her to return, but Rachel had talked him into a reprieve. But she felt restless, eager to get on with her life.

Since her excursion with Lucy Albright, school had become tedious and boring. Traveling with Lucy to her home near Bull Run had been a life-changing event for her. Seeing those brave young men and ministering to those young, injured soldiers so far away from home was the greatest thing that had ever happened to her. Now she was back at school and the war was in the doldrums. There had been no major battles in Virginia. It seemed that both sides lacked good generals. She had heard that General McClelland and President Lincoln did not see eye to eye on battle strategy and that President

Davis had yet to appoint the right general for the forces in Virginia.

Laura shook her head thinking about it. Why couldn't they come to terms with each other and avoid bloodshed altogether? She thought about Uncle Drew and Rachel. They surely had different political views about slavery and the South, but they came to terms. She smiled, remembering Rachel's fire and Andrew's patience. The sparkle in both their eyes when they looked at each other left Laura with a deep yearning that someday, somewhere there was that someone who would complete her world as Rachel had Uncle Drew's.

She sighed. Fat chance of meeting someone while stuck here in this girls' school. However she had heard rumors that the school was sponsoring a ball for the officers of the regiment nearby. What a grand idea! She could learn first hand what was going on in Virginia and maybe all those dancing lessons and instructions on how to be a proper lady might prove useful after all. However she would have to admit that the skills she was learning at the local infirmary seemed much more relevant. Even now she was part of a local ladies guild making bandages and putting together supplies for the local regiment. She couldn't help but let her imagination take her where those items she worked on would land.

As far as the war and her efforts, it was not that she wanted the war to go on. Far from it, seeing those wounded and ill young men made her realize the seriousness of what was coming. Her prayer was that it would conclude rapidly and spare both the North and South their finest. She was a Southerner from her very depths, but those soldiers in blue had families who loved them, shed their blood when wounded, and experienced fear in the face of enemies just like the boys in gray. But this one thing she knew ... if the battles came near, she would want to contribute, one way or another.

Lucy burst into the room they shared squealing with delight. "It's true, Laura, we are going to a ball for the soldiers!"

"The school is sponsoring it?"

Lucy made a face, "No, you know they wouldn't do anything so exciting. It would be too forward for a girl's school to sponsor one. Also 'they have a responsibility to the parents to maintain proper supervision of us'."

"Then where is the ball and how can we go?" Laura puzzled.

"We have permission to spend the night with my Auntie Elizabeth."

"Auntie Elizabeth?"

"You know Mrs. Elizabeth Donohue."

" I know who you meant but you said WE?" Laura questioned.

"Oh I signed your name to the request."

"I still don't understand."

"The ball will be at Aunt Elizabeth's friends, the Carlyle's across town."

"And?"

"And we are invited guests!!!"

Laura laughed. "I'll not begin to ask you how you arranged that. Mrs. Donahue is not even your aunt."

"No, but I would like her to be. She is soooo much fun."

"Yes, but she does occasionally raise some eyebrows," Laura protested, not altogether comfortable with Lucy's arrangement.

"The town gossips are jealous of her because Colonel Devonshire likes her so much and gives her special attention."

"That's not all that raises eyebrows."

"You mean because they say she is a spy."

"Shh. That's not even funny, Lucy. You could get her in a lot of trouble."

"If she were a spy, it would be for the South, not for the other side. Anyway whatever is there to spy about...you know, 'all is quiet on the Potomac." Lucy tossed her red curls, and changing the subject, looked in the mirror. "Whatever will we wear? We must be the most beautiful ladies there."

Laura laughed, "No matter what you wear, without a doubt you will be the loveliest fair maiden attending. Who can compete with those flaming red curls, blazing green eyes and skin like porcelain?"

Lucy furrowed her brow, "Only the one with hair of spun gold and eyes that sparkle like diamonds and are blue as a cloudless sky. You're right, we will be the belles of the ball!!"

"What are the ramifications of getting caught going to the ball? You know it will get back to the school."

"Where's your sense of adventure, Laura? We'll worry about that later."

"I can only imagine having to face Uncle Drew and tell him that I have been suspended from school."

"They wouldn't dare suspend you. They need your uncle's money too bad. Didn't you say something about an endowment or something?"

"Yes, but that wasn't a condition for my coming here. Rachel has a heart for the school and just wanted Uncle Drew to set up an endowment."

"Well, whatever the reason, they would think twice before kicking you out. Now me, that's a different scenario."

Laura laughed, "You have been in trouble a few times. Kinda strange with your father a clergyman and all."

Lucy waited for a few seconds then admitted, "I guess I've tried too hard to prove that I'm not different."

"Your infractions have not been serious, more mischievous."

Lucy nodded her head, "But still have caused my family some anxiety. I guess they keep wondering what's next."

"Which brings us back to the issue at hand. What kind of problems are we inviting by going to Miss Elizabeth's and attending this ball?"

"None at all. I know how you are about going by the rules, so I got permission. They said as long as Miss Elizabeth is going with us."

"Well, what about her 'reputation'? Is she in good standing with the school?"

"Oh, yes. You know those endowments we were talking about?"

"Oh, Miss Elizabeth?"

Lucy nodded her head. "BIG one. The school is not the problem. It's more my parents."

Laura frowned. "OH?"

"What they don't know can't hurt them."

Laura shook her head. "No, Lucy. Until you get permission from your parents we aren't going to go."

The tone in Laura's voice told Lucy there would be no adventure until she won her parent's approval, no matter how much they wanted to go.

A broad smile parted Lucy's full lips. "Got you! I know how you are, and I already have their permission. In fact, I had to have it before the school would agree."

"What about me?"

"Oh, you never get in trouble so you didn't have to have permission."

"That sounds a little strange, but I'll take it!"

Excitement of the coming events consumed the girls in the following days. The next three weeks seemed to pass in turtle fashion. Lucy bemoaned the fact she had nothing suitable to wear while Laura had a closet filled with finery. Laura laughed and invited her to select something from her wardrobe. Many of the gowns had never been worn because of lack of opportunity.

Finally, the long awaited day arrived. Lucy greeted it with her usual exuberance. The gown she had chosen was sea foam green with a sweetheart neckline and a lace overlay skirt. It seemed made just for her. The sweeping skirt accented her tiny waist and the lovely diamond pendant that Laura loaned her brought out the sparkle in her eyes. She turned from the mirror, satisfied that truly no one would be lovelier or dressed finer than the two of them.

Laura's gown of sapphire velvet along with the excitement of the evening turned her eyes to cobalt. With her hair caught up in curls, golden tendrils escaped to frame her face, her beauty turned heads as she entered just behind Elizabeth and Lucy.

A tall, handsome young man with dark hair stood in the corner with a group of young officers laughing and talking until Laura and Lucy swept in. Suddenly his eyes riveted on Laura and missed what his friend was saying. "Uh, what were you saying, Joel?"

"I said you are staring, Josh."

"I don't think I have ever seen anything as lovely as that." He nodded his head toward the women.

Joel nodded his head, "And which one is your pick? I'll give you first choice."

"There is only one choice for me, the lady in blue. She's mine for the night," Josh murmurs, "and maybe forever."

The group standing with them laughed at their friend, then Walter protested, "Whoa, what makes you special, Joel, Josh? We'll see who the fair maidens prefer."

The objections pelted the backs of the two young officers as they rushed to the side of the two young women in question.

Josh lightly touched Laura's arm as she paused and turned the full force of her cobalt eyes up to his warm brown ones. A slight smile lifted the corner of her lovely mouth. "Would you do me the honor of saving your first dance and all of them for me?"

Laura lifted one brow. "And you are?"

Josh blushed. "Allow Aunt Elizabeth to introduce us."

By this time all three of the women had halted and Elizabeth laughed, "This overeager young whelp is my nephew. Laura, may I present Josh Douglas, my nephew? Josh, this is Laura Meredith from Georgia who attends Turner's Ladies Academy."

Josh took Laura's hand and bowed over it. "An honor to make your acquaintance, ma'am."

Laura's laughing eyes greeted him even as her heart skipped a beat. "I'm glad to meet you, Josh Douglas, and you may have my first dance. As for all of them, I'm not so sure."

"Believe me, you will," Josh responded, a mischievous glint in his eyes. "I will save you from an evening of boredom with these other guys."

"So this is merely a matter of protection?" Laura laughed.

"Well, er," Josh stammered as two other young men pushed between them, clambering to be introduced.

Elizabeth laughed and made the proper introductions. The two grabbed Laura's dance card and filled it with their names, leaving Josh standing in the middle of the floor as one of his friends whisked her away across the dance floor. Laura looked back at the abandoned young man and smiled, mouthing, "I'm sorry."

Josh retreated to the sidelines, his mood thunderous, as he watched her dance away from him.

Joel meanwhile had taken Lucy's hand and led her across the dance floor before Elizabeth could make the introductions and the other young men could interfere, leaving their chaperone shaking her head and chuckling with delight.

Laura was whirled from partner to partner, leaving a chagrined Josh who refused to dance with anyone else. Every once in awhile when she would float by him, she gave him a broad smile. Finally she pleaded with her partner to give her a respite so she could get some punch. She didn't know when she had enjoyed anything as much as all the attention that she was receiving. Perhaps the dancing and etiquette lessons that she had considered so boring weren't a waste of time after all.

The fruit punch, smelling of citrus and pineapple, soothed her parched throat. Placing her cup on the table she turned toward the young man who had followed her to the refreshments when a strong arm captured her waist. Suddenly she was spinning around the ballroom in the arms of Josh Douglas. Looking up into his warm brown eyes, she lowered her lashes in a provocative manner and said, "Why, Mr. Douglas, you have just broken in line. I don't think you were the one scheduled for the next dance."

Josh growled, "No, but the rest of the dances are mine."

Laura smiled, lifting her card to look at it. "Really? Let me see what my card says."

Josh closed the card with one hand, "You can believe me, the rest are mine."

"Is that any way to treat your friends?" Laura chided.

"Have you not heard that all is fair in love and war?" he asked.

"Love and war?"

"We are at war you know."

"I'm well aware of that but I didn't think the war was between the two of us."

"We're not at war, but it gives urgency to the first part of that equation."

"Why, Mr. Douglas, are you in love with someone?"

"Miss Meredith, have you ever heard of love at first sight?"

"Yes, but I don't believe in it."

Josh paused, his face suddenly serious. He captured and held her eyes before replying, "Neither did I, until tonight."

Laura blushed as a strange and wonderful sensation engulfed her.

Elizabeth had enjoyed watching the girls make new friends until her own dance card filled. Afterwards she had little time to watch the girls as she was whirled around the floor from one waltz to another. Many both young and older men enjoyed the company of the lovely and articulate woman. After an especially lively tune, she begged her partner's indulgence so she could catch her breath as he had reserved the last two dances on her card. She excused herself and stepped onto the balcony. She was enjoying the brief respite when a deep voice behind her spoke, "You are looking lovely tonight, my dear."

"Why, Colonel, I didn't know you were here. I noticed a distinct absence of your name on my card," she teased.

"I only just arrived. I couldn't leave without telling you goodbye."

"Goodbye?"

"I'm afraid so."

Tears welled up in Elizabeth's eyes. "For how long?"

"I have no idea. They are sending me to the west. Things are heating up over there, and Johnston needs some help. Seems General Fremont has issued an emancipation proclamation on his own and although Missouri voted not to secede, he has stirred up a lot of secession sentiment in the state. Guerilla fighting has started, and we could take advantage of it with the right organization and leadership. Also, the Mississippi River is there and we can't let the feds get control of it or they will have a stranglehold on us."

"Is it as bad as that?"

"With Lincoln blockading all of our Southern ports and, if he takes the Mississippi, then we have no way to get the goods, guns, etc. that we need. Right now our ships are faster and smaller and have been able to elude their ships. But it will only be a matter of time until they seal our ports because they are building ships and increasing their navy rapidly. The South doesn't have the means to adequately build the ships we need nor manufacture the guns and weapons that are essential to us. We are dependent on foreign trade for that. President Davis wants me to go to Missouri and assess the situation and make a report to him personally."

"You'll go behind the lines?"

"I'm not at liberty to say how I'm going to evaluate the situation."

"Oh, Doug, that sounds so dangerous."

"War is dangerous."

"I shall worry about you and pray for your safe return every day."

"Thank you for that, Elizabeth. It will be a comfort to know I am in your thoughts and prayers."

"You are a dear friend and we have had such good times together," she remarked, averting her eyes so that he might not see the sadness there.

"I wish we had had more time and then perhaps we could become more than dear and compatible friends." His voice broke.

"Perhaps, but the war intrudes."

"Yes, the war intervenes and changes our objectives. We are not free to plan our tomorrows because we don't know if we have any."

Tears spilled over and coursed down her cheeks as the pain of a thousand couples who had to say goodbye to face a challenging, perhaps lonely future touched her heart, "But for another time and place..."

"Yes, another time and place love might have visited us. But as it is, I won't presume on a future for which I have no promise. I have no right to speak my heart, but I wanted to tell you goodbye and to tell you how much these past months being with you has meant."

Taking her hand, he kissed it, and he grinned. For a brief moment the Doug she had grown so fond of peeked out and he warned, "Elizabeth, don't guard you heart too closely. Whatever is in the past, let it go or you will miss the joy of love."

And suddenly she was alone again with only the leaves rustling in the trees to whisper Doug's warning.

Chapter Eight

"You've got to do what, Drew?" Rachel exclaimed.

"I've got to go to Savannah and check on Daphne."

"I thought Philip was going to take care of her."

"When I went to town yesterday, there was a letter waiting for me from Philip. He said something has happened to Daphne."

Rachel's heart thudded. "What do you mean, happened to her?"

"She has disappeared under some very strange circumstances. Her home was ransacked and there was blood on the rug," Andrew explained, his jaw tight, bracing for the conflict that he knew was ahead.

Rachel looked up into his eyes and noting the pain there, walked up to him and placed a hand on his chest. "I am truly sorry, darling. Of course you must go. Shall I come with you?"

"I want you to, but I really need for you to stay here. Roger is out of the area. He went to visit our troops and will be gone for about two months. The equipment we ordered is scheduled for delivery. I really don't need to be gone."

"But you must go! You won't rest a minute until you find her. I can take care of what needs to be done."

Andrew gazed at Rachel in disbelief. "You really mean that?"

Rachel smiled, "Surprised? Yes, I truly mean that. I had rather you not go, but you should. I don't understand your commitment, but I accept it. Now tell me what Philip said."

"He said an unsavory character came to see him last week telling him that Daphne was hiding fugitive slaves. He was a slave patrol and went to her house to apprehend the slaves. When he entered the house, she tried to kill him."

"How did she do this?" Rachel puzzled, remembering Daphne's petite frame.

"Said she brandished a large iron bar on the end of a pole and hit him in the head with it. Said that she obviously had it for just that very reason. Said he was nice to her and tried to talk her out of doing anything foolish, but she wouldn't listen. Said she was like a wild woman, and the next thing he knew he was laid out on her rug, and she was gone."

"So he turned her in to the slave patrol authorities?

"That's what is strange. He told Philip he didn't want to cause us, meaning Philip and me, any trouble. So he wanted to see if Philip had heard anything from her and, if he did, would he try to talk some sense into her. He claimed to respect the two of us so much that he was trying to protect our reputation."

"Well, that was considerate of him."

"Considerate enough to request two thousand dollars in gold as hush money."

"What?"

"Right. Daphne may be dead for all we know. That's clearly extortion and I told Philip to go right to the authorities and turn him in."

"Well I hope he did."

"He didn't."

"Why?"

"I don't know. All he said was I had better come."

Rachel nodded, "You must leave at once. Where do you think Daphne may be, that is if she is alive?"

Andrew replied shaking his head, "That's not all. Agan seems to be missing as well. My only hope is that they are together somewhere, otherwise I don't know why he would be gone."

"That's not likely. I saw the way Daphne looked at him the first night I was in Savannah. She looked as if he would be the last person in the world she would go to in time of trouble."

"Then where is she? And what has become of her? Where is Agan and what has happened to him?" Andrew sighed as if the whole world were on his shoulders.

"When do you leave?"

"In the morning. The train for Savannah leaves early. Meanwhile I'll try to tie up the loose ends here, so you won't have so much trouble handling the equipment when it comes in. You will have to pay for it, but Ambrose in the factory will get the men to set it up. You might supervise where you think the most efficient place is to put it. The men are real excited about it. We were fearful that it might not run the blockade, but it did. Now whether or not the next shipment will make it is just a guess."

The house seemed so empty with Andrew gone. The memory of his parting kiss still lingered on her lips. It told her how much he didn't want to go. Her response told him she didn't want him to. But it transcended what they wanted, and sacrifices could strengthen a relationship or make it weaker. How it would affect theirs was up to her. Could she put aside the emotions that threatened to drive a wedge between them?

Funny she had lived almost a year without anyone here but her and a servant. Now she had a houseful of servants and a home that was the envy of all the area. Rachel paused to look about. Her hand reached out to stroke the lovely dining table. The wood, a rich walnut, had a hand rubbed finish that left a warm patina. The aroma of lemon oil filled the room, and she knew that Jose had just polished it.

The formal dining table would seat a party of twenty, and she had entertained more than that several times since she and Andrew were married. Her guests didn't fool her. She knew that they were still reluctant to embrace her into society, but they needed to sell their cotton to Andrew so they accepted her. Tongues still gossiped as they are apt to do in a small community, but her husband had insisted, and she had complied. She had made a handful of friends, but her dearest was Bertha Emory. More surrogate mother than buddy, she knew she could always depend on the ample blue-eyed woman to be loyal and to tell her the truth whether it was pleasant or not. She had been her defender when the world seemed set against her and her encourager when she wanted to give up. Bertha had been Andrew's biggest fan when he set out to win her heart. She didn't know where she would be today if God hadn't sent both Roger and Bertha into her life.

Now she shuddered. She still had a burr in her soul, as Roger called it, and both he and Bertha were gone so how was she going to deal with it? She wanted with all her heart to be the wife Andrew needed and wanted. But until she settled this issue concerning Daphne she knew she couldn't be all that he needed. She trusted Andrew explicitly but his attachment to Daphne gnawed at her soul. If she trusted Andrew as she said she did, then what was it about Daphne that stood between them?

She knew what Roger would say. He would tell her to ask the Lord about it. She had been hesitant to. Guess she was afraid what the Lord might reveal. Wasn't that the case so often? She didn't go to Him because she really didn't want to find out that she was the one at fault. Even though she felt that Andrew was wrong not to explain to her concerning his commitment to the beautiful young woman, her resentment went deeper than that. Why? What was it?

The woman might even be dead. Then what? How would Andrew react? Would he be inconsolable? If so, why? And how would she react? In all honesty would she feel just a smidgen of relief? Guilt flooded her soul as she considered the possibility.

"OK, Lord, my heart hears you. Why do I feel as I do, and what shall I do about it?"

Rachel wandered into the library and picked up Andrew's much worn Bible. She loved the room. It bespoke of him. The fragrance of leather and oil, pine and wood smoke hit her full force and the longing for him overwhelmed her. Feeling the worn leather beneath her fingertips, she opened the pages and saw the notations he had made on almost every page. She sat down in the lounge chair of supple oxblood leather where each night he studied, often reading to her and they would discuss certain passages. Tears blinded her for a moment, realizing that he was not here tonight to show her a passage that would answer her question. In reality, it was a question she couldn't even discuss with him. She had already said too much when she told him she didn't like Daphne. The problem was a bone of contention between them and she had to have an answer. Would the Lord show her without Andrew or Roger to tell her?

Rachel flipped through the pages. Several hours passed before she knew it. God's dealings with the Israelites fascinated her as she read through Old Testament passages. Her own heart told her that her foolishness seemed mirrored in theirs. She was overwhelmed with God's wonderful grace and love to receive and forgive them when they repented. What joy they must have felt when He restored them. She could understand how they must have felt, for she, too, had received His forgiveness. Then she read the story of Moses' sister, Miriam, and her criticism of his wife. God was not pleased with Miriam's prejudice, and he severely chastised her.

Rachel's heart began to race. Was that her problem? Clearly God was not happy with prejudice. It stemmed from pride and according to what Andrew had read to her out of the Scriptures, pride was one of the sins God hated most. Was that her problem?

No, surely it wasn't. Perhaps it was merely a clash of personalities; hers and Daphne's were so different. It could be a little jealousy of Andrew's attention to another woman. Surely God would understand that. That wouldn't be a sin, would it? Didn't Scripture say that He was a jealous God?

On and on Rachel argued with the voice that spoke to her heart, trying to rationalize her feelings toward Daphne. Then, like a gentle spring rain on a parched soil, memories came of a Savannah waterfront and her thoughts toward the beautiful young woman of color as Andrew Meredith assisted both of them into the carriage with equal deference. She remembered the indignation she had felt that he had treated them both the same. She experienced outrage at his equal treatment because she was white and Daphne wasn't. Rachel gasped as the truth of her issue with Daphne became clear. It was an issue of pride, a sin that God hated.

Her tears began to fall gently at first, then flowed freely as into her mind streamed other occasions where racial pride had blinded her eyes and controlled her actions. With her soul laid bare, Rachel asked for forgiveness and received it and with it came an acceptance of why Andrew had freed Sweetwater slaves.

Long after twilight had come and gone and Jose had lit the lamps, Rachel continued to read. How joyous to find affirmation in the New Testament that Jesus Christ had come to not only remove the sin that separated God and man but also would remove the wall of separation between people. Rachel prayed for that miracle and had received it. Now she asked God to bring her emotions in line with her new revelation and commitment.

The few days turned into a week, and a telegram arrived from Andrew with a terse message that he had not found what he was looking for. She knew that he had not located Daphne. Rachel's heart constricted for the anguish her husband must be feeling and fear for the young woman's safety gripped her. Questions ran rampant through her mind. Was Andrew safe? Would he do anything foolish? Then irrelevant, was he missing her as much as she was missing him?

She laughed at her own self-absorption. There was nothing like a little separation to remind her not to take their relationship for granted and to cherish every moment that she had with him. She sighed and questioned why had God chosen to bless her in such a wonderful way. With it came the thought "for to whom much is given, much is required". She shuddered, willing away the fears that rushed in.

Two nights later, just after dark, a sharp pounding at the door interrupted Rachel as she sat at Andrew's large desk paying bills and checking invoices. Since the servants had retired for the night, she made her way to the door, puzzled as to why anyone would venture out in the torrent of September rain that was falling outside. The insistent pounding began again and she hurried toward the door, mindful that she was alone except for the cook who slept in a room far in the back of the house next to the kitchen.

Peering through the sidelights, she could barely make out the outline of a large man who seemed to be carrying something. Reluctant to open the door she paused beside the door until a familiar voice tinged with an island accent yelled, "Miz Rachel, I need your help. Please open the door."

Rachel jerked the door open and standing before her was a rain-drenched Agan holding a limp Daphne in his arms. "Agan! What happened?"

"It's Daphne. She's sick. We've been traveling for days. Hiding in the woods. I wouldn't have brought her here, but she's going to die if I don't get her help." The haughty demeanor that usually characterized Agan was absent and in its place, fear and frustration.

"Take her upstairs to the first guest room on the right. It is the largest and most comfortable. I'll get both of you some dry clothes. Where have you been and what has happened? Andrew is in Savannah looking for Daphne."

"It's a long story, ma'am. But first things first. If you could get us some dry clothes and something to eat. We haven't eaten in two days and Daphne is having chills."

Rachel ran to the cook's room and told her to go get Louisa, Jose and Adam as she needed them. Instructed her to warm up the soup and venison they had for supper and to get a pot of water boiling. Next she ran to her room and began to pull out some of her clothes, then shook her head and went to the wardrobe to pull out winter things. They were cold and needed something to warm them. She finally settled on her warm flannel nightgown and some of Andrew's heavier working clothes.

With socks and warm clothing in hand, she arrived at the door just as Agan knelt beside Daphne, anguish written on every line of his exhausted face. His hand reached out and, with tenderness so uncharacteristic for him, stroked her face. She made no response but remained still as death, her breathing rapid and shallow. He whispered something to her, but so quietly that Rachel failed to make out what he said.

"Here, Agan, put these clothes on. I ordered Louisa to heat some water and Adam to prepare a warm bath for you. You are chilled to the bone."

"No, I need to see to Daphne."

"I will take care of Daphne's needs. She will need you later, and we don't need two of you ill," Rachel commanded gently. "Soon as you are dressed and have eaten we will talk."

Taking a dry soft towel, Rachel gently dried Daphne's hair. Louisa helped remove her soaked clothing, replacing them with the ones she had found in the wardrobe. She briskly rubbed her arms and legs with the towels, but still Daphne didn't respond.

Rachel paced the kitchen floor, pondering what to do. She needed to send for the doctor, but she did not know if he was home and then there remained the problem of this torrential rain. She had heard there had been a bad storm on the coast of Florida and assumed that it had made its way here. How long had Agan and Daphne been out in it? Where had they been? Where had they been staying?

Agan entered the kitchen and she turned toward him. "We changed Daphne's clothing and I have ordered some soup for her. If she doesn't gain consciousness we will have a hard time getting it down her. How long has she been ill?"

"Three days. It started with chills and fever. We had to go through the swamps to avoid slave patrols. She must have picked up something there."

"Did you drink the water?"

Agan nodded his head, "We didn't have a choice. We were thirsty and didn't dare show our faces. Not many fresh springs where we were forced to travel. We figured every patrol from here to Savannah was looking for us."

"Tell me what happened."

"Daphne told me she had killed a man, so I had to get her away from there. I had no plans to come here, but it seems here we are." A sad smile softened his tone.

"Yes, here you are," Rachel agreed.

"It looks like she needs Mr. Andrew Meredith and his protection after all," Agan declared, bitterness in his voice.

"Is that what you think, Agan?"

"That's what I know. It is obvious I couldn't protect her. Look at her now." A sudden vulnerability displayed in this usually self-sufficient and confident man.

"Her condition is not your fault. You did what you could, putting your own safety at risk. Maybe things aren't as bad as they seem," Rachel encouraged.

"They couldn't be worse. It will be only a matter of time before the authorities put two and two together and trace her here. She committed a crime. Mr. Meredith will be prosecuted for harboring a criminal."

"Maybe not."

"There is no maybe to it. You don't understand because you are white." Agan said, his teeth clinched.

Rachel gave a mirthless chuckle. "I've been told that before."

"Well, it's true."

"True or not, things are not exactly what you think."

"How is that?"

"For starters, Daphne didn't kill anyone. She did injure a man. How that little girl did so is a mystery to me, but obviously she did knock a man out; however, he didn't go to the authorities." Rachel explained.

"He didn't? Even when hitting a white man is a criminal offense?" Agan's eye widened at the news.

"It seems he thought extortion would be more profitable so he went to Philip instead and asked for money not to report it to the authorities."

"And what did Lord Duval do?"

"I'm not quite sure because I don't have the whole story, but I gathered he gave him the money."

"That won't be the end of it."

"I'm sure. Andrew is in Savannah seeing what he can work out."

"Of course." Agan commented, his lips in a thin, tight line.

"He doesn't even know whether Daphne is alive or dead. He is beside himself. I will be so happy to telegraph him with the news that you are here."

"This may be disrespectful, but how can you abide that?"

"What?"

"Your husband's obvious attachment to another woman."

Rachel's face flushed as anger surged through her. Controlling her voice, she answered quietly but firmly, "You are correct, that was very disrespectful, but I will forgive that statement on the grounds that you are beside yourself with worry. As for your question, I don't know what you mean by 'attachment', but I assure you his only involvement with Daphne is motivated by the goodness of his heart just as he did for you, Agan Chero. And as you know from experience, my husband has a very good heart."

"Yes, I have received his generosity, but it never led to this devotion that Daphne has for him."

"Maybe hers is appreciation which is sadly lacking in you, I'd say."

"What she feels for your husband goes far beyond appreciation, and that's the core of my problem. Why does she feel thus? What has been between them all these years that would foster that kind of loyalty and er, 'affection'? At one time she loved me. Your husband never encouraged that."

Pain and doubt gripped Rachel's heart for a moment, then determined she countered, "I can't answer those questions, Agan. But this one thing I know, I trust my husband completely. And whatever has transpired to weld her attachment to Andrew Meredith is honorable and above board."

"How do you know that, Mrs. Meredith?" Agan questioned quietly.

"Because he is that kind of man, honorable in every way. Furthermore, you will not sit in my home ever again and allude to any evil attachments between Daphne and him. Do you understand?"

Agan took a deep breath. "I understand. And forgive me for any disrespect that I displayed toward you. You are correct, it is my state of mind. Even so, it is inexcusable to talk to you as I have. You have been very kind taking us in, and it truly is wonderful to observe the love and trust you have toward your husband."

"Now to the present situation. As soon as you have your supper, get the carriage and go find Dr. Tim Hutson. Elijah will give you directions to his house. If he isn't at home someone will tell you where to go. When you locate him, tell him that we have need of him right away."

***

Through the midnight hour and beyond, Rachel sat at Daphne's bedside. When chills struck her, she covered her in quilts, then when sweats followed, she removed the covers and wiped her brow with cold cloths. Little by little she was able to get a few drops of water through her parched lips. All efforts to get soup into her failed because for the most part she remained unconscious except for brief periods when her eyes would open and she would moan, "Oh I have killed him, what shall I do, Mr. Andrew?"

Just before dawn, Rachel's relieved ears heard gravel crunching under buggy wheels. She ran to the window and peered out. The light in hallway spilled into the darkness and illumined Agan and Dr. Tim alighting from the buggy. Both ran up the wide veranda steps. The rain had finally subsided, and now the wind howled, bending the trees and hurling branches from the them.

***

"What do you think is wrong, Dr. Tim?" Rachel whispered as the young doctor finished his examination.

"I can't be positive, but from what your man told me..." Dr. Tim began.

"You mean, Agan," Rachel corrected.

"Yes, Agan. What I learned and what I see here, her symptoms seem to be that of miasma, but I don't understand where she could have contracted it."

Rachel looked over the doctor's shoulders and met Agan's eyes, dark and forbidding, daring her to explain to the good doctor.

"You know that she is from Savannah. They have just arrived in this area."

"No, I didn't know. I've only been in this area for a few weeks, and I've yet to learn much about the residents. Mostly, I've been out delivering babies and checking on the health of the slaves. You know how you and the other plantation owners value your possessions."

Rachel saw Agan's jaw tighten and she remarked, "Perhaps some of us value them as people not possessions, Dr. Tim."

The doctor squinted his eyes and gazed at her before replying, "I didn't mean to offend, Mrs. Meredith. I hail from Boston and I just assumed...."

"That's the problem with most northerners, they assume before they have the facts. In fact I am surprised that you are here instead of Massachusetts since we are at war."

"The war caught me in Savannah. I was visiting some friends there and someone told me about the therapeutic springs around the Marietta area so I journeyed on up here to see for myself. I found quite a lot of union sentiment there and thought I might just ride out the war here. Surely, it won't last long and I doubt that it will reach here."

109

"I pray that what you say is true, Dr. Tim, but you best keep your union sentiments to yourself if you want a practice here. You are correct in saying that there is some union sentiment here, in fact my husband was against secession."

"Well there, you see, I've found a friend already. I shall look forward to meeting your husband."

"Let me warn you before you do. He was against secession, but he is a southerner to the bone and will fight to the death to defend her."

"I see. Thank you for your advice, Mrs. Meredith. I'm just getting my bearings in this wonderful part of Georgia, and I don't want to offend anyone, nor judge the culture too harshly. I would like to make my home here. The climate is so much better than Boston, not to mention the beautiful young ladies I have met."

Rachel laughed, "I can see where that would be an incentive for a young man of your age and profession. Just be careful and stay away from politics, and pray your assessment of the war proves true. Now what about Daphne?"

"Since you told me she just recently came from Savannah, then I am sure my diagnosis is correct."

"Then what's to be done? Does it just run its course? What is the prognosis? Can it be deadly?"

"As weak as she seems to be, the outlook is not good, I'm afraid." Dr. Tim shook his head.

Agan stepped up to the bedside and looked down at Daphne, a grimace distorting his face.

"Is she your wife, Agan?" Dr. Tim asked, sympathy threading his voice.

"No, just an old and dear friend. Mr. Meredith brought both of us from the islands when we were just teenagers."

"You two belong to Mr. Meredith then."

"No, we belong to no man. We both are free," Agan answered, his voice hard.

"Oh, you bought your freedom?"

"No, Mr. Meredith freed us voluntarily. But what can we do about Daphne? Is she going to die?" Impatience raised Agan's voice.

Dr. Tim cocked an eyebrow and shot Rachel a questioning look.

"That's right, doctor. What about Daphne?"

The doctor sighed, then shook his head. "I'm not God, you know. But I am sure this is a miasmic condition, and I have heard of a treatment that some doctors have experimented with."

"Anything, doctor, that will give her a chance," Agan's usual arrogance lost in his pleading.

"I prescribe giving her five grams of quinine every two hours, and if she doesn't improve bump it up to ten grams."

"I thought that was a preventive treatment."

"There is some discussion that if it can prevent then it could be a treatment."

"What have we got to lose?" Rachel asked.

"Everything if we don't try something," Agan concluded.

"He's right. Without something done, it would be a miracle for her to survive. It will be anyway even if the medicine works."

"Do you have some with you?"

"I don't know why...we usually don't need it in Boston. I hardly thought I would need it here, but somehow brought it with me from Savannah."

Rachel gave him an exhausted smile, "Another miracle."

"Mrs. Meredith, I will show myself out and I'd advise you to get some sleep before I have two patients."

111

She nodded. "Thank you, but I need to stay up and get that medicine into her."

Agan turned from Daphne. "Mz. Rachel, I will see to Daphne. You go to bed. I appreciate all that you have done for her...for the both of us."

Rachel nodded her head, "Call me if you need me. I am going to stay in the guest room down the hall so I will be near."

A puzzled look washed over Agan's face. "Why? Why are you doing this?"

"You could call it a 'spiritual awakening'. " With a mysterious smile Rachel left the room leaving a puzzled Agan in her wake.

Rachel slept fitfully through dawn and a few hours beyond. With the sun streaming through her windows, she sat up with a start. A soft knock at her door awakened her, and she heard the voice of Agan calling her name. She smoothed her rumpled clothes, her heart racing with concern for Daphne and opened the door. "How is she?"

"She seems to be some better. I was able to get more liquids in her, but I did increase the quinine. I thought you might like a cup of coffee and a scone." He nodded toward the tray.

Opening the door wider, Rachel took the tray. "Thank you, Agan. I didn't realize how hungry I was until I smelled this coffee. I will be in to relieve you as soon as I finish."

"No need to hurry. I made a pallet beside her bed so I got a little sleep between her medications."

Midmorning Rachel had her carriage brought about, knowing that she had to get a message to Andrew. She left for Bertha Isaacs house to see if Jacob would go to Marietta for her. The day proved glorious; the air had a hint of autumn and washed crystal clean from the storm the night before. The very essence seemed to dispel the cobwebs and lingering doubts from her mind. Since Agan was caring for Daphne and Dr. Tim was to visit again, she decided to make the trip into town herself. She needed the time to think.

Rachel arrived at the train station to send her wire just as a loud whistle announced the arrival of the train from Atlanta. A moment of longing for Andrew's presence filled her being. If he were here, he could lay all this fear and doubt to rest, but he wasn't. It was an exercise in faith as the doubts bombarded her, and she refused to give them entrance.

Jeremy looked up and smiled, "Hello, Mz. Meredith, I was just going to send Daryl out to your place. You have a wire from Mr. Meredith. It came yesterday morning, but the weather was too rough to get it out to you. I hope it wasn't too important."

Rachel snapped, "Of course it was important! That's why I drove all the way into Marietta to send Mr. Meredith a wire. If I could make it, surely you could have delivered it by now."

Jeremy dropped his eyes and muttered, "I'm sure sorry, ma'am, but I just came to work."

"Well, you better tell me who was working because----."

Suddenly a familiar voice spoke behind her, "Because my wife is going to have someone's skin, if they don't take more responsibility for their duties."

Rachel whirled around and threw herself into Andrew's waiting arms, "Oh Drew. You are home at last."

"Yes, darling, home at last and what a welcome! Maybe I need to go off more often." Meredith chuckled, his smile lightening his tired features.

"You look so tired, dear."

"I am and frustrated. I still have no word on Daphne. Seems she just disappeared." Andrew explained as he assisted her into the carriage.

"Daphne and Agan are at Sweetwater."

Andrew gave a relieved sigh. "Wonderful. That's why I'm home. I figured that since all else failed, they probably would land here, but they can't stay. That rascal will soon make the connection as to where I am and follow."

"It's not all good news, darling," Rachel warned.

Andrew's brow wrinkled, his eyes questioning.

"Daphne is very ill. She may not recover."

Pain washed Andrew's face, turning it pale.

"What happened?"

"With exposure to the elements and nothing to eat she came down with what Dr. Tim calls miasma."

A stern look turned Andrew's eyes cold, "They had nothing to eat?"

"When they arrived at our door, both were soaking wet and Daphne was unconscious. He said they had had nothing to eat for two days."

"Why didn't Agan look after her better?"

"He was trying to avoid slave patrols. He thought Daphne had killed the man, and his friends had removed the body,"

"Well then, as soon as they made it to our area why didn't he bring her to Sweetwater?"

"He was reluctant to seek our help."

"What kind of fool notion is that?" Andrew roared.

"You'll have to ask Agan for that explanation yourself," Rachel replied, a new coolness in her voice.

"You can count on it, I will."

"Then you had better be prepared for his answer."

"What do you mean by that, Rachel?"

"Just what I said. Obviously there has been a volcano brewing within him for some while and you've either been oblivious to it, ignored it, or thought it would just go away."

Andrew smiled and reached for her hand. "I've been a bit busy and wildly distracted."

"This started long before me, Andrew. Even I noticed the tension, though I didn't know what the source was until last night."

"Well, what is it?" he queried.

"It's not for me to explain, it's something between you and Agan."

"Stars above, woman," Andrew bellowed, "I've been nothing but good to Agan, I've given him every opportunity, and I have never wronged him."

"Except in the area of his heart."

"Now what's that supposed to mean?"

"Like I said, you'll have to ask Agan about that, but since it touches an area that you don't like to address, be prepared for an answer you won't like," Rachel advised, ending the conversation.

The two went by the livery and picked up Andrew's horse, hitching it to the back of the carriage, for the long silent trip home.

———————————

Andrew went straight to the room where Daphne lay. Finding Agan by her side, he merely nodded at him. "How is she? Has there been any change?"

Daphne stirred and opened up her eyes. When she saw Andrew, she reached toward him, ignoring Agan, "Oh, Mister Andrew, I am so sorry. I have put you in great trouble."

Andrew took her hand and asked, his voice tender, "What are you talking about, little one?"

"Didn't Agan tell you? I killed a man." Tears streamed down her cheek. Andrew's heart broke. He'd never seen her cool facade dissolved in this manner. No matter what faced her, she was always stoic.

"Hush now, you didn't kill anyone."

"Yes, I did. Please listen to me. He's dead, and now I am as good as dead." Daphne moaned. "But, most of all, I have put you at risk. I mustn't be here. You must send me away."

Agan spoke, "Daphne, Mr. Meredith is correct. You didn't kill anyone."

"He's alive?" she questioned, turning her head from Agan to Andrew, "How do you know? Have you seen him?"

"I haven't, Daphne, but Philip has. He did not turn you in to the slave patrol," Andrew explained.

"I can't believe it. A miracle. I'm safe." A relieved smile lifted her dry and cracked lips as she drifted off to sleep.

Andrew turned to leave the room and motioned Agan to follow. Rachel remained behind to moisten Daphne's lips. She felt her head and smiled. The fever had left, at least for a while. For the first time in nearly twenty-four hours she breathed a sigh of relief.

Making her way down the stairs, Rachel heard Andrew's voice coming from the library and followed. She paused at the door, hesitating to go in but able to hear the conversation between the two men. Feeling that she was intruding, but compelled to stay, she didn't move.

"Agan, I don't know what you were about, putting Daphne through what you did. She could have died."

"I did the best I could, Mr. Meredith. I don't possess the advantages that you have to protect her. And then we didn't have the information that you have." Sarcasm tinged his voice.

"Had you stayed in Savannah, you would have."

"I couldn't take that chance. Would you have taken that risk? I know first hand what those slave patrols will do," Agan stated through tight lips.

"That's my very point. You put Daphne at risk involving her in who knows what kind of mischief."

"It was anything but mischief, sir. But you are quite right. I did put her at risk, and I regret it deeply."

"Regret just won't do, Agan. What in the world did you do to entice her? Philip said whatever it was, and now we are pretty sure what it was, he could not dissuade her."

"I didn't entice her. I showed her a world that she didn't know existed. She made her own choice."

"Did you not care that you put her at risk?"

"Respectfully, sir, did you, Mr. Meredith?"

"What in the world did I do to put her at risk?"

"You freed her, educated her, then imprisoned her in your world by elevating her above her own people and allowing her to be ridiculed by yours. Her only world is and was you. Even in her delirium, it was you she called out for, your welfare for which she was concerned. You used her, and then you cast her aside when someone better came along! You robbed her of any chance of happiness with someone else."

"I never prevented her from having a life of her own, someone to love, to love her."

"What about me, Mr. Meredith?"

Andrew shrugged, "What about you, Agan? I'll admit I discouraged a relationship when you both were younger, but that is because you were too young, and I was protecting you from the passions of youth."

"Or saving her for your passions, Mr. Meredith?"

A crashing sound sped Rachel into the library where she found Agan sprawled on the floor, and Andrew standing over him, shouting, "Don't you know, you ungrateful whelp, why I protected her so fiercely, and why I care for her so much? She is MY SISTER!"

A hush filled the room; only the ticking of the clock down the hall could be heard. Rachel's gasp broke the silence, and Agan sat up, rubbing his jaw, too stunned to respond.

Suddenly, all the tension drained from Andrew, and he collapsed in his chair, his head in his hands. Rachel went to him, and kneeling beside him, caressed his face. He captured her hands. Forgetting the presence of Agan, he confessed to his wife. With a single tear escaping down his cheek, the strong self-made man removed the bone of contention that had hampered their marriage. "The humiliation of what my father did has followed me all the days since I ran away from home. I have tried to make up to Daphne for the violation my father visited on her mother, but I have carried the shame of it in my heart, too great a shame to share even with you, my darling. It was wrong, and, as Roger once told me, caused a burr in my soul."

"Roger knew?"

"Yes, Roger figured it out."

"He never told me."

"It wasn't his to tell. It was my responsibility to deal with that burr in my soul. I was stubborn and didn't. And because of it I've put you through pain and doubt. Will you forgive me?"

"There is nothing to forgive. What you have tried to do for Daphne was a testimony to the kind of man you are. That you couldn't bring yourself to share this with me or anyone is understandable."

Andrew turned toward Agan, still sitting on the floor, trying to take it all in. "Agan, you are right. I did imprison her, but it was by overprotecting her, not using her for my pleasure. I did discourage that budding relationship between the two of you, not because I had anything against you, but because you both were too young. Later, I would have had no objections, but somehow the attraction between the two of you seemed to have evaporated."

"No, sir, it didn't evaporate. I killed it by hating you and making her choose between loyalty to you or to me. She chose you. I thought for the wrong reasons. Now I know how wrong I was."

"You hated me? What have I done to you?" Pain darkened Andrew's eyes.

"I blamed you for stealing Daphne's love."

"But I didn't."

"I understand that, now, but it doesn't erase the past."

"No, but sometimes there could be a new beginning. Like now."

"What do you mean, sir?" Agan asked.

"It's obvious that the two of you can't stay here. It's only a matter of time until that scoundrel finds his way here. When he exhausts all the money he can garner from us, he will seek his revenge on Daphne, one way or the other."

"So what's to be done?" Agan questioned.

"I talked to Philip, and he suggests that Daphne go to Charleston, catch one of the blockade runners and go to Boston. The curator of a gallery there wants more of her paintings and wants to meet her. I had a home there that Daphne is quite familiar with and now belongs to Philip. He said he would quite willingly sell it back to me for her a residence if he could stay there when he comes to Boston.

Sadness dulled Agan's eyes as he took in what Andrew said. He slowly nodded his head agreeing, although his heart ached at the thought. "That sounds like the best solution. She surely could support herself and have a safe place to live."

"To tell you the truth, I have had second thoughts about that solution."

Alarmed, Agan frowned. "Second thoughts?"

"Yes, in light of what you have said, and the gossip that Daphne has already endured, I don't think it would be a good thing for Philip to stay at Daphne's when he is in Boston."

"Why Philip wouldn't lay a hand on Daphne, Andrew," Rachel exclaimed.

Andrew laughed. "Just trying to alleviate any gossip, Bostonians notice what's going on, I assure you. They will remember Daphne, and who knows what they thought about our relationship."

"But that was such a generous offer from Lord Philip. Won't he be offended?"

"Of course not, but he might have some problems with my idea."

"And what would that be, Drew?" Rachel asked, puzzled.

"That Daphne have someone with her. I propose Agan go with her. In that case Philip would lose his manager at Balmara."

"Well what good would that do? Where would Agan live? He couldn't stay there with her. You would still have a man and a woman improperly living in the same house."

"It would be totally proper as soon as Agan convinces Daphne to marry him. How long will that take, Agan?"

"I believe as long as it takes me to convince her that my priorities have changed, and that I no longer hold any resentment toward you. One of us will have to tell Daphne who she is. Who will it be?"

Andrew replied, "As long as I am into confessions, I will. Anyway, it is my responsibility. As soon as she is well enough, I'll see to it."

Several weeks passed before Daphne recuperated enough to make the long journey to Charleston. During the interval, she reveled in the knowledge of who she was. It changed nothing concerning her relationship with Andrew, but it had answered the many questions that had plagued her over the years. Meanwhile, Agan's constant attention without his former bitterness stirred the embers of times past, and they began anew. By the time she was strong enough to make the trip, Roger arrived home, just in time to perform the wedding.

Because several weeks passed and there was no word from her pursuer, Daphne questioned Andrew about staying at Sweetwater. The tender light in Andrew's eyes told her that was an option that he preferred, but instead answered, "Philip was right, Daphne. I kept you from your best. You have a greater and broader future in Boston. Are you not excited about the potential of your art? And there waiting for you is your own home with Agan and perhaps children down the road. No, as much as I will miss you, your place is in Boston with your husband. There will be no opportunity for you here, and just because we have not heard from that despicable George doesn't mean he won't land on our doorstep seeking his revenge. For your own protection and for the good of your future, you must leave." Andrew reached out and took her hand, capturing her eyes he said, "But I will miss you terribly. My heart and Rachel's go with you."

Daphne smiled through her tears, remembering Rachel's care of her. "Yes, I think even Miss Rachel will.

A week before her wedding, Daphne asked Rachel if she could talk to her about something, and Rachel agreed, puzzled about what might be concerning the young woman. Everything seemed to be progressing as planned. The expression on Agan's face had made a complete change from cool haughtiness to warm and inviting. His admiration for Andrew grew each day as he shed the last vestige of his resentment. His happiness in winning Daphne's trust and love appeared boundless. He could barely restrain his eagerness to claim her as his own. He stood amazed at the dreams that had risen from the wreckage of his former questionable ambitions.

Rachel found Daphne waiting for her in Andrew's study. When Daphne asked Rachel to close the door behind her, Rachel raised an eyebrow questioning.

"I don't want us to be interrupted. I just don't know when this new man, Agan, will bounce in." Daphne explained with an unsure smile.

"I know he's excited about the two of you and the promise of your future together."

"It's more than that. Something happened to him after Mr. Roger came back. He said he would tell me all about it, once we're married."

"He has loved you for a long time."

"He said since the day he first laid eyes on me. I told him that was crazy, I was just a skinny little thirteen year old gal."

"You must have been more than that to him."

"He said I was beautiful, and I wouldn't even look at him. I did notice him, but I didn't want him to know it."

Rachel laughed. "We women do have to keep up our mystique."

" I don't think it was that. I was just scared of everybody. My ma was so afraid someone would send me off that I made myself aloof from everyone. That wasn't what I wanted to talk to you about."

"Oh?"

"I wanted to thank you for all you did while I was sick. You may not know that I knew, but I did. Every time I would moan or wake up, you would be wiping my forehead or giving me something to drink. My question is why? Something has changed in you, Miss Rachel. In the past, we didn't like one another very much."

Rachel laughed. "Are you admitting you didn't like me?"

"It was more that I didn't want to like you. You threatened my world. And sure enough, you did end the world that was mine. I didn't know what I would do. How was I to know that a better world awaited me? Aunt Tilde always talked about a God who had a plan for our lives. I guess I would like to know more about Him. When I was in that terrible trouble, and when I came so near dying, I realized that I needed Him. Do you know what Aunt Tilde was talking about?"

"As a matter of fact I do, Daphne."

"Would you tell me, then?"

"She was talking about a personal relationship with God. Not just hearing about Him or saying with our lips we believe there is a God, but to know Him in a personal way."

"How in the world can you do that? I believe that there is a God in heaven, and that He created the world and all that is in it. But how can you connect with Him in a personal sort of way?"

"That can only come through His son, Jesus Christ."

"How does that happen?"

"Daphne, do you ever feel as if there is a wall between you and God, or you and someone else?"

"Yeah, you."

"And by your own admission you don't feel connected to God."

"That's right. He's way up in heaven, and I'm down here."

"Have you ever considered that the separation is something called sin?"

"I've never done anything really bad so how come it's sin separating me from God or from you?"

"The Bible is God's word to us. It tells us about Him and what He expects from us. His word states 'all have sinned and come short of the glory of God.' Now that means everyone, you, me, Andrew, Agan. All of us have failed to reach the mark God has set up for us."

"Now what mark is that, Miss Rachel?"

"Perfection. We have to be perfect in every way. Are you perfect, Daphne?"

"Of course not. Nobody is, so how can anyone know God and go to heaven?"

"That's the dilemma." Rachel smiled at the earnestness reflected on Daphne's face.

"So what's the answer?"

"The scripture tells us that the wages of sin is death."

"I thought there was hope; does that mean we are all condemned?"

"There is a penalty that has to be paid for sin, no matter how little or how big, same penalty, death."

"That's not very encouraging," Daphne sighed. "But there must be an answer for it because you are happy, Andrew is happy, Mr. Roger is very happy. I don't understand how could you have any peace if you knew that there is no hope? That your sins were going to have to be paid for?"

Rachel's smile was glorious, "That's the right question, Daphne. The rest of that verse says that although the wages of sin is eternal death, which we know is separation from God, the gift of God is eternal life through Jesus Christ, His Son."

"How is that possible?" Daphne asked her voice low with a tremble in it.

"Have you ever heard about Jesus dying on the cross?"

Daphne nodded her head.

"That's what it was all about."

Suddenly, Daphne's eyes brightened, and she caught her breath, "He paid the wages for my sin, and I don't have to die? I can have a relationship with God?"

"That's right, Daphne. Because He paid the wages for our sin by his death on Calvary, our sin debt is removed, and our separation from God is over. You don't have to face eternal death because He died in your place and my place."

"You mean everybody's going to heaven because Christ paid their sin debt?" Daphne asked, puzzled.

"Not exactly. The availability is there for anyone who accesses it, but not everyone does."

"How do you access it?" Daphne's heart began to race.

"The first thing that we have to realize is that we are sinners and have a desperate need for His sacrifice. The next thing is to repent, which means to turn from whatever is keeping us from Him, and to acknowledge that we are sinners and lost without His sacrifice. If we ask Him to forgive us on the basis of what He has done for us when He paid for our sin, and invite Him into our lives, He comes into our heart. It is then that we have a personal relationship with God. It appears pretty simple but that one request makes an eternal difference." Rachel smiled and stood up. "I think I hear a ruckus outside the door, and I think your guy is just about to bounce in."

Daphne returned the smile, uncertainty gone, an inner glow lighting her eyes.

The house seemed empty after Daphne and Agan's departure. Andrew stayed busy at the mill, but Rachel had time to think. What a difference these several weeks had made. She would never have thought that she would miss the beautiful girl. But she did.

She hoped that they would know sooner rather than later if the couple made it to Boston safely. Philip would somehow get the word to them. The plan was for him to meet them in Charleston with Daphne's paintings in tow. He would then accompany the two to their new home and introduce them to Carlyle.

They were sailing on one of Philip's new fast steamers and although he felt their chances were good to run the blockade by outrunning the federal gunboats, there were no guarantees. Rachel would breathe easier once she knew for sure they had made it. It was necessary that they went as soon as possible because the net continued to tighten around the South, and it wouldn't be long before Philip had some decisions to make for himself. He could hardly continue to have a foot in each world, so to speak. He continued to balance a ship building business in Boston and a plantation in Savannah. Rachel shrugged. Those were problems too big for her to work out!

A loving smile lifted her lips. How good it was to be able to turn her problems over to Andrew's strong and capable hands. How different from two years ago when her life was in shambles and she lived at the mercy of her evil neighbor. Regret washed her face as the memories of what she had risked and nearly lost because of her stubborn bitterness flooded in.

Willing away the unpleasant memories, she thought about the newlyweds. How excited they were! The Daphne with the cool and unshakeable facade appeared a new woman. Her eyes glowed with soft love lights in them when she looked at Agan, leaving no doubt that the emotions and attachment which began so long ago had returned in abundance. That Philip rescued her paintings, all except the river scene, proved an added blessing. They would have the income from her art along with the gold she had brought with her to support them until Agan found work.

Their ability to be self-sufficient appeared paramount to Agan. He had conveyed to Andrew that the house he had provided in Boston was enough, that from that time forward, her husband would be the caregiver for his wife. Andrew seemed to understand and willingly relinquished his care of Daphne to Agan.

Rachel entertained no worries about their survival. Philip had said that Daphne had no idea of the depth of neither her gift nor the commercial success it offered. Once again she marveled and treasured the gift Daphne had left her and Andrew.

On the day prior to Daphne's wedding she had presented to Rachel and Andrew the exquisite painting that she had been working on during her recovery. Andrew had ordered paints and canvas shipped from Savannah, hoping that they would comfort and encourage Daphne's recovery. And it did. As soon as her strength permitted, she found a sunny alcove where Agan set up her easel, and she began a painting.

She covered it each day and had dared anyone to touch it. Curiosity built as to what the painting was and if she would have it finished in time. Although they entreated her to give them a peek, she remained adamant they must wait. She seemed to relish the mystery and, in fact, it seemed to aid in her recovery. Andrew and Rachel assumed it was one she hoped to sell along with the others Philip was bringing. It should prove a valuable boost to their nest egg.

So they all looked forward with anticipation and curiosity to the unveiling of the painting. Rachel was especially curious since she had never seen any of Daphne's work.

The moment finally arrived when Daphne brought the shrouded painting into the library where Rachel and Andrew were reading. Agan trailed behind her, a pleased look plastered on his face. With a shy smile she announced that she had finished, and it was time for the unveiling. Putting their books aside, the two of them moved to the edge of their seats, both conjecturing whether it would be a seascape or a portrait.

With a flourish, Daphne pulled the shroud off and Andrew and Rachel sat speechless, their eyes locked on the painting, both in shock, disbelieving. There in living color before them was Rachel on the Savannah dock as Andrew had seen her that first day, her hair in wild profusion, green eyes blazing. It was the day that forever changed their three lives. It was so real, it seemed that she could have stepped from the canvas, a living and breathing person.

Daphne frowned, watching their expressions. "Have I offended you? Is it not a fair likeness of you, Miss Rachel?"

Andrew found his voice first, "I shall treasure it until the day I die."

Rachel smiled an uneasy smile. "Is that the way you saw me, Andrew?"

"Exactly, and my heart never recovered."

"I didn't realize that I looked so fetching in disarray." She stood up and moved toward the life size painting, touching it gingerly. "Actually I'm quite beautiful. Did I really look like that?"

Andrew laughed, "Unerringly, my dear, and Daphne you will not take that to Boston. I will give you whatever price you want for that."

Daphne stuttered, "You, you're not o-offended?"

Andrew countered, "Offended? It's the most beautiful portrait I've ever seen, but how did you reproduce it without Rachel modeling it?"

"It was etched in my mind, a scene never to be forgotten. Are you offended?" Daphne turned to Rachel her eyes questioning.

"Offended? No, I'm beyond flattered, but I'm with Drew. We don't want this going to Boston."

"Absolutely not, it will go on the wall right there," he said pointing to the most prominent spot over the mantle. "That way I can drown in those glorious eyes whether she is here or not."

Daphne smiled her relief. "That is my going away present to the two of you for saving my life and giving me a new one."

And so, Daphne was gone, but in her work, the essence of her remained behind.

Chapter Nine

"I can't believe it." Laura exclaimed, as she threw the letter down on the bed.

"What can't you believe, Laura?" Lucy murmured, her attention fixed on the book in her hands.

"That Daphne has gone away to Boston and that she and Agan are married."

"Who is Daphne?" Lucy questioned, absentmindedly.

"Lucy! Don't you ever pay attention to anything I say?"

Lucy raised her head and gave Laura a puzzled look. "Are you talking about your servant?"

"How dare you call her that!"

"Well whom are you talking about then?"

"She is simply the most beautiful woman that you would ever see in a lifetime."

"Then she is that servant girl you told me about. See I do listen to what you say."

"I'm sorry, Lucy. I guess I am upset. I do so miss home. Especially when something big happens."

"You think it is something big when a servant girl marries, and you need to be home for that?" Incredulity washed Lucy 's features.

"You don't understand. Daphne is not simply a servant, she is more like family."

"Is she a slave?" Lucy asked, her attention now captured.

Laura sighed. "Lucy, you just never listen. Of course she's not a slave. Never has been. Uncle Drew freed her."

Lucy probed, "But she is a woman of color?"

"What does that have to do with anything?"

"Everything. How could she be like family if she is a woman of color?"

Laura threw herself into the adjacent chair, a frown on her face. "I never thought of that."

"Of what?"

"That she was a woman of color and that it should make a difference in the way I feel."

"I'm just trying to understand, Laura. Especially since you said I never pay attention to what you say. Of course we don't own slaves. Can't afford it, but even if we could, I doubt we would. I don't think Pa would feel right about it, being a clergyman and all."

"That's not the way it is in Georgia. Many of the churches supported slavery. Fact of the matter, Uncle Drew and Aunt Rachel received the cold shoulder when they attended the community church because my uncle opposed secession."

"What happened?"

"They warmed up soon as they realized that Uncle Drew would buy their cotton for his mill. Anyway, it wasn't the parson, just some of the town folk. But that's the way it is where I came from, but in north Georgia there is still quite a bit of pro union sentiment."

"What's your uncle going to do?"

Laura shrugged. "Who knows? I'll expect he will fight for the South although I don't believe he is a strong supporter of slavery."

"Why do you say that? Didn't you say he had a lot of slaves?"

"I was just going by the way he treats them, and there is Daphne and Agan."

"Yeah, back to them. Why is it you feel like this Daphne is family, and you are upset about them marrying without your being there?"

"I grew up with Daphne in the house."

"Oh she took care of you. Isn't she a bit old to be marrying or has she been married before?"

"No on both accounts. She was young when she came, and we treated her as one of the family. When she grew up, she became the one who looked after everything. Cool, beautiful and efficient, she went about her business with devotion and due diligence."

"So she was a housekeeper." Lucy sighed, tiring of the conversation and going back to her book.

Laura settled back on her bed with a dreamy look on her face. "I thought Daphne hated Agan. How romantic! They practically grew up together, then something happened to come between them, and finally love triumphed. Who could ask for more than that?"

Lucy looked up a mischievous twinkle in her eyes. "Speaking of love, what's going on with Josh? Now that's one lovesick puppy, if I ever saw one. He's smitten, no doubt about that."

"Don't be silly, Lucy. We are just very good friends," Laura corrected primly.

"Huh! That's not friendship that causes his eyes to follow you everywhere you go."

Laura smiled, pleasure lighting her eyes. "Does he really do that?"

"Absolutely. Joel said he is just no fun anymore. Not a whit interested in any other girls. Wish Joel looked at me the way Josh looks at you. That first night at the dance, do you know he refused to dance with anyone after his friends spirited you away?"

Laura sighed, "No, I didn't know that, but we did get to dance."

"Yes, finally. That was a dirty trick his friends played on him. Joel told me that the moment you walked in he said you were his."

"Really? Now who does he think he is to make that kind of statement? I will be the one to make that choice." Laura tossed her head.

Lucy laughed, "And who would you choose?"

Laura giggled, "No one but Josh."

"So when are you going to see him next?" Lucy questioned, her voice low as if she were afraid they would be overheard.

"I don't know. I hate to keep bothering Miss Elizabeth. We've been spending every weekend with her."

"That's the only way Joel and Josh can come calling. These old school rules are antiquated. They teach us how to be a proper lady and wife and then give us no chance to meet anyone."

"Perhaps they think we are too young."

"No, they don't want the problem of chaperoning us. It's added responsibility to protect our good name and theirs and they won't accept it. But don't you worry one bit. Auntie Elizabeth enjoys having us over. Anyway she seems sad lately and that's not like her. To tell you the truth I think it has something to do with Colonel Dunbar's leaving. I believe she is sweet on him."

Laura's eyes widened. "Oh how exciting! Do you think she would tell us if she is?"

"I don't know. She might. You know she has no family nearby, many acquaintances, but few close friends, if any. I think the women are all jealous of her. She is so beautiful and rich. They don't know why she isn't married. They kind of see her as fierce competition." Lucy whispered.

"Do you think the school will let us spend another weekend with her?"

"Of course. They think she is my aunt."

"Now, Lucy, where did they get that idea?"

"Guess because I call her Auntie Elizabeth, and my folks gave them permission for me to have overnight visits. Didn't your uncle give permission, too?"

"Yes, seems that Uncle Andrew knows her. I don't know how, but there is some connection, and he thinks well of her."

"So there. We will get our things ready!!! It's almost Friday."

Laura giggled. "Josh did say he definitely planned to call at Miss Elizabeth's on Friday evening and hoped that I would be there."

"I'm sure it's Auntie Elizabeth whom he plans to see," Lucy teased.

Clouds danced across the moon, softly shadowing its full October glory, giving the scene an ethereal ambience. Josh sat facing Laura on the expansive porch of Elizabeth's home, his usual exuberance absent. He leaned in toward Laura, a frown wrinkling his brow. "Laura, do you think Aunt Elizabeth would allow us a walk in the garden?"

"I guess so. The moon is bright, and it's not as if we would be out of sight." Laura replied after a moment considering the request. "Are you not enjoying the porch? It is such a beautiful night."

"Of course I enjoy anywhere you are, but it is you who makes the night beautiful."

Laura's face flushed in the semi-light as his gaze captured hers. Then attempting to regain her composure protested, "Why, Josh how you do go on! You must have practiced that flattery on a lot of girls to perfect it so well."

"You know very well, Laura Meredith, that was not flattery. What more do I have to say or do to convince you that you have all my heart."

Laura squirmed under his scrutiny. "Josh, lower your voice, your aunt will hear you."

"I don't care if the whole world hears me. However, I do want to go for a walk because I have something to say that is for your ears only."

Laura's brows went up, her heart raced. "Miss Elizabeth, may we take a stroll in the rose garden? We shall not be out of sight."

Joel chuckled, "What's the matter, Josh? Are we cramping your style?"

Josh nodded. "I can't hear myself think with all that laughing you and Lucy are doing. I imagine you are giving Aunt Beth a headache."

"What do you have to think about which is so serious that we are disturbing your thought processes? You need to lighten up, Josh, and be a little fun. My stars, you are probably boring Laura to death," Joel teased.

"He is not boring me, Joel Landis. And don't you dare say that about him. He takes life a bit more serious than you. I like that," Laura defended with a toss of her head.

Elizabeth laughed to herself, noticing with interest Josh's serious expression. "Certainly you can go for a stroll. Put your shawl on, Laura, even though it is unusually warm for an October night, the breeze beyond the porch might have a chill in it."

135

Laura picked up her shawl and started down the steps with Josh following. Carriage lights on the drive illumined their way.

"Don't you think Lucy and I need to come with you two? To keep Laura from being bored?"

Josh clenched his jaw and remarked between tight lips, "You stay right where you are, buddy. You're the one from whom we're trying to escape."

"Only you. I bet Laura would like for me to come along." Joel teased prompting Lucy to strike him with her glove, poking her lips out in a petulant frown.

"That's enough, Joel. It's obvious Josh has something on his mind that's bothering him. A good friend would try to cheer him up, not anger him. Be a little more considerate." Elizabeth commanded quietly.

"I've tried that. He has been a sad sack since we received our orders yesterday. I tried cheering him up but to no avail. I thought seeing Laura would help, but obviously it has done no good."

Lucy turned to him, her eyes widened. "You received orders, Joel? No wonder he is serious."

"I don't know why he is taking it so hard. This is why we joined. I'm excited that we are finally going to see some action. No offence taken but to "I didn't join up to go to balls and sit on porches with beautiful young women." Joel explained, failing to notice Lucy's growing frustration.

Laura and Josh reached the edge of the torchlight placed near the walkway leading to the house, then stepped into the shadows of a large magnolia tree. Laura shivered and turned toward Josh, "Is what Joel said true? Are you leaving soon?"

Josh nodded, "That's what I wanted to tell you. I'm sorry you had to hear it from him."

"No matter from whom I heard it, it's news I don't want to hear." Suddenly Laura was aware of Josh's closeness, and she dropped her head, hoping she could hide the riot of emotions clamoring inside her.

But he had seen, and he moved even closer. Reaching toward her, he lifted her chin just as a single tear escaped. "You care?"

"Of course I care. Who wants to see their friends go into harm's way."

"Just a friend?"

"Of course you are my friend. Friends care what happens to friends."

"What if being just a friend is not enough for me, Laura?" Josh's ebony eyes were large and questioning in the stream of silver moonbeams diminishing the darkness. He reached for her, placing his hands on her shoulders.

Laura stepped into him, resting her head on his chest. She shuddered, "Oh, Josh, I care for you deeply, but we are so young. Much too young to be thinking of anything beyond friendship."

He drew her closer, enfolding her in his embrace. She didn't resist, and he spoke more softly, his voice husky, "I may be young, but I'm old enough to go to war and old enough to know that I love you."

Laura raised her head, looking directly into his eyes, pain reflected in her. "Josh, you don't know that what you feel for me is love. How do you know that it is not a passing infatuation?"

Josh took her hand and placed it against his thundering heart, "Would infatuation cause my heart to race, to have the vision of you invade my dreams every night and take command of my thoughts no matter what I'm doing?"

"It could be." A sad smile tilted one side of her lovely mouth.

"Very sure. I know how I feel, and it is real and genuine. The question is how do you feel?"

"Thrilled every time I think of you, delighted each time we meet and honored that you would feel as you do toward me," she confessed.

"But are you in love with me?"

"I don't understand these emotions that you stir in me." Laura shook her head. "They might lead us where we shouldn't go."

"Don't even suggest that, Laura," Josh's voice rose. "What I feel for you is honorable. I would never take advantage of you or do anything to shame you."

"I know you wouldn't, Josh." An uneasy smile parted Laura's lips, then added, "perhaps my emotions are not to be trusted. They frighten me."

A relieved grin relaxed the tension that had bound his face. "Don't be afraid. I'm not asking for a commitment from you. I know you are young, we both are, but I had to know how you felt about me. If, in fact, I could hope that there is a future for us."

"We both can hope. My feelings for you run deep and when we are older..." she paused.

"And the war is over?" he added.

"Yes, and after the war is over, perhaps we can plan a future together. But now my heart is aching at the thought of your leaving and going into harm's way. Promise me you will take care and not try to be a hero." Her voice trembled with emotion and fear.

"You have given me the strongest reason to take care, but, ironically, you also make me want to conquer worlds for you."

"Make sure it's not a battlefield you try to conquer." She looked up; her eyes bright with tears as he bent his head down and placed a tender kiss on her lips.

Lifting his head, he smiled and whispered just as Elizabeth called their names "That seals our bargain, and I shall take it in my heart and replay it a thousand times in my mind. You are the only one for me, Laura Meredith, and I shall not be content until you are mine."

Chapter Ten

Laura tore the letter open, her first from Josh. He had been gone two weeks and rumor of a battle on the Potomac had reached the school. She knew Josh was assigned to Col. Nathan Evans' regiment and word had trickled back that his regiment had been involved in a victory against Gen. Stone.

His letter verified the rumors. It was true indeed, his unit had fought with Nathan Evans' Mississippi regiment at Ball's Bluff and had driven the Northern troops into the Potomac. Many of the opposing soldiers were forced off the bluff into the river, some of them drowning and over 500 surrendered to the Confederates. She had even heard that one of the union officers killed was a U.S. Senator and a good friend of President Lincoln. She shivered when she heard that bodies of the federal troops who drowned were washing up on the shores of the river in Washington. That could have been Joel or even Josh. War was not romantic. It had lost its splendor when she had ministered to the wounded at Manassas. Now with someone she cared for involved, it proved a nightmare.

Relief engulfed her to learn that Joel and Josh came through unscathed, but it proved short lived when she read further in the letter only to discover that he and Joel had been transferred to General Stonewall Jackson's division.

The two young officers were elated with the transfer to the famous general's forces, which came with a promotion for both. Laura's apprehension only increased with this news as she discovered both promotions had come as a result of extraordinary valor on the battlefield. The good news was they would enjoy a brief leave before joining Jackson's forces, and they were coming here rather than going home.

Her heart raced at the thought of seeing him again. The memory of their last night together and the tender kiss that had sealed Josh's declaration kept playing through her mind. It brought new explosive emotions with which she scarcely knew how to deal. How would it be when she saw him again? Would the wonderful friendship that had blossomed between them be strained? Would these new dynamic feelings that raged inside her compromise the lighthearted give and take they had enjoyed? Were they ready to go on to the next level? In reality, what was the next level?

Suddenly Lucy burst into the room. "Laura, they are coming back!"

Laura nodded her head, "I know. I just read Josh's letter. Did you get one from Joel?"

Lucy shook her head, her eyes sad. "No, Auntie Elizabeth told me. Seems he will be staying at her house with Josh. That presents a problem for us."

Laura looked at her, a puzzled expression wrinkling her brow.

"You know, how can we see them? We certainly can't go stay with Auntie when they are there, and they can't come here."

Disappointment consumed Laura. "Then why are they coming here and not going home?"

"We've got to think. They simply can't come here without our seeing them," Lucy wailed as she plopped down on her bed.

"Shh, Lucy. Miss Malboro, the hall monitor, will hear you, and then we will both be in trouble."

"Right now I don't care. If I can't see Joel, and he is going off to war, I'll just die. I don't know how long it will be before we can see them again. Laura, don't you even care if you don't get to see Josh?"

Laura let out a long sigh, responding quietly, "Oh I care, Lucy. More than you know."

"That's right, Laura, it is more than I know. Something happened that night in the moonlight between you and Josh, and you haven't shared one iota with me. I ask you is that anyway to treat a best ever friend?"

"Nothing really happened."

"Yes it did! Your face is turning red!!"

"No, it's not. It's just hot in here."

"Is not! Come on, Laura. Tell me what happened. Did he kiss you?"

Laura's face turned crimson.

Lucy giggled. "Why, Laura Meredith, I'm surprised at you!!!"

"It's nothing to be giggled at, Lucy," Laura reprimanded.

"Then tell me everything that happened. What does it feel like to be kissed?"

"It was a very solemn moment, and one I will carry to my grave." A dreamy expression captured Laura's deep blue eyes as the scene played out in her mind for the thousandth time.

"Oh, how romantic. Why can't Joel be romantic like that?"

"It was more than 'a romantic moment'. It was a life-impacting event. I've never felt this way before."

"How many suitors have you had before?" Lucy giggled.

Laura rolled her eyes. "None. You know that!"

"So no wonder you've never felt that way before."

Laura frowned, then nodded in agreement, misgivings suddenly marring her euphoria. "That's right, so how can I determine what I am feeling?"

"Did Josh declare his love to you?" Lucy probed.

Laura nodded. "But he agreed that we are very young to have such feelings and will wait until we are sure they are real."

"Does that mean that you can't go to the balls and dance, or see other young men or he can't see other young women?" Lucy poked out her bottom lip in disapproval.

"Of course not. How else will we be sure?"

"Oh, why do you two have to be so sensible? Many young women your age are marrying before their beaus go off to battle. That's what I would do."

"No, you wouldn't. You just think you would. When it came right down to it, you would realize you are too young and this is your first experience with love so how will you know it is real?"

"All I can say is Joel better not give me the chance," Lucy avowed.

"Oh, poo, Lucy. You know you wouldn't want to miss all the balls and young men admiring you." Laura's melodious laugh broke the solemn mood in the room. "Anyway, from what I've seen, I don't believe Joel is ready to commit just yet. I think his mind is on fighting military battles, not heart issues."

"You can say that again. I've not received a single letter from him while Josh took the time to write you."

Laura leaned back against the pillows on her bed, "It seems like a lifetime. What are we going to do about getting to see them?"

"We'll ask Auntie Liz. She will have an answer... I just know she will." Lucy's indomitable spirit restored.

Laura nodded her head dreamily. "Someway we will be able to see them."

The days seemed to drag and still Josh nor Joel arrived. Laura questioned Lucy and Elizabeth, but neither had heard anything more from the two young men. Meanwhile rumors concerning federal troop movements toward their area kept emotions running high.

Finally, a hastily written note from Josh arrived confirming that their leave had been delayed. Seems they had been ordered to join Gen. Jackson immediately, and they were on the move.

Apprehension constricted Laura's heart. Worry for Josh engulfed her as anxiety for their own predicament teased her senses. She questioned whether or not she had made a wise decision not to fol-low Uncle Drew's request for her to return to Sweetwater. It was true she did miss her family, but she felt that war was coming to this area and soon if the rumors flying about proved true. When it came, she wanted to be useful, to make a difference. War had not come to Georgia yet and perhaps would not at all. If the Confederacy contin-ued their successes, maybe the war would end soon.

And then there was Josh. Her heart thundered. Yes, there was Josh. If she stayed, then she would be nearer him, perhaps be able to see him. It would give them time to sort out these strange emotions that bombarded her each time his profile teased her memory. In Georgia that would be impossible. She was sure that Rachel would be fine without her help as long as Uncle Drew was with her. But how long would that be? Would he go to war? No, he was too im-portant at home. The mill would provide necessary provisions for the army. Hadn't they said they were gearing up to make uniforms? Laura shook her head, trying to calm her racing heart. No, it was unthinkable. Uncle Drew couldn't go to war. She wanted him safe. She needed that security, knowing she had a haven to return to.

But meanwhile, as she heard of skirmishes and troop movements, she doubled her efforts with the local guilds, even volunteering with the doctors to learn nursing skills. The staid woman's academy surprised her when they allowed her to participate in the volunteer work; it certainly involved non-ladylike endeavors. But she loved it. As she worked with the local doctor, she discovered a latent interest in medicine. If she were a man, she would love to be a doctor. Perhaps after the war she could continue her education and become a doctor. That is if she and Josh ... she diverted her thoughts, not wanting to invite the avalanche of questions that threatened to overwhelm her.

The palette of golden and crimson leaves of fall gave way to the stark empty branches of winter. Still Josh and Joel remained with Jackson's forces, unable to get home. His letters told of fierce training and discipline. Long marches up and down the mountains in all kinds of inclement weather, and she could tell from his letters that the youth who had left her with such sweet memories in the fall had changed. The youth had become a man. As the heat of the furnace strengthens steel, so circumstances and training had transformed him. And she wondered, had the sentiments he felt toward her changed? What would he be like when she saw him again? How long must she wait?

As Laura left the local doctor's office where she had been assisting, a blast of artic cold smashed into her, taking her breath away. Walking with her head down, she pulled the hood of her cape up

against the biting November wind. She failed to see the neatly beard-
ed tall officer dressed in Confederate gray standing just outside the
door. His broad brimmed hat was pulled down low against the cold.
His dark, somber eyes fastened on her as he leaned against a lamp-
post. She passed him by without seeing him, her thoughts on what
the doctor had just told her and the preparations he was making for
the battles that would surely come. In her mind floated images of
Josh, the battles he faced, the danger....

The tall soldier moved in behind her, content for the moment
just to watch her walk. Then his long legs caught up with her, and
touching her arm, she raised her head, in alarm at first, then shook
her head as warm, familiar brown eyes peered over a new, neatly
trimmed beard. Her heart caught in her throat. Then with a shout of
joy, she turned toward his open arms and fell into them.

"Josh! Is it really you?" She cried as her hands caressed his cheeks.
"What's this on your face?"

He laughed. Even his laughter had a new depth in it, "Yes, it really
is."

"What, how, how long?"

He placed his finger over her lips. "General Jackson is here, setting up his headquarters. I don't know for how long. But for now, it's
a dream come true."

"Oh, Josh. You're really here. Where is Joel?"

"He'll be here later. Right now, he is helping the general."

"Is your presence not required?" She stammered, her heart in her
throat.

"He gave me an hour off for good behavior," Josh laughed, a
glimpse of the old Josh peaked out, then was gone just as quickly.

Laura stepped away, pushing Josh's hands away that now encir-

146

cled her waist and looking around to see who might have witnessed their tender reunion.

Josh laughed. "There are no old tattle tales around to report you."

Laura smoothed her cape, "You never know around here."

"And who cares anyway?" Josh teased.

"Well I do. If I get sent home to Georgia in disgrace, then you'll have even a harder time seeing me, not to mention my having to face my uncle. Now that's one man you wouldn't want to disappoint."

"Sounds like an ogre."

"Who? Uncle Drew?"

Josh nodded, a smile tilting one side of his mouth.

"You've mistaken my meaning. I wouldn't want to disappoint him because I love him so. He is the finest and kindest man I know."

"Present company excepted?" Josh's brow wrinkled.

"Oh, Josh. You know what I mean."

"Maybe. But is he going to be someone I have to compete with for your affections?"

"Compete with?"

"A husband has to be number one in his wife's heart."

"I don't have a husband," she reminded. "When I do, then my Uncle Andrew will relinquish his place in my heart, but I will never stop loving my uncle. You would like him, Josh."

"If he is anything like you, I know I would."

"He is nothing like me!!"

"Then I shall honor and respect him for the fine job he has done of rearing you."

"What a wonderful thought!" Laura cocked her head to one side, a blond curl escaping from her hood. "But let's don't talk of Uncle Drew. I want to hear all about your adventures."

A solemn expression dimmed the lights in Josh's eyes, "War is not an adventure, Laura."

"I'm sorry, I didn't mean to make light of war. I just want to know all about what you have encountered. It's been so long since I have seen you."

"Too long. Much too long." All brevity had left his face.

"Yes, it has." Laura paused and looked up, then added, "You've changed."

"You mean the beard?" He rubbed his face

"It's more than just the beard. Come let's go to Miss Elizabeth's house. Then we can properly talk."

"I only have an hour or so."

"You know I am inviting trouble being seen with a young man without a chaperone."

Upon arriving in Winchester, Gen. Jackson had requested President Davis to place him in command of all forces serving in the Shenandoah Valley. He knew that control of the Valley was vital to winning the war. Lincoln's objective was to capture Richmond. If Jackson gained control of the Valley, he could protect Richmond, harass Washington, invade Maryland and perhaps later invade Pennsylvania.

The Valley, known as the garden spot of Virginia because of its fertile soil, provided a prime source of food for the armies fighting in the state as well as the citizens of Richmond. In 1860 it had produced over two million bushels of wheat and was rich in livestock. Essential rail line located in the Valley transported food and supplies to Confederate forces. If the rails should fall into enemy hands, they would need to be destroyed to hamper enemy movements and supplies.

President Davis gave Jackson his old Stonewall Brigade along with Gen. Loring's division but rather than the 15,000 men he requested, he had to make do with only 11,000.

He assembled all the cavalry forces under Colonel Turner Ashby. Due to Josh and Joel's horsemanship and the fact they were receiving two fine horses from home, it seemed only good judgment to place them in the cavalry. The two were overjoyed as all the intense ground maneuvers were not to their liking.

The days marched on toward Thanksgiving and Josh snatched time away from duties whenever he could to spend with Laura. Her work at the hospital and her studies along with his duties hampered their time together .

Laura's heart still raced when Josh entered the room, but their conversation no longer ran along the frivolous. Josh resented her work when it interfered with the few moments that he could steal away from his duties. The lighthearted give and take that they had enjoyed in the past vanished, and they quarreled often. Both had matured and changed.

Laura resisted the new urgency that seemed to drive Josh. Finally one night in Elizabeth's parlor, with tears threatening, she exclaimed, "Josh, what has happened? We both agreed that we are too young, too inexperienced to think of anything more than a deep friendship with perhaps a future together after the war; yet you seem to have forgotten. I am not ready for marriage and neither are you."

"You want to know what happened? War has happened. The young boy who confessed his tender feelings to you under a bright

October harvest moon has looked death in the face and has had friends die in his arms. These experiences made me realize that the future is now. We have only the promise of this moment, and I want to spend it with you. I love you, Laura. Marry me, now."

"I ca-can't. Not now. You mustn't rush me."

"Don't you love me?"

"I care deeply for you. I'm just not ready for marriage."

"If you really loved me, you would."

"You don't understand. I have never felt for anyone the way I do for you. My heart skips a beat when I see you. I love to see you laugh, to feel your eyes on me, to spend time with you. Is that love? We must be sure. The war puts a different perspective on everything."

"That's what I mean. It gives us no promise of tomorrow, only what we have now. I want you for my wife."

"And we both are too young."

"I grew up on Bell's Bluff when I watched men die, when I wondered any moment if the next bullet had my name on it. I watched our 'enemy', who in reality are my brothers- in -arms just wearing different uniforms, dodge our bullets, struggle in the river, and drown in front of me."

Josh dropped his eyes as he continued, "I met one of our boys in gray, a young sergeant who carried the first national flag for the 8th Virginia Infantry or the Blue Ridge Boys as they were called. He was way over six feet tall, some say he was at least 6'7" tall with flaming red hair. His name was Clinton Hatcher. He had discontinued his college education at Columbian University in Washington to join the Confederacy because he was a strong secessionist. After his first taste of battle at Manassas, he joined the 8th. He was only twenty-one years old when he was killed in battle that day. A fine and brave soldier, but his life was snuffed out, he has no future."

A tear trickled down Laura's cheek, and her small hand grasped Josh's. "I'm so sorry, Josh. What a horrible time you've been through."

He turned to her then, his eyes bright. "That's war, Laura, and I'm not whining about it. I'm trying to explain the urgency. You see, Clinton had a girl he was in love with. He told us all about her and how his hopes were high that after the war they would get married, but it proved only a pipe dream. They had no future. I don't want it to happen to us like that."

"I don't either, Josh. But I don't want the urgency of the war to cause us to make a mistake."

"I see." Josh responded, a thread of cold steel in his voice. He rose, dropping her hand. "I'll let myself out, and please tell Aunt Elizabeth that I do appreciate her hospitality and trusting us enough to give us some privacy. I'll be going now."

Laura shook her head, her voice raised in exasperation, "I don't think you see at all! When will I see you again? This week?"

"I think not. I believe I need to give you some space. Some time to think."

"I don't want space from you, Josh."

A wry smile parted his lips, but not making it to his eyes. "Perhaps I need some from you. Time to sort out some things. All I know is that when I stood in battle and saw the carnage something happened inside me. I saw that the Yanks bleed just like we do. We share a common heritage, so what in the world are we fighting for that is worth the cost? I don't even believe in slavery anymore, so why am I fighting? In short, Laura, suddenly the only thing in this crazy conflict that I am sure of is my love for you. But it is obvious that our opinions are not compatible so I best bid you good day," and then he was gone as icy fingers of terror gripped Laura's heart.

Thanksgiving came and went. Had it not been for the hospitality of Elizabeth, it would have proved a lonely vigil. Josh was as good as his word, and week followed week without Laura seeing him. Finally, she heard that his horse had arrived. He was officially assigned to Ashby's cavalry and had volunteered for a scouting mission. She wondered if the 'scouting missions' were raids on valley railroads about which she had heard rumors. Ever the daring one, Joel had volunteered, and so both rode off together with a small contingent of other young riders, much to Lucy's consternation.

Her friend had proved uncharacteristically quiet on the subject of Laura and Josh. She seemed to sense that the problems the two were experiencing needed to remain between them, and so her usual exuberant questions were absent.

Elizabeth invited the girls to spend the holidays with her. A round of balls and parties kept homesickness at bay, but reinforced the memories of lively brown eyes and tall broad frame that remained missing.

The lovely mansions in Winchester proved a feast for the eyes. Decorated in splendor, they posed as if the war were only an illusion. Society went about its business of celebration and pleasure, ignoring the fact that Washington and the federal troops were less than seventy-five miles away. But amidst all the splendor and good intentions of the season, the thought rarely left Laura's mind that somewhere between her and those seventy five miles, Josh was shivering in the cold December nights. No party could dull the ache that those reflections brought to her mind nor the memory of their last encounter. His heart wrenching confession haunted her day and night.

He rode into town on Christmas Eve as carols drifted from the church services on Main Street. Laura was leaving Dr. Martin's office when she saw him. He paused, mounted high above her and tipped his hat to her. Her heart thundered as her eyes scanned his face. Weariness lined it, yet something in his eyes offered comfort. The former sternness had softened, and his mouth turned upward in an accepting half-smile. His eyes were clear, the former anguish missing. Leaning forward he spoke, a new tenderness in his tone, "And how is my lady doing this chilly Christmas Eve?"

A radiant smile parted Laura's face, "Now, I'm quite wonderful! You're here, and you are safe."

In one fluid motion, Josh was out of the saddle and holding her in his arms.

Ignoring any curious eyes that might be watching she nestled into his broad shoulder as relief released the tears that had been bottled up for weeks and dampened his coat.

Chapter
Eleven

Rachel sighed as she stared out the wide expanse of windows that graced her office nook. She seemed restless and anxious for Andrew to be home. Somehow lately she wanted to cling to him. It was as if any moment he would be gone, and she would be alone again.

She chuckled to herself and ran a hand over her hair, smoothing it in place. He loved her hair. She had given it little notice until he had admired it. Now she reveled in its abundance. He also loved her eyes; she had never noticed the lights in them until he had pointed them out. She had taken her beauty for granted, until Andrew. She stood in awe of his love and cherishing of her. It humbled her that she could be so blessed.

How far she had come from that Miss Independence who had scorned the need for anyone. That had been an ill concealed charade for sure, but it had almost cost her Sweetwater and Andrew. Cold tentacles raced up her spine. Why couldn't she even yet separate the two? Was this place still too important to her? Andrew said that someday she would come to him without Sweetwater. Couldn't she now? If there were a choice...? She shook her head. But there was no choice, Andrew was the love of her life and with him came Sweetwater. He had provided her with everything her heart had desired, had fulfilled her wildest dreams.

Lately, he had been trying to talk to her concerning his provisions for her, what she should do if he were not around, if somehow he didn't survive. She knew he was alluding to the war. When she told him she wouldn't hear of it, he had quit talking to her about it. She could only hope that he had given up the idea of going to battle. She knew better. If he thought it was the right thing to do, he would go despite her objections. But for him to go made no sense. He didn't believe in secession and, after all, he had agreed to Governor Brown's request that they divert the factory into making uniforms and tents for the army. That should be contribution enough for the war effort. Goodness knows doing so had cut their profit margin in half. And now the governor was pleading with them to stop growing cotton and grow corn. What was that all about?

Suddenly, Andrew appeared on her horizon. She smiled as she watched him striding across the back lawn from the stables, master of the manor and her heart. How much these two years had wrought, how her heart had changed, her emotions revealed. How could she have been so wrong about this man among men? His strength, his courage in the face of opposition, his tenderness and devotion to her, characterized the man he was. She came so close to disaster. She could have lost him, nearly did. But was Roger right? Did it take all that to appreciate and value what she had now? Perhaps. But it hadn't just affected her; it had impacted Andrew and others. She remembered Roger's gentle warning in that lilting brogue of his, "Yea,

Missy, the consequences of sin ne'r stops with only the guilty, but hurts the innocent, too. The biggest devil's lie is you can sin and get 'way with it. Ye can't. Nay, it hurts the blameless as well as the guilty."

Her guilt had been one of bitterness and clinging to the past, a willful blindness to the blessings that could be hers. Roger had accused her of having a false god. He claimed that she had worshipped Sweetwater and was willing to sacrifice everything to it. What about now? Was that sin still lurking in her heart? Roger had warned her to be mindful. Sometimes sin creeps in when we are unawares. Old attitudes rear their ugly heads, causing us to stumble.

She looked around her, then shook her head. True, she enjoyed immensely what the place had become. Her life's dream was fulfilled in being the mistress of Sweetwater Plantation, but worship it? No, enjoyment was not the equivalent of worship, and there was no harm in appreciating what she had and the promises of the future. She smiled pushing aside the question that nagged her now and then. How willing would she be to give Sweetwater up? She breathed a sigh of relief. No chance! Andrew had seen to that. And the war? Well, it was all in Virginia, and an invasion this far south was only a mere possibility.

As Andrew stepped inside the door, Rachel threw herself into his arms. He could always extinguish her fears. In his arms, she was home, Sweetwater was just icing on the cake.

A broad grin spread across his face as he looked down into her eyes before he planted a kiss on her forehead. "And to what do I owe this enthusiastic greeting, my love?"

"I, I was just thinking about how thankful I am for you and our life together. And...," she dropped her head suddenly timid.

"And, what?" He probed.

She tightened her arms about him, nestling her head on his shoulder, murmured, "How much I love you."

He lifted her chin and placed a long kiss on her lips, "I'm glad of that, Mrs. Meredith, for the feeling is mutual."

Arms entwined, they turned and made their way into Andrew's study. A roaring fire greeted them dispelling the December chill as they sat down side by side on the supple leather couch. Christmas had been a solitary affair for the two of them. Roger had been away visiting friends, Phillip on one of his blockade running missions and Laura away at school. Now they awaited the New Year and what it would bring..

"Oh, I have a letter from Laura." Andrew announced, extracting an envelope from his coat pocket.

"When did that come?"

"It was waiting for me when I arrived in Marietta and I forgot to mention it."

"Forgot? You know how I look forward to her letters."

He smiled, mischief firing his eyes, "Something did distract me a bit when I arrived home."

Rachel reached for the letter, ignoring his remark, as a blush tinted her face. "We are receiving precious few these days," Rachel exclaimed.

"The war is hindering the mail, I'm sure."

Rachel shook her head. "I think it's more than that. I don't think she is writing."

"Think so? I thought we received about what you would expect from someone who is busy with school and volunteer work."

"Uhmm, I don't think so. I believe something is going on with that little miss." Rachel murmured as she extracted the letter adding, "Do you think she has met someone?"

"I should hope she has met quite a number of people. After all, didn't we send her up there to learn the social graces along with getting a real education?"

"Oh, Drew, you know what I mean!"

He shook his head a puzzled expression on his face. "No I don't know what you mean."

"I mean someone special."

"Special? Well I guess there are Lucy and Elizabeth."

"No, I mean a young man."

"What? Laura? Don't be ridiculous. She's far too young to even be thinking about young men in that light. Besides that girls' seminary is quite strict about that sort of thing." Drew dropped his head then murmured, "That's one reason I chose it."

Rachel laughed. "Andrew Meredith, Laura is a young woman and a beautiful one. She probably has dozens of admirers. And don't think because the school is strict that she has been isolated from the opposite sex."

"Really?" A frown wrinkled Andrew's forehead.

"Yes, really. I went to a girls' school, so I know how the system works or at least the ways to circumvent the rules."

"I didn't send her up there to have dozens of admirers. I sent her up there to get an education, and if that's not what she's doing, then it is time for her to come home."

Rachel smiled, merriment dancing in her eyes. "You talk like she is a child."

"She is."

"She is marrying age," Rachel observed.

"She is not. You were much older than she."

"And, if you remember, I was already classified as a spinster. My aunt was trying to marry me off from the time I was Laura's age."

Andrew picked up her hand and kissed it. "I'm glad she was unsuccessful. Although I can't imagine how or why."

"Because I refused to marry for any reason but love. Drove my aunt witless." She chuckled at memories that were no longer painful.

"Now whatever gave you the idea that Laura has met someone 'special' as you put it? What has she said in her letters to give you that idea?"

"Oh, men! You can be so dense!" Rachel laughed. "It's what she hasn't said."

"Let me get this straight. I'm to conclude that Laura's heart has been captured by someone because she hasn't said anything about this 'someone,' so therefore there is definitely a someone? And because I have not reached that conclusion, I'm dense?" Andrew shook his head, a bewildered expression wrinkling his brow. "If I am dense, it is in the area of understanding a woman's logic."

"Not logic, Drew, woman's intuition."

"Or romantic notions."

"Make light of it if you will, Andrew Meredith, but you just wait. You will see that I am right."

"Well, my dear, if there is anything to this suspicion of yours, don't you think it would behoove us to find out the whole story?"

"Now you're thinking straight."

"I'll write the head mistress tonight and get it in the post when I go to Marietta next week."

"Oh, no, Drew! You can't do that."

"And why not? We have given that school enough in endowments that she should be glad to take the time to apprise me of any situation that might be impacting my niece or interfering with her getting a proper education."

"Oh, Drew, don't sound so, so..."

"So what?"

"So stuffy. We are talking about matters of the heart."

"I'm being practical. Seems that at least one of us should keep a level head and get to the bottom of your speculations."

"What you are proposing is not logical. It's emotional."

"You just accused me of being 'stuffy.' "

Rachel tossed her head. "You get that way sometimes when you are emotional."

Andrew dropped his head and shook it, trying to hide a smile. "Will I ever make any progress understanding the feminine mystic?"

"That's what keeps us irresistible."

"So that's what it is. Must be working because you are a mystery that I revel in unraveling. Everyday with you is a new adventure. Now educate me as to why my approach is wrong. Don't we need to get information? We both agreed on that."

"You said that they had very strict rules. We don't want Laura to get in trouble or to be forbidden to see her young man, however she is managing that."

"Her young man?" Andrew all but shouted.

"Now listen to you, Andrew Meredith. You sound like an outraged father."

"Father, no. Outraged, yes."

"Oh my! What an uphill battle Laura will have if she has any suitors."

Andrew nodded his head. "That's right. They will have to pass a strict inspection. For her to have an admirer way up there in Virginia where I can't meet him and evaluate him is just not acceptable. She is young and very wealthy in her own right and I don't want any fortune hunters trying to capture her heart."

Laughter rolled from Rachel until the tears streamed down her face, "Drew," she gasped between waves of merriment. "This is not a horse you are procuring for her. Love is an affair of the heart, and it might surprise you to know that you can't rule Laura's heart."

"All the same, emotions aside, there is a practical side to this sort of thing."

"Andrew Meredith! There you go again with your 'practicality.' Some things transcend the practical. Have you not learned anything about affairs of the heart?"

Andrew looked up, a bewildered expression in his eyes, amusement gone.

"Do you not remember the 'business proposition' you made to me when you asked me to marry you? You never mentioned love or your feelings for me."

"Didn't get me very far, did it?" He chuckled.

"No, you almost lost me to Philip."

He reached for her, pulling her against his shoulder and burying his face in her hair, he murmured, "I thought offering you Sweetwater was my only chance to have you. How was I to know you loved me? You never gave me a clue."

"I fought against my heart. How foolish I was," Rachel admitted.

"How foolish we both were, but that is in the past. Seriously, I don't want to make a mistake with Laura. I'm the only father she's ever known, and I feel responsible for her. What do you suggest?"

"I think your idea of doing some investigating is right, just not the school authorities."

His eyes suddenly widened, and he snapped his fingers, "I know whom I can write. Elizabeth. Hasn't Laura spent some weekends at Elizabeth's?"

"Good idea. By the way, just who is this Elizabeth, and how do you know her?" Rachel demanded, her eyes sparkling.

"Just an old flame of mine." Andrew sighed.

"Extinguished, I trust."

"Actually Elizabeth grew up down the road from me. She was considerably younger, in fact no more that nine or ten when I left home. It was quite a surprise when I ran into her in Boston. She had married one of the wealthy Boston merchants who lived on the same street as my Boston brownstone. We met occasionally at social functions, and then, when I moved to Savannah, I heard that her husband, who was many years her senior, had died and left her a very rich widow. I believe her family arranged her marriage. They would have wanted her to make an advantageous match because she was dowry poor. The father had dissipated the family fortune."

Rachel nodded her head. "I can relate to that."

Andrew smiled. "You might find you both have a lot in common. She is very beautiful, too."

"Oh?" Rachel arched a brow.

"But not as beautiful as you," he assured.

"You are learning, Mr. Meredith!" Rachel chuckled, not the least bit threatened.

"It might take a lifetime for you to teach me!"

"I look forward to the adventure!"

A contented smile warmed Andrew's eyes as he pulled her even closer. "So what are we going to do about our little miss?"

"I think your idea about contacting Elizabeth is our first line of action. We won't question Laura, just yet. I will write her about everything going on here and what news we have had of Philip, etc."

"Which by the way, I did have a word from Philip. Seems he arrived in Boston earlier this month and...."

"How could he go to Boston from down here?"

"He is an Englishman and can freely travel across both lines. At least for now. However, he was on his ship that ran the blockade safely. It docked in Boston, and he attended to some business in the ship yard and visited Daphne."

"How is she doing?"

"Painting fast and furiously and making a good living. Her income has allowed her to establish a way station for escaped slaves on their way to Canada."

"So she is continuing what she started in Savannah?"

"Yes, except on a larger scale."

"What is Agan doing?"

"He is working for a large mercantile company as both clerk and procurer. Seems that Mr. Carlton, the curator of the gallery where Daphne's paintings are for sale, was so impressed with Agan, he recommended him for the job. He is doing quite well, but Daphne says he is restless."

"Restless?"

"Yes, wants to get in the battle fray. If the feds ever allow the blacks in, then Daphne feels sure he will enlist."

"How does she feel about that?"

"Philip didn't say."

"I can only imagine how she feels. I'm so glad I don't have to face that."

Andrew sat up sharply and turned toward her. "Rachel, you may very well have to face that if this war is not over soon. I thought it would be a quick defeat for the South, but the North has made so many military blunders it may result in an extended conflict. If so, I will go."

Rachel's throat constricted, heart pounding, "You can't. I won't let you. I can't survive without you."

Andrew took her face in his hands. "I don't want to go. I don't want to leave you, nor fight for a cause in which I don't believe, but my duty calls me to support the South I love."

"What shall I do? How shall I make it?"

"Rachel, if our people don't run off, you will be fine. You can raise food, you have a manager at the mill, and I will bring Laura home. You are strong as a willow tree. You have faced adversity before and conquered."

"Only because you recued me!"

"You have learned vital lessons from what you went through, lessons that can carry you through what we are facing. Your faith will be your strength, your knowledge and experience in the land will help you, and I have put in your name and Laura's a large amount of gold bullion in England. If all else fails, you both can go to England with Philip, I have made him executor of my estate."

"What do you mean if all else fails we can go to England? Sweetwater is free and clear, you told me it was. You gave me the deed."

"I did, my love, but if we are invaded by the north, nothing is safe."

"I can't believe we will be invaded or that anything will happen to Sweetwater. I don't understand why you have to go. You are doing your part for the cause. We are losing money as it is so that our soldiers can have uniforms and tents. And now we have stopped cotton production so we can grow corn to feed them. How can I, a woman, do that if you are gone?

"I hope, too, that we won't be invaded, but no one knows what the future holds. We must plan. And as for you, a woman, what can you do?" He chuckled, "I remember a beautiful woman with porcelain skin, donning homespun and a palmetto hat digging in the dirt and growing a field of cotton."

"That didn't come to fruition," she reminded.

"But it wasn't your fault the weather turned nasty."

"I had help."

"And I think our people will remain loyal and help you now. Think of all the women whose men have left, and they are alone with no servants to help them raise a crop to feed themselves and their babies."

Rachel shuddered. "I don't like to think about that. I am blessed far above most women. Forgive me. I was thinking only of myself. I can't stand the thought of your putting yourself in harm's way or life without you; but I know there is a bigger picture, one of deprivation for thousands of people."

"Maybe in some small way we can use Sweetwater to bring relief to some and supplies to our men on the battle front. You're right. It is time we think beyond ourselves."

Tentacles of fear ran Rachel's spine. Then taking a deep breath, she raised her chin, determined to face whatever came with grace and wisdom. "Now you best get that letter off to Elizabeth, and I will write to Laura."

Days turned into weeks before they heard from Elizabeth. Finally toward the end of the month, a letter addressed to the both of them arrived and they retrieved it on a trip into Marietta on a warmer than usual January day.

Andrew put it in his pocket and walked to the carriage, Rachel clinging to his arm. As soon as they were seated, Rachel clamored, "Open it, Andrew!"

He looked at her, quirking his brow, "Open what, Rachel?"

"The letter!"

"Oh, I thought we would wait until we get home where we could leisurely read it. We still have a lot on our list to attend to and it is getting late."

Rachel grabbed for his pocket, "Give me that letter!"

Laughing, he placed his hand over his pocket, deflecting hers. "Don't be so impatient. Whatever Elizabeth has to say can wait until we get home. I'm sure she is going to explain that Laura's volunteer work and school has kept her too busy to write us, just like I suggested."

"Andrew, give me that letter."

Andrew threw back his head and laughed. "Very well, my dear, if you want to read it here. I thought we might go in the Fletcher House and have a cup of coffee and a muffin while we read it."

A broad smile parted Rachel's lips, showing the tips of her teeth. "You do like to tease me!"

"Yes, I do. Since you were an only child and missed the harassment a brother can be, I try to fill in the gap a little now and then."

"Did you harass your little sister?"

A frown darkened Andrew's countenance for a moment as memories of a painful past threatened to intrude. "No. Our family was not what you call normal. We were quite restricted by my father. I learned by watching other happier families."

Rachel reached out and placed a comforting hand on his. "Neither was my childhood normal. Perhaps, we have learned from our experiences so that our children will have a better home to grow up in."

Andrew looked at her, "Our children? Is there something you haven't told me, Rachel?'

She smiled, her eyes bright. "Not yet, but soon I hope."

Andrew's emotions ran rampant at the thought of her giving birth. More than anything he wanted children, but with the future so uncertain, he had grave misgivings.

He shook his head dispelling the painful past and his fear for the future. This was the moment he had, and he would treasure it, refusing to let anything cloud this time he and Rachel had together.

As soon as they had ordered their snack, he opened the letter and together they read it.

Elizabeth told them that indeed Laura was busy, that she had been working long hours with the local doctor in town and keeping up her studies. Her grades were exceptional, and she had developed an avid interest in medicine. She was not only assisting the doctor, but studying under him. She had even mentioned an interest in becoming a doctor.

Andrew sighed deeply when he read that, but seemed to experience some relief until he read the next paragraph where Elizabeth explained that she felt uncomfortable about betraying what might be a confidence since Laura had failed to tell them about the young man she was seeing. However, she continued, she understood how they must feel, and she wanted to assure them that her nephew was the young man in question. He was a lieutenant in General Jackson's regiment assigned to Col. Ashby's cavalry unit. He had fought gallantly at Ball's Bluff and earned a battlefield commendation. He was well mannered, his family wealthy and was head over heels in love with Laura.

When Rachel read that she exclaimed, "I knew it!"

"But the question remains, what does Laura feel toward him?"

"Maybe she will elaborate if you will let me finish the letter!"

"Yes, here she says that Laura is behaving in a very mature and sensible fashion."

"What in the world does that mean?"

"I don't know. Oh! There is more on the back."

"Oh, dear, she says that anything more about how Laura feels or what she and this 'Josh' are planning will have to come from Laura," Rachel read.

"Stars above!" Andrew practically shouted, turning the heads of the few patrons in the dining room.

"Shh, Andrew. People are staring."

"Am I going to have to go up there and find out what's going on? It's obvious that Laura isn't going to tell us. I'll just go bring her home."

"Think about that carefully, Andrew. Suppose he is the one God has picked out for her. Would you want to get in the good Lord's way?"

"No, of course not. But this not knowing...,"Andrew growled.

"What you mean is not being in control."

He took a deep breath, then covered her small hand with his and reluctantly agreed "Of course, you're right. I do like to be in control. I like to protect and take care of my own."

"An admirable trait, but sometimes we have to relinquish our control and turn the outcome over to God."

Andrew's mouth turned up in a half smile, "When did you get so wise?"

"Learning from my husband and the circumstances that God has allowed in my life."

"So what should we do?" Andrew asked, slumping back in his chair.

"Trust Elizabeth when she states that Laura is behaving sensibly. I would think that means she is not planning to run off and get married anytime soon."

Andrew nodded. "However, the war and the threat of death put a lot of pressure on young people to seize the moment. My prayer is that she will confide in us soon."

———

Time and circumstances contributed to Laura's sensible behavior. When Josh had ridden in on Christmas Eve night, Laura's relief knew no bounds. When he held her in his arms on that cold and windswept street, her heart told her that it belonged to him and him alone.

Since Laura and Lucy were spending the holidays with Elizabeth, only his duties and her work kept them from spending all their waking hours together. Once more they were at ease in each other's company, and Laura decided that perhaps she was not too young to love or perhaps even to be married in these uncertain times. If Josh raised the conversation again, she would not raise her same objections. No telling how soon he would be facing death again.

She shuddered at the thought of telling Andrew and Rachel, but she decided that she would write them and tell all. But maybe she could wait until after the New Year began. Anyway, she didn't have anything definite to tell them, except she had met this wonderful young man who set her heart to racing. She laughed when she considered giving them that explanation. It would hardly do. She could only imagine Uncle Drew's response.

By the end of Christmas week the weather turned balmy for December. On the last day of the year, Josh arrived at Elizabeth's home just as they were having breakfast. His usually warm, brown eyes were somber, and Laura's heart fell. Somehow she knew their separation was imminent. How could she bear it?

Elizabeth invited Josh to breakfast with them. After finishing her second cup of coffee, she excused herself, and told Laura she would be in the garden room mending some clothing.

Josh rose from the table and took Laura's hand and pulled her up. "Let's go for a walk in the garden. The sun is warm, and I believe you won't be too cold."

Laura tried to smile despite the strange heaviness that bound her heart. "You mean another walk in the garden?"

Josh smiled. "You remember?"

"How could I ever forget?"

"Come then. We don't have much time."

Laura jerked her head upward and cried, "Wha-what do you mean?"

"I need to talk to you. What a wonderful week this has been, being with you, hearing your voice, watching you laugh. I've tried to store up the memories to keep me warm on the cold winter nights I am facing. I've just received orders...we are pulling out tomorrow, and I don't know when we will be returning. I couldn't leave without telling you how sorry that I am about what happened when we were last together."

"I am sorry, also, Josh. I should have been more understanding, but you were right in one thing. I did need to sort out my feelings."

"And they are?"

"I love you and am willing to marry you whenever you want me to," she declared boldly, a blush tinting her face.

Josh chuckled. "Laura, that is the most unflattering statement that a man in love could receive."

"What?"

"That you are willing to marry me."

"But I am!" Laura exclaimed, her blue eyes wide.

"Willing and wanting are not the same thing! When you come to me, I want you to want that with all your heart."

"But I do love you with all my heart," Laura protested.

"Perhaps, but I have had some time to think also. That last mission Joel and I were on gave me some space from you and time to sort out all the conflicting emotions that I had about this war. First of all you were right. Now is not the time for us to marry."

"You don't want to marry me anymore?"

Josh shook his head. "That's not what I mean. The timing is wrong. I have a job to do."

"And I would hinder that?"

"Yes. I would be worried about not coming home to you, or coming home, maimed and not be able to take care of you. I can't have a divided mind, if I'm to fulfill my duty here. I can't worry about whether or not I will survive, or whether or not an injury I might receive would tie you down for the rest of our lives. Our first plan in this very garden to see what the war and the future holds for us is the best plan." He paused, "I have thought carefully about this, and I want you to go back to Georgia where you will be safe."

"No, I am staying here as long as I can. I want to be near you."

"My heart's desire is to be near you, to have you by my side always, but that is selfish. I don't know how long I will be gone, or even if I will return to this area. I know if we don't block McClelland's forces from getting to Richmond, the war is lost. We must control the Valley to keep potential reinforcements from going to McClelland. That is our major objective. While we are at it, we hope to put a scare into Washington at the same time. If we are successful they won't know when we might show up on their doorstep!" Josh laughed, a little of his former enthusiasm lifting his countenance.

"Do you feel different about your involvement in the battles?"

A sad smile lifted his full lips. "I have reconciled my reservations. I hate the war no less. It is senseless but I love the South. I will defend her until my last breath and will do so with all my heart, hoping that it will bring this bloodbath to a more rapid end."

"I'm glad you have made peace with your misgivings. I, too, want to do my part. That's why working and learning with Dr. Martin has been so important to me," Laura explained.

Josh took her hand. "I understand how you feel; however this area is going to be rife with war, and I want you out of harm's way. McClelland is building pontoon bridges across the Potomac, so they can get troops into this area. There will be many fearsome battles fought over Winchester because of its vital location just south of the Potomac. Since it is situated on the lone route between eastern and western United States, it connects directly to Washington D.C. This location is a transportation hub, and each side will consider it vital to their success and will fight for it."

"I will stay until Uncle Drew makes me go home," Laura stated, her voice determined. "If there is a chance to see you, I will be here, waiting."

"Don't you understand, Laura? If you delay with the hope of seeing me, you may not be able to get home? Even your Uncle Andrew might not be able to manage your escape."

"You really think we will be occupied by Union forces?"

"Absolutely. At some point our forces will have to leave Winchester; even now we leave only a small contingent holding the area. When word gets back to Banks, and it will because of the Union sentiment in town, then he will occupy."

Chapter
Twelve

Jackson moved out on January 1st with nine thousand men, leaving only a small force to guard Winchester. Joel and Josh left with Ashby's Brigade. With their sabers glistening in the bright sunlight, the cavalry rode out behind their striking leader. Ashby, dressed in Confederate gray, had golden lace on his sleeves and around his collar. His broad brimmed black felt hat with a long black feather streaming behind and his brightly polished high top boots with spurs finished a dashing outfit. However, it was his personal appearance that completed the romantic picture. His build was muscular and wiry, his complexion dark, his eyes a warm brown, and his black beard covered his chest. It was said later that he had the look of an early Crusader. However, Laura's eyes were glued not on the dashing colonel, but on the young, now captain, who rode just behind his leader with Joel on his right. With his eyes to the front, they never made contact with the girl he was leaving behind. Determination set his jaw and resolve drove him forward. Laura wept, not only for Josh but for all the brave young men galloping forward to who knew what? How many would return and would she ever see Josh again?

That night the warm weather that had heralded an early spring turned bitter. The first night they were on the march a winter storm hit turning the roads into sheets of ice. The temperature dropped so low that icicles clung to the men's beards. Travel became miserable and almost impassible, but the general pressed on, causing federal troops to evacuate Bath and retreat to Maryland. Although the enemy's position kept Jackson from crossing the river into Maryland, he bombarded the Baltimore and Ohio Railroad with artillery, destroying a section of it. Afterwards, he continued on to Romney and occupied the town on January 14. He had planned to use the town as a base for advancing into Cumberland, Maryland but the morale of the troops remained so low that he canceled his plans. Leaving Loring's Division in Romney, Jackson returned to Winchester on the 24th. Ashby and his men were with him. After only twenty-four days, Laura and Josh were together once again.

Early in February the head mistress of the school called a meeting of all the students, which had now dwindled to less than twenty. When she announced that the school would close in mid March, Laura panicked. She realized that if Andrew found out, he would require her to return home. Her conscience bothered her because she had failed to relay important information about the key events that were impacting her life. Her heart told her she was being deceitful with ones who loved her. But how could she leave Josh and the work she had come to love? If she told them, then home she would surely go. Her heart tore between the love for them and her desire to stay where she was. What a dilemma, was there no answer to it? Would she ever be willing to go home and leave Josh and her work?

Elizabeth offered her home to Laura until Andrew could make arrangements for her to return to Sweetwater. Lucy would be returning home to Front Royal. How could she get along without her high-spirited roommate who was more a sister than friend? Who would cheer Laura on when she worried, and who would offer Lucy the level headed practicality that she so often needed?

Meanwhile, she delayed writing a letter telling Rachel and Andrew about Josh. What and how would she explain him to them? Could she announce out of the blue that she was in love without ever having mentioned him? What a shock, even then how could she explain their relationship? She didn't quite understand this new level herself. Now she had one more bit of news to add that would affect all their lives.

Lucy left for Front Royal and home at her parents' command while Laura stayed more and more with Elizabeth. The school had become lenient in their waning days allowing her to remove all her belongings to Elizabeth's home. Her friend greeted her warmly and seemed to especially enjoy Laura's company; her normally independent spirit appeared somewhat curtailed of late. She looked lonely for the first time since Laura had met her.

When she received word that her friend, the Colonel Devonshire had been killed in action, Elizabeth was grief-stricken. In her grief, she finally confided in Laura. She recounted the conversation that she had had with Doug before he left. She said that it had caused her to re-evaluate her life. He suggested that she had built a wall around her heart. She came to realize the truth of what he said, and now she was ready to dismantle it, to consider love. In short she yearned for someone with whom she could share her life. She explained that her marriage had been arranged, and her husband abusive; therefore, she thought she would never risk love. And then she met Doug. Although she was not in love with him, he had breached her heart's barricade and showed her that all men were not like her deceased husband. He was kind, caring and winsome, and she had enjoyed his company. She had hoped that when he returned their affection and friendship might deepen into something else. He had suggested that his feelings for her ran deeper than friendship. Now he was gone and she would never know.

And as her tears began again, Laura had no idea what to say in the presence of her friend's deep sorrow. So she sat by her side and patted her shoulder, conveying her deep concern in the only way she knew how. Unwittingly Elizabeth had stirred the terror bound in her own heart for Josh's safety. Her friend's anguish magnified it. Each moment that Josh was in town and they spent together became more precious than the one before.

Meanwhile, Jackson's victory at Romney had been short lived. The troops under Loring became so discontented during the inclement weather that they had petitioned the Confederate Secretary of the War to withdraw them from Romney, claiming that their position was exposed to isolation by the Union troops. They were granted their petition and were reassigned out of the Valley reducing General Jackson's forces to around 4,000 men. At Loring's departure, Federal troops once again occupied Romney, this time under General Lander.

With Loring's withdrawal and the subsequent arrival of federal troops in Romney, Jackson realized his ability to defend the lower Shenandoah Valley was so greatly impaired that he would be forced to evacuate Winchester.

On March 9, facing Union General Banks and a superior force approaching, Jackson and his men left Winchester. Laura said her tearful goodbyes to Josh and shortly thereafter watched forlornly as the enemy seized Winchester. Now in an occupied zone, it looked doubtful that she would be going home or seeing Josh anytime soon. School closed, and she and Elizabeth continued on with their lives. Elizabeth met secretly with the Ladies Aid Society knitting socks and providing other needed items for the Confederacy, and Laura worked with the Dr. Martin. She redoubled her efforts to learn, as she didn't know how much longer she would have the opportunity. Now instead of men in gray, she ministered to casualties dressed in blue, and all the while she was left to wonder about the whereabouts of Josh. Was some nurse or doctor dressing his wounds?

The only good thing about the Federal occupation was that the much-needed medicines, which were previously in such short supply, were now plentiful. What a relief it was to have morphine to dull the pain of young enemy soldiers who cried out in agony. Their pain proved just as intense; their blood as red and they, too, fought for a cause they believed was just. Each time she helped a soldier, her prayer was that if Josh were ill or wounded someone would watch over him.

Finally, Laura wrote the long delayed letter, doubting that it would make it through enemy lines, but easing her conscience all the same. She merely told them about the young soldier who was a very dear friend whom they would like and admire if only they could meet him. She added that he was away in harm's way and she didn't know when or if she would ever see him again. She told them of the school's closing and her sense of accomplishment working with the doctor. She said that she didn't know when or how she could come home. She assured them that she was safe and would stay put in Elizabeth's home until further notice.

When she read the letter to Elizabeth, her friend smiled and then gently suggested that perhaps she was not totally forthcoming about her friendship with Josh.

Laura grimaced and defended, "But I don't know anything to tell them other than this." She choked and her eyes filled with tears, " I don't know if I shall ever see him again, and I know if I have to leave and go home to Georgia, there will be a great distance separating us. He will be here and I, far away. Will we ever meet again?"

"Oh, my dear," Elizabeth encouraged, "Josh loves you. He will search for you until he finds you."

"I believe he loves me, but he has changed his mind about marriage."

"He is considering your welfare, what's best for you."

"Perhaps, yet I don't know if we shall ever enjoy more than a deep friendship, no matter how much my heart hopes otherwise. To tell Uncle Drew 'what might be' is not an option at this moment. Josh made it very clear... any decision that is made will be after this horrible war. Then there will be time enough to prepare them."

Elizabeth nodded, agreeing that she saw Laura's point. They waited to post the letter with some unknown courier who might agree to carry her letter beneath her hoops through the lines.

What she left out of her letter were the conditions in which the two women found themselves. General Banks imposed a strict curfew on the Winchester citizens and confiscated food, hay, and grain to feed his men and horses. Where previously there had been plenty, now food and comfort proved sparse. He imposed further indignities by appointing provost marshals to rule their daily lives.

What had been high Confederate feelings among many women turned to something darker. The denial of their constitutional rights hardened the Secessionist sentiment in the women. Mary Greenhow Lee stated that her contempt toward the Yankees banished all fear.

It would later cost her her home.

When one soldier remarked to a lady's maid that her mistress was very beautiful, she replied, "My goodness, mister, she jest as soon cut yore heart out."

Many of the women donned 'Jeff Davis' bonnets to hide their faces from the soldiers. Their bold impudence antagonized an already explosive situation even more. After a visit from the U.S. Secretary of War, he described his impression of the town as, "the men are all in the army, but the women are the devil."

Although her heart was breaking and the two of them were suffering deprivation of sustenance, comfort and freedom, Elizabeth and Laura failed to support the open hostility that marked so many. Laura continued her work as more wounded came in and both of them carried food to the many homes that had been confiscated as hospitals, feeding both Union and Confederate wounded.

When General Johnston received information that General Banks was preparing to split his forces and return to Washington, he ordered General Jackson to prevent General Banks' forces from leaving the Valley. Jackson readied his small 3,000-man force for an attack on Kerns town, nearby. As the battle raged and artillery heard in Winchester, their hope rallied that soon they would once again be in friendly hands. It was not to be so.

Not realizing that he would be facing a force of 9,000, Jackson attacked. After a fierce battle, his men were forced from the field in defeat, but the Union failed to pursue. Although they lost the skirmish, it did disrupt the Union's plan of transferring troops to reinforce the forces fighting on the Peninsula in Virginia. On the bigger picture it proved a strategic victory for the South, even though it failed to bring the much hoped for relief to Winchester.

It was not until several weeks later that Laura's letter reached a grim Rachel and Andrew. By this time they were aware of the occupation of Winchester. Andrew had tried to come up with every possible solution to extract her from the area, but up to now every plan had reached a dead end. Meanwhile the mill was going full blast, trying to supply the army what they needed. It proved a mammoth endeavor considering the limited supply of cotton that he had managed to procure. He had heard that bales upon bales of cotton lined the wharfs of Savannah and Charleston waiting to go to England, but with Fort Pulaski in the hands of the Union, the blockade had tightened. Philip could no longer slip out of the Georgia port with his fast blockade running ships. Andrew's only answer was to buy the cotton at exorbitant prices and ship it by train to his mill and the New Manchester Mills.

So far only a few of the slaves, now free men, had fled, and his crops of corn showed promise. He planned to transport the corn by rail to the armies fighting in Virginia and Tennessee, if the rails remained accessible. He knew that the fighting men needed food. He planned this over Governor Brown's objection that they be stored in the state's coffers for future needs. Andrew refused to be so selfish. His heart told him that in some small way maybe it would benefit Laura and open the way for her to return to them.

In April, the war that Rachel had determined would never reach Georgia, had its first military raid into the state, not only the state but had breached their area. It brought an abrupt end to her illusion, forcing her to face reality.

A group of men devised a daring plan to destroy the Western and

Atlantic Railroad between Atlanta and Chattanooga, thus hampering the delivery of supplies and reinforcements to Confederate forces fighting in the Tennessee campaign.

They planned to hijack a locomotive on its way to the Tennessee city and destroy bridges along with the rail and telegraph lines thus cutting communication between the two cities as well. On the tenth of April, James J. Andrews, a civilian scout and spy, arrived in Marietta, Georgia. Union Soldiers from three Ohio regiments along with one civilian, William Campbell, volunteered for the mission. Dressed in civilian clothes, they traveled in small groups in order not to raise suspicion. They met at the Fletcher House where they stayed until the morning of April 12. Early that morning they boarded the train as passengers only to seize the train at "Big Shanty" when it stopped for breakfast where both passengers as well as crew vacated the train. Due to a spirited chase and dismal weather, their grand scheme failed. They had to abandon the train, north of Ringgold, GA, just eighteen miles south of Chattanooga.

They managed to do little damage to the rails, and thanks to an intermittent rain, they failed to burn any bridges. Although they failed in their objective, it proved a wake up call to both Andrew and Rachel. The war moved ever nearer to them with no end in sight. Even now, battles raged in middle Tennessee with Chattanooga perched on their near horizon. If the Tennessee city fell, the next major target would be Atlanta, which was the transportation hub and food basket of the Confederacy.

Soon Andrew would have to make his own decision about his further involvement in the war. He decided he could make no move until Laura arrived home safely. Before he would leave he wanted to see that Sweetwater crops were on their way to Virginia to feed the troops fighting there. He wanted to be available if any conflict should develop with Governor Brown over shipping his goods out of Georgia.

The year marched on and with what little information Andrew could garner, Winchester was in the middle of fierce fighting with it changing occupation forces several times during the year. They had had no more word from Laura. If the casualty reports were anywhere near accurate, he felt sure that she was getting much practical experience in medicine to go along with her studies. However there was scant comfort for him in those thoughts. He was not at all sure that he supported her involvement. He only hoped that Union soldiers respected young ladies as Southern gentlemen were trained to do. Rachel tried to reassure him by suggesting that the North had not declared war on women and children. They were not monsters; they were Americans. He nodded, though not convinced. Rachel had reminded him gently once again that Laura was an adult now, and he needed to relinquish control. But deep in his heart, he wanted her home where he could keep her safe. Or at least try to.

Remembering his wife's sage observation that he could not control everything, he dropped to his knees entreating the Almighty to protect that precious girl he loved as his own.

December arrived in Winchester and this year there were no balls or brightly decorated houses. The wind blew cold and bitter in the Union occupied city. It had changed hands between the North and South multiple times during the year. At times even the main street of town saw intense fighting. When Jackson would reoccupy, there was jubilation in the streets. At times even civilians would join in the fray and shoot at fleeing Yankees.

Laura had seen Josh briefly in June before Banks had reoccupied Winchester. Lean and strong, he held her for a moment before he left to join the rest of his regiment and whispered his love for her, telling her to be brave.

A few days later she heard that they had been involved in a battle near Harrisonburg where their beloved Ashby was killed. With his horse shot out from under him, he continued on foot until he was shot through the heart. His last words were, "Forward my brave men." Laura wept when she heard and wondered about the whereabouts of Josh and Joel who had come through that battle unscathed, despite trying to rescue their commander. Both had received field commendations, and Josh had been promoted to major and Joel to captain.

One year after the poignant reunion of Laura and Josh in that cold windswept street on Christmas Eve evening, the command in Winchester changed once again. The day dawned dark and dreary on December 24 when Union General Milroy and his troops arrived in town.

Shortly after his arrival, the general issued an edict stating that his will would be absolute law and none should dare contradict or dispute his slightest word or wish. He stated that many had heard terrible stories about him before he came and supposed him to be a Nero for cruelty and blood. He confessed that he felt a strong disposition to play the tyrant among the occupied citizens whom he considered to be traitors.

And he didn't disappoint. Determined to conquer the indomitable secessionist women, he played the tyrant to the hilt. Being a rabid abolitionist, it was said that he had a strong desire to execute Virginians. He set up tribunals, ignoring constitutional authorities, and sentenced the townsfolk to execution by firing squad.

What Elizabeth and Laura experienced under Banks' occupation proved child's play compared to the harsh treatment under Milroy.

He provoked such terror in the hearts of the women of Winchester that they walked down the middle of the streets for fear of accidently brushing up against a Union soldier. He seized their beautiful homes and cast them out with no place to go. Elizabeth and Laura housed those castout until their house was at capacity, all the while fearing everyday that his men would come with eviction orders if not something worse.

When Union troops brought in a group of wounded confederates, Laura raced out to help. Her eyes touched each face looking for that special one, but relieved for a moment that he was not among them. She then scurried inside the hospital to garner aid and supplies to help the casualties.

She divided the most serious cases from the least severe and began to work. She had finished with the first young soldier when she felt a cold steel barrel in her ribs. Looking up, she stared straight into the beady eyes of General Milroy. "Missy, you will not use Union supplies to treat these vermin infested traitors."

"They will die without treatment, and they are not traitors. They are soldiers in proper uniforms, Sir."

A smirk contorted the general's face, "You call these rags proper uniforms?"

"Proper or not, they are soldiers in uniform, and it is my duty to care for them whether their clothes are grey or blue." She drew to her full height; her face flushed, her cobalt eyes blazing.

"The only duty you have, missy, is to obey my commands." He snarled at her.

"Oh, no, sir. I have a higher duty than that," she disputed, fearlessly. Sudden anger boiled up in her.

"You dare oppose me?"

"I do." Her chin rose, determination in every line of her body.

"Do you know the penalty for that?" Milroy barked, his irritation escalating because she didn't tremble in his presence.

"No, sir. I do not know the penalty for doing my humanitarian duty and following God's commands."

"And that is...?" He shouted

"Love thy neighbor as thyself and whatsoever you would have done unto you do likewise. If I were wounded and injured, I would want someone to care for me, wouldn't you? These men need me," she stated, her voice calm and firm, her back ramrod straight.

By this time a curious crowd had gathered on the street watching the spectacle. Milroy motioned with his handgun. "Missy, you go to my headquarters and I will deal with you later." He turned to his aide. "Take her to my command center."

The young lieutenant took her arm gently, and nodded his head toward the expansive mansion down the block. It was the home of an outstanding citizen in Winchester who had been evicted along with her daughters, one who was very ill. Refused enough time to gather any of her belongings, she had to leave the medicine that she needed. Troops escorted her to the county line exiling her over an unsubstantiated charge of possessing contraband. As soon as she was evicted Milroy moved his wife in and established it as both his residency and headquarters.

The young man who escorted her remained silent, but Laura

186

could sense his discomfort. When they arrived at the door, he turned to her and said, "I'm sorry, Miss Laura."

Laura quirked a brow at him. "How is it you know my name?"

The young lieutenant blushed. "Even enemy soldiers can appreciate a pretty lady, ma'm."

Laura turned to him and beamed a radiant smile toward him, "Where is your home, Lieutenant?"

"Northern Virginia, ma'm"

"I thought so. Your polite manner and the way you said ma'm. How did you come to join this war?"

"I believe in the Union, and I don't believe it's right to own another human being."

"Many of our boys believe just as you do, but they felt an intense loyalty to Virginia. They joined the Confederacy when the state seceded."

"Then I guess they are as sick as I am over this fighting. When I joined up, it never occurred to me that I would be shooting my neighbors or treating ladies like they have been treated here. I've watched you work with our wounded. You make no difference between yours and ours. I appreciate what you're doing despite how you've been abused."

Laura looked over his shoulder. "Your commander is coming, and I don't want you to be in trouble, but thank you for your encouragement."

"I fear you'll be needing it. Now I'll be bidding you a good day." And he tipped his hat to her, just as the general approached, scowling at his young officer.

Laura bounded up the steps, her spirits lifted somehow.

Milroy marched into the room and nodded his head to his staff.

Pointing to an office off the wide spacious foyer, he said brusquely, "In there, young woman."

He sat down behind his desk, leaving her standing and said in a voice loud enough for everyone to hear, "As I stated from the beginning that disobeying my orders is a capital offense. You, young lady, have publicly defied me, and that I will not tolerate."

"I'm sorry, Sir, if you consider what I said a defiance. Have I not abided by all the rules you have set for this town? I concur that you have the authority over me, except in this case."

Milroy lowered his voice and spoke between his teeth, "Why this case?"

"Because there is a higher authority."

"Not in Winchester. I am the sole commander here."

"Perhaps in military terms, but in truth, we both have a higher authority. When there is a conflict, I must recognize and obey Him." Laura said quietly. As her anger subsided, she had no desire to embarrass him in front of his staff.

"I don't recognize a higher authority here than me."

"That's up to you, Sir. But I know that you do recognize one from Washington, and it is my understanding that your President recognizes the same Higher Power that I do."

Milroy frowned; he didn't want to be reminded of Washington. He'd had a few complaints, but what did they know about war? They were just politicians. Besides they were there, and he was here. "We are not talking about Washington, we are talking about Winchester, and the way you have behaved."

"But ultimately Washington will hear." Laura insisted.

"Are you threatening me?"

"No, Sir, just reminding you."

"I'm a half a mind to make an example of you that will make this town know I mean business." His eyes slid over her making her shiver.

He laughed a little seeing her response. It pleased him. This was more like it. "So you are afraid of me. You should be."

"You misunderstand. I'm not afraid of you, I just don't approve of the way you looked at me. I did nothing to deserve that."

"All Southern women deserve whatever I want to say or do. Hell is not full enough; there must be more of you Secession women of Winchester to fill it up. You best remember it is I who holds your life or death in my hand."

"I beg your pardon, Sir. You do not hold my life or my death in your hands," she contradicted once more.

"If I don't hold your life in my hand then who does?" Milroy queried with a frown, startled but intrigued despite himself.

"God does. And until I have completed the work He has for me, no one can take my life away."

"And if I execute you according to my edicts, then you figure you have finished with your God's work?" He sneered.

"That's right. It's not up to you, but Him. I will not arrive in Heaven one minute late or one minute early." She stated calmly, then added. "But I don't think He's finished with me yet."

"Really? Why?"

"Because there are many wounded soldiers, both confederate and union, that need me and honestly, so do you, General Milroy."

"Why in the world would you think I need you?"

"Because your medical team is out in the field. All you have are the women volunteers whom you have mistreated, Dr. Martin, me and a few orderlies for your many casualties. If you fail to provide help for

189

all of them, our prisoners and your men, you will be in trouble with your government, and it will look very bad on your record. And besides that, if I may be so bold, there were many Union sympathizers in this community before you came who are changing their minds because of your harsh treatment."

Milroy growled, "You are an impudent young woman, and I really think I should make an example of you. Where is your home?"

Surprised that he thought Winchester was not her home, she replied a longing in her voice, "Georgia."

"What in blazes are you doing up here?"

"I was going to school."

"Are you going to school now? I didn't know there was a girl's school in town."

"It closed."

"Then why didn't you go home?" he barked, wishing she had.

"I can't. Your people are in my way. Besides, I have a job to do here."

"Oh, we are back to that, are we?"

"Yes, sir. I do think that's our point of contention."

"Do you know some people have said that I shot people who were treating the rebel wounded?" He smirked.

"Yeah, I heard that, but I don't believe it."

Milroy obviously taken aback, "Why not?"

"Because as despicable as you are, I don't think even you could commit such a horrible act."

"So you think I'm despicable?" He smiled, the bully in him satisfied at last that he was getting through to this renegade girl.

"No, I think you want to make people believe you are."

Milroy frowned, looking toward the door to make sure his officers hadn't heard this remark; this was not going at all the way he had intended. "Captain Dodge, take this female and put her in the jail in solitary confinement until I decide what must be done with her."

So Laura spent the first of many cold nights in a dark lonely cell while Milroy agonized over what to do with her. He knew the truth of what she said. Washington would frown on any punitive actions toward her. No question about it, it would get back to them; yet, he couldn't let her defiance toward him go unpunished. And it was defiance toward him, no matter what she said about having a "higher authority".

He couldn't abide insubordination. Besides if he let her get by with it, he might lose control of the loathsome women in this town. No, he would have to make an example of her. But how? He would have Washington to contend with if he proved too harsh. And then she was right. He needed her medical skills. His men told him that she was quite gifted. He sighed, if only she had responded like most. He could have scared her, threatened her, and that would be the end of it. But no she had to defy him.

When the news of Laura's altercation reached Elizabeth, her heart constricted with fear. Now she had to get word to Andrew, but even then what could he do? He had not been able to extract her from this situation so far. The few times the South had reoccupied the town proved too brief to get word to him and give him time to arrange transportation out.

Elizabeth decided her first attempt would be to send a letter by courier, but by the time a letter reached Georgia, Laura might be...she didn't want to finish the thought. Surely the despicable man would not execute a young girl for giving medical aid to the wounded no matter which side they were on.

Elizabeth wrote the letter and attempted to find out from her source in town if a courier was expected anytime soon. She said no one knew. Since Milroy's occupation intelligence gathering had diminished to almost a stand still. Couriering had been at a minimum. Elizabeth's heart plummeted. What was to be the fate of the young woman she had come to love as a younger sister? Bitter tears streamed down her face at her helplessness as she sat in the shadows of her parlor looking out on a bleak landscape.

A knock on her door revived her from her unpleasant thoughts. When she encountered Lucy standing at her front door, she cried for joy, "Lucy, how did you ever get in here from Front Royal?"

"Simple. I have traveling papers. I've come to see my Aunt Elizabeth," Lucy chirped, "I heard you weren't feeling so well. So I've come to see about you."

"Me? Not feeling well?" Elizabeth queried a puzzled look wrinkled her brow.

"Yeah, you remember, you're all alone...?"

Understanding brought a smile to Elizabeth's face, "Oh, yes. You may be more accurate than you know, my love."

"I was so bored at Papa's." Lucy shrugged her shoulders as if that explanation would prove sufficient.

Elizabeth embraced her young friend, exclaiming, "Oh, the good Lord knew I needed you today. Laura is in terrible trouble."

Lucy pushed by Elizabeth and entered the broad hall, "I heard."

Elizabeth frowned, "You heard?"

"Yeah, bad news travels fast."

"Only through certain sources." Elizabeth corrected, truth dawning. "Lucy, not you, too."

"Not me, too, what?"

"Putting yourself in harm's way."

"Whatever do you mean, Auntie? You know me. Life is just a party, not a thing serious about me. By the way, I hear you have lots of parties around here, just like we used to." Lucy grimaced.

"You know better than that, and I want to know what you are really up to Lucy!"

"Why just visiting my sick auntie who needs me."

"Your 'auntie' is not sick but I do need you so."

"Tell me about it."

"I need to get some help for Laura, and I don't know where to begin."

"How about wiring her uncle? And then a word to Washington wouldn't hurt. This ogre needs to have his wings clipped."

"Sounds like a great plan, except as far as we know, no courier will be coming our way. Milroy has clamped down on the town, and he is so suspicious of everybody that getting any intelligence out is almost impossible."

Lucy took a furtive look behind her and closed the door, "What if I get it out for you?"

"You, Lucy?"

Lucy nodded her head. "I have a friend in Front Royal, perhaps you have heard of her----?

"You mean Belle Boyd?" Elizabeth whispered.

Lucy nodded, then lifted her skirts where packets of medicines were tied to her hoops. "She couldn't make it so I'm the delivery lady. Anyway, she couldn't come. She would raise all kind of suspicions right now. Since I went to school here and you are here, I seemed the logical choice."

"Wherever did you get those, Lucy?" Elizabeth's eyes widened, fear darkening them.

Lucy shrugged. "Don't know, I'm just the delivery person. They were attached to my hoops at the lady in question's home and I have an appointment to dispatch these between here and Front Royal. All I know for sure is that our troops are in dire need of what I am transporting. Meanwhile I am to visit with you, gather information about troop strengths and any other information from these boys in blue." Lucy batted her eyes coquettishly.

"There will be no charming these boys in blue, even though you have the charms of a Delilah. Milroy would have their heads. Unless you are a known Unionist, they are forbidden to associate with any females in this town. The only thing they are allowed to do is insult us."

"Then I shall gather information on my own and transmit it. The most important is the information that we need to get out to Washington and Sweetwater about our sweet Laura."

"Oh, Lucy. Do you think we could?"

"If I can get through without a hitch it is as good as done. I meet my contact noon tomorrow. My pass is only for two days," Lucy explained, her voice barely above a whisper.

"I pray for a miracle, for your safety and Laura's release."

"You keep praying, Auntie. We all need it," Lucy entreated, her carefree facade dropped.

Chapter
Thirteen

Andrew stared in horror as words on the wire blurred. The familiar clickety-clack of the telegraph machine faded into silence while the message on the page sunk into his innermost being. A sense of helplessness washed over him, weakening his knees so much so that he sat down on the bench pressing against his leg.

He had come to Marietta to meet the train that carried a shipment of cotton he had purchased and had shipped from Savannah. It had cost a small fortune to get it, but it proved necessary if his mill could meet government demands. Savannah and Charleston Factors were holding the cotton on the wharves with the disillusioned hope that soon England would throw in her support for the South. Then it would be on its way to Europe, garnering them a substantial profit. It was true England wanted the South's cotton, but to get it she would have to show some semblance of acceptance of slavery. That wouldn't set well politically with the British.

Andrew knew the factors' hopes were nothing more than pipe dreams. With Fort Pulaski now in Federal hands, shipping from Savannah proved impossible. The days when fast sailing blockade runners could avoid the Union blockade and get out of Savannah were at an end and before long there would be very few ports left where it would be minutely possible that one could get in or out of the South.

He had arranged for Delmeade's to make delivery to the factory but he had wanted to assure himself that the shipment had arrived in its entirety. Since Philip seemed to have disappeared and Agan was gone he had few contacts left in Savannah to handle his affairs. Suddenly the wire he held in his hands pushed aside anything but the horror of the words seared into his heart. Laura was in imminent danger, and he had no means to rescue her.

Andrew dropped his head into his hands and groaned, heedless of watching eyes. His heart cried out to his Maker. "Oh, God, what must I do? Give me wisdom for only you can resolve this issue. Please rescue Laura. I've tried to take care of my family. I thought I was strong enough, rich enough and smart enough to handle any of their problems. But I'm not. Please, Lord, I need your help, Laura needs your help."

Andrew's distress was so intense that he failed to hear the train as it rolled into the station nor did he see the handsome, blond giant step through the door. Only when he felt a hand grasp his shoulder did he look up straight into the concerned azure eyes of Philip , "Drew, my friend, what has happened?"

Andrew silently handed the wire to Philip.

After reading it, he handed it back to Andrew and shook his head, "What are we going to do about it?"

Andrew shuddered. "That's the problem, I don't know what I can do about it. I've been trying for months to get her out of there and every avenue closed. According to this, that hate-crazed man just might execute her."

"He wouldn't dare."

"He must have gotten by with a lot so far, if his reputation is accurate. This is almost enough to make me a flaming secessionist. Maybe what I need to do is join up with Jackson and then maybe I could rescue her."

"Get yourself killed in the meantime and then you would be no benefit to Laura or Rachel. We need to think. Let's get a cup of tea. You know an Englishman thinks more clearly after a cup of tea," Philip said trying to lighten his own heart and the heart of his friend at the terrible news.

After Andrew's coffee arrived and Philip had had his fill of tea, Andrew remarked, "By the way, Phil, what in the world are you doing here? Been trying to chase you down for months."

"That's a strange thing, Andrew. I got home from that last blockade running venture out of Wilmington, barely by the skin of my teeth I might add, and planned to meet with my manager, plan the crops for the coming year and unwind a bit. Suddenly I felt an overwhelming need to come to Georgia. When I saw you and the condition that you were in, I realized why. Do you suppose God sent me?"

"More than likely. I needed a friend today and Rachel will need you tonight. How will I ever tell her what has happened to Laura?"

"If God sent me, then He has a plan."

"Do you know what it is?"

"Maybe."

Andrew's eyes widened. "What, man, what?"

"I will go after her."

"Oh, I thought you had a plan." Andrew groaned.

"Don't be so dismissive." Philip countered. "You underestimate my powers of persuasion."

"You know you can't get across enemy lines and waltz into Milroy's quarters and demand Laura's release. If that were an option, I would have been in Winchester months ago." Andrew shook his head, "I should never have let her go up there and should have made her come home when Virginia seceded."

"Friend, visiting the 'what ifs' is never productive. Now hear me out," Philip quietly commanded.

Andrew sighed, "I'm not going anywhere."

"Andrew, there is a difference between you and me."

"That's pretty apparent." Sarcasm laced Andrew's voice.

"No, listen. The biggest difference is I'm British, and you are Southern."

"So? We get along fine."

"I can see you are not your usual alert self. I'm not talking about our relationship; I'm talking about the freedom and privilege that I enjoy as a neutral. You are at war with your country, I'm not."

Andrew's eyes brightened. "That's right! You can cross enemy lines without impediment."

"If my papers are in order, and they are."

"What is the plan?"

"Simple. I just go to Winchester, however I can get there and bring Laura home to Sweetwater."

"Just demand of this Milroy to give her to you? I'm sure he is not a cooperative individual. From everything I've heard and what's in this wire, he won't give her up easily."

"When I get through, I believe he will."

"What makes you think that?"

"I have a persuasive card up my sleeve."

"And that is?"

"I'll go to Washington. The Secretary of the Navy wants more ships. They have been requesting that I build them some. So far I've been too busy."

"Making blockade runners."

"They don't know that. I've just turned them down."

"If it takes building them a ship to release Laura, build it!"

"I hope that it won't come to that, but if worse comes to worse, it will be something with which to negotiate."

"When can you leave?"

"As soon as a train heads north."

———————————————

The trip to Washington proved challenging. There were bits by rail, hours on end by buggy, and at one point by horseback, but on arriving in Washington, Philip obtained his objective quickly.

When he introduced himself to Secretary of War Stanton and showed him Andrew's wire, he ushered Philip in to see the President himself. After a brief meeting, Philip left a very angry President, who gave him a pass for safe passage and an order for General Milroy.

Philip found the seventy or so mile trip to Winchester less challenging and he arrived in town just at dusk. He shook his head as he observed the war ravaged town. Many of the former show places were in disrepair with the public buildings down Main Street damaged by the fierce fighting that had taken place in the town. He kicked up swirls of dirt as he left the station and walked down the center of town. Officers in blue stared at him, their curiosity high, yet much to his surprise they failed to detain him or ask any questions. Finally he approached a young man in blue lounging against a shell pocked building and inquired as to which house was Elizabeth's residence.

The soldier grinned. "You're not from 'round here," He observed without answering his question. "Good thing 'cause our general ain't in no accommodating mood for any locals. He hardly trust any of them even when they claim to be Union sympathizers."

Philip laughed, "Good observation, young man!"

"You sound like one of them Englishmen."

"I am, and you sound like a Southerner. So what are you doing wearing a blue uniform?"

The tall thin man shrugged. "I'm from North Alabama ,and I didn't have no slaves and warn't gonna fight for nun. I knowed they tol me twarn't jest about slaves, but about whether or not them politicians in Washington had the right to tell a state what they could and couldn't do. I don't know jest what it really is all bout so fer me it boiled down to being conscripted into the Confederate Army where I know I'd starve and not have a weapon fittin' to shoot or join the blue. I joined the blue; thought I'd have an easier time of it. I knowed the South ain't rich enough or got enough guns to hold out fer a long war, but to tell you the truth, though, I wish I wuz anywhere but here."

Philip frowned. "And why is that?"

"Can't speak agin my commander or it would be a court martial fer sure, but let's just put it this way. I warn't gonna fight for slavery, but I never wanted to kill my neighbors or treat wimmen like they are being treated. Some of my reb neighbors been brought in here wounded. Shore brought to mind who I mighta been shootin at even when I can't see their faces. A little lady tried to help them, but she didn't get nothing but trouble for it. Might have been different if she hadn't been a Secesh. By the way, Miss Elizabeth's house is just down

200

the street. It's the big white one with the wide porch." Lowering his voice, he added, "When you see her, you'll git what I mean."

Philip's heart sank. If Elizabeth's treatment had been so ruthless, in what condition would he find Laura? He thanked the young soldier and hurried to his destination.

He knocked several times. The dark house appeared deserted. Just as he turned to leave, she opened the door. Philip's breath caught in his throat. Elizabeth stood there in the open doorway, her eyes wide, an unspoken question in them. The last glimmer of light surrounded her like an aura, and the fragrance of lilacs wafted from her, teasing his nostrils. Never had he encountered such sweetness in a countenance. His eyes took in her lustrous brunette hair, her warm mahogany eyes with long lashes and her full lips that turned up in good humor. Her tattered dress clung to her shapely body, and his heart leapt in his chest. For a long moment words failed the usually gregarious duke. Who was this beautiful woman? Elizabeth? If so, then why had Andrew not prepared him for this exquisite creature standing before him? Was the man blind? He should have told him.

"Yes?" Her voice was as melodious as her beauty was captivating. "Yes?" she repeated. "Can I help you?"

"Uh, uh," Philip stammered. She carefully observed this elegant, handsome stranger. Although his clothes were rumpled, and he appeared road weary, his attire proclaimed him a civilian and a wealthy one.

Suddenly a radiant smile parted her lips and ignited warm, bright lights in her eyes. She stepped forward and extended her small delicate hand to welcome him. "I don't know how or where you came from, but you must be the miracle we prayed for and expected."

"No, ma'm I'm no miracle, I'm Philip . I've come to take Laura home where she belongs." He had recovered his poise and flashed his heart-stopping smile on her.

"Then indeed you are the miracle we have prayed for. I'm Elizabeth Donahue."

He took her hand and raised it to his lips. "Laura never told us her friend was so beautiful."

"Ah, if you think so now, you should have seen me before the war." She laughed, completely at ease with this handsome stranger.

"If you were anymore beautiful, I could scarce take it in," he said and meant it.

"So you are the Sir Philip that Laura has told me so much about. The one who loves adventure and was in love with her Aunt Rachel."

Philip laughed and placed a hand over his heart. "That's history! I've met a new love."

Elizabeth quirked an eyebrow, lights danced in her eyes. "Laura neglected to mention you have an outrageously flattering tongue."

"Not flattering, just the truth."

Elizabeth laughed out loud, relief over the past days of worry proving delightful. "Come in, you must tell me the plan. How in the world are you to get Laura away from that monster?"

"Tell me what has happened since she was arrested," Philip directed, all light-hearted banter extinguished.

"Milroy is a fiend. He kept her in solitary confinement for two weeks with only bread and water. Then so many casualties came in, he marched her down to the hospital to work, but under guard. Now that the casualties have lessoned, I'm fearful she will be back in solitary confinement. I was able to see her every now and then and take her what food I could muster up. As you can see foodstuff and all essentials are in short supply for us. The troops have plenty.

They have confiscated all our supplies and had more of their own shipped in, but General Milroy considers us traitors and wants us to be treated likewise. I'm fearful he will set Laura's trial soon. He hates her and will make an example of her perhaps even executing her. He has threatened me. He knows I am her friend."

Philip shook his head, sorrow dimming the merry lights in his bright blue eyes. "He will pay for what he has done. At least Laura will be set free from his tyranny."

"But how is it to be done? He honors no one's request or authority but his own. Just because you are British won't have any influence over him. I tell you he despises Laura and won't let her go."

Philip reached out and took her small shapely hand in his, "Where is your faith? Didn't you ask me if I were a miracle?"

She chuckled, "I hoped."

He stood up and patted his pocket. "I may not be the miracle, but this is."

Elizabeth's eyes widened. "What is it?"

"Orders from the President of the United States to release Miss Laura Meredith into my care and to give her and her party safe passage to Atlanta, Georgia."

Elizabeth jumped up and squealed for joy, throwing her arms around the surprised, Philip, engulfing them both in the sweet fragrance of her. He reveled in every second of it.

"Oh, I am sorry, Sir Philip," she said pulling back as a blush tinted her lovely complexion. "What happy news! Our Good Lord was looking after us after all."

"Indeed He was, ma'm. Now I must find the dishonorable General Milroy and garner Laura's release before she has to spend another night in those horrible circumstances."

"God speed. I shall make a bed for you and for her. The women who were formerly staying here have moved out of Winchester, and I am alone."

"And the neighbors? Will they not gossip at your entertaining a male stranger overnight?"

Elizabeth laughed. "Do you think I care? The only neighbors I have are either dressed in blue or are Unionist, neither of which I give a whit about what they think."

"I shall be on my way if you'll point the way to his headquarters. Don't want to risk having Laura spend another night incarcerated."

"It's not hard to find. Just look for the most elaborate mansion in town and that will be both his home and headquarters."

Philip shook his head with disgust and rose to go.

───────────────

Milroy's aide answered the door. "Have a seat here, sir. I will see if the General is available."

"Oh he is available. I have an important message for him."

"If you'll give it to me, I will take it to the General. Then he can decide if he needs to see you."

"No, I'm to deliver it in person, and he very definitely needs to see me."

"Very well, sir. I will tell the General."

Philip heard a commotion in a room just beyond his view and a gruff voice demanding, "Who does he think he is interrupting my evening meal? I have finished for the day. Tell him to come back tomorrow."

Someone responded too quietly for Philip to make out what was said, then he heard the General's voice, "Very well then, I will see him, but it had better be important."

The general entered the room, without jacket and his collar askew. "What is so important I can't finish my meal? State your business and do it in a hurry."

"You might prefer to transact this business in your office." Philip counseled.

"Never mind my office, I decide where to transact my business so state yours and leave. I'm tired and you are wearying me further."

"As you please, General Milroy. I am here to get a certain Laura Meredith released into my care and custody."

"You disturbed me for that?" the General shouted, "The word is never. She is my prisoner, and she will stay my prisoner. I am not relinquishing her into anyone's custody. Why in heaven's name do you think I would release her to you?"

"Because I am British and neutral. She is a very dear friend who has done nothing to deserve this fate. I want her released without delay," Philip warned, his voice low and threaded with steel.

"Ha! You must be jesting. I hold no respect for the British and care not what you want. Now I will be wishing you a good day, sir. I strongly suggest that you take the first opportunity to leave this community or I shall forget your neutrality."

Philip laughed, "I don't think you can do that, Sir. Your government greatly desires to stay on good terms with ours, lest we give our support to the Confederacy. As in the case of the two officials from Britain who were jailed."

"You mean the two apprehended on a blockade runner?" Milroy spat out, "Should have hung 'em!"

"The very same. I remember your President's response. He stated that he only wants one war at a time. I believe he still feels that way. And I might add my country would not look in good favor on anyone infringing on my neutrality. Oh, pardon me for my oversight, I am Sir Philip . My father is Duke of Session."

"Titles don't impress me and be that as it may, refusing to hand over to you this little troublemaker won't start a war."

"You are refusing me?"

Milroy growled, "Yes, I'm refusing you. Enough of this, be gone man."

"Before I go, perhaps you should read this letter," Philip encouraged, a twinkle in his eyes.

Milroy frowned, then took the letter. His bluster subsided, and his face paled when he recognized the official seal of the President on the envelope. He motioned Philip into his office. Sitting down at his desk, he put on his spectacles and read the letter. Then called his aide-de-camp and barked, "Bring our prisoner to me."

A few minutes passed before Laura entered the room. Her eyes looked even larger in her thin face, but they were still luminous. That she had been deprived of the food she needed was evident. Her homespun and tattered dress hung from her shoulders, and Philip's heart ached. She marched straight up to Milroy's desk, her chin high, never looking to the right or left; thus she failed to see her friend standing in the shadows. Philip closely observed her, marveling at her apparent courage. She appeared unafraid, despite what she had experienced at the hands of this loathsome man. Even though she had suffered greatly, her spirit seemed undaunted. The lovely young girl, privileged and pampered, whom Philip had last seen in Savannah now stood before him, transformed into an even more beautiful woman matured by the ravages of war.

"You wanted to see me, General Milroy?" she asked, her voice calm, almost accommodating.

"I am releasing you. You may go home."

"Sir?""

"You can go home!" He almost shouted, frustration written in every line of his body.

"Home?"

"Yes, I mean home. Georgia, home. I don't want to see your face again and take that woman, Elizabeth, with you!"

"Beg your pardon, Sir. But how am I going to get home?"

"That's his problem!" Milroy snarled pointing to Philip.

Laura turned toward the shadows where Philip waited.

"Philip," she cried, as she ran across the room, throwing herself into his waiting arms, "Oh, Philip! It's been such a long time."

"That must be the understatement of the year," he chuckled as he gathered her thin body into his embrace. "Let's go find Elizabeth. She is most worried about you. Then tomorrow we have a long journey ahead of us."

"Yes, the long journey home."

Chapter Fourteen

It took several days to procure transportation out of Winchester, and all the while, Laura and Philip pleaded with Elizabeth to accompany them. When they feared they would never convince her to leave her home, Milroy made the decision for her. He sent an eviction notice confiscating her home and another notice exiling her from Winchester.

Philip's heart soared at the thought of the beautiful Elizabeth accompanying him and Laura on the long journey home. In just a few days, the young nobleman had lost his heart. The trip would offer a time for them to get to know one another. What better way to learn about a person than to observe each other under pressure? He was well aware of the stress the three would endure on their journey. They would have to traverse around battles, perhaps find themselves in the midst of one. He knew that she would be a great comfort for Laura in the hardships they might be facing. The deep friendship and affection they shared bonded them more like sisters than friends and would prove invaluable in facing difficulties ahead.

Philip told himself Laura was the reason Elizabeth must come, but in reality the thought of parting with her before he could persuade her of all his attributes seemed intolerable.

The journey proved no less taxing than Philip imagined. They traveled by train, by carriage, on horseback, and where rail was pulled up and destroyed by troops, they hiked by foot. While he had experienced complications traveling to Washington, this trip proved much more challenging. His gentle heart ached when he saw the hardships the ladies had to endure, but they never complained. His admiration for both of them grew with each tortuous mile they trod, and his love for Elizabeth flourished with each day's dawning.

What he thought would be a better route through Virginia into Tennessee and on to the train in Chattanooga turned out to be long with many difficulties. In hindsight, he wished that they had gone to Boston and sailed south to Wilmington, hoping to evade the blockade and capture.

They carried only necessities with them because Milroy gave them little time to leave. In fact after his edict, they had only hours to escape. They had to leave behind their few remaining beautiful gowns that had not been cut up for bandages and other uses. Now they hung limply in an armoire in Elizabeth's home, the contraband of war. They were blessed that the spring weather stayed uncommonly warm, and they had experienced little need for heavy coats. At times when the wind blew cold , they huddled together for warmth. Philip would wrap them in army blankets secured from a kind officer and hold them in his arms for extra warmth until they could find suitable shelter. Through it all, Elizabeth never complained, only expressed gratitude to her benefactor for his assistance. When she did, Philip vowed in his heart that someday he would give her all the comforts that the world could offer if only she would say she would be his.

They crossed the lines between Union and Confederate forces multiple times. When the Union sentries saw the pass with the President's official seal on it, they were waved through without question. When they came to the Confederate lines, Philip showed his papers of neutrality, and most times they were waved on through without incident. But once as they circumvented a battlefield, sentries took them to the colonel's headquarters. When they found out that Laura and Elizabeth had been in Winchester and described what they had endured, they received the warmest hospitality. Laura asked if anyone knew Major Joshua Douglas, but no one could give her any information. It was as if time had swallowed him up. She asked how she might contact him, and they told her if she knew his regiment, write him a letter and address it there. Perhaps the letter would find him, but she was no longer sure of anything. Where was he? His regiment had been divided, a new commander had taken over, and she had no idea where he was or how to contact him. The colonel suggested she write to the last place she knew. When she told him that she had already done so, he shook his head sadly.

When they approached near enough to a battle that they could hear the distant boom of artillery, hope stirred in her heart. As irrational as it seemed, she dreamed of encountering the cavalry and seeing his precious face once more before she left Virginia. She recognized the possibility as unlikely, but still she hoped. Jackson had marched his troops and cavalry across the mountains to join Lee and the Army of Northern Virginia where they were in heated conflict. If only she could know his whereabouts and let him know hers. Had she just waited, perhaps Josh would have made it back to find her.

She shook her head, that was not an option for her, he had much more on his mind than worrying about her, for he must be serving in a different theater of war. If by some miracle he did make it back to Winchester, she remained confident someone would tell him.

After weeks of travel and a convoluted route, they finally reached Chattanooga. The end of the journey appeared a possibility. Both women suffered from exhaustion, and Philip was weary to his bones as well. They rested for a couple of days in a local hotel, enjoying the comforts of bed, food and bath before they could catch a train south. He immediately wired Andrew that they were on the last leg of their journey home. On the third day, Philip was able to purchase three tickets for a train leaving for Marietta the next morning. At the station, he wired Andrew the happy news that they would be arriving in Marietta mid-day.

Rachel was beside herself with excitement. Philip was bringing Laura home! It was a miracle almost too wonderful to comprehend. Her world would be complete. Her family around her, the mill refurbished and running at full strength, enough food put away to have plenty. What more could she ask for? To say that she was thankful would be an understatement. She realized from where the blessings had come, and how thankful she was that God had provided Andrew Meredith as His instrument to bless her.

She gazed out her windows at the rolling acres that met the river beyond. It was May again, and her mind traveled back four years ago when she had arrived at Sweetwater. What a difference these four years had made. From what seemed disaster had grown blessings exceeding her wildest dreams. Everything she had ever wanted was hers. A home, a love and now a sister. Not that Laura was really her sister, but they had bonded in her brief time here, and she had filled that empty space in Rachel's heart which had always longed to have a sibling. Amazing that she had seen so much of herself in Laura. Now she wondered how the hardships she had endured might have changed her. According to Philip's wire the changes were all for the better.

Rachel frowned as she considered the past months and their anguish over Laura's welfare. It had hurt her to see Andrew so distressed with his inability to rescue his niece. It was so unlike this self-confident man to allow obstacles to defeat him. However these circumstances seemed beyond his control, actually beyond anyone's control. It was a strange time. He experienced defeat in every way he turned. Why? Did it really defeat him or was this a period of learning in his life, of teaching him to be willing to relinquish control? Whatever it was, a new peace seemed to permeate Andrew. He seemed more relaxed and perfectly accepting that Philip, and not he, had been the one who had rescued Laura and her friend, Elizabeth.

Rachel's musings suddenly turned from the much-anticipated return of Laura to this mysterious woman, Elizabeth. How would she affect the balance at Sweetwater? Would she fit in? Would Rachel like her? She shook her head, appalled at the path her thoughts were taking her. How self-centered her thoughts had turned. Where had her compassion gone? For a moment the old Rachel threatened to show up. It mattered not whether this stranger had a compatible personality. It was both her duty and privilege to offer home and comfort to a refugee from the war. Then a mischievous smile played at the corner of her mouth. Actually she couldn't wait to welcome this woman of mystery. Besides with Andrew, Laura and now, even Philip, holding her in the highest regard how could she feel otherwise?

Thinking of Andrew, she turned as his footsteps sounded in the hallway. "Rachel, let's be on our way. We don't want to be late to meet the train."

Turning a radiant smile on him, she replied, "I'm ready, darling, and I can't wait to get that little miss home and restore her to health and happiness."

"And Elizabeth...?" Andrew reminded.

Rachel frowned before answering, then smiled with confidence. "And, yes, Elizabeth, too."

<hr/>

The train pulled in two hours late with an impatient Rachel and Andrew pacing the station floors. Finally Andrew went to the Fletcher house securing three rooms for the night along with reservations for dinner that evening.

When Philip bounded off the train, he turned to give his hand to someone just beyond Rachel's view. When she stepped into the waning sunshine, Rachel caught her breath. Even in much worn clothing, a more beautiful brunette, she had never seen, but it was the way Philip looked at her that brought a smile to Rachel's lips. With Elizabeth on the ground, Laura followed and Rachel gasped. Waiflike and fragile her beauty was almost ethereal. Her eyes appeared even larger in her thin face but glowed with some new inner, indefinable beauty. Rachel embraced her with tender care, fearful that she might crush her. Then she turned to Elizabeth who waited with Philip in the background, watching, not wanting to intrude.

"Welcome to Georgia, Elizabeth. We are so happy Philip brought you to us," Rachel said, with a warm smile, meaning what she said and confident that she would share a friendship with this beautiful woman who had the most compassionate eyes she had ever seen.

"I don't know how long I will have to impose on you, Mrs. Meredith, but I greatly appreciate yours and Andrew's hospitality. I had no other option but to leave Winchester as General Milroy exiled me from the town."

"Because of me, Rachel," Laura explained. "She tried to help me and lost her home because of it."

"I pray that it won't be a permanent loss." Elizabeth smiled at Laura.

"For your sake, I hope not. I can understand what your home must mean to you. I almost lost mine but meanwhile, our home is yours as long as you need it or wish. And by the way, please call me Rachel. I know we shall be great friends," Rachel assured her.

Andrew nodded his agreement as he took Elizabeth's hand. "Rachel couldn't have been more accurate. I'm so thankful that all three of you are out of that hellish place and home, safe and sound. I don't know for how long we will be exempt from the fighting."

"Oh, Andrew, spare us those dire suppositions," Rachel protested.

Andrew turned an indulgent smile in her direction and chuckled, "You are right, my dear. We need not darken this homecoming by focusing on the dark clouds on our own horizons, and we don't need to stand out here further tiring these travelers. We need to feed you and let you get some rest. We are staying here for the night."

Exhausted, the three nodded their heads in relief that the last leg of their long journey would wait until morning.

As soon as Andrew saw to their meager luggage, he herded them into the Fletcher House. It was the dinner hour, and many of the patrons looked with curiosity at the party of five, their eyes especially taking in the two women in tattered, dusty clothing. The more people stared the more agitated Rachel became. Then she looked at both Laura and Elizabeth and saw that they, too, recognized the stir they were creating. Why didn't Andrew do something? This was rude and insulting behavior. These people needed a reprimand, and if he wouldn't, then she would. She started to rise and felt Elizabeth's restricting hand on her arm, "It's alright, Rachel. They mean no harm, they are just curious."

Before Rachel could respond, one of the ladies sitting closest to them turned toward Laura and asked, "Forgive my staring and curiosity but are you the young woman imprisoned in Virginia for trying to help our wounded soldiers?"

A broad grin grew across Laura's face. "I am, and this is my friend, Elizabeth Donahue, who was exiled because of her attempt to help me. We made it out, thanks to Sir Philip, with not much more than these clothes on our backs."

"Oh my dears, what a tortuous trip that must have been."

"You couldn't exactly call it a carriage ride in the park," Laura chuckled.

"I'm surprised you could even make it. How did you come? All the way by train?"

Laura and Elizabeth looked at each other and laughed, "By train, by boat, by carriage, and by foot. Sometimes we bypassed skirmishes and in one instance a major battle."

"I'm so glad the two of you escaped. If I can do anything to help you, please let me know. I am a member of the Ladies Aid Society, and this is the closest that we have come to any of the women who have been exposed to combat. I would like for you to come and address our next meeting here in Marietta. Why, you are virtual heroines." When the stranger said that applause erupted in the dining room.

"No ma'm we are not heroines. In trying circumstances you do what you have to do and pray to the Good Lord to give you courage, strength and wisdom to carry you through," Laura protested. "but how did you know about us?"

The good lady blushed and stammered, "Uhm, let's just say that news has a way of traveling no matter the circumstances."

Rachel rolled her eyes and looked at Andrew, "Jimmy!"

Andrew chuckled. "Our teletype operator. I guess he couldn't help it. The tidbit was too good to keep."

"Heaven help us if there is news that shouldn't be broadcast!" Rachel exclaimed.

Andrew patted her hand, a loving smile lifting the corner of his mouth. "He wouldn't. He values his job too much."

The trio ate heartily of the delicious stew and warm bread while Rachel and Andrew watched approving their appetites. Elizabeth marveled that food of this quality was available, even if Georgia was the breadbasket of the Confederacy.

Andrew queried them about their trip, reluctant to draw Laura into conversation about her ordeal in Winchester and regretted that strangers had brought up the subject. He knew there would be time enough for that.

As he asked what battles they had to circumvent, Rachel grew uncomfortable. She didn't want to think about the war. She wanted it to stay in Virginia or Tennessee or wherever it was. Her mind tried to block out the warnings Andrew had issued to her and the raid into

Georgia that had disturbed her peace. But she couldn't. The more they talked about the war, the more agitated she became.

Finally she blurted out, "Andrew, don't we have any other subject of conversation?"

Andrew's smile was gentle, "I don't know. What would you suggest?"

She raised her eyebrows and asked weakly, "The crops?"

Laughter greeted her answer and Andrew patted her hand. "Thanks for reminding me again that tonight needs to be a celebration, not a wake. We've plenty of time for discussing the more disturbing subjects that are primary right now."

Rachel tossed her head, "Don't be condescending, Drew. I was thinking of Laura and Elizabeth. I know they have had enough of this war to last a lifetime. Now that they are here, safe and far away from it, we need to help them heal and put it behind them."

"It is my fervent prayer that we can, but I'm not as confident as you that we won't feel the effects here."

"We have the best generals and seem to be winning most of the battles. Don't you think that will force the North to come to their senses and let us go our own way?" Rachel insisted.

"I wish it were so, but I see no end in sight. I said from the beginning, we don't have the assets to win a long war and the battles have gone on for over two years. Already the South is experiencing great deprivation, both our troops and civilians."

Rachel dropped her head, "I know. I just don't want to think about it."

"I'm afraid you must," Andrew encouraged.

"We have prepared for the worst and I don't plan to dwell on that until I have to."

Philip laughed and, trying to lighten the mood, agreed, "Don't borrow trouble, eh?"

"Well didn't our Lord, himself, admonish us not to worry about tomorrow because today has enough worries on its own?" Rachel added.

All of them laughed as Andrew answered, "Yeah, something like that."

A commotion at the door turned their attention to a young man who just entered. In a loud voice he exclaimed, "We indeed have sad news. Our great commander General Stonewall Jackson was mortally wounded at Chancellorsville and has died."

A stunned silence greeted his announcement as the enormity of the loss impacted the room. Then here and there women began to weep. As Laura's heart tore remembering the General with fondness, an even deeper pain penetrated her heart and mind as she thought of Josh's whereabouts, feeling in her heart that he would be near his general. A tear trickled down her face as she longed for a word from him, assuring her that he was safe, that he had not suffered a similar fate.

Morning found Philip and Elizabeth refreshed and ready for the trip to Sweetwater, but Laura remained pale and wan with a nagging cough that worried both Rachel and Andrew. After discussing it privately, they decided that she should see Dr. Tim before making the trip to Sweetwater.

Over Laura's objections and Andrew's insistence, Rachel and Laura arrived at the doctor's office just as he was returning from an all night delivery of twins near Powder Springs. Although he was ready to get some sleep himself, he agreed to see Laura after Rachel's insistence.

Dr. Tim's practice had grown exponentially in the prior months, and now his well-equipped office would equal any physician's in Atlanta or Savannah. After examining Laura, he concluded that the cough represented nothing serious and that rest and proper nourishment would have her back to normal in a relatively short time. Curiosity led him to ask questions of how she came to be in her current situation. She told him of her work with the local doctor in Winchester and her subsequent imprisonment because of her attempt to help Confederate soldiers.

His eyes brightened with interest before she finished relaying her story. After asking her numerous questions, he suggested that she might assist him when she fully recuperated.

Rachel frowned. "Marietta is a good distance from Sweetwater, Dr. Tim. I don't see how Laura could do that."

Dr. Tim looked at Laura, ignoring Rachel and remarked, "I don't know how we can work out the logistics of this, but I need an assistant. Your knowledge is very profound for one who has not attended medical school which proves you have an avid interest in medicine."

"I have studied at every opportunity, and it is my passion."

"Perhaps we could set up a clinic several days a month at the mill town, and people from both Sweetwater Mills and New Manchester could take advantage of the services. As it is now you either have to travel a great distance out in the country, or they have to come in to Marietta, missing an entire day's work or worse if they are very ill." Rachel suggested.

Laura's smile beamed across the room to Rachel.

"That is an excellent idea, Mrs. Meredith," Tim agreed with enthusiasm. Then turning once again to Laura, "And as for you, young lady, you get well soon as possible, I need your help."

The reluctance Laura had experienced about going to the doctor turned into excitement at the prospect of a new venture. Already her weariness seemed to lessen as she contemplated a new endeavor. Perhaps it would help to dull the pain of separation that pierced her heart. Nothing could take away the longing for Josh; but if she kept busy in a work that was fulfilling maybe she could keep the loneliness at bay.

The warm days of May gave way to the warmer days of June. With the advantage of youth along with proper rest and nourishment, Laura made a rapid recovery. Soon she regained the weight she had lost and a rosy bloom returned to her cheeks, but the physical recovery did nothing to extinguish the sad lights in her eyes. She had yet to mention the young man about whom she had written to them. When Andrew and Rachel were alone, they speculated aloud to each other about him, but neither wanted to broach the subject with her, feeling it would be best if she volunteered the information that they were so anxious to hear. They felt that with Laura home, it would be an invasion of her privacy to ask Elizabeth so they waited and watched as the sadness dampened her usual effervescent personality.

Elizabeth, too, flourished under the tender care she received from Sweetwater. "I have not lived in the country since I was a child and quite forgot how wonderful roaming the fields and pastures can be. What a glorious feeling to have good horseflesh beneath me and to ride like the wind across the land!" She exclaimed to Rachel as she and Philip entered the drawing room one afternoon after her daily ride with Philip.

He smiled down at her, delight illuminating his countenance. "So you like the plantation life, my dear?"

"It's wonderful. I've hardly missed my home at all. How could I? I have never been so well treated or been made to feel so welcome. Truly, Sweetwater is the essence of Southern hospitality. I couldn't be more grateful. When I think of all those women who were displaced in Winchester with no place to go, I almost feel guilty. Who am I to have been blessed so graciously?"

"It's not as if you haven't suffered. You endured much hardship to get here," Rachel reminded.

Elizabeth nodded, pain dimming her joy for a moment, "I wish with all my heart this terrible war would end. The loss of property is negligible when compared to the loss of loved ones."

Philip's eyes scanned her face, as he looked for an answer that would solve the mystery that kept him at arm's length. He clamored for the key that would give him access into an area that she had sealed off from him. His frown deepened when he observed the tear that escaped and trickled down her cheek. Would she ever let him in? Yes, she would because he would not give up until she did. His heart had found the one with whom he wanted to spend a lifetime. This time he would not be denied.

She quickly wiped the tear away, her embarrassment obvious at revealing her emotions. "Perhaps soon it will all be over."

"I'm sure of it," Rachel announced with determination.

"Ever the optimist, dear Rachel," Philip chortled.

"Or ostrich?" Andrew observed dryly from his favorite chair, a book bound in fine leather held lightly in his hands.

An uneasy silence rested in the room, and the pleasant aroma of lemon oil enveloping them did nothing to ease the tension that suddenly flared between the couple.

Rachel pursed her lips, her eyes suddenly the color of an angry sea, and turned toward her husband. "Ostrich? You think I am burying my head in the sand?"

Philip walked over to her and took her small hand in his, answering for Andrew, "I'm afraid so. The news is ominous."

"What news did you hear when you were in town?" Andrew questioned.

Philip turned a questioning eye toward Rachel.

"Oh go ahead, Philip, tell us the news. I know that I can't keep the war at bay much longer. If the nation will have no peace, at least I want peace with my husband. I will face whatever comes, but I refuse to borrow trouble."

"The siege of Vicksburg is still going on, and it does not look good for our forces."

"Vicksburg is a long way from here," Rachel insisted.

"What happens in Vicksburg will impact all of us. If Vicksburg falls, then the Confederacy will be cut in two. Besides that, Rachel, half of Tennessee is already in Union hands. Except for Virginia, more battles have been fought there than anywhere else."

Andrew spoke up, "That's true. The North wanted to get control of the major transportation routes. Now they have the Tennessee River and much of the Mississippi River."

"Why do they want that control?"

"To transport supplies for their own forces and in some cases for troop movement as well as preventing the South from being able to supply their men. Not only are they focusing on the waterways but the roads and railroads, thus the reason for the raid here in Georgia."

"So what are you saying, Andrew?"

"I'm saying look at the geography, Rachel! Tennessee joins Georgia, and our crops are needed to supply the troops. Would it not stand to reason that Atlanta, a transportation hub in the South, would be in their target sites? Unless this war ends soon, the war will come here to Georgia."

Rachel dropped down on the settee, her body sinking into the down cushions, and sighed, "So what are we to do?"

"Plan for the future."

"How did the people of Winchester plan?" Rachel turned toward Elizabeth and Laura who had just joined them.

"Most didn't make any plans and when they were exiled they had no place to go. Those who had stored up food and supplies lost them. Except what you have done and are doing, I don't think there is anything else you can do. Maybe increase our prayer lives."

Rachel nodded. "We certainly need to do that. Our garden is beginning to mature, so we will be putting up more produce, and I have a supply of bandages and first aid supplies on hand. I have to have that for the slaves anyway. I mean field hands."

Elizabeth and Philip frowned and asked in unison, "Field hands?"

Rachel's smile wiped away all traces of her former frown, "Didn't Andrew tell you?"

"Tell us what?"

"He freed our slaves!" She exclaimed, pride in her voice.

"All of them? Even your household servants?"

"That's right!"

"How did that go over?"

"Smooth as silk."

"You mean you concurred?" Philip could scarcely believe his ears.

Rachel poked her lips out playfully, "Not at first. Objected fiercely, but you know Andrew."

"If he thinks he is right, he acts."

"He did and he was right. Only a few left, but we provide housing, food, an acre of land and a stipend, much like before except now they are free."

"And can sell what they grow on their acre." Andrew added. "Some of them are quite thrifty and industrious. Roger is really the reason why this has worked so well. He has shown them how to live free. He is an inspiration and an instructor for them."

"I feel the same way you do about slavery except I don't have a Roger to assist me. But I may be forced to shut down my operation."

"How so, Philip?"

"I can't continue to have operations in both North and South and expect to claim neutrality. I can no longer sell my cotton to Europe. Because of the blockades, it is impossible to get it out. If I sell my food and cotton to the Confederacy, then I'm not neutral. That's how I evaded promising to build a ship for the Union when I saw the Secretary of War. I told him as a neutral I could not build them ships."

"What did the President say?"

"We didn't get around to that discussion. He is pretty pressed for time, he has a war on his hands. When he read the wire you received from Elizabeth, he was infuriated with Milroy and dispatched me with his direct orders. Good thing, too or Milroy never would have released Laura."

"And we can't thank you enough for what you did." Rachel replied for both of them.

"It was all in God's planning. Just think if I had not come just when I did and had not made that trip to Winchester, I would have missed out on the highlight of my life."

Rachel and Andrew laughed, "And what in the world could that have been?"

"Meeting Miss Elizabeth." Philip grinned as Elizabeth blushed.

"Now, Philip, there you go again with your absurdities," she added with a laugh.

"It is only absurd if I can't convince you to come home with me."

"Philip, you know I can't do that. You are a single man. What about my reputation?"

"It didn't seem to bother you in Winchester."

"That was different. Laura was with us, and we were at war."

"You have provoked a war in my heart, Miss Elizabeth."

"Oh, Philip, you say the most outlandish things!" Elizabeth retorted her eyes wide as she looked up at him.

"Truth can be outlandish," Philip replied, his heart in his eyes.

Elizabeth flushed and turned from him and stammered, "You don't know what you are saying."

Andrew looked at Rachel, his eyebrow raised.

Rachel shook her head, shrugging, then questioned with a laugh, "Would you two like to finish this conversation alone?"

Elizabeth caught her breath. "Of course not. Our friend Philip is full of mischief tonight. He gets a real delight out of teasing me. He knows we are just very dear friends."

Philip frowned, the twinkle in his eyes extinguished. "You are a cherished friend, my dear, along with the three others who inhabit this home. Who would have ever believed that an English nobleman's dearest friends would be on this side of the Atlantic?"

Andrew relieved with the turn of conversation asked, "Why do you think that is so, Philip?"

"You are real. There is no pretense and no false sense of social barriers that we experience in England. That is one of the things that drew me to Rachel when I first met her. Of course how was I to know she was not really who I thought she was? But her love of country drew me here, and I, too, have grown to love this country. That's why it saddens me to see this bloodbath, but I believe when the conflict is over that a solidified nation will emerge, which then will live up to its potential."

"Philip you are talking Yankee drivel. The South wants to go her own way."

"I'm sorry, Rachel, but the South is wrong. They have been treated badly in many instances, but the nation must survive as a whole." Philip shook his head.

"So what are you going to do?" Andrew asked.

"Ultimately go back to England. That probably will be sooner than later. My father is growing impatient with my absence, and the blockade running is getting too dangerous. The profits are no longer worth the risk. You know I am an only son. My father sent me a reminder of that. He is getting older, and for all his crustiness I think he misses me. Of course, he would never admit that." Philip gave a mirthless chuckle, a brief moment of pain dimming his eyes.

"You said that you might have to shut down operations at Balmara."

Philip nodded. "As long as the plantation was bringing in a good profit, my father was pleased. Most of our properties are managed in the old ways and present more drain than asset. What I've been able to do over here with the ship building, plantation goods and, yes, even the blockade running, have been quite lucrative. But the war has curtailed the profits here, and he is objecting. His objections are valid. I do have a responsibility to him to be a good son, regardless of his disposition."

"Do you have a plan?" Andrew asked.

Philip nodded his head and turned a wary glance toward Rachel. "She's not going to like what I have to say."

"So what's new, Philip? I haven't liked many of the comments you have made since you brought Elizabeth and Laura home."

"Oh, my, Rachel, aren't we testy tonight," Philip responded gaining his composure, his eyes serious. "Sometimes the truth is not pleasant."

"Go ahead. Tell us what you are thinking," Andrew encouraged.

"I'm thinking that at some point you may have to evacuate Sweetwater."

"Never!" Rachel snapped. "Sweetwater is our home."

"As Winchester was mine, Rachel. Never in a million years would I have dreamed of leaving. In fact, Philip had the most difficult time persuading me."

"I couldn't, if you remember. General Milroy banished you," Philip reminded.

"And you are saying the same thing could happen here."

Philip nodded his head. "Something Elizabeth said to you about people having to leave with nowhere to go gave me pause. I think you need to make plans in the unlikely event that it should happen here."

"What do you have in mind, Philip?" Andrew asked.

"Visit me at Balmara."

"Why ever would we go there? " Rachel asked, her eyes wide.

"A place to escape if the need arises."

Andrew nodded his head. "I've never considered that possibility."

"If the Feds come here and the rail lines are still open south of Atlanta then you could theoretically ride the train all the way to Savannah. You'd have to move before Atlanta fell."

"Why would your place be any safer than Sweetwater if it comes to that?" Rachel pressed.

"It may not be, but the way I see it, Atlanta is a transportation hub and, if it is taken, the produce raised further South will not be available to the Confederate troops therefore making the city a prime target for the Yankees. In order to take Atlanta they will have to cross the Chattahoochee, and I would guess Confederates would make a strong defense at the river. That puts you squarely in the line of fire, but with proper warning gives you time to escape."

"I believe you are right, Philip. I had been wracking my brain for a way of escape, but I'd never considered that possibility," Andrew observed.

"But isn't the coast vulnerable also?" Rachel asked.

"That's true. There have been small raids and one major massacre on the coast, but so far no real effort to take Savannah and the surrounds. Only Fort Pulaski has been captured and that was to strengthen their blockade of the Savannah port. There is a reason you would be safer there that we haven't mentioned and the most important, I think."

"And that is?" Rachel inquired, agitated with the direction of the conversation when confronted with scenarios that she had pushed aside in the past.

"Philip is a British subject and therefore neutral," Andrew answered.

"And they can't legally arrest me or seize my property."

"Unless you are caught harboring rebel fugitives." Andrew added. "If you hide us and they find out, you forfeit your neutrality. You've been playing with fire ever since this war started with your blockade running, not to mention your single handed charge on General Milroy in Winchester."

"If you remember, I did have a little help from the President."

"Yes, and that, too. You are certainly not one faint of heart."

"Except with fair maiden." Philip smiled and looked at Elizabeth.

"Philip, we would never want to put you in harm's way," Elizabeth objected. "How could we in good conscious gain our freedom in exchange for the loss of yours?"

Philip walked over to her and took her hand. "Don't you understand, my dear? Without you, my freedom is worth little."

Elizabeth blushed and dropped her head, unwilling to meet his eyes and the love glowing in them.

Rachel sighed and looked toward Philip, then to Andrew. "You really think it will come to that?"

Andrew reached over and took her hand, "No one knows the future, Rachel, but we need to plan. I think Philip's idea is something to consider."

A shiver ran down Rachel's spine as reality sank in, destroying the happy tranquility of the past days. "Very well. We shall make some plans...just in case."

"And since we are making plans, I have a few of my own that I need to share. I guess now is as good a time as any," Andrew said, his voice low, hesitant.

Rachel's head jerked up, and she gasped, "No, not that! You can't, Drew."

Andrew nodded his head, "I'm afraid that I must. That's the reason it is so important to have an escape plan that you can implement."

Philip and Elizabeth looked at each other. Then Philip suggested, "Perhaps this is something that you, Rachel and Laura should discuss privately. Elizabeth and I will have tea on the front veranda."

"No need for that, Philip," Rachel replied, her voice trembling. "We have nothing to say that can't be discussed in front of you."

"But, Rachel, we don't want to intrude." Elizabeth protested.

" I know what Drew is about to tell us. He thinks he needs to leave us in order to fight for a cause he feels is lost and one in which he doesn't believe. I will never understand that reasoning if I live to be a hundred." Rachel lifted her hands frustrated.

Andrew sighed, rising from his chair. "Rachel."

She turned toward him, a sad smile lifting the corner of her full lips, "I know, darling. It is your conviction that you should go and if you think it is the right thing to do...!"

"He does it," Philip and Laura spoke in unison.

"That's right, he does it," Rachel said looking up at Andrew, her heart in her eyes. "And that makes him the man he is, and one of the reasons I love him so."

Andrew pulled her up and into his arms, "Thank you, my Love. For understanding."

Rachel laid her head on his shoulder and chuckled, "Understand? Never in a million years. But support your decision because you think it is right...always."

Ignoring the other three, Andrew tilted her head and place a long slow kiss on the lips turned up to his as Rachel melted into his arms.

Suddenly, an indescribable longing filled Elizabeth, and her eyes grew bright with tears as she witnessed the tender scene before her. What would it be like to love and be loved like that?

Philip took notice, and encouragement raced his heart.

Chapter Fifteen

The days proved lonelier than Rachel could have imagined without Andrew by her side. He had left to join the forces fighting in Tennessee. Shortly thereafter Philip had left for Savannah, promising to return as soon as possible. Suddenly, the three women found themselves alone to face the challenges at home.

Andrew had arranged capable management at the mills. Thanks to his wealth he had been able to secure enough resources to continue their operations. He had even added a leather factory where a couple of cobblers made boots for the troops. Rachel knew that the future of the shoe-making endeavor would be short lived because the blockade obstructed their supply of leather from the west coast.

Philip had failed to persuade Elizabeth to join him on his trip to Savannah. She protested that Rachel might need her since Laura was now fully involved with Dr. Tim and his practice. Rachel's heart tore at the disappointment registered on Philip's face but was overjoyed to have Elizabeth's company. Not only was she a pleasant companion to Laura and her, but also her knowledge of all things practical proved an invaluable help as they readied for whatever might be ahead.

In the mornings Rachel traveled to the mill to go over operations for the day. After lunch she assisted Elizabeth in overseeing the canning and drying of the abundant fruits and vegetables that were ripening in the orchards and gardens. When the fruit cellars were packed to the brim, her friend suggested that they have the workers dig more places for storage near the spring and deeper into the woods. Remembering the confiscation that took place in Winchester, she stressed that the stores of foodstuff and other necessities be hidden away and difficult for enemy troops to find which might prove crucial to their survival.

Rachel agreed with Elizabeth and had the most trusted of her workers go far into the forest away from the plantation house to build fruit cellars for food. They also erected paddocks to stable and hide the best of Sweetwater horses and barns for the cattle, which would be needed for food and milk. There were young children among the workers, and she wanted to make as sure as she could that they would not be denied the sustenance they needed to remain healthy. What a different mindset Rachel now had from the Rachel of old who had cared so little for the needs of life beyond her own.

Unknown to the mistress of Sweetwater, the activity deep in the forest was watched by the very eyes that Andrew had encountered on his wild ride before their marriage when he searched for a witness that could clear Rachel of murder charges. The old toothless woman who had rescued and nursed him back to health, nodded her head, pleased that her 'girl, Miz Rachel' was thinking and planning ahead. She would personally see that no harm came to these provisions.

How strange it was that this hidden world of abused renegade slaves, knew what was happening in the outside world and rejoiced over potential liberation. Overriding any elation she might have of the coming liberation, was Agatha's fear of the future for her precious Rachel. How happy she had been when Rachel married that rich and powerful Meredith man who had taken such good care of her. Now he had gone to war, and she watched from the shadows ready to protect and provide for her former charge if the need arose. Yes, she was willing to give her life for that white girl she loved like her own.

Agatha cackled remembering the stubborn free spirited little girl who had been in her custody from birth. She sho' nuff had been a handful, but now she was a woman grown and matured. Her old wrinkled face contorted as she recalled the heartache her girl had suffered. First that terrible disease took her beautiful mama. Then her papa, who was so selfish in his own grief, let her suffer alone. Finally he sent her off away from him 'cuz she reminded him of his wife. After that, he lost her inheritance through riotous living. Sho nuff it wuz their neighbor, that awful Walter Banks, who tricked the master, but if'n he hadn't been in his 'cups' most of the time, he'd had more sense. He woulda knowed that scoundrel wuz cheating him. She growled...etched in her memory were Rachel's emerald eyes, wide and fearful as she left home for the last time. She remembered how her own heart had wrenched like something had been torn from her.

Agatha shook her head at the memory, and then a satisfied smile divided her face. Despite everything, that young girl had survived. Now she faced the future unafraid, so the old woman had been told. Her charge turned out strong and resilient, and Agatha had helped shape her. The good Lord used Andrew Meredith to smooth out the edges. But hard times were a comin' and Agatha stood ready to step in again if it became necessary. Hidden deep in the forest, she could watch over Rachel and her provisions. If she needed a place of refuge, then Agatha would see to it she got it. "Ain't no Yankee gonna bother my girl," she muttered.

To say Rachel faced the future without fear was not accurate. She stayed busy from dawn until after dusk, but when she had a moment of quiet or solitude, fear threatened to engulf her. Not fear of enemy troops or fear for her safety, but the fear of losing Andrew. Her heart had never known such happiness as it had with him. He cherished her as no one had ever done. His provision and care of her proved boundless. It was not losing what he did for her nor what he gave her that prompted her terror. It was the thought of never feeling his arms around her again or never to look into those warm mahogany eyes that devoured her with tenderness. The thought that she might have to spend the rest of her life without laying beside him, listening to his gentle breath, feeling his touch proved unbearable. She missed seeing him walk across the yard, the sound of his voice calling her name, his kiss planted tenderly on her lips. When he left, she felt as if she had been torn asunder. It was as if the better part of her were missing, and she hated the war all the more for it.

Laura meanwhile kept a frantic pace, learning all that she could from Dr. Tim. It was not long before she began to make the sixteen-mile trip into Marietta to assist him in his office. Rachel insisted that she take a driver with her because she often returned after dark. She would fall into bed, almost too tired to speak, but nothing erased the pain in her heart. Finally Laura poured her heart out to Rachel. Rather than receiving a rebuke, Rachel opened her arms to the younger woman and let her weep until no tears remained. How could she do less? Her own fear and heartbreak gave her an understanding heart.

The weeks passed, and the news worsened on the war front. On Independence Day both Vicksburg and Gettysburg were lost. The South reeled from the news. How long could she survive? Already men were deserting, returning home to help their families who were destitute.

Andrew had arrived in Tennessee and received a commission from Gen. Braxton Bragg in Chattanooga. And he had more alarming news for the South. General Rosecrans of the Union Army of the Cumberland had outmaneuvered the confederate Army of Tennessee and driven them out of middle Tennessee. They had retreated to Chattanooga where even now Rosecrans threatened the city.

Rachel rejoiced over the news that Andrew remained safe and out of harm's way for the moment. The army rested between lulls in the battle. He told her that after a meeting with Bragg, he became the general's liaison and received a captain's commission. He remarked that morale was low, which was understandable, but it seemed complicated by the senior officers' dissatisfaction with the general's leadership. He said that he had not been around long enough to ascertain if their criticisms were valid, but he did know as long as Gen. Bragg remained his commander, he and the other officers owed him respect and loyalty.

It pained him to see conflict within, as they needed to be united in purpose to be victorious. He said that the recent defeats that had driven them to the Chattanooga position were in large part due to the lack of communication between the general and his subordinate leaders. Rachel could just imagine Andrew shaking his head at the situation. With his wisdom and ability to prioritize, he must be frustrated that all could not put aside their complaints to see the bigger picture. Victory depended on cooperation, and they were desperate for a win.

Rachel read and reread the letters from Andrew. At night she would read then and place them beneath her pillow, imagining that they still had the fragrance of wood smoke and fresh air that always seemed to cling to him. In short she longed for the touch, sight and smell of him. She knew that once the battle heated up again letters would be scarce so she treasured each one.

Laura had written Josh many letters, addressing them to what had been Ashby's Brigade, but still there had been no word from him. She finally gave up, knowing that no response could only mean one of three things. He was fighting with another unit, and he hadn't received her letters, he was in a Yankee prison somewhere, or he was not alive. Her heart refused to accept that those vibrant eyes were closed forever and tried to convince herself that her letters had never reached him. But, try as she would, sorrow would overcome her in an unguarded moment and the tears would spill down her face. For in her heart of hearts, she knew that if he was alive and received her letters, he would respond.

Dr. Tim had proved a welcome diversion with his offer of work. Laura only worked three days a week, but the rest of the time she filled with studying when she was not assisting Rachel and Elizabeth. To Rachel's surprise, on one of Laura's days off, the handsome young doctor arrived at their door carrying a bouquet of flowers.

"Is Miss Laura available, Miz Meredith?"

Rachel raised her eyebrows and looked as his flowers.

A flush tinted his face, and with a sheepish grin explained, "I thought some posies might bring her a little cheer."

Thus began a series of visits, and before long Tim's visits became a regular occurrence. He would regale the ladies at dinner, and then he and Laura would retire to the parlor and play a game of whist. Some evenings Tim would bring a puzzle, and all of them would sit around the game table in Andrew's library and put it together until late in the evening. His visits proved therapeutic for all three ladies. His charming ways and inventive recreation gave a momentary relief from the stress of their daily lives.

Rachel's delight knew no bounds the first night she heard the tinkle of Laura's laughter ring from the parlor. Relief spread through her and she realized how worried she had been for this young woman she had come to treasure. Maybe she had turned the corner and could go on with life. If Josh were gone, then would Tim be a suitable prospect for her heart? Perhaps ease the pain of loss? They shared a passion for healing. That was a starting point. And he was charming and quite good-looking. Rachel shook her head as she acknowledged to herself that she was running way too far ahead! She sighed and determined to rejoice that Tim had provided Laura with brief respites from sorrow.

Elizabeth continued to receive ardent letters from Philip. Rachel, though consumed with curiosity, refrained from questioning her new friend about her feelings for him. She noticed that after each letter the beautiful young woman received, her demeanor became flushed and quiet. Rachel felt with all her heart that Philip could look the world over and find no equal to this woman to whom he had lost his heart. And as for Philip, except for Andrew, he was the finest man she had ever known. What was the problem? Did Elizabeth have some ghost in her past that prevented her from accepting this perfect (in Rachel's mind) match for her? Rachel had to bite her tongue and resolve every day that she would not interfere. Yet it proved so difficult. They seemed so right for each other.

———————————

A glorious dawn broke the eastern sky and Rachel sat in her usual spot in the keeping room where she always began the day. Thinking of Andrew and praying for his safety, she placed his Bible that she read every morning on the table beside her. The sun would soon be up heating the day. She decided that her trip to the mill would be early and brief. She felt compelled to go so that she would be able to answer Andrew's questions about its progress in her next letter.

She paused mid step. Out of the side of her eye, she thought she glimpsed the fleeting outline of someone, rounding the corner of her house. Alarmed she moved closer to the window to look. All was calm. No movement or form appeared in her line of vision. She dismissed the incident from her mind and credited it to an errant bush moving in the breeze or a servant up early. She turned to make her way to her room to finish dressing when she heard a distinct though quiet, knock on the kitchen door. She alone was up, so she made her way to the door, puzzled. Maybe it was a servant in need of assistance.

Pulling her dressing gown securely around her, she paused and brushed her hand through her hair, which hung in lush profusion down her back. For some reason her heart began to race as she reached to answer the door, and she jerked her hand back as if it were a snake. She shook her head. What was this all about? Why should she be frightened? The Yankees weren't here yet. She chuckled at her own edginess. A memory flashed in her mind of a night long ago when the sheriff and Walter Banks had arrived at her front door with ominous tidings. Cautiously she reached for the doorknob uncertainty in every move.

"Yes, who is there?" She questioned through the closed door.

Someone murmured something she failed to understand so she opened the door. "How...?

She stopped, and, covering her mouth with her hand, her eyes widened.

The man was tall and scrawny, with a scraggly beard and in much need of a bath. He reeked of sweat and rum. His thin lips parted in a malevolent smile revealing a mouth full of tobacco stained broken teeth and rancid breath. His eyes leered at her, slithering up and down her form, and he drawled, "Well, well, what do we have here? So we meet again."

Rachel's eyes fluttered as she fought the light-headedness that threatened to overcome her. The memory of a hot Savannah dock and three men who had attacked her rushed in as she looked straight into the eyes of one of those very assailants. He pushed her backwards into the kitchen and slammed the door behind him.

Rachel backed away from him, and he grabbed her arm, pulling her so close to him his foul breath overwhelmed her. She wrenched her arm from him demanding, "What do you mean invading my home?"

"You remember me do you, missy? Or should I say missus? So the great Mr. Meredith took you in." He chuckled relishing his good luck.

"He is my husband, and you get out this minute before I call him. You've already experienced what he will do to you. But trust me, it will be much worse this time."

"Don't you go trying to fool me. You ain't got no husband here and all yore servants are asleep and won't be in fer another hour'r two."

"You are mistaken."

"I ain't mistaken. I been askin' 'round, and I been a watching. Ain't nobody in here 'cept three wimmen and them pampered servants out there in their little huts fast asleep." He laughed and added, ogling her. "I jist didn know one of them wimmen wuz you. More good luck than I expected."

"If you don't leave immediately, you are going to experience anything but good luck." Rachel threatened through clinched teeth.

"I ain't leaving 'til I get what I'm here for," he threatened, grabbing her shoulders and gripping them until pains shot down both arms.

"Beg your pardon?" Rachel gasped as she tried to wrench free of his strong bony fingers.

"You jest be still. Give me what I want, and I'll be on my way."

Rachel shuddered. "Wha... What do you want?"

"I want that high yella wench who tried to kill me," he growled.

"What are you talking about?"

"You know exactly what I'm talkin' about. Yore husband's other bedfellow. I say it makes it kinda cozy having both of you under one roof, now don't it?" He snarled so close to her face, she felt his breath on her cheek. Nausea boiled up in her throat.

Rachel jerked her arm free and with lightning speed burned her hand across his face. "Get out! Daphne is not here."

Stunned for a moment, the tall man rubbed his cheek, then shoved her against the wall and roared, "You get me that wench, or you will be the one to pay,"

Rachel struggled against him, but he proved surprisingly strong for so gaunt a man. She failed to budge him.

"You might as well quit struggling and do my bidding," he commanded.

"How can I give you something I don't have? Anyway you have been paid royally for what you claimed Daphne did. There will be no more payment coming. Daphne is not here, never will be here again, and she is far from the likes of you. You might as well be on your way."

He threw back his head and laughed. "Be on my way? And who is going to see to that? Not your servants, certainly not your husband, and you are too far from town to get help. If I can't have the wench, then I'll take my pleasure from you and whoever else is in this fancy house. I will take what I need or want from you, rich white lady."

Rachel struggled, but he moved his forearm to her neck and pinned her to the wall, leaving one of his hands free. He ran it down her arm in a caressing motion and reached for the belt securing her dressing gown. Laughing, he said, "I'll finish the job I started four years ago. This time there is no one to interfere."

"Except me," came a quiet voice behind him.

George jerked his head around and encountered the steady gaze of Elizabeth Donahue holding a 36-caliber colt revolver, with the hammer back and pointed directly at him. With eyes bulging, he turned toward Elizabeth as he yanked Rachel to his side. "Lil lady, who do you thank yore a scarin? Ain't no day of the week I cain't handle two wimmen like you. As fer the gun, that's a joke. We both know you don't know how to use it and if'n you did you wouldn't have the stomach fer it. So jest hand it over."

"I don't think so Mr....."

"George. Call me by my first name cause we will be pretty familiar in a little while." He sneered.

"OK, so George it is, but understand this, we won't be familiar at all now or later. One way or another you are about to be on your way, whether it is in this world or the one to come. If that's the case, it won't be a pleasant experience. So release, Rachel, and leave while you still can," she warned, her voice calm and steady.

George laughed and lunged toward Elizabeth, grabbing for her gun. A loud explosion parted the air, ripping through the kitchen and reverberating through the house as Elizabeth pulled the trigger. The bullet pierced her target precisely where she had aimed it. The arrogant assailant fell to the floor head first, a startled expression on his face as his blood pooled on the wide pine boards beneath him.

Rachel, wide eyed, stood immobile while Elizabeth walked over to George and looked down murmuring, "I don't think he will bother you anymore, Rachel."

"Oh, Elizabeth!" Rachel cried.

"We need to send for Dr. Tim and for the sheriff. He's very still, probably dead." Elizabeth observed as if in a trance.

Laura bounded down the stairs. "What in the world was that noise...? Oh my!"

Elizabeth remarked, "I just shot a man. Would you see if he is alive?"

Laura kneeled beside the intruder, searching for a pulse. "No, he is dead. What happened?"

"I, I shot a man." Elizabeth stammered, her face paled as she collapsed on the floor.

Rachel ran to the side of her friend. "Get the smelling salts, Laura. You know where I keep them."

Rachel bathed her friend's face with a cool towel as Laura waved the acrid potion beneath her nose. Elizabeth's eyes opened, and she pushed Laura's hand away from her. She shook her head and looked to her right toward George's body sprawled exactly where he fell. She sat up and a shudder engulfed her. Then the sobs began. "I didn't know I could ever do it, kill a man! When I saw him and what he was doing to you, it all came back to me."

Rachel sat down beside her on the floor, her arm around Elizabeth's shoulders as Laura looked on in amazement. "Laura, go tell Elijah to go to town and fetch Tim and the sheriff. I don't think we can clean up here until they come."

Laura responded, "I think maybe I should go with him. I don't exactly know what happened, but I suppose it was a case of self-defense."

"Absolutely and it would be better if you went with Elijah. Elizabeth, let's go in the parlor. This is not a scene that we need to monitor. George is not going anywhere, and obviously he is beyond our help."

Elizabeth sat on the down settee, her eyes darting back and forth. Rachel observed her and asked, "Do you need a cup of tea or coffee?"

Her friend shook her head without speaking. Then her whole body began to tremble, and she covered her eyes with her hands, dropping her head.

Rachel sat down beside her. "Would it help to talk to me, Elizabeth?"

Elizabeth nodded as a new set of tears coursed down her cheeks. "Maybe it's time I told the whole story to someone."

"You said that it all came back to you. What was it that came back to you, Elizabeth?" Rachel probed.

"My past. My husband, the man who was supposed to honor me, protect me, and love me. Instead he was a monster, a master of abuse. I vowed to never let that happen again. I purchased a weapon, and I learned how to shoot it. I determined never to put myself in a position where I couldn't protect myself."

"You were going to shoot your husband?"

Elizabeth shook her head. "No, I purchased the weapon after his death. I don't know what I would have done had he continued. Escape was not an option because who would have believed me? He told me if I showed my bruises to anyone he would accuse me of infidelity and say someone else had beat me. More likely I wouldn't have survived."

"The abuse stopped at some point?"

Elizabeth nodded. "He became very ill and died. The physical abuse stopped with his illness, but the verbal abuse continued up until the day he passed away. I can honestly say that I never let that deter me in performing my duties. I looked after him as a good wife should, but I admit I had no regrets when he died."

"I'm so sorry you had to endure those horrors, Elizabeth. Why did you marry him?"

"For money. My parents married me off to him."

"How could any parent do that to a child?"

"They didn't know. He had a public side and a private side. He was a pillar of the community with an impeccable reputation. In private life when we were alone, he was a demon. Those scars won't go away. They still haunt my dreams at night."

"Is that why you hold Philip at arm's length? He loves you, you know."

Elizabeth nodded, "How can I ever trust a man again? I so want to."

"Philip is different. Not all men are monsters." Rachel said.

"How do I know? My husband, to all who thought they knew him, was a fine man."

"Did you ever see him in difficult situations before you married him?"

"No, I barely knew him and neither did my parents. We met at a neighbors' ball, and he began a whirlwind courtship. In the end he made my parents an offer they could not refuse. You see, we were little more than destitute thanks to my father's careless ways."

Rachel nodded. "I can relate to that. I, too, was penniless without dowry when Andrew married me. But God was gracious to send me a kind, gentle yet strong man who cared nothing about a dowry or lack of it. I can categorically say that all men are not brutes. And I know that Philip is what he seems to be."

Elizabeth sighed. "I want to believe that, to trust him. But when I think I am ready to, then all those memories flood in."

"The one thing that I have learned, if we are to embrace a new tomorrow, we must let go of the bondage that ties us to yesterday. I almost waited too long to accept that truth and I risked my only chance at happiness. Learn to trust again. Philip is worthy of that. How do you feel about him?"

Elizabeth smiled through her tears. "I could love him, but there are other barriers."

Rachel frowned. "Other barriers?"

Her friend tilted her head toward the keeping room where George's motionless body lay. "Him! Will Philip even want me now? When the sheriff comes, I may be arrested. Can you imagine Philip's father's reaction if he married a jail bird?"

"You won't go to jail."

"Even so, I killed a man. I don't think that would go over well with the duke."

"As far as I'm concerned and any other sensible person, you are a heroine. It was a clear case of self-defense, and you have a credible witness. We were both in grave danger. You did the only thing that could save Laura and us. You heard his threats."

"Yes, he made very specific threats. By the way what did he mean when he said he was going to finish what he had started?"

Rachel winced, and then smiled. "You know in the Bible what Joseph said to his brothers about what they meant for evil, God meant for good?"

Her friend nodded her head.

"That's what happened to me. When I arrived in Savannah from England, I became impatient to get off the ship so I decided to go on my own rather than waiting for the captain to escort me. Bad decision, and just the first of many that year, I might add. Anyway, I walked down the docks, and when I reached a rather secluded area, these three men attacked me. George was one of them."

Elizabeth's eyes widened, and she leaned forward, "What a small world. Then what happened?"

"Andrew arrived, rescued me, and the rest is history. I don't know to this day what disciplinary actions he carried out against George and his crew, but I know they looked terrified when he gave them into the custody of his 'man,' who was nearly seven feet tall and brawny. Whatever happened, it must not have been pleasant and today he was out to get his revenge."

"So he came all this way for revenge?"

"Not against me. He was looking for Daphne."

"Seems you have a long history with George."

"Quite true. He had attacked Daphne once, and she cracked him on the head and escaped. Since she is a woman of color, he planned to either have her arrested or get money from Andrew to keep him quiet. I think that ultimately he had a more vindictive plan. He was angry that she had bested him and wanted more than her arrest or even money. When I answered the door, he remembered me and thought he had found the mother lode. He could triple his revenge against me, Andrew and Daphne. That is until you intervened."

―――――――――――

"Miss Elizabeth, there will be no charges here. In my book you are a heroine, and it comforts me to know that you women can look after yourselves so well. I fear you'll need it if the Yankees come. I've heard some disturbing news about what they did on the Georgia coast. The burning and killing of innocent residents, both black and white showed what their leaders are like," Sheriff Doyle assured.

"Laura and I have experienced some of their abuses, but I choose to believe that most of their generals are men of honor," Elizabeth disputed.

"Maybe some of their generals are, but they don't always know what their men out in the field might be up to. You just keep that revolver loaded 'cause you may have occasion to use it again."

Elizabeth's face paled at the thought and she winced. "I pray that I will never be put in that situation again. To have taken a life, no matter how evil, will haunt me to my grave. The look on that man's face, his blood spilling out and to know that I did it---. Well what can I say, I have blood on my hands."

"Not innocent, blood, ma'am. You saved the life of your friend and your very own along with Miss Laura's. He couldn't have done what he planned to do and left you alive to identify him. He was an evil man. I am thankful that you were prepared. I wish more of the women around here were. I feel it in my bones, trouble is coming."

⸺⸺⸺

The hot days of July gave way to even hotter days of August and Rachel kept watch over Elizabeth with a loving eye. As the days distanced themselves from the traumatic event of George's death, Elizabeth seemed to recover her equilibrium. When they received a wire that Philip planned to join them soon, she received the news with excitement.

Rachel and Laura hoped that his visit would find Elizabeth in a more receptive mood toward their friend. Laura had written him about the horrible experience of George's visit but neither she nor Rachel let Andrew know. Rachel feared it would worry him and that a divided mind would put him at greater risk. They had handled the situation thanks to Elizabeth and with God's help they would face and handle whatever the future held.

Rachel's heart failed her when late on Saturday, August 22, Laura arrived home from Marietta with the news that Union forces had reached the Tennessee River across from Chattanooga. It was under heavy bombardment, and the brief respite had ended. Andrew was again in harm's way.

Early in September, she received a brief letter from Andrew telling her that they were unable to hold Chattanooga, and he now was encamped on Georgia soil. By the time she received his letter, the Confederates had garnered a major victory at the Battle of Chickamauga on September the 19th and 20th. Hearing how intense the battle had been, anxiety preoccupied her every endeavor until she could know that Andrew came through it unharmed.

Rachel's worry was so intense that even Philip's arrival did little to lift her spirits, Elizabeth and Laura also shared her concern, but both of them welcomed him with open arms. Elizabeth's warm greeting set the young lord's heart racing as new encouragement infused him. Maybe this trip would bring him the one thing in the world he wanted more than any other. To have Elizabeth for a lifetime was his heart's desire, and he determined to pursue her until she agreed that they were meant for each other.

Finally early in October, Rachel received a letter from Andrew. Brief and a bit tattered, it eased Rachel's heart. He was safe, for the moment. However, an uncharacteristic frustration permeated his letter. As always he spoke of his love for her and how he yearned to hold her. He told her he hungered to stroll across the fields hand in hand with her and to have their morning cup of coffee on the balcony outside their room. He told her how he dreamed of her at night and how much his heart ached to see her. She relished the words. In her mind she could almost hear his deep voice speaking those words of love to her. They brought to her remembrance his whispers of her beauty when the nights were still, and she nestled in his arms. Tears blinded her for a moment as the images raced through her memory.

While he told her all the things her heart longed to hear, there seemed to be an air of resignation between the lines that bothered her. Things were not going well and he, too, was becoming alarmed at the battlefield decisions or non-decisions being made. For the moment their troops were entrenched on Missionary Ridge and Lookout Mountain. As Bragg's liaison, he traveled between both entrenchments transmitting Gen. Bragg's messages to his disgruntled generals.

He regretted the fact that they had not cut off the escape route when the Union forces retreated from Chickamauga nor pursued them before they could regroup in Chattanooga. Instead they were looking down on Chattanooga from their lofty position and attempting to cut off the supply lines to the city. Meanwhile Gen. Bragg was too distracted by the infighting among his leaders to make aggressive battle plans.

Andrew added with tongue in cheek that one of the events in their favor was the rumor mill that claimed Rosecrans was so stunned by his defeat at Chickamauga that he, too, was unable to make a decision. The rumors said Lincoln remarked Rosecrans seemed so 'stunned and confused he was like a duck hit over the head.' It would seem that the two opposing generals were equally short on decision-making.

Gen. Bragg told him that the Union forces had only six days of supplies left. It would be just a matter of days until they would be forced to abandon the city since most of the supply lines were in Confederate hands. Andrew found it difficult to believe Lincoln would allow withdrawal when the North, contrary to the South, had men and supplies to relieve the city. He expected shortly they would be facing a larger force and be required to fight or retreat.

Another bit of good news was Gen. Wheeler's raid on a sixty mile stretch of a mountain road in Alabama. The road proved to be a main conduit for supplying Union forces. The general had captured a train carrying 800 wagons, which he burned along with destroying mules and horses that his men couldn't use.

Andrew wrote about a young colonel attached to General Wheeler's cavalry whose deeds had made a lasting impression on him. They never met; he only saw him from a distance. Handsome, tall, and erect, his reputation was one of intelligence, bravery and common sense tactical ability. He had been cited for bravery numerous times and had been a part of Ashby's regiment, transferred to Wheeler's recently. Since Ashby had fought near Winchester, he hoped to meet him soon and ask him if he knew Elizabeth. If what he heard about him was true, young men like him were truly the hope for the future. Alas! No time for civilities. The war hindered normal civilized exchanges.

The warm golden days of October drifted into the cold barren days of November, and Andrew's prediction proved accurate. Grant replaced Rosecrans and Sherman joined him with 20,000 troops, and they reopened their supply lines. On the 24th of November, they took Lookout Mountain and on the 25th they captured Missionary Ridge after a fierce battle. Southern forces retreated to Dalton, Georgia where they wintered. On November 29 General Braxton Bragg tendered his resignation and much to his chagrin, Jefferson Davis accepted it. For a few days at least, Rachel could breathe easy. Andrew had survived to fight another day and now he would be on Georgia soil as they advanced ever near Sweetwater. But she no longer cared about slavery, about the Southern way of life or even Sweetwater, she would be willing to forego all that had been so dear to her if she could only have Andrew back safe and sound with her.

Chapter
Sixteen

After receiving word that Andrew was safe for the moment, Rachel joined Elizabeth and Laura in relishing Philip's visit. It proved a lengthy visit. Arriving in October, he lingered until December. In the wake of the unfortunate encounter with George he appeared reluctant to leave. The young lord went to great effort to make sure that Sweetwater provided as much safety as possible for the women and servants. He instructed Rachel and Laura in the handling of a weapon. He made them take target practice despite their objections, and he continued to monitor Elizabeth. She seemed to rebound from her trauma. Rachel felt sure that it had to do with Philip and his help, but also the conversation, which she had with her that fateful day. It proved true that heartaches bottled up have a difficult time healing, and once she shared it, the mending process began.

And as for Philip, Elizabeth had restored his usual vitality by her warm greeting when he arrived and her continued attentiveness. Always the thoughtful and considerate friend, he insisted that the four of them enjoy a much-needed diversion. He also included Tim, who had been a regular dinner fixture since Philip's arrival. He planned an exclusive dinner at the Fletcher House. He found three young women who played string instruments whom he hired to entertain them with chamber music.

The three women dressed in their finest. Rachel provided one of her gowns for Elizabeth. The cloud of pale yellow silk highlighted her dark beauty. The bodice accentuated her tiny waist above a skirt that flared wide over hoops with flounces of tiered Belgian lace cascading down the front of her dress. She glanced in the mirror and smiled. It had been a very long time since she had been to a ball or wore a beautiful dress. There seemed little reason to pinch her cheeks. They were rosy with excitement. She had no need for the jewels she had left hidden in Winchester because the lights in her eyes shone brilliant as diamonds.

Philip waited at the bottom of the stairs and looked upwards when she appeared like an apparition before him. His breath caught, leaving him speechless for a moment. No words came. He could only gaze at her, his heart rampaging in his chest. Had there ever been such a vision of loveliness? Finally the paralysis ended, and he held out his hand to her in silence. There was little need for words... his eyes had said it all.

***

The meal proved delectable as the main ingredients came directly from Sweetwater's coffers. Some food supplies were in short supply for the public so Philip transported meats and vegetables in for the dinner. In Atlanta corn sold for $10 a bushel and flour for $120 per barrel while a cord of firewood garnered $80. There was little doubt that times were more than difficult and would get more so if the war continued to march southward. Although so far Sweetwater was shielded from the deprivation that many experienced, the war was no less a heavy burden to Rachel. No physical accommodation could relieve the heaviness her heart bore.

Tonight she endeavored to put aside the ache in her heart so she would not dampen the spirits of those around her. She enjoyed the lively conversation and for a few moments, put aside the worry that hounded her every moment. The classical music playing throughout dinner proved both soothing and entertaining.

Neither Rachel nor Laura could help but notice the light in Elizabeth's eyes as she gazed at Philip. Laura caught Rachel's attention and raised one brow. Rachel chuckled and nodded her head with delight. Maybe at long last, Philip had made some progress. As for Philip, his vibrant personality bubbled over with excitement.

Just as they were finishing their after dinner tea, Philip excused himself to speak to the musicians. The ladies and Tim assumed he went over to dismiss them. They watched the young ladies face light up in response to something Philip said. He returned to the table as the trio talked excitedly among themselves.

"Well, ladies. Our dinner music has ended. Now the fun begins," Philip announced as he nodded to the musicians.

At that point the three began a lovely waltz and Philip held out his hand to Elizabeth, "May I have this dance, my lovely?"

A delightful grin parted Dr. Tim's face as he held out his hand to Laura.

Before long the two couples were floating across the floor and other patrons in the room joined them.

After the first dance, Philip and Elizabeth returned to the table. "Now it's your turn, Rachel," Elizabeth offered.

Rachel looked up with a smile. "Thank you, but I shall not dance until Andrew can hold me in his arms." She paused as tears brightened her eyes, "I hope that will be sooner than we think. Truly I am enjoying watching you."

Philip cocked his head, "I believe you mean that. You're turning me down? You don't know what you're missing."

Rachel laughed, banishing the sad moment, "You forget, dear boy! I've danced with you before. I'll wait for Andrew, thank you!"

"I won't try to persuade you. Come, Elizabeth. We'll show these people how it's done." Philip laughed, eager to capture Elizabeth in his arms once more.

The young trio played waltzes and reels. Those who chose not to dance tapped their toes, and Rachel enjoyed herself despite her heavy heart. Finally after many tunes, it was time to end it. When the last tune began, Rachel caught her breath, and tears filled her eyes.

The violins were playing "their" song. Memories flooded in of their wedding reception and that last dance when Andrew had held her close. They had floated across the floor, and before the tune had finished, he had whisked her to the stairway and up to their room. Ignoring her objections and concern for their guests, he had retorted with a laugh that they had all stayed too long anyway, Philip could take care of them. Andrew had waited all his life for her. He was unwilling to wait another moment. The lovely tune followed them up the stairs and permeated their sanctuary.

Longing and loneliness suddenly overwhelmed her, and she dropped her head with her hands over her eyes. How much longer could she bear this pain of separation?

Someone touched her shoulder and she resented the intrusion until a familiar voice commanded, "I believe this is our dance."

"Drew?" She whispered, afraid to look up; afraid it wasn't true. It couldn't be true. He was in the midst of battle.

"Yes, my love. I'm home."

Leaping to her feet, she knocked the chair over as she threw herself into his waiting arms.

His arms pulled her to him in a crushing embrace. Then without a word, he moved her onto the floor. They moved as one to the sweet sounds of the violin and Andrew whispered in her ear, "I believe we never finished our dance."

She looked up, mischief firing her eyes, and whispered, "Oh, yes we did, and it was a glorious finale."

A flush tinted his face as the music stopped.

Walking back to their table, he said, "I have someone with me. I hope you don't mind. He was given a few days off also, and it was too far for him to go home."

"I don't care how many you bring with you, as long as I have you. I just want to know how you got here, and how long you can stay," she demanded with a smile, emerald lights sparkling in her eyes.

Arriving at their table, Andrew shook hands with the young doctor and Philip while Laura hurled herself into his arms.

"Miss Elizabeth, you are looking quite beautiful," Andrew exclaimed when Laura finally released him. His arm reached for Rachel as if he could hardly let her go for a moment.

"Philip, did you know Uncle Drew was coming?" Laura demanded.

"I did not. I had hoped this little party would be a mood lifter for all of us, I had no idea that it would be this good. Can I plan an evening or what?" Philip bragged.

Elizabeth took his arm and looked up at him, her heart in her eyes. "Now don't get all puffed up. It was a great evening, but the Good Lord had it already planned!"

"I guess you're right, but it has been most rewarding."

Dr. Tim exclaimed, "Thank you for including me. It was a great evening. So glad to see you, Captain Meredith. I'm anxious to hear all about your experiences when you have time. Not tonight of course as you have more important things on your mind. But I have been around quite regularly in your absence, looking in on the ladies and trying to be of some help to them. I hope to continue to enjoy their hospitality."

Laura patted his arm with a warm smile, "And you have been a very delightful diversion. We are all very appreciative of your efforts."

Rachel and Elizabeth murmured their agreement.

Andrew looked at Tim, and then gazed at Laura, a question in his eyes. "Oh, I almost forgot. The young man that I brought with me is trying to arrange for accommodations."

"There is no need for that, Drew. We have more than enough room for him. And if he is far from home, I'm sure he would enjoy our home more than a hotel. I would hope someone would offer you the same consideration in similar circumstances," Rachel objected.

A broad smile parted Andrew's face, "I told him that, but he didn't want to intrude."

"Go get him at once."

Andrew turned toward the door, "Here he is now."

Laura's face paled as she whispered, "Josh!" and sank into her chair.

A frown marred Tim's pleasant countenance when he glanced

from Laura toward the handsome young soldier who strode across the room, headed straight for Laura.

Rachel's wide eyes went from Josh to Andrew who had a broad, pleased smile pasted across his face. Elizabeth's face beamed with delight, and Philip looked puzzled.

Josh kneeled by Laura as he took her hand in his, raising it to his lips, "Hello, my love. It's been a long, lonely time."

Tears streamed down Laura's face as she sobbed. "I thought you were dead. Why didn't you answer my letters, let me know that you were alive? Do you know what torment I have suffered because of you?"

Josh took both her hands and bowed his head over them. "I received no letters from you and no answer to mine."

"Surely someone told you where I was when you went back to Winchester."

"I haven't been back there. I have been shifted from one regiment to another, at one point I was captured. That's when I got separated from what was left of Ashby's unit. I escaped and joined Gen. Wheeler's regiment. For some reason the high command pulled me from his regiment when Gen. Bragg sent him north into Tennessee, so I landed in Dalton with your uncle. That's when I found out where you were. I wasn't sure you wanted to see me since I never heard from you," Josh explained as he looked up and fastened his eyes on Tim.

"Not want to see you?" Laura repeated between sobs, "How could you even think that?"

"You did mention that you were very young, and I thought maybe you had second thoughts. Or maybe you had met someone else," Josh countered, once again glaring at Tim.

"Did you have no more confidence in me than that, Josh? Even if I had changed my mind, I would have told you."

"Have you?"

"Have I what?"

"Changed your mind?"

"Not in a million years!"

"And who is this young man with you?"

"Oh, this is Dr. Tim Hutson. He is just my employer," Laura explained as if that settled any misunderstanding.

Rachel and Elizabeth winced as they watched an uncomfortable Tim squirm, his face flush.

Josh stood and reached his hand out to Tim, and glancing around the table said, "Forgive my lack of manners. If you have ever lost something you treasured more than life itself and found it again, then you can understand how I felt just now when I walked through that door. I knew from Captain Meredith that she was here, but to see her, well what can I say? She pushed everything else from my mind. Dr. Hutson, I'm Joshua Douglas."

"That was pretty obvious," the doctor commented with a wry smile.

Josh turned to Rachel. "Mrs. Meredith, I assume. I would have known you anywhere. Your husband's description of you was very accurate."

Rachel lifted a questioning brow, a smile on her full lips.

Josh chuckled, "He said you were the most beautiful auburn haired beauty that ever walked this earth and that the sparkle in your eyes would put emeralds to shame."

"My husband said that?" Rachel asked, surprised that Andrew would reveal his emotions to Josh.

"Yeah. We were both feeling a little down. I won't tell you what

259

I told him. But I can see with my own eyes that his was no idle talk" Josh explained, "I must admit that I thought he was exaggerating, but I can see he wasn't. All I can say is that I've never been in the company of three more beautiful ladies."

Reluctantly, Josh left Laura's side and went to Elizabeth who stood and held out her arms, "So glad to see you safe and sound. This puts a perfect end to a perfect evening"

Elizabeth turned toward Philip and breathlessly said, her heart in her eyes, "Philip, this is my nephew, Joshua Douglas. Josh, this is my dear friend, Sir Philip ."

"So glad to meet you, Josh. What an evening! We searched for you on our journey through Virginia. Anytime we came near a battle, Laura sought out the commanders to ask about you, but no luck. Our little gal here was not a happy traveler. I think she would have willingly stayed in that prison in Winchester if she had been sure that you would come back."

"Prison?" Josh asked, alarm dimming the delight in his eyes. "You were in prison, Laura? Captain Meredith didn't tell me about that."

"She was, and it took the President of the United States to release her." Philip stated.

"Philip rescued both of us. If it hadn't been for him, Laura might have been executed, and I would have been homeless. We can never thank him enough for all the trouble he went through to get us here," Elizabeth said, as she gave him a loving smile.

Philip chuckled, "Oh, I can think of a way you can thank me."

Josh looked from his aunt and then to Philip taking in the chemistry between them. Then grinned. "I think you should take care of that right away, Aunt Elizabeth. While he is willing."

Elizabeth blushed as Philip took her hand. "I've been pleading with her for six weeks. Maybe with your help I can convince her. I don't have much time left to do so."

Elizabeth frowned, "Why, Philip? Are you leaving us?"

The young lord nodded, "This is why we had our party tonight. I leave for Boston day after tomorrow."

"Oh, what will we ever do without you?"

"It is my fervent hope that you won't be without me. Agree to be my bride, and I will delay my trip by a week. We will be married, and you can go with me."

A flush turned Elizabeth's face crimson as she protested, "Philip! This is a private matter."

Philip shook his head, "I have been begging you privately for all these weeks. I thought perhaps I could call in the troops, literally." He nodded his head toward Andrew and Josh.

"This is not a war," she protested.

"There is a battle raging in my heart that only you can quiet."

"We will discuss this later and in private, I might add."

"Hooray! She is going to discuss it with me. Finally she is taking me serious."

Elizabeth smiled at him, her eyes sparkling. "Very serious."

Her tender gaze set Philip's heart to galloping with hope.

Andrew and Josh were home for the entire month. They would get to celebrate Christmas at Sweetwater and return in mid January before the spring conflicts would start. Andrew had put in for leave as soon as Gen. Bragg had told him of his plans to resign. When the general discovered that the Sweetwater Mills were manufacturing fabric for tents and uniforms and that Andrew had the means to buy the cotton at the going rate, he urged him to take his leave in order to escalate production as much a possible. It was true ... the army suffered from deprivation of goods and uniforms. In Bragg's opinion, Andrew's contribution far outweighed what he could do on the battlefield.

Many of the troops had boots with holes in them and morale continued to fall. If they were cold from lack of proper clothing, it was easy to understand why the tide of war didn't turn for the South, Bragg had observed.

When Andrew had told Josh of his plans to go home to check on his mills, the young man's eyes brightened with excitement. "I'm past due for a furlough. I haven't had one since I've been in this war. Do you think you might need an assistant at the mills?"

Andrew laughed. "I need all the help I can muster. By the way this sudden interest in Sweetwater Mills wouldn't have anything to do with a certain blue-eyed miss that just happens to be my niece, would it?"

"It has everything to do with her even though I am doubtful of the reception I will receive. I know she is very young and might not have known her own heart," he had commented sadly.

"I wouldn't be too concerned, Colonel. Laura is young, but she is mature for her age, and she doesn't make decisions lightly," Andrew tried to encourage. Rachel had written him about the regular social calls the young doctor was making and images of Laura and Tim together wafted through his mind.

Could Josh's absence have made her heart grow fonder for someone else? Time and Josh's visit would answer that question.

And time did answer the question. Laura blossomed in the weeks

Josh stayed at Sweetwater. Love brought a radiance to her at which her uncle marveled. There was no doubting, she was a woman grown and in love. Where had the time gone? Where had his little girl gone? His heart contracted in fear for them. Josh's future loomed unsure. If he rejoined the cavalry, his was the most dangerous position in battle. They went in first; they ferreted out the enemy, and they were all known for brashness and bravery. The young colonel had already received four commendations for bravery. The most notable one was for attempting to save the life of Ashby, his commanding officer. Yet, so far, he had come through unscathed, but it would take only one bullet strategically placed to destroy the heart of his niece.

Everyday when the weather permitted, the couple rode with carefree abandon through the countryside as if there were no war and that their prospects promised only golden days of togetherness. Much to Tim's irritation, Laura excused herself from work. Once when he had showed up in the evening unannounced, it was obvious he was odd man out.

He chaffed at losing his help at work, but more than that he had believed, given time, he could have made Laura forget that phantom who had stolen her heart. But phantom or not, he had appeared in the flesh, and he was no longer just a fading memory. In fact, he was anything but. He couldn't deny the bloom had returned to his assistant's cheek and a sparkle in her eyes. Tim encouraged himself with the thought that Josh would be leaving soon to who knew what, and he would be here with Laura.

Then that soldier boy might get a surprise. He and Laura were well suited, both passionate about their work. Something this saber rattling youth would hardly understand. He and Laura made a handsome couple. He knew that she held him in high regard, and he thought that she had begun to look on him as someone special. That is, until she introduced him at the Fletcher House. Even now he flushed remembering her words. "He's just my employer." He determined to change that attitude. He had made up his mind. Laura Meredith would be his someday if he had anything to do with it. He would just bide his time. Joshua Douglas would be gone soon, and she wasn't Mrs. Douglas yet.

The weather turned unseasonably warm with the sun brilliant in an azure sky. Laura and Josh packed a lunch and lounged on the banks of the wide river, speaking of their love and planning for a future together, neither daring to mention the uncertainty of their tomorrows. Josh questioned her about Tim, and she gave him a puzzled look. "Why all this interest in Tim?"

"I'm not interested in Tim. He's not my type." Josh teased.

"Then why all the questions?"

"I was just trying to find out about your work. You seem passionate about it." Josh hedged.

"You were not, Josh Douglas! You're jealous."

"Just scouting out my competition."

"Oh, Josh, how could you even think that?"

"You're beautiful, young, and I'm the first beau you ever had. I want you to be sure."

"I was never more sure of anything in my life. You are the only one for me."

"That gives me great comfort, but I know the two of you share a common interest. Tim is a nice looking, pleasant chap, and it's obvious he is smitten with you."

"If he is then I'm sorry for him, because he doesn't stand a chance."

"I'm not so sure. I have to leave, and he gets to stay."

"And you are planted firmly in my heart whether you're here or away." Laura reached up and caressed his cheek.

Meanwhile a disappointed Philip had traveled on to Boston without Elizabeth at his side. He rejoiced in the fact that he had finally captured her heart. After the night he had declared his love publically, he tried once more to convey his love to her. They took advantage of the spring-like weather that had visited Sweetwater in the midst of December. They strolled through a garden of camellias blooming profusely of reds, pinks, white and candy stripped flowers. The tall and stately bushes shielded the couple from view, giving them privacy that Philip sought. He determined that today was the day he would breach the self-imposed barriers that Elizabeth had erected around her heart. Philip paused to pluck a vivid red blossom, nestled on a lower branch among the glistening green leaves. He reached toward Elizabeth and tucked it in her abundant curls, letting his hand linger and tracing his finger down her cheek in a tender caress.

Her hand covered his, and the tender smile she bestowed on the handsome golden giant warmed his heart.

He took her hand, then captured the second and moved closer to her. His brilliant blue eyes, devoid of their usual exuberance and filled with determination held hers. "Elizabeth, do you know how much I love you?"

"How much, Philip?"

"I would give everything that I have or hope to have if I could have you as my wife."

"Would loving me cause you such a sacrifice?"

"Of course not. My point is compared to my love for you, nothing else has any value."

"Then I am indeed a most blessed woman."

"Only if you will accept my love and return it."

"I do accept it. I love you with all my heart," came Elizabeth's soft response, little more than a whisper.

Philip reached out and enfolded her in his arms, placing a long and tender kiss on the lips turned up to him. For a moment he held her, and then when his emotions were under control, he asked, his voice husky, "My Beth, do you know how long I have hungered to hear those words?"

"Perhaps as long as I have yearned to say them and resisted," she said as she stepped back from his embrace.

"Why, my darling?"

"Many reasons, some too painful to articulate." she murmured.

"Forget them. Be my wife, Elizabeth Donahue, and go with me to Boston."

"There are obstacles, Philip." She shook her head, sadness overriding her joy.

"Nothing that we cannot overcome. If it is something in your past, it is over. If it's something in your future, we will face it together. The only important issue is whether or not you love me."

"Oh, yes, I love you, more than I can find words to express. You almost make me believe that we can overcome anything."

"We can. Believe me, believe in me. I will love you, protect you, cherish you and provide for you until my last breath. I will never mistreat you, ask you to violate your principles or abandon you. I will spend my life treasuring you."

"Rachel told you?"

Philip nodded. "Do you mind?"

Elizabeth sighed, "No. Really, it is a relief. I so wanted to love you, but I was fearful and ashamed."

"Fearful?"

"Afraid to trust anyone. Afraid to let my heart love."

"Ashamed?" Philip probed, knowing she needed to tell him, but not wanting to hear. Hardly able to bear the thought of what she had been subjected to.

"Yes. Somehow when a woman is abused, she often feels as if it were her fault, something she did to cause it. I know that I didn't; yet there was a shame that attached itself to me. Rachel helped me so much, and your love has helped me realize my worth."

"I am amazed that you have survived such horrors with your sweet gentleness and kindness intact. Most would be bitter."

Elizabeth shook her head. "I'm not bitter. I realize the blessing God has sent in my life when he sent you. He has used my unpleasant past to give me a new insight and compassion for those going through heartache of all kinds."

"When I first saw you I was overcome by your beauty and the compassion in your eyes. I think I fell in love at first sight, and it has grown steadily since. Come be my bride and go with me to Boston."

"Philip, what will your father say?"

Philip bit his lip and paused before answering.

"Just what I thought. An American widow, homeless and unacquainted with the mores of English noble society would be anathema to him."

"I'll have to admit. He might have some objections, mainly because he has selected whom he thinks would be suitable. But his opposition won't matter. I love you, and I will have you if I have to give up everything."

"Would that happen?"

"I don't think so. I'm an only son. He has few other options. He would have done something different a long time ago if he could. I've proved an extreme challenge to him."

"Why? How?" Elizabeth pressed.

"I refused to play the typical role of a noble's son."

"And that is?"

"Riding to the hunt, card playing, imbibing, chasing women and just living the frivolous life of a wastrel."

"Why would he want that of you?"

"Then I would stay out of the business of looking after the estates."

"Why?"

"He is very adverse to my suggestions. You see, I have been unwilling to settle for leaving things the way they have always been. I am excited about the opportunities that America offered before the war and will after the conflict is settled."

"You want to stay here?"

"No, I can't nor do I want to give up my native land. I just want to incorporate some of the ideas I have tried in running our estates. Father was outraged at some of what he called my revolutionary plans. That's the reason I invested over here. I wanted to prove to him that my ideas were profitable and attainable and could be applied successfully to our holdings. This Civil War has curtailed the progress I made, but nevertheless I proved my point. I am eager to establish some new concepts in management that I think will profit us and benefit our people."

"Do you think he will be more open to them now that you have proved that they work?"

Philip shook his head. "He is a stubborn man, and he is reluctant to share any of his control with another. I wish he could treat me like an adult who possesses some credibility. So for the moment, we are at a standoff. Sometimes I don't know if I shall ever go home."

"Someday you will have to return."

"When father dies. That is if there is anything left of our estates. They haven't been profitable for years."

"Then how has he sustained them?"

"Out of the reserves from the past and on the profits I was generating in America, but there is a limit. The war has cut into my profits, and when the reserve is depleted, our estates are at risk. I wanted to try something to save them, but I got nowhere with him. In fact we had a great row my last trip home."

"How long ago was that?"

"Right before my Winchester trip. Sailed on one of my blockade-runners out of Wilmington. Wanted to see what it was like to go all the way to England on one. I have about decided that if father is determined to run our operation in the ground then, so be it. I can make a life for myself over here."

"You can't do that. As an only son, you have a responsibility. Philip, you can't deny that. What are we to do? On top of everything else you've chosen an unsuitable woman to love. I really want your father's blessing on our marriage. Wouldn't it be wiser to go home and attempt to make peace with him and ask for his blessing before we marry?"

"Appealing to him would do no good, and I refuse to let him choose whom I'm to marry. I've already explained his way is the only way."

Elizabeth dropped her head on his shoulder, "Philip, there is something you don't know about me that might make a difference with your father."

Alarm froze Philip's countenance. "What, my love?"

"I am a very wealthy woman."

"You are? What does that have to do with anything?" Philip dismissed.

"Maybe that would have your father think better of the marriage, if he knew."

Anger flushed Philip's face. "Whether you are a pauper or the wealthiest woman in the world, will have no bearing on our marriage. The money is yours, and I refuse to purchase my father's approval."

"Since his approval is so important to me, would you at least give him a chance to give us his blessing, and, if my wealth would make a difference, use it?"

"You are asking too much! That would mean I would have to wait for you at least another six months."

"Call it an investment, Philip, a down payment on our future happiness. Additional conflict with your father would put stress on our marriage. If he knows I wanted you to get his blessing first, then perhaps he would realize that I'm not a scheming widow who is after your money and position. I can't help but believe that my wealth would help to reassure him."

"Come with me," Philip begged. "Once he meets you, he will understand."

"No, Philip. Petition for his blessing first."

"And if he doesn't give it?"

"I will marry you anyway," Elizabeth promised.

"Let me think about it," Philip demurred. "I've had to wait too long already."

Elizabeth's laughed. "You impatient man, it has been less than a year! Four or five more months to give our marriage a good foundation is not too much to sacrifice. Besides, somehow or some way you need to make peace with your father."

Philip reached out and once again enfolded her in a tight embrace. "Beth, now my Beth. I want to shout it to the world; 'she loves me and will be mine.' I don't want to wait. What if something happens to you? To me?"

"Then perhaps we were not right for each other," Elizabeth suggested against his shoulder.

"Nothing in this world and the world to come could make me believe that we were not made for each other."

While Elizabeth and Philip argued over what they should do, Philip received a wire that made the decision for them. His dad was ill and asking for him. Forced to leave at once, he left alone and with a heavy heart, not knowing what he would face when he arrived home. He determined that no matter what, he would come back for Elizabeth. Life without her was unthinkable.

Chapter
Seventeen

For Elizabeth the holidays proved bittersweet. Sweetwater was decked out in her finest for the yuletide festivities, and she rejoiced when she remembered the conditions of her former Christmas. Yet the joy of her surroundings did nothing to assuage the emptiness that Philip's departure had left in her heart. Although she tried to banish them, doubts plagued her. What if Lord Duval refused to give Philip his blessing? How could she bear being the source of more conflict between them? Her heart ached for Philip. She believed that in every man's heart a little boy resided coveting the approval of his father. Whether or not Philip would admit it, he yearned for acceptance.

Five days before Christmas a package arrived in Marietta for her with strict instructions that delivery be made immediately. When she saw the box and the return address on it, she tore into it, disregarding the fact it might be meant for Christmas. Inside the box was a letter and another box.

He told her in the note that he had made it to Boston by way of

Wilmington and a blockade-runner. It had dropped him off the coast of Boston where a small boat had ferried him into the harbor and his factory. It had proved a harrowing trip as they were nearly captured twice and only the superior speed of the small ship he was on and its maneuverability enabled them to escape. Despite his longing to have her with him, he thanked the Good Lord that she remained safe and secure at Sweetwater. The trip made him realize the risk that he had asked her to take and the selfishness of his urgings.

Elizabeth held the letter to her heart as tears welled up in her eyes. How different could two men be? Memories from her painful past threatened to overwhelm her, but she resisted. Instead she focused on the selflessness of the man to whom she had pledged her heart and rejoiced in the goodness of God. Truly even in the midst of her agonizing past, God had a plan for her life, a plan for good and not for evil. Even the disgusting General Milroy proved a stepping-stone to the promise of a rewarding future. Without Milroy banishing her, she would never have escaped with Philip. Without Laura's imprisonment, Philip would not have come, and their paths would have gone their separate ways. Looking back she could see God's unmistakable hand leading in the journey of her life. Examining her own life she acknowledged that too often she could only see the hand of God in her life in hindsight and failed to have the faith to know His hand was guiding her in the present, no matter the circumstances.

She sighed and chuckled. "Sometimes we humans are a pitiful lot."

Elizabeth tore the ribbon from the last box, eager to see what Philip had sent her. His note clearly instructed her not to wait until Christmas, and her eagerness would have hardly allowed her to anyway.

Laura and Josh strolled into the parlor just as Elizabeth lifted the velvet lid. Gasping, she gently lifted a ring with a large sapphire resting on a bed of diamonds and a card that read, "This was my Mother's given to me to place on the finger of my betrothed. I wish I were there to slip it on myself, to see it on your hand; however not even the beauty of this ring can equal yours nor the glitter of these gems equal the fire in your eyes or the flame of love that warms my heart. Wear it always and everywhere so people will know you belong to me."

Josh's eyes widened and he whistled, "Quite a bauble, Aunt Elizabeth. Quite a tribute to his love of you."

Tears streamed down Elizabeth's cheeks as she responded, "How can I wait? I love him so."

Josh took Laura's hand in his and replied, "I know exactly how you feel."

The days rushed forward toward the time Andrew and Josh would have to leave. Rachel attempted to push the dread of it away, to cherish and savor each moment of having him by her side. She abandoned herself to the pure joy of his presence.

They roamed the fields together on horseback. She showed him all the preparations that she had made deep in the forest and glowed with pride when he praised her forethought. They visited the mills, and Andrew praised her management there. She relished his approval in every area and was relieved that when he had to leave, he could go with the confidence knowing his affairs were in good hands.

The most precious moments were spent in the privacy of their own suite. Despite the morning chill, they bundled up and sat on their balcony drinking steaming cups of coffee and speaking words of love. Andrew determined that before he left, she would know exactly how much he loved her and the joy their union had brought to his life. He wanted her to have those words seared upon her heart to comfort her during the lonely nights that stretched ahead.

She knew that, after he left, each time she held a cup of the hot beverage in her hand and the pleasant aroma teased her nostrils, she would remember Andrew's voice speaking of his love for her.

Christmas proved a joyous occasion, even though the time of their departure loomed imminent. They exchanged gifts, and the servants prepared a sumptuous buffet from the bounty that Elizabeth and Rachel had put away. Andrew and Josh ate their fill and then some, knowing that when they returned to the battlefield, rations would be scarce.

During the glorious days of Andrew's return, one heartache dampened Rachel's heart. As successful as she had been in pushing away the dread of his departure, this anguish refused to retreat. Earlier in the year while her husband was with her she had acknowledged that she had everything in life that she wanted. Her contentment seemed complete. After he left and she knew the danger that he faced, she yearned for a child. She wanted to give Andrew a son, a son that would bear his image, dark and handsome, one who, when he became a man, would walk in his father's strong moral fiber. But most of all she wanted a child that should anything happen to Andrew, she would still have a part of him. The yearning became so acute at times that it was a physical pain.

The night before he was to leave as she nestled in his arms, the yearning triggered an avalanche of tears that dampened his shoulder. "Don't cry, my love. Whatever lies ahead, we have no regrets."

"But I do, Drew," she sobbed.

"What?" He asked, alarmed, turning her face up to his so he could look into her eyes.

"I have failed to give you a son."

"Oh, Rachel. You are all I need."

"You don't want children?"

"Of course I do if God chooses to bless us with them but, if not, your love is sufficient for me. Can you imagine my worry if I were on the battlefield and you were with child? Talk about a divided mind!" He chuckled. "Don't you give that another thought."

"But I think about it often."

"Because you think I'm disappointed?"

She nodded. "But it is more than that. I want children, your children."

"And we shall, only now we have to get through these next few months."

"I know you are right. Do you think the war will end soon?"

"I don't see how the South can hold out much longer, but I'm fearful that we will suffer greatly before it ends."

"We, meaning us or the Confederacy?"

"Both. I want you to promise me that if the war draws near here, you will leave. Follow our plan and escape to Balmara. I have had the servants prepare rafts at a crossing down river in readiness and some of our horses and a wagon are secured in a stable out of sight on the opposite side of the river. The servants will see to them while I am gone and will be in readiness if you need them. But when the fighting reaches the northern part of Cobb County, you must not tarry."

"I will never leave you here and go."

"Promise me. I need that peace of mind knowing you will be safe."

"And you think we will be safe at Balmara?"

"Safer. Promise me you will go."

"If you will also."

"I don't know where I'll be, but this one thing I know if you are in danger I will be beside myself and unable to do my best in battle."

"Then I promise. I don't want to do anything that would put you more at risk."

He took her hand and kissed it, "Thank you. My mind will be much easier."

After the men's departure in mid-January the warm weather of December gave way to a winter blast of artic air and stinging rain. The heavy skies that draped the horizon reflected the atmosphere within the palatial manor. The three women remained alone except for the servants, each experiencing their own private angst.

Elizabeth waited for a letter that never arrived. Questions bombarded her mind. Had Philip arrived in England? What was the condition of his father? Had he broached the subject of their marriage?

The weather precluded any outside diversions. The bitter wind made riding an impossible venture. Even indoors, the usual warm and cheery kitchen with the scent of freshly baking bread failed to entice the trio. In fact, the aromas drifting from the kitchen seemed odious to Rachel. All she could think of was Andrew out in the cold with hard tack his only sustenance. Disgusted with herself for letting her emotions affect her appetite, she forced herself to eat. But the food had little taste and even her usual robust health and energy seemed to falter.

After a week of the dismal atmosphere in the house, Laura determined to go back to work despite the inclement weather. She knew that many people were sick, and Tim could use her.

She had not heard from Tim in the last few weeks. In fact the last time she had spoken with him, he had been anything but cordial. He appeared disgruntled with her because she took the time off to be with Josh. Accused her of not taking her work commitment serious. Laura frowned remembering her conversation with Josh about Tim. She had never considered Tim anything beyond an able doctor and her employer. They were working toward a warm friendship but nothing more. Tim had never even suggested he had any deeper feelings for her. Josh's arrival had curtailed Tim's visits. She didn't know why he had stopped coming unless he felt Josh disliked him. In a way she was glad he hadn't come around. She was jealous of any time she had to share Josh's full attention. But she did wonder all the same, why the doctor had stopped coming.

There was no way Laura wished to offend the young man. He was welcome to come again, and she felt it would be a good thing for Elizabeth as well as Rachel. Maybe a visit from him would lift their spirits. They seemed to enjoy the games and puzzles that he brought, and he certainly enjoyed the food. So she made up her mind. When she went to work, she would invite him to visit, dismissing Josh's suggestion that the young doctor had a romantic interest in her.

"Well, well, who do we have honoring us with her presence today?" Tim chortled as Laura opened the door letting a blast of the frigid outdoors in with her.

Her cheeks were rosy from her ride in the carriage and her eyes were shining. It was good to be out and about. She determined not to let her former anxiety take over her life. Josh was in no less danger, but at least she knew where he was and that his heart toward her had not changed. She realized that in part she had worried that her not hearing from him might have meant he had had a change of heart. It would seem that he had entertained the same reservations about her and all because their letters were lost somewhere in this horrible war.

She smiled a warm smile and relished the acerbic medicinal smells that greeted her. Walking over to the heater, she warmed her hands and gave Tim an enchanting grin. The roaring hickory fire had the office toasty and inviting. As much as Laura had savored Josh's visit and the time spent with him, she suddenly realized that she had missed the work.

"Well, boss, I'm reporting for duty," Laura said with a salute.

Tim chuckled, "Aren't we in a good mood? I thought you would be in the doldrums for weeks like you were when you first came home."

"No, no more doldrums. It's good to be out, and I'm looking forward to getting back to work," she explained as she took off her bright red fur lined cape and hung it beside his jacket.

Tim looked at it hanging on the wall and remarked, "They look good hanging together."

Laura cut her eyes toward him and frowned. Maybe Josh was on to something after all.

"What's different this time? Did you find that maybe you weren't so in love after all? Maybe Mr. Perfect had some imperfections?" Tim asked.

"No, nothing like that. I've just determined that I am going to have a little more faith this time and not allow fear to rule my life. But as for being in love, I am and as for imperfections, we all have them. To pretend anything differently would be foolish."

"Your decision is welcome no matter what brought it about. As you can see, we have a waiting room full of sick and injured folks so let's get to the business at hand. Your apron is in the cabinet over there." Tim directed quietly, mulling over her remark that everyone had imperfections. Maybe things were not perfect in paradise. A smile teased his lips as he whistled a merry tune. Things were looking up.

After several hours of work and the last patient had left, Tim invited Laura to the Fletcher House for a warm cup of chocolate to which she agreed. It would help fortify her for her cold journey home.

Mindful that she couldn't stay long because of the weather, they exchanged pleasantries and Laura invited him to continue his visits to Sweetwater. She told him that Rachel and Elizabeth must not have made the same determination as she for they were definitely experiencing the doldrums if not depression. She could understand Elizabeth being so anxious waiting to hear from Philip as not knowing was worse in some ways than knowing, but Rachel seemed worse than she was before Andrew came home. She wasn't eating and her energy level was nil. Laura confessed that she was worried about her.

Tim smiled a broad smile and remarked, tongue in cheek, "You honor me, Miss Laura, that you think my mere presence could be therapeutic. Shall I charge for a service call?"

Laura's laugh tinkled through the dining room as she protested, "I don't think so. The way you devour the food at Sweetwater, I would say you are overpaid!"

"Very well, just trying to make a profit."

"At your friend's expense! How mercenary you've become, doctor," Laura chirped, thoroughly enjoying the repartee.

"Well you know what they say. 'Make hay while the sun's shining.'
"

"I don't think you lack for sufficient profit, Dr. Tim. Your business has tripled here in town, and now you have Powder Springs and the mills. I would conclude that you are doing quite well, especially for a transported Yankee. I don't know how you did it, but you've convinced us 'Rebs' that your heart's in the right place."

"Just doing my job and trying to watch my p's and q's. As far as profitable business, I don't know that it will last long. When the war comes here, it will be battle casualties to treat, and the civilians will be on their own. Already medicine is getting scarce."

Reality crashed in on Laura bringing back memories of Winchester and the wounded there. "I don't want to think about that just now." She replied softly.

Tim took her hand and murmured, "I'm sorry, Laura, I didn't mean to bring up painful memories. We were having such a delightful time."

Laura patted Tim's hand holding hers, then pulled it away "I know. You are a good friend, Tim. Thank you for your understanding. Now I really must go."

Andrew had written Rachel that the army had settled in for the winter under their new commander, General Johnston, and he felt that morale would improve. The men respected the general's experience and reputation, but he was concerned because enmity between Jefferson Davis and Johnston was well known. He hoped that this time both men would put aside their differences and work toward a common goal. If they didn't, only disaster could follow because according to rumors, they faced a much superior force and a feisty, battle savy general.

General Johnston used the cold winter months to fortify Rocky Face Ridge five miles west of Dalton, Georgia where his 55,000 troops were entrenched. The tall ridge soared seven hundred feet high and extended north and south nearly ten miles. The army's position gave them a broad view of the valley below and a superior tactical advantage. During the lull of the winter months, the troops had dug so many trenches and built so many earthworks the enemy referred to it as the Georgia Gibraltar. The situation promised disaster for any army foolish enough to assault it head on.

Finally, in May Rachel received a brief note from Andrew explaining to her that she might not hear from him for a while because he would be very busy. It seemed that Sherman had moved his superior forces into Georgia. From his vantage he could see the valley awash in blue uniforms. Sherman was on the move, and the battle was to begin. He told her not to worry for their position was impregnable. Johnston hoped to hurl the advancing Federals back into Tennessee with a stunning victory, then pursue them and retake the vital state.

Rachel received the news with mixed emotions. Her anxiety heightened that Andrew would be in harm's way, but encouraged that the war might turn away from Georgia. What Andrew failed to tell her was his concern that Sherman, known for his surprising and successful battle tactics, might just outflank their line. With only 50,000 men, Johnston could not adequately guard the entire ridge with three gaps through it. One of them, Snake Gap, led to Resaca and the railhead, which was their supply line.

And that was exactly what happened.

On May 4th, General Sherman marched his army of 100,000 men into Georgia and on May 7th, the battle for Atlanta began. Knowing it would be an impossible task to assault the Confederates head on from their impenetrable positions, he decided to send General McPherson with a force of 25,000 around the southern end of the ridge and strike Resaca and the railhead. Heavy fighting ensued on the 7th and 8th of May from an area north of Dalton along the ridge south to Dug Gap. The Feds made no headway but they prevented Johnston from sending men to guard Snake Gap. When McPherson's troops reached the gap on May 9th, they found it open and marched through with high spirits planning to take Resaca and the railhead, thus striking Johnston a crippling blow.

Andrew wrote Rachel that Johnston had sent him to Resaca to check on General Polk who was supposed to be arriving with 15,000 reinforcements from Mississippi and to get back to him. His journey proved perilous as he encountered numerous troop movements and had to resort to making his way through the thick underbrush, never knowing when he might encounter the advance guard of the enemy. He wrote her that he never imagined he would be so thankful for a dark horse. He blended right into the pines and it proved necessary many times as one company after another passed. But he would have to admit that they were not very vigilant. It was as if they were out for a holiday full of self-confidence that the battle would be theirs. And why not? They found a major pass unguarded.

He recounted how he had doubled his efforts riding steep ridges and places where his mount barely had footing in order to reach the pass before them and to warn the brave men at Resaca that a large force was heading their way. His letter continued,

"I found Josh there. Wheeler's forces were guarding the bridge at the Oostanaula. Only a force of 4000 comprising an advance element of General Polk's army was in Resaca to face a much superior force. I heard later that it was McPherson with a regiment of 25,000.

Even though I had to return with a message for General Johnston, I knew they needed all firepower they could get, so I stayed. As usual Josh fought gallantly along with the other cavalrymen. They put up a lively fight against superior forces until they joined us in a line of defense.

Why McPherson didn't push his advantage and take Resaca and the railhead is a mystery to me. Perhaps the stubborn resistance of our forces fooled him into thinking we were a much larger force. For whatever reason, he drew back to the Snake Creek Gap, and I returned to General Johnston with all the information I had garnered.

Sherman finally gave up trying to drive us off Rocky Ridge and moved his forces to Resaca. Johnston followed suit where we had another fierce battle. Once more Sherman circumvented us forcing us to retreat. We crossed the Oostanaula at night as Johnston expected to find a better terrain in which to draw the Feds in a deadly assault, but alas it was not to be found. We had lost our advantage in Dalton, retreated *from Resaca, Adairsville and abandoned Cassville. Morale is low, and I fear that our soldiers have lost the confidence that they once had in our leader's abilities. As for me, I think probably some mistakes have been made but we are up against a far superior force and a wily general who flanks more than fights."*

I know, my darling, that the news is not good, and I hate to burden you with the particulars, but we are steadily retreating toward our hearth and home. I want you to put into place the plans we have made. Please don't wait so long to leave that you can't get away. My greatest anxiety is that you will be in harm's way.

Words are inadequate to express the loneliness I feel without you by my side. The hardship of soldiering, the danger I face each day cannot be compared to the deprivation I feel not being able to hold you in my arms and to drown in those glorious eyes. Each time that you look into the mirror remember that image is what I carry to sleep with me at night and into battle on the morrow. I love you and I pray that this hellish conflict will soon be over and that we will be together, never to experience separation again."

Your faithful husband,
Drew

Rachel wept when she received the letter. The horrors that she pushed from her mind came crashing down as she read his account of the battles and his participation in them. Until she read them from his own hand, she could push away the details. Now in vivid color she could see him in the smoke of battle and hear the whir of bullets as if she were there.

And then there was his edict that she must prepare to leave. Surely it was premature. If Johnston found the perfect place to make a stand, then the tide of war could still turn, she fooled herself into believing. The truth of the matter was, as long as Andrew moved this way, the hope that he could join her never left her heart. To leave here without him seemed unthinkable.

And then there was Laura. As the war drew nearer, they were already receiving casualties in Marietta, and she refused to budge. She told Rachel that she had no intention of leaving with Josh in battle nearby. If somehow he were wounded, then she would be there to care for him. "What about Uncle Drew," she asked. "What if he is wounded? You can't leave, Rachel."

She had echoed the very emotions pummeling Rachel's heart. But she had promised. Besides there was another reason she should heed her husband and the promise she had made to him. Rachel was with child.

When her malaise had refused to let go of her, and nausea with lightheadedness adding to her discomfort, she had feared that she had a serious medical problem. Laura and Elizabeth noticed Rachel's weight loss, and Elizabeth voiced her concerns to Laura. She feared Rachel's condition was due to worry. She had tried all she knew to do to divert her mind from the war. Dr. Tim's visits did little to cheer her, and she had stopped her daily visits to the mill; instead Elizabeth filled in for her. Her friend went each morning to check on production and supplies while going over the books with the manager. It was something she enjoyed, and it helped her not to focus on where or what Philip might be doing and the uncertainty of their future.

One night while Elizabeth and Laura were putting a puzzle together with Tim, the young doctor inquired as to why Rachel retired so early. When he heard that she had not been feeling well, he asked why she didn't come in for a visit.

Laura explained that she thought Rachel had worried herself sick and observed that there was no pill to cure that.

Tim insisted, "But what if it is something else as well?"

"I think she is better."

"Why do you say that? Does she have more energy? What about her appetite?"

Elizabeth shook her head, "No. But the weight loss has stopped. In fact I think she has gained a little weight."

A half smile lifted Tim's face, "You said she has been nauseated, low energy, lack of appetite and light headed?"

Laura nodded.

"And she has lost weight, then gained weight?"

Elizabeth nodded placing the final puzzle piece in its place.

"All over?"

"All over what?" Laura frowned.

"Has she gained weight all over?"

Laura and Elizabeth looked at each other a flush tinting both their faces. "No, just…"

"Around the middle?" Tim pushed back his chair a lopsided grin lifting his mouth. "I wouldn't know for sure until I talk to her or examine her, but I think she is probably expecting a child. And I would guess that she is about four or five months into her pregnancy." He announced a pleased smile on his face. "Do you think she would see me?"

"I don't know. She has already retired."

"Go see if she is asleep. We need to allay any fears about her health. Besides that it will give her something positive to focus on rather than the danger Captain Meredith is in."

Laura knocked on Rachel's door when she saw a ribbon of light beneath it. She had been reading and seemed relieved when she heard the doctor's request. She readily agreed to have Tim see her.

When he finished his questions, Rachel's eyes questioned his. She asked, "Do you think it is anything serious? I just couldn't put another burden on Andrew. He has enough on him just keeping alive dodging those hateful Yankee bullets."

He smiled warmly at her and remarked, "Mrs. Meredith, I don't know for sure until I examine you, but I think it is possibly the best news a woman can receive."

Rachel's mouth dropped open and she stuttered, "You mean, you think, oh I can't believe it!"

"From what you have told me, I think you are expecting a baby, probably about September."

"Oh no!" Rachel replied.

Tim looked perplexed, "Most women rejoice at the news."

"Oh, I do, I do. It's just that Andrew said if I were with child, he would worry too much." Rachel explained.

"What's to worry about? You are strong and in excellent health. Didn't you suspect that you were expecting?" Tim asked.

"No. I thought every symptom was because I was so worried about this war, Andrew, Josh, and the Yankees coming. I completely missed it. And then I have been married awhile and, you know..."

"Haven't conceived." Tim finished.

Rachel nodded her head, her heart pounding in her chest. The news pushed worry about her uncertain tomorrows aside. What glorious news. Couldn't wait until she told Andrew. Then she frowned.

The most wonderful news could not be shared with the one who would care the most. She refused to put any additional worry on him. She would carry that news close to her heart until she could present him with his son... or daughter, her heart reminded her.

Chapter
Eighteen

May saw a steady stream of Confederates battling and retreating as Sherman flanked and pushed steadily on toward Atlanta, marching ever closer to Sweetwater. Rachel had one bit of hope. Andrew wrote her that they were entrenched at Allatoona Pass, and Johnston hoped that he could draw Sherman into battle and stop his push south. Finally he had found the strong position for which he had been searching.

But once again Sherman refused to take the bait. Instead, gave his men a short rest and then he started toward Dallas, a small community fourteen miles south of the Etowah River. On the 24th of May Sherman was closing in on Dallas, but when Johnston learned of his plan, his forces met Sherman's at a little Methodist church called New Hope on the 25th. The Federals found the Confederates determined and encountered a storm of bullets each time they attempted to advance. General Thomas lost fifteen hundred men with the Confederates suffering only a few losses.

Andrew wrote Rachel how hard it was to be within riding distance of her and not be able to see her, but he had to spend the day searching for the best place to position the troops. He said the general was dependent on him because this was his home ground. "Little does he know," Andrew wrote, "I'm not overly familiar with the woods and briers of this area. I spoke at churches in the area before the war, but traveling through these ravines and jungles was not part of my agenda."

Rachel smiled, remembering Andrew's passionate attempts to save the union and the controversy surrounding his efforts. She had refused to appreciate what he did then, but now she wished with all her heart that he had been successful. How different their life and prospects would be now if Georgia and the rest of the states had not seceded.

But mourning over what might have been provided only an exercise in futility. Her current dilemma was what she should do presently. In each letter Andrew pressed her to go, yet her heart urged her to stay.

Laura arrived home the night of the 27th, exhausted and downcast. She barely toyed with her supper and asked to be excused early. Rachel looked at Elizabeth and arched her brow, questioning. Elizabeth nodded and followed her upstairs where she found Laura sobbing.

"My dear, whatever is the matter?" Elizabeth asked.

"The wounded started pouring in today. There was a terrible battle at Pickett's Mill."

"We lost many men?"

"No, our losses were minimal next to the Federals, but the men told me of the terrible conditions. With this incessant rain bearing down on them in those jungles, they were subjected to continuous sharpshooting, stench of the dead in this terrible heat and the cries of the wounded. Some called it the Battle of Hell's Hole."

Elizabeth sat beside her on the bed and patted her hand, "At least our casualties were fewer."

"Yes, but where is Josh? Would he be one of those wounded crying out? Maybe someone hasn't found him," Laura moaned.

"Laura, I hardly think what you have described to me would be a suitable environment to send in the cavalry."

Laura looked at her and smiled, then frowned. "You are right; he probably wasn't there, but what about Uncle Drew? We mustn't tell Rachel about the battle. She mustn't know."

Andrew survived the battle and it turned out that Josh had been there, dismounted and firing across Pumpkin Vine creek. When Laura received a letter from him, he reiterated the horrors of the scene. He told her that he actually felt sorry for his enemies. He wrote, "Our bullets swept the ground like hailstones. The Feds didn't have a chance. It transcended war; it was butchery. Some of the brigades lost more than half their men. I will be so glad when this conflict is over. I am tired of seeing men killed."

Fear gripped Laura. He must not lose heart or he would not survive.

The loss stunned Sherman, and he retreated eastward. His troops needed a rest. The rain proved incessant, hampering their movements, so he halted his advancement briefly. He set up his headquarters in the top of a cotton gin in Big Shanty where he had a clear view before him of Kennesaw Mountain, on his right Pine Mountain and beyond Lost Mountain. From his vantage he could see Johnston's signal stations on each of the heights and his men busy felling trees and building batteries for the coming engagement.

After a few days rest, Sherman's forces began to move despite the rain. He pushed Johnston's forces back from Brushy Mountain on their east to Lost Mountain on the west. Finally facing the formidable six-mile entrenchments extending over Big and Little Kennesaw toward Cheatham Hill and beyond, he chose to envelop their flank and threaten the railroad.

When the ladies heard that Johnson had made a stand at Kennesaw Mountain, they greeted the news with mixed emotions. A battle was bound to ensue. That meant greater risk for Andrew and Josh; yet, maybe Johnston would finally be able to beat Sherman back.

On the night of June 21st, Josh moved with the last of Hood's forces from the eastern Brushy Mountain line west to Mount Zion Church to protect Johnston's line of communications that the Federals threatened.

The night was hot and humid, and Josh rode exhausted in his saddle. He had been with the cavalry at Lost Mountain, barely escaping capture. Now he was with Hood, and he trusted that the sacrificing of another night's sleep was worth it. His hope was that the Feds would be unaware of their movement.

But it was not to be so. Hood was unaware of the full force of Union forces awaiting him. On the 22nd of June Union cavalry waylaid Josh and a small contingent of other cavalry officers scouting in the Kolb's Farm area, and a heated skirmish ensued. Outnumbered, they fought gallantly but were pushed back. Just as they entered dense underbrush, a loud explosion sounded near Josh's ear and a searing pain tore through his left shoulder. Both horse and rider fell to the ground as a vision of dancing blue eyes and hair of gold filled his mind.

"I'm sorry, my darling," he whispered as pain closed in and chased away her image.

***

Fully expecting an increase in casualties, Laura left for Marietta, despite the steamy June weather. It was not her day to work, but she went anyway telling herself that Tim would need her. The truth of the matter was, she could scarcely stand not being in town because that was where she could get the latest news of what was going on in battle. And if something serious happened to Josh, he would be brought there. Many of the public buildings on the square, including the Fletcher House, had been opened for the wounded. Tim along with several other doctors went from one building to the next, doing what they could. As the casualties increased, supplies dwindled.

When she arrived on the 22nd, the wounded were already pouring in. Soon she was too busy to worry about how the battle was going or even where Josh might be. Relief brightened Tim's eyes when she appeared, and he always insisted that she work by his side. It was almost as if he felt more confident when she was there. They made a great team. She seemed to anticipate what he needed before he asked. Sometimes her observations proved beneficial to his diagnosis and treatment.

She worked on throughout the afternoon and early evening. When she noted darkness approaching, she called Elijah in to tell him she would be staying in town for the evening. She directed him to go home and bring Elizabeth the next morning along with all the medical supplies they could muster up. She told him to tell Rachel that she should not come. If they needed her later she would send

294

him for her. And she further added for them not to worry, the hotel had a room available for her.

"Laura, we need something to eat," Tim suggested.

"Do you really think we have time to eat?" Laura asked. "I just heard that General Hood has encountered a large force of Federals at Kolb's Farm and has been hurled back with many casualties."

"More the reason for getting a bite to eat now so you will have the strength to work later. It will take a while for the wounded to get here." Tim smiled and took her hand into both of his. "I don't want my helper to get sick on me, I need her too much."

Laura withdrew her hand from his, uncomfortable with the message she saw in his eyes. That he had begun to care for her was evident, and she had no desire to hurt him. Her heart belonged to Josh. "Perhaps you are right, Tim. I don't know if I can eat a bite but I will try."

They sat together in a small corner of the dining room that now had been boarded off to make a place for the wounded. Laura toyed with her food, worry and anxiety capturing her once again. Tim looked at her and frowned. "You've got to get hold of yourself, Laura. This worry will destroy you."

"I wish I could, Tim. You just don't know how it is to love someone the way I love Josh."

Pain touched Tim's hazel eyes. He took her hand, looking deep into her eyes and replied, "Don't I?"

Laura frowned and shook her head, "I'm sorry, Tim. I had no idea."

"Not an inkling?"

Laura hesitated, "I treasure our friendship."

"I want so much more than that, my dear."

Laura looked up at him and shook her head, "I'm sorry."

Tim smiled and patted her hand, "I know. Your heart belongs to another, but I just wanted you to know that if anything changes, I'm here for you."

Laura sighed, "Thank you for understanding."

"And now it's time to get to the job at hand! I believe I see more wounded arriving." Tim exclaimed, his manner all business.

They worked on through the night. As the clock rushed toward the midnight hour, Laura stood at the door trying to catch a breath of fresh air in the stifling heat and a break from the smell of blood and dying. A wagon arrived, and she walked out to greet it when she noted two cavalrymen riding behind it. Her heart lurched in her chest. Could it be possible? Was Josh and his cavalry with Hood? She thought that he was in the Lost Mountain area. His last letter had said he was there.

She ran to the back of the wagon as one of the men dismounted. "Ma'am, let me help you. The colonel is in a bad way. He may not have survived the ride in. We didn't find him 'til several hours after the blue coats ambushed us. The bushes hid him. Just as well or the Yanks would have found him."

Laura peered into the wagon, her body trembling. "Josh," she whispered and collapsed in the young soldier's arms.

———————————

Josh was alive but just barely. His injuries were serious and the delay of medical attention compounded his problem. Tim would have to perform surgery on him, or he would not live. However the procedure was so near his heart that any movement might be fatal. It would require chloroform, but they had given out of the drug earlier in the afternoon.

Tim shook his head and nodded toward Josh who was thrashing back and forth with pain. "Laura, the risk is too great to go in without chloroform."

"But we have to do something or he will die."

"You must understand and accept, he may die anyway."

"But, for sure, he will if you don't operate."

Tim nodded his head sadly.

"Then we will get some chloroform."

"Where?"

"The Yankees have some!"

Tim sighed, "And how are you going to get it?"

"Steal it if I have to!" Laura cried.

"Don't be silly. Let me think. If you had a pass, then I know of a house in Kennesaw that has some."

Laura's eyes widened, "How do you know that?"

Tim smiled. "That's what I'm paid to know. No, before the Unions occupied Big Shanty I got some chloroform from them when we ran short before. But you don't have a pass so you can't get across the lines and besides that, they may have already sold what little they had."

"You just tell me where it is!"

"Don't be foolish."

"Tell me, Tim. What can they do to me if they catch me? They have much too much on their minds to worry about me. Sherman is trying to figure out a way to get Johnston off Kennesaw Mountain."

"Let's look at the map. Maybe you can bypass their picket lines. However that carriage of yours is hard to hide."

"I'll go by horseback."

"In the dark?"

"Better to elude the enemy."

Dark clouds hid the waning moon, plunging the countryside into darkness. A couple of times Laura lost her way, but she made it to her destination without ever encountering a patrol, either Confederate or Union. According to Tim's rough map, she crossed the lines several times. Rain threatened but held off until she reached the house, isolated in a wooded area several miles from Sherman's headquarters and in the area temporarily controlled by Confederate forces.

There was a light in the window, and she could see shadows moving about. Strange that they would be up so late, but thankful all the same. Now if they only had what she needed.

She knocked on the door and the door opened a crack. A gruff voice asked, "Who are you? What do you want?"

"I'm looking for Jim or Hazel. Dr. Tim Hutson sent me."

The door widened and a hand grabbed her and jerked her in the house. "What in tarnation are ye a comin' this time of night?" the man growled.

"The same reason you are up, I gather." Laura replied, her chin raised in defiance.

"We're up 'cause we got to move! Them Yankees are a moving. They will be all over us before we know it. Now what does Tim want now?"

"Chloroform. I need as much as I can get. Hood had a great number of casualties, and we have many wounded."

"I ain't got that much, but you can have all I have since we gotta get outa here, that is if'n you have the gold."

"Gold?" Laura asked, her heart dropping.

"Yeah, gold. That Confederate money ain't worth anything and whether or not the Rebs win or the Yanks, gold will spend."

"But I don't have any gold."

"Then I guess you won't get any chloroform."

Laura sank down on the bench by the door. "Surely we can work something out. I'll bring it back to you."

"You won't be able to find me. We're packing up as you can see."

Laura put her hand to her throat and rubbed it, trying to think. Her hand closed over the diamond pendant nestling beneath her dress. Andrew had given it to her on her sixteenth birthday. Beautiful and expensive, it was worth far more than the price of what she was trying to purchase. Treasured because it had been a gift, reluctantly she reached her hand behind her neck and unfastened it. Holding it out to the garrulous man, Laura said, "This is far more valuable than your asking price."

Greed flashed in the man's eyes, then he reached for it. "Well, let's see about this. I guess it might cover about half of what you want."

"Oh, no, mister. You give me everything you have. You know this pendant is worth far more than what I am purchasing. Now get me the medicine, men are dying while they wait for you." Laura commanded, disgusted with anyone who preyed on misfortune to make his living.

"Okay, little lady. Don't get all fired up. The medicine is right in here."

"It is pure, undiluted?"

The old man's eyes widened. "Now would I sell you inferior stuff?"

"That's for you to know and me to find out!"

"It's the real stuff. If it warn't then I couldn't do business. Now, ma'am, you need to be on yore way as the Yanks are a moving and daylight will be here soon."

Laura grabbed her package and started out the door.

"One more thing, ma'am. You need to be hiding this here stuff."

"Hiding?"

"Yeah, you know, under yore uh uh ."

"Skirt?"

He nodded.

"Turn your head. If you have some string I will tie it on my hoop."

He handed her a ball of twine and turned his back.

The air was still heavy, and rain threatened as Laura trotted down the unfamiliar road. Moonlight would have helped her find her way, but the darkness helped conceal her. She had been on the road for about an hour when she heard horses behind her. With her heart racing, she left the road and entered the dense woods that bordered it. She dismounted and led the horse deeper into the woods, not giving a thought to the nocturnal copperhead reptiles that roamed the area. Her heart was with a dreadfully wounded young man whose lone chance for life was attached to the hoops beneath her dress.

The small unit of cavalry soon passed, and she led her horse back on to the road. Mounting, she turned at the next crossroad and prayed that the Union soldiers had continued on the road she had left behind. Letting the horse have its head she endeavored to make up the time she had lost arguing with the supplier and her trek into the woods. Streaks of dawn broke the morning sky, and Laura hoped that she was now riding in Confederate territory.

All she could think of was Josh and the urgency that drove her to get to him. Suddenly before her, a lone soldier stood in the road. In the dimness she could not make out whether he wore blue or gray. The picket held up his hand for her to stop. Tempted to race on by him, she paused instead. The darkness seemed to swallow the trooper in his deep blue uniform. Laura noted, surprised that he was black. Her heart thudded What was she to do? She had no pass.

The soldier spoke, his voice with the familiar tempo of one from the Islands, "Ma'am this seems a strange hour for you to be out. We expect some skirmishes to develop in this area. Wouldn't want you to get hurt, now would we? May I see your pass?"

Laura's heart was beating so hard, she could scarcely hear his question. "Oh, my! I seemed to have misplaced it."

"Did you have one, Miss?" The soldier picked up the lantern by the side of the road and held it to Laura's face. "Miss Laura! What are you doing out here? You are in the middle of Union forces on the move."

Laura looked puzzled in the lamplight. Then her eyes widened as the light illumined the soldier's face. "Agan, oh Agan. What are you doing here?"

"Fightin' for my country, ma'am."

"Oh, yes. So what are you going to do with me? Are you fighting women folk, too?"

He shook his head. "What about your pass, Miss Laura? And what are you doing here? Sweetwater is a long way from here."

"You know I don't have a pass, so just take me to jail or whatever you call it. But know this if you do… the blood of men will be on your hands."

"Ma'am?"

"I'm a nurse. I went after chloroform from a disgusting old man who took advantage of me."

"He did what?"

"No, not that. He just took advantage monetarily. Anyway, the man I love is in desperate shape and will die without this medicine. So just go ahead and shoot me or whatever you're supposed to do."

"What about if I escort you through our sentries?" Agan grinned.

"You would do that?"

"And more if I could."

"How will you?"

"My horse is tethered in the woods, and my replacement is just arriving."

Daylight hidden under the heavy sheet of clouds greeted Laura as she rode into the square. Leaping from the horse, she bolted into the hospital a question on her face.

Tim smiled a tired smile, "He is still hanging on, just barely. Were you able to get our merchandise?"

Laura nodded and asked, "Who in the world was that horrible man?"

"One with whom we were forced to do business. It's a seller's market."

"Not anymore. He moved out tonight, and I obtained the last of his supplies."

"And where is it?"

Laura grinned and pointed downward. "I once objected to wearing hoops, but I've changed my mind. They make wonderful conveyors."

Tim's skill and Josh's youthful stamina brought him through the surgery, but whether or not he would live only time would tell. An exhausted Laura would not leave his side. Tim, concerned for her health, felt a burden lift when Rachel arrived with Elijah. Maybe Laura would listen to her counsel.

Rachel came in Elizabeth's place and left her to look after their affairs at the mill. Laura protested that she was putting herself and the baby at risk. But she replied that she wanted to be here closer to the news. Finally Sherman, impatient with his progress, had begun a frontal assault on Johnston's line at Kennesaw Mountain. She knew that Andrew would be involved so she wanted to be nearer to him, just in case.

Tim assured them both that she would not endanger the baby in any way and was probably better off here than at home worrying about how the battle was progressing. Anyway he could use an extra hand, especially since his chief assistant was occupied.

Sherman's uncharacteristic frontal attack failed. His troops could not budge the entrenched Confederates, and in their attempt to do so he lost 3,000 men. They heard later that one Federal soldier described reaching the crest of the ridge. He said that it was as if the "Confederate trenches vomited fire and smoke, raining down leaden hail in our faces." Other Southern soldiers added to their discomfort by rolling large boulders down the mountain on the advancing troops.

Andrew watched as gunfire ignited the underbrush putting many of the wounded men in blue in danger of burning to death. A Confederate colonel from Arkansas jumped from his trench and waved a white handkerchief, shouting to the Federals to come get their wounded. All gunfire ceased until they recovered their men. Even some of the Confederate soldiers helped rescue their enemy's wounded and take them back to their lines.

When Sherman realized his mistake, he stopped the slaughter of his men. Meanwhile Schofield had circumvented Johnston's line and secured a place closer to the Chattahoochee. From there he could strike the railroad and wreak havoc with the Confederate's supply line.

When the news of Schofield's position reached General Johnston, he called Andrew into his field office. "Captain Meredith, you own a mill out on Sweetwater Creek?"

"Yes sir."

"And I heard you have some ownership of the railroad."

Andrew laughed. "I did until the state confiscated it for their purposes."

"Oh, yes, that's unfortunate but I would think that you still have some say, anyway a pass from me should do the trick." He said as he wrote a pass and handed it to Andrew

Andrew frowned, wondering where this conversation was heading.

"I have an assignment for you."

"Anything you say, General."

"You make uniforms at that mill of yours?" Johnston barked, battle weariness lining his face.

"Yes, sir, and boots."

"Our men are in sad need of refurbishing. I want you to go get all the uniforms and boots that your mill has on hand. See to it that it runs full steam to make all it can between now and the time we cross the Chattahoochee."

"Sir?"

"Yeah, we're moving out or Sherman is going to beat us to the Chattahoochee. The river is our major defense of Atlanta. I have good defense works built on the other side of the river. Once we get there they can't get to Atlanta over us, but we've got to get there first. He has already flanked our left line. Do you have a way of getting those uniforms on the other side of the River?"

"Yes sir. There is a ferry. We can operate it if the operator has left." Andrew added with a chuckle, "And I doubt seriously he will be there."

"Good. Once you do that, I want you to go south and check out the rail all the way to Savannah."

Andrew's heart pumped with excitement, as he thought "Rachel, Rachel, I can meet you in Savannah."

"Now be on your way. That's a tall order for a short time period."

Andrew saluted. "Yes, sir, I'm on my way." And he was.

When Rachel and Laura heard the news of Schofield's advancement, they knew that Marietta would shortly be in Federal hands. Laura asked Tim if Josh was able to travel to Sweetwater. He told her that it would be hard on him but so would a Yankee prison. However, if the Federals got to the river, he questioned whether or not he would be in less danger of arrest at Sweetwater.

That was the big question that plagued Laura. Rachel urged her to make a decision because she needed to go home. She had made Andrew a promise. They had to prepare to leave. It broke her heart to think of leaving without Andrew but she had waited long enough. She fervently hoped that she had not delayed too long. If she didn't keep her promise and something happened to the baby because of it, she would never forgive herself. Besides Elizabeth must be beside herself with worry.

In the end they loaded Josh in the carriage, shielding him in everyway they could and headed for home. They carefully mapped out a route where they hoped there were no Federal troops. The longer they waited the more difficult it would be to get home.

Josh seemed no worse for the trip. In fact when they arrived at Sweetwater, he grinned his heart-wrenching grin and said, "Now ladies, how do you propose to get me up those steps?"

"If our servants have not all abandoned us, then they will assist Elijah, and I shall threaten them with their lives if they breathe a word about your being here," Rachel rejoined with a smile as she viewed the relief registered on Laura's face.

Elijah jumped down from the carriage and said, "Don't you worry none, Mr. Josh. We'll make a litter for you and have you in the house 'rite soon."

"Thank you, Elijah. A good bed and pleasant company sounds most appealing. Fact is I was in doubt that I'd ever enjoy pleasant company again." He looked toward Laura and tears welled in her eyes. "I guess the Good Lord wasn't finished with me yet."

Before long Josh was situated in Laura's room, which was a corner room with broad windows on two walls. Rachel chose to place him there because the windows provided a cross breeze which gave some relief to the stifling heat of the day and an expansive view of the drive and side lawn. Laura moved her essentials to the guest room just down the hall where she could hear him if he needed assistance.

The long bumpy ride had exhausted him, but Laura was pleased that it had not opened his wound nor started him to bleeding again. Tim had told her that if he could tolerate the trip to Sweetwater, then he probably would recover. She was to use the antiseptic that she had purchased from Jim to keep the wound clean and infection free.

Before long Josh saw Elizabeth galloping up the drive at a fast pace. Calling to Laura who was down the hall, "Aunt Elizabeth is tearing up the drive. Why do you suppose she is in such a hurry?"

Elizabeth slid off her horse and threw the reins to a waiting stable boy and ran up the steps, calling "Rachel, Rachel."

Rachel rushed into the hall just as Elizabeth approached the stairs, "Oh, there you are. I just wanted to tell you that Andrew is at the mill."

Rachel's hand went to her throat. Afraid to believe what she heard, she whispered, "Andrew here?"

"No, at the mill."

Tears of relief spilled down Rachel's cheeks as she turned toward the door, "I must go to him."

Elizabeth reached out to her friend. "No, he was very definite about that. He said you are to get ready to leave."

"He is going with us?"

"He hopes so, but he has to load all the uniforms and boots into wagons and take them across the river. He doesn't know how long that will take, and he wants us to go. Marietta was occupied by the Union troops at 8:30 this morning. It won't be long until they will be here."

"What will we do about Josh? How can he travel? If we leave him here he will be arrested, and if Andrew returns here, he might be arrested. What a dilemma! I must go to him. I want to see him."

307

Elizabeth laid a restraining hand on her arm. "No. He is angry enough because you have not left yet."

"Did you tell him about Josh?"

"I did and that seemed to mollify him some."

"What are we to do?"

"I'm going back to the mill to see if there is any way I can help Andrew. He has got to get out of here before the Feds get here."

"You think they are going to be here soon?"

"Johnston has pulled out and is crossing the river. Andrew says that the general feels he can defend Atlanta adequately there. Hurry, Rachel, get your things together we need to be ready to leave shortly."

"What about your things?"

Elizabeth laughed. "Did you forget? I travel light. My reticule is already packed."

Josh called from upstairs, "Bluecoats coming up the drive."

Fear gripped Rachel. Josh would be arrested and so would Andrew. And now they were blocked from leaving. She should have listened. Was that to be the story of her life...failure to heed advice? She shuddered.

Elizabeth turned toward the grand stairway and directed calmly, "I'll see what we can do about Josh. You answer the door."

Rachel saw a group of perhaps fifteen soldiers pause in front of the house, then two officers dismounted and climbed the steps with deliberation. She paused, waiting for them to knock. The pounding began, and she still waited, hoping to give Elizabeth enough time to hide Josh.

"Mrs. Meredith," a deep voice called. "Please answer the door. We are not here to harm you."

Rachel took a deep breath and proceeded to the door, her heart racing but her demeanor calm. "Yes? Can I help you?"

"I am Col. Turner, and this is my aide, Justin. We have come to requisition supplies for my men." He tipped his hat.

"Such as?"

"Foodstuffs and food for our horses."

"How much do you need?"

The colonel smiled. "All that you have. I've heard that you have raised a great deal of grain and other foodstuff to feed your armies. They will taste equally as well to our troops."

"Are you asking my permission?"

"No. Just letting you know what we are doing."

"That's kind of you." Rachel responded with sarcasm.

"Now, Mrs. Meredith, we aren't required to let you know what we are doing."

"Yes, I know. 'To the victor belong the spoils.' "

He chuckled, "Something like that."

"I could say 'be my guest,' but I'm not quite ready to say that."

"We are looking for a place for our headquarters. This place is really nice. Do you mind if I look around?"

"Would it matter if I did?"

He smiled again. "Not really. By the way, you're not hiding any Reb soldiers are you? Maybe your husband?"

"I haven't seen my husband in months." Rachel answered.

"Then you won't mind if we check your house out?"

"Now?"

"As good a time as any."

Rachel's heart beat a rapid staccato, even as outwardly she remained calm. She held out her hand and with a sweeping gesture replied, "You won't find my husband here. As I told you I haven't seen

309

him since January."

Col. Turner walked past her, then turned and inquired, "You own the mills on Sweetwater Creek?"

"Which mills?" Rachel asked. "Not the mills at New Manchester."

Turner shook his head, "I know that. Colonel Silas Adams with the Kentucky cavalry visited them yesterday. They are no longer in operation. I'm talking about Sweetwater Mills."

"My husband, who is away defending our state against your invasion, owns them."

"And you manufacture Confederate uniforms and," Turner looked at his paper, "boots, I believe."

"Then if you have all that information why are you asking me?" Rachel asked, delaying him all that she could.

"Just a formality."

"Where do you want to start your inspection of my property?" She asked, anger replacing fear in Rachel.

"Suppose we start in the kitchen. I imagine your cupboard is well stocked."

"I thought the rules of war left food for the victims."

"Pardon me, Mrs. Meredith, but I don't think you qualify as a victim. You are supplying the Confederate army with food and clothing. General Sherman considers that treason. It also gives us limitless ability to take what you have."

Rachel shivered as they made their way into her hot July kitchen. Bessie her cook, stood in the middle of the room, her eyes wide with fright.

Colonel Turner looked at Bessie, and then said with a snarl, all his former pleasantness abandoned, "You don't have to do anything else this lady orders you to do. You're free now, we're here."

Bessie found her voice, stood up straight and put her hand on her hip. "I wuz free a' fore you got here. Mr. Meredith he done free me."

"Is that so? Then why is he out fighting against the Union?"

"Like I said before, he's defending our state against those who have invaded it," Rachel answered for Bessie, her teeth clinched.

Ignoring Rachel, the colonel asked Bessie, "How about cooking me and my officers a good supper?"

"I'll have to ast Mz. Meredith."

"I give the orders now, and I want a good supper. Put on the fatted calf. I know you must have one." Turner sneered.

Bessie looked at Rachel, her eyes questioning.

"Go ahead fix the dinner you had planned. Just prepare for a larger crowd. There will be how many more, Colonel Turner?"

"About fifteen of us plus you of course."

"And my niece and good friend."

"So there is someone else in the house."

"Of course. Servants and then three women."

"I thought I heard some scurrying about upstairs."

"Scurrying? You must be hearing things," Rachel dismissed. "Or maybe you are scared of ghosts? I promise you although the house is old it has no ghost... only my heart."

"Your heart?"

"Yes, I love this place."

"If you do, then I would advise you to cooperate with me. General Sherman has said that anyone who fails to or rebels against our occupation will suffer the consequences."

"I've heard. You've put some beautiful places to the torch for no good reason."

"That's a matter of opinion. Just be forewarned. Cooperation is the key to riding out the storm. It would be a pity to see this house destroyed," Turner warned. "Shall we finish our tour? I see that you have a very well stocked larder, and I assume you have root cellars as well? Justin, you check the cellars while I check the upstairs."

Rachel nodded, "Do you plan to leave us nothing to eat?"

The colonel chuckled. "Let's just say you won't be eating quite as sumptuously as you did before I came."

Rachel led the way from the kitchen into Andrew's study. The colonel walked over to a shelf lined with books. Bound in supple leather, their rich hues of brown and burnished copper, burgundy and green gleamed in the soft afternoon light filtered through gossamer curtains He cocked an eyebrow at Rachel, "Not just your ordinary southern farm boy, I see or are these just here for ambience?"

"I don't know what you mean by that. My husband is a well read man."

"He has some very fine books here," the colonel observed, pulling out a volume here and there.

"His library is close to his heart. I daresay none of my husband's collection will be needed to replenish your army."

Colonel Turner walked further into the room and then stopped as if transfigured before the fireplace and Rachel's portrait. "This must have cost your husband a small fortune."

"Why do you say that?"

"I've seen some of this artist's paintings up north. They are exceedingly expensive. I can only imagine what it cost you to have commissioned her to paint your portrait. And I might add, it's very fetching." Turner smiled his eyes turning toward Rachel with a look in them that disturbed her.

"You may have commandeered all that I have at your disposal,

Colonel, but I will not tolerate unsuitable comments about me, my friend or my niece. We are ladies, and you will respect us as such."

Surprise lifted the colonel's brows and he remarked, "I understand. Do forgive my inappropriate remarks. I will respect your wishes. I'm not so sure about others who will follow me. However, I believe that I might come again to claim this portrait as the spoils of war before someone else does. It would be a shame if it were destroyed or fell into the hands of someone who doesn't appreciate art. I am fascinated with it. Sure would like to know the story behind it, but of course you are under no obligation to share it."

"That is correct, and I won't," Rachel declared her lips in a tight line.

"Well, then, shall we survey your upstairs?"

"And why must you? I've already told you my husband is away. I have not seen him since January."

"Then you shouldn't mind my having a look."

"I do mind. You are invading my sanctuary for no reason and will disturb the other ladies unnecessarily."

"Nevertheless, lead the way."

With her heart in her throat, not knowing where Josh was, Rachel led the way up the grand staircase. Colonel Turner paused to admire the intricate carvings beneath the smooth walnut handrail. It was obvious that he was a man who appreciated the finer things in life. Thinking to distract him she asked, "And what did you do before this horrible war?"

"I was a professor in a small college in Massachusetts ."

"Your family is there?"

"My parents and siblings."

"Then you aren't married?"

"No. Not yet."

"Betrothed?"

"No. Never met a woman who tempted me to give up the joys and freedoms of bachelorhood."

"As you can see, this is the main bedroom suite."

"Very luxurious. Yours?" Colonel Turner commented as he walked around the room taking in all the fine furnishings and opening closet doors

"Yes, mine and my husband's."

When they visited the next four guest rooms, Rachel noted that there was no sign of Laura's things. Elizabeth remained nowhere in sight. She could scarcely breath. Laura's room and Josh were next. Where was he? Did they have time to get him into the attic? But then they had searched the cellars, they would probably comb the attic.

Just before they entered Laura's room, Elizabeth rushed out, almost colliding with the colonel. She held a cloth and a basin filled with water. An agitated expression marred her smooth brow as she said, completely ignoring the officer. "I'm so glad you are here, Rachel."

Alarmed, Rachel asked, "What's the matter, Elizabeth?"

"It's Laura. She's not well," Elizabeth explained, somewhat breathless.

Belatedly Rachel pointed to Colonel Turner, who stood transfixed, his eyes devouring Elizabeth. "This is Col. Turner, and he thinks he needs to search our house."

Elizabeth hardly gave him a glance as she scolded, "Very well, but do hurry, and don't distress my patient. It's bad enough to intrude in the privacy of private homes, but to disturb a sick young woman who has been faithful to nurse wounded soldiers both blue and gray.

314

Seems to me you would have some consideration even if it is war."

Colonel Turner's mouth dropped open. "I'm truly sorry ma'am. You said she looked after wounded union soldiers? And where would that be?"

"In Winchester. Both of us were there when that terrible General Milroy occupied the area." Then Elizabeth looked up straight into his eyes, hers innocent and pleading, "I hope you are nothing like that evil man."

The colonel shook his head, taking a moment to recover his voice, "No, ma'am. I have heard about the conditions during that occupation. I sincerely hope nothing like that takes place here."

"But you are taking all our foodstuff and such?" Elizabeth pressed.

He nodded his head and admitted apologetically, "General's orders."

"Oh, yeah, that general. Does he carry a torch to bed with him at night?"

Rachel stood quietly by, speechless at the performance that her friend was giving.

"Ma'am I need to peek inside the room just to tell my superiors that I have made a thorough search and found no renegade Rebs."

Elizabeth drew herself up to full height, "Very well then, you may peek in but be quiet. Maybe she has fallen to sleep. I do hope so. And please do not refer to our brave soldiers as 'rebs.'"

Rachel opened the door for the colonel who took one step inside. There laying in bed with the covers drawn over her was Laura, her cheeks crimson as if she had a high fever. She thrashed from side to side, muttering unintelligible sounds.

Colonel Turner's eyes widened, and he backed out of the room, alarm written all over his features, "Have you sent for a doctor?"

"And how would you suggest we do that? Our doctor is under Federal occupation and so are we."

"What do you think is wrong with her?"

"We can only hope it's not the fever. The fever could spread through your ranks. Good enough for you I'd say," Elizabeth chirped to the colonel's retreating back.

"Aren't you afraid you will get it?" He hurled behind him.

"Oh, no. What's she got, I've already had."

Rachel nodded, "Me, too."

Turner replied, "I haven't. I'm from Massachusetts, we don't have the fever up there."

Colonel Turner canceled his dinner demands and had his men empty out all the food contained in the fruit cellars and the butter and milk stored in the springhouse. Leaving the indoor pantry untouched for another day, his men set up camp on the front and back lawn with the task of making their own dinner from the bounty they had confiscated.

Rachel rushed over to Laura and placed her hand on her head, "Why, Elizabeth, she is burning up."

Laura opened her eyes and threw back the covers, "You would be too if you had all these quilts on you."

"Where is Josh?"

"Under the bed. We've got to get him out before he does get a fever. Wonderful performance, Elizabeth. You should be onstage," Laura exclaimed, mischief sparkling in her eyes.

Chapter
Nineteen

Weariness settled into Andrew's bones as he slowed his pace toward Sweetwater. It had been a hectic day. He had assisted in the loading of two wagons filled with uniforms and boots, working fast and furiously while praying he could get ahead of the Federals before they crossed the Chattahoochee. He didn't relish being taken prisoner, but above that he wanted the impoverished soldiers to have the uniforms. They were in desperate need of both baths and clothing. One soldier had remarked that if a uniform had one hole in the seat of his pants it was a captain, two holes represented a lieutenant and if the whole seat was out must be a private. Andrew hoped quite a few privates would receive both a pair of pants, some boots and maybe have time for a bath in the river before the conflict heated up. He wished he could have provided more, but production had begun to slow because of a shortage of raw materials.

Civilians were in no less need. With all the resources going to the army, it proved impossible for regular citizens to get thread, yarn, fabric or even needles. They became so desperate, that a group of women robbed wagons on their way to Atlanta loaded with yarn and fabric from New Manchester Mill. Other seizures had taken place across the state. So far the Sweetwater Mill had been safe even though Governor Brown refused to provide any armed guards that the mills had requested.

He breathed a sigh of relief. Hoping for a night with Rachel and a bath himself, he picked up his pace. He decided to ford the river a few miles to the south and west of Sweetwater, just in case the Feds had made it to the ferry. Andrew had just exited the river into the dense brush when a movement spooked his horse. He pulled back on the reins, just as a shadowy apparition appeared in front of the horse.

Andrew placed his hand on his holster, "Who's there?"

"Don't you go a shootin' me, white man," a familiar voice called out of the darkness.

"Agatha?" Andrew questioned, relief flooding over him. He swung out of the saddle onto the ground.

"Yeah, I be Agatha alright," the old woman cackled.

"What are you doing out here? In the middle of the night?"

"More to da point, what you doin out here, dis time o night?"

"I'm going home."

"No you ain't."

"And why 'ain't' I, Agatha." His tone was curt, fatigue eroding his patience.

"Cuz yore yard done covered up with them blue coats."

Andrew's heart fell. Rachel had waited too long.

"I've got to get to my family," Andrew protested.

"You ain't got to git nowheres, Cap'n," Agatha disputed. "If you go in there, you ain't gwine git nothin' but arrested. Then what my Ra-

318

chel gonna do? I dunno why you thought you had to go off to that war anyhows and leave my baby. She gonna have a baby, and you done left her to flounder on her own. I is mighty disappointed in that turn of events. Thought you'd looks after her better'n that."

"Baby? Rachel is going to have a baby?" Andrew croaked.

"I reckon ye didn' know'bout that." Agatha's pleased cackle parted the darkness.

"No, I didn't. And how did you know?"

"I knows ever thang that happens in that big house and all 'round it. I makes it my business to know," Agatha bragged, then added, "And I know ye ain't gwinna go home tonight."

"I am."

"No, ye ain't. I gotta a safe place for you and for my lil gal and them other folk at yore house. We gotta bide our time and git them soldiers out o' there first."

"How? If the Yankees are already here, they will be swarming all over this place."

Andrew could hear the smile in the old crone's voice, "Maybe here, but not where you and my Rachel will be. Nobody can find it 'cause nobody wants to go through that jungle, or what looks lac a jungle."

"Ok, Agatha, lead on. I'm your prisoner,"

"You remember that Do jest what I tell you to do, and we'll do jest fine."

"I am anxious to see my wife, even if I did tell her to leave, and she didn't obey me."

Agatha chuckled. "Did ye 'pect her to? She done always have a hard time taking advice."

Andrew sighed, "Don't I know it."

319

Rachel paced the floor, anxiety for Andrew keeping her up. She feared that he would arrive home unawares of the Yankees parked all around their house. She was desperate to warn him, but how? If he came toward the house unawares, then arrest would be inevitable. Maybe the soldiers would leave tomorrow. They hadn't stayed at New Manchester or burned the mill there. Hope ignited, then fizzled. Where could Andrew stay until the Yankees left? Sentries must be posted in the woods beyond the house. Then again they may have already found him. Did Elizabeth say he was coming back here? She couldn't remember. On and on her worried mind raced, battered with questions that had no answers.

Shortly before midnight, a soft knock sounded at her back door. Pulling her dressing gown closely about her, she paused before moving toward the door, uneasy about who and what waited outside. Was it an errant soldier, bent on doing harm, robbing or even worse? She caught a movement out of the corner of her eye and she turned her head. Elizabeth moved just inside the keeping room and leaned up against the wall.

"You can go ahead and answer the door, Rachel," she encouraged quietly as she lifted the revolver she held in her hand.

Rachel opened the door to find one of the young servant boys standing on the back porch. He lived in one of the quarters just behind the house. Rachel held her lantern up and saw that he was carrying a stack of wood.

"Amos?"

In a loud voice he answered, "Yassum, this here is the wood you needed. I shore hope Miss Laura gits to feeling better. I knowed you

320

needed this here wood to bile that water."

Rachel looked at him, puzzled. What was this all about? She stepped aside as he brought the wood into the house. He placed it in the already overflowing wood box then moved two logs aside and pulled out a white piece of paper.

A cry caught in her throat. The handwriting was Andrew's. He was somewhere nearby.

His message was terse and brief. She smiled as she read, noting his impatience with her from the tone of it. He was safe and was biding his time until he could retrieve them and take them to safety. She was to be packed so they could leave at a moment's notice and that he hoped this time she would follow his instructions. He finished by cautioning her that her life and his depended on it. And, by the way, he understood she had some news to share with him.

"News to share?" Rachel thought. "Did Elizabeth tell him about the baby?"

"What did the note say, Rachel?" Elizabeth asked from the shadows.

"It's from Andrew. He is safe, will come to get us when and if the Yankees leave. And that he had heard I had news to share with him. Did you tell him, Elizabeth?"

"Absolutely not. I would never do that unless something happened, and he needed to know and not then without your permission. I wonder how he heard?"

"Just like how he got this message to us? But then, maybe it isn't the baby he is talking about."

'I guess there is a network around here that we know little about." Elizabeth conjectured.

"The same one that helped Andrew clear me of murder charges

before we were married. There was always something mysterious about that. As much as I would ask him, he wouldn't give me the details of his trip into the deep woods."

The soldiers stayed in the area for several more days. As with the New Manchester Mills, they dismantled the equipment and stopped any hope of future production. Col. Turner approached the house once again, declining to come in and inquired why there were no finished goods to be found in the mill.

Rachel laughed, "If there is nothing there then you have no evidence that proves we have been supplying the army anything."

"I don't need evidence. This is war and you are the enemy. A lovely one, I might add. The fact that all goods are gone will not go well with the general. He was counting on that fabric to ship north for our own use. I wouldn't be at all surprised if he doesn't torch the mill. Now if you will cooperate with me, I promise you this beautiful home that you love so much will not be burned."

"What kind of cooperation are you talking about, Colonel?"

"Perhaps your neighbors have far more than we have been able to find. Just a little information is all that I'm asking for. And of course you would have to tell me where your husband is. I know he was here, probably still is."

"You think I would betray my husband to save this house?" Rachel stammered, unable to believe her ears.

"It is a lovely estate, and I am acquainted with some of the local gossip concerning you and this house."

"Local gossip?"

"Yes, how you came to have this palatial home. Rather like a marriage of convenience, I heard." Turner chuckled.

"Then you have the wrong information. There is nothing in the world that would induce me to tell you where my husband is."

With a shake of his head, Turner clucks, "You could save all this in exchange for a little information. I'm sure no real harm would come to your husband, and you would be saved the loss of your dreams. No one need ever know."

Anger flushed Rachel's face. "And it is time for you to leave, sir."

"I or someone will be back, and the next time it will not be a friendly visit." Turner threatened.

Rachel slammed the door behind the Colonel's retreating figure as tears streamed down her cheeks, she whispered, "Oh, Andrew, nothing in this world means anything without you."

To Rachel's relief and surprise Colonel Turner and his men vacated her property but not before they had raided the rest of her stored food, and carried off all the livestock, chickens, horses and wagons that he could find. After taking her carriage, Colonel Turner sent his aide and a few men inside to raid her cupboards leaving only a small amount of dried beans, rice and a little cornmeal for them to subsist on. They leveled the cornfield where the ears of corn were just ripening and the wheat field ready for harvest. If they remained at Sweetwater, there would be no cornmeal or fresh flour for baking bread, the soldiers had seen to that.

She watched as they pulled away and smiled when she thought of Elizabeth's wisdom at building storage facilities deep in the woods where they might be overlooked. So far they had escaped the occupying army's notice, but for how long? A thorough reconnaissance of the surrounds might lead them to their stash, and then what would the consequences of hidden resources be?

She fully expected to hear from Andrew shortly, but how could they escape? All vehicles and horses were gone from the stables. The ones hidden away in the woods were inaccessible to her now. Her house was probably being watched and Josh couldn't ride a horse anyway. Could he survive such a monumental move even if there were transportation available? She shook her head. Andrew would figure it out. He could do anything.

They had just finished their meal of rice and beans, spiced up by Bessie from her own limited cupboard at home when a note arrived. The ladies and Josh were just thankful they had something to eat. It was terse. "Be ready at midnight. The Feds have moved out of the area temporarily, and we have to take a chance now."

Rachel's heart constricted. How could Andrew be sure all the troops were gone, that there were not watching eyes in the area? Never the less, she would be ready. She intended to be with him whatever happened.

Midnight arrived and Rachel, Elizabeth and Laura waited by the kitchen door with Josh on a litter that Elijah had helped them maneuver down the stairs and to the door.

Rachel turned to Elijah, a sad smile lifted one corner of her mouth. "Elijah you have been a faithful servant to Andrew all these many years, and I want you to have this." She gave him a handful of gold coins.

"Thank you, Mz Rachel. You no call to do this. The servants who are left are loyal to Mr. Andrew and you. We ain't 'gwine to tell them Yankees nothing."

"I know that Elijah. I don't know what's ahead for you and the others. I feel sure that Sweetwater will be destroyed. The 'liberators' may destroy your houses as well in retribution against us. These gold coins will be valuable in the days to come to get you a new start somewhere else. You know where the extra store of food is, if the soldiers don't find it. Use it for the people's survival and if by some miracle Sweetwater survives. Stay here if you want and continue as if we were here."

"Will you ever be back, Mz Rachel?"

Tears filled Rachel's eyes and spilled down her cheeks. "I don't know. This may be the last time I see your face this side of heaven, and I may never walk down the halls of this beloved old house again. I can't see what the future holds, but I do know what is important. I am open to a new beginning whether it is here or somewhere else. Here are more coins for the other servants. I am putting you in charge of the dispensing of them. You are wise, trustworthy and understand their needs."

Just as she finished, the sound of wagon wheels rumbled through the night and she threw open the door. Parked in the shadows and beneath a large magnolia tree, Andrew climbed down from the seat and Rachel was across the lawn before he could reach the door. Flinging herself into his arms, she cried, "Oh, Drew, how long it has been. I knew you would come."

He gathered her to him in a fierce embrace, his impatience with her forgotten. The only thing that mattered at the moment was that they were alive, and she was in his arms again.

The journey into the deep forest took several hours. It proved rough and sometimes challenging as they encountered steep ridges and deep ravines not suitable for wagon traffic. Josh moaned now and then and finally slipped into a semi-conscious state when the pain grew unbearable. Laura sat beside him, and finally moved where she could cradle his head in her lap.

"However did you find this place, Drew?" Rachel questioned as she perched next to Andrew on the bouncing seat.

He turned toward her. "I didn't, it found me. When you were facing arrest and I came looking for Timothy who could clear you, I fell off my horse somewhere near here and the people of the village found me."

"So there really is a village. Is that where we are going?"

"Not exactly. There are some caves that will be more secure until we can escape to the river and on to Atlanta."

"How did you determine we could go there and how did you find it?"

"You might say that I have built an unlikely connection with these people."

"You're being mighty mysterious. I can understand our servants having a loyalty to us, but not these renegade slaves. And that is what populates the village is it not?"

"Exactly, and they are looking forward to the Yankees setting them free."

"So then why help us?"

Andrew chuckled. "I think you will better understand when we get there."

The first streaks of dawn parted the eastern sky when they paused before what appeared as a large dense thicket of beech trees with dense underbrush of briers beneath and vines entangling the trees.

Rachel sighed, "How are we ever going to get through that?"

Andrew smiled, "Just wait."

All of a sudden the trees parted as if by magic, and the wagon rolled right over the underbrush to the mouth of two caves, side by side. Dark forms pushed the trees back, and then replaced them as soon as they were through.

Rachel marveled, "What a perfect hiding spot. How on earth did you find this?"

"You might say a friend of yours provided this for us."

"A friend of mine?"

"I think she is coming to meet you now." Andrew grinned tilting his head toward the cave.

Rachel squinted her eyes trying to see through the wagon lanterns into the dark entrance to the cave. She could barely make out the outline of a gnarled form emerging from the cave. Andrew alighted from the wagon and lifted Rachel to the ground, lingering a moment, relishing the feel of her in his arms.

Suddenly, standing next to Rachel, was the form, which had emerged from the cave.

"Now, child, you bes' be gittin to bed. I bet you ain' had no sleep this here night and you gotta pertect that baby you be carryin'," came the command from a familiar and beloved voice from Rachel's past.

"Agatha!" Rachel shouted throwing her arms around the old black woman who had been her nurse from the time she was a baby. "Where have you been? I have needed you so."

"Hush up, child. You hadn't been a needing me. You've had this big man lookin after you." Then she gave Andrew a glare. "'Sept lately and he done left you to fight then Yankees and sho nuff you need me now. You gotta git outa here."

"And you will come, too." Rachel insisted.

"No, honey chile, I'm done too old fer traveling and jest as soon as you and the Cap'n git outta here, you ain gwine a need me no more. These people need me. They gonna be liberated, but they's don't know what to do wid it. So it's up to me to teach 'em." The old woman smiled, showing a mouth full of broken teeth.

"Agatha, if you knew I was back, why didn't you come to me? What happened? Why did you abandon me? I had nobody."

"I got my pride, Rachel. When you left I wuz a fine looking woman. When you came back, I was a ruint one, thanks to that Mr. Walter Banks. I wuz too ashamed fer you to see me."

"What did he do to you?"

"He beat me till he thought I wuz dead, then throwed me out in the woods. I warn't dead. Night and day, as I could, I crawled through the woods, living on berries and sech until I ended up here. After awhile I felt like I wuz gonna live, I made a place fer myself where nobody cud find me. 'Fore long, other abused slaves begin to hear, and finally we had a village. I knowd you wuz home, and but there wuz too many people depending on me. 'Besides, I knowd you needed this here man. If'n I had a helped you then, you might not have him now. Baby, you can be a mighty stubborn little miss." Agatha shook her head. "It warn't easy to see you suffer, but I knowed you had to be in a hard place afore you would realize what wuz really going on, and who it wuz you needed."

"And you think if you had come to me, I wouldn't have realized I needed and loved Andrew?"

Agatha nodded her head and murmured, "Uh huh, some of us has a harder head than others. Yores is mighty hard. But you is on the right track now, that is if'n these Yankees will give us a break to git you outta here."

Elizabeth had climbed out of the wagon and was standing, mesmerized at the scene unfolding before her. Then she asked quietly, not wanting to interrupt, "What shall we do with Josh? He is in a lot of pain, and we need to get him out of the wagon."

"I have a cot fer the young soldier. My boys will get him outta the wagon, and then we'll have a look at him. Might be I've got something that will hep 'im."

The day passed as Laura and Elizabeth worked feverishly over Josh. The trip had re-opened his wounds and renewed his bleeding. Andrew insisted that Rachel get some rest after chastising her for not telling him about the baby. He could not keep a stern face for the news of the baby had kept a perpetual smile on his face since he had Rachel safe within the reach of his arms.

Finally, Agatha came with potions and poultices and shooed Laura and Elizabeth from Josh's bed, suggesting they get some sleep as well. Before the day was out, Josh's bleeding had stopped, and he was awake and taking in some thick broth that Agatha had concocted.

Laura's eyes were bright when she went to his side after her nap and saw how much he had improved. She looked at Agatha and asked, "What in the world did you do for him, Agatha?"

The old woman cackled. "Them's my secret, girl. Old Agatha has been working wonders ever since I found myself in these here woods where we only depend on the Good Lord's remedies."

"I'd buy a bushel of that," Laura exclaimed.

"Naw, that only comes from time, age and experience. You ain' got none of that."

"But I am studying medicine."

"Hmp!" Agatha said in disgust. "All them doctors wanna do is cut off arms and legs. They is plenty they could do 'afore they do that."

"I want to learn about your natural remedies, Agatha."

"Well, maybe I'll teach you what I cin before you leave. And maybe I'll giv you a sack ful of my favorite concoctions. If'n you be a good girl."

"Oh, I'll be the best." Laura promised.

———

As is the case in any hurried move, the three ladies discovered things they had failed to bring. Andrew told them that there was nothing left behind that couldn't be replaced. He demanded that they forego their complaints and worries of what they had forgotten. Soon they would be leaving, and all would be facing a new life, a new beginning. Whatever they left behind needed to be left behind. He was very adamant in his declarations until he found that Rachel had left her portrait behind.

"You did what?"

"I got so worried about you and then so excited that you were coming, I forgot it. Anyway it was so large, the frame and all."

"My dear, all you had to do was to take it out of the frame and roll it up. Small package but an irreplaceable item."

"But you said everything we left could be replaced," Rachel reminded.

"I was wrong," Andrew admitted.

As they were eating a savoring stew that Agatha had brought them for dinner, Elizabeth sat down beside Andrew, obviously upset. She asked, "Andrew, you said that we had horses nearby that Agatha's people had rescued from our stables?"

"That's right. Enough for each of us to ride. We will have to ford the river further down stream, but the trail is not as rough as the one we came from the house on. Why?"

"I need to go back to the house."

"Absolutely not."

"I have no choice."

"We don't know when the Yankees will be back, and if they find you there, then who knows what could happen. Anyway, the trail is too difficult for you, and you couldn't find your way back anyway."

"Agatha said she would send someone with me until I reach familiar ground."

"Why would she even consider that?"

"She wants Rachel's portrait."

Andrew grimaced. How could he give it up? But he had rather Agatha have it than the Yankees, besides he owed her a lot. Even his life and Rachel's.

"What have you left behind that is so important you will risk heaven knows what by going back there?"

Tears weld up in Elizabeth's eyes. "Philip's ring."

"What?" Andrew shouted.

Elizabeth nodded, "It can't be replaced. It was his mother's, has been in his family for generations and is very valuable. I took it off and hid it. I thought that I had included it in my reticule, but it isn't here. I didn't wear it when the troopers were around for obvious reasons."

"Oh, my dear. Philip had rather have you than a dozen rings. He would never want you to take the risk."

"I could never face him without it," she sobbed.

"You are determined?" Andrew asked, touched by her anguish. She nodded.

"Very well. Tell Agatha to get someone to fetch you a horse and be on your way. But understand this, Elizabeth, you put us all at risk."

Elizabeth dropped her head, "I know, Andrew. But I swear to you that I will not reveal where you are if I am taken."

"They can be very persuasive; they want me and will be very angry that you all have escaped."

"I know. But do not wait for me to return. If you need to leave and I am delayed, please go."

"And what will you do? I owe Phillip to see to your protection."

"At the risk of losing your baby?"

Grimness darkened Andrew's countenance and he shook his head. "If we get the chance to leave, we must. Josh is so improved that in another day I feel he will be able to ride."

"Then you must go tomorrow whether I have returned or not."

"And if we leave without you, then what?"

"Agnes will take care of me until she can think of something."

"Very well, then, when we get to the other side of the river, if Johnston is still holding on there, we can rest before going on to Atlanta to the train and south to Savannah. So speedy return is of the utmost importance."

Elizabeth nodded. "I shall not linger."

With a more encouraging lift to his voice, Andrew encouraged, "A journey by horse will be much quicker than by wagon. With a guide, there will be shortcuts you can take, and I pray that you will return before we have to cross the river."

"I understand. I will leave within the hour."

The trip through brush and deep forest through ravine and up steep embankments proved challenging even for Elizabeth's expertise on a horse. A flash of a smile briefly lifted her full lips as she thought of all the Virginia hunts in which she had participated. How ironic that God could use even the frivolous in one's life to prepare for something vital in the future.

An hour into the perilous ride, the terrain evened out into gentle hills and valleys, and the forest became less dense. Thirty minutes later she saw the river and soon the regal lines of Sweetwater Manor materialized through the trees. Breathing a sigh of relief, she slowed her pace and asked Jon, her young guide, to wait for her in the edge of the forest.

She rode onto the large expansive back lawn that swept up to the kitchen door. Dismounting she entered the kitchen. A heavy silence engulfed the room, and she called out for Elijah. As she called for him, Elizabeth made her way throughout the house wondering where the loyal servant had gone. The eerie hush permeating the house propelled her toward the light in search for evidence of someone somewhere. She stole a peep out the window... the entire premises seemed devoid of life, both human and livestock. A tremor raced down her spine. Had the Yankees come back?

She raced up the stairs toward her room, her heart pounding. Had she come too late? Would she find her ring still hidden behind the cleverly concealed cubbyhole she had discovered in the ornate walnut dresser gracing her room? She turned the corner and gave a sigh of relief. The room appeared as she had left it, neat and undisturbed.

She rushed to the dresser and opened the secret drawer. When she removed the false bottom, she discovered the ring. Its sapphire encircled with brilliant diamonds beamed up at her. Relief surged through her. Grabbing it, she placed it on her finger and stopped to enjoy it, her heart rejoicing for a moment over its significance.

Love for Philip suddenly engulfed her as she reveled in the promise of a future with him. She shook her head. A future, that is, if time and circumstances allowed the two of them to find each other again. Maybe he would be in Savannah when they got there. Reality burst in on her pleasant musings, and she grabbed a ribbon. With reluctance she removed the ring from her finger and looped the ribbon through it and hung it around her neck. Hidden beneath the neckline of her dress, it nestled close to her heart where it would be safe from curious eyes.

She ran down the stairs and into Andrew's study with only one thing on her mind. Get the painting and get out of there. For some reason, she felt an urgency permeating the calm, deserted situation that greeted her Why was it deserted? Where had the servants gone? Something seemed unnatural, yet, the house appeared undisturbed.

She lifted the portrait from the wall and looked around frantically for a tool to extract it from the frame. Andrew told her to roll it up and bring only the painting, transporting it would be easier that way. A sad smile lifted the corner of her mouth, acknowledging that Andrew would have to give up this prized possession to the woman who had rescued them. What a predicament! The strong and capable Andrew Meredith having to take orders from an old broken down woman, but one whose love for Rachel almost rivaled his own.

She ran to the kitchen, and finding nothing better, she retrieved a dull dinner knife. It should do to pry the work of art from its housing. Rushing back into the dim library she began the tedious job of removing the painting without damaging it. Elizabeth was so intent on her task that she failed to hear footsteps on the porch. Just as she finished her task with a sigh of relief and rolled it up, a dark hand reached out from behind her and captured the rolled up canvas.

"I'll take that, ma'am. You won't need that where you are going. I will be keeping it because something that lovely belongs in a safe place."

Elizabeth whirled toward the intruder, her eyes wide with fright. "Wha what do you mean? You will keep it? That doesn't belong to you. It is Rachel Meredith's."

A sad smile parted the handsome golden brown face beneath a sergeant's blue cap. "I know who that is and to whom it belongs."

"Then why are you confiscating it? Did Colonel Turner send you after it?"

"No, ma'am, he doesn't know I am here. I am taking it for safe keeping."

"I will keep it safe. And anyway why do you care what happens to it?"

"I care because it is an exquisite piece of art and because my wife is the artist."

"Are you Agan?" Elizabeth whispered, hope renewing.

"I am. And you are?" he asked, his island lilt noticeable.

"Elizabeth Donahue, a close friend of the family. I was staying with the Meredith's. Laura told me about how you helped her escape capture the other morning." Elizabeth turned the full force of her gaze on him, her eyes pleading. "Let me take it to the rightful owners. It means so very much to them."

Agan shook his head. "I wish I could. The only thing I can do is attempt to preserve it. I rode on ahead to make sure it didn't fall into the wrong hands."

"Turner's," Elizabeth snarled, a frown of disgust marring her beautiful features.

Agan nodded. "We were here yesterday, and I saw the painting. Colonel Turner bragged about the priceless artwork that would be his as soon as he returned. I knew I had to get here first."

"Then I must leave it with you." Elizabeth turned to go and remarked over her shoulder, "If Andrew can't have it, then I'm sure it would please him that Daphne would have it back."

Agan reached out to restrain her, "Ma'am, you can't go. Even now your house is surrounded. Soon they will be in here to arrest anyone in this house."

Elizabeth's face paled. "Arrest? For what?"

"The charges are treason."

"How can that be? I am a guest in this home."

"Guilty by association I suppose."

"Help me, Agan," Elizabeth pled.

Agan sighed, as he dropped the painting behind the sofa, "If I could, I would. As you can see, they are already at the door."

Elizabeth dropped her head unwilling to let Agan see the rampant emotions that racked her soul. Where would all this end? Would she ever see Philip again?

"What is in store for me?" she asked, grasping for some small kernel of encouragement.

Sadness dulled the bright lights in Agan's eyes. "I wish I could be hopeful, but all that I know is General Sherman issued an order for the arrest of all the workers and owners of the mills in the area making supplies for the Confederate army. They are to be charged with treason, marched to Marietta to be put on trains and sent north where they can do no more harm. Already the Roswell Mills have been vacated and burned. Even at this moment Colonel Silas Adams has arrived at the New Manchester Mills and the troops will carry out those orders. I had hoped that the family had vacated the premises."

"Why would they arrest me? I was only a visitor in the Meredith's home. I have no ownership in the mill."

"I feel sure you may suffer simply because the family has alluded capture. The general is intent on making it difficult to all he encounters. He said that it is his plan to make Georgia howl and end the war more quickly. Personally I wish there was a more humane way to accomplish that goal. I am ready for it to be over and get back to my wife."

"I hardly see how he could hold me responsible for what goes on in Georgia. I'm a refugee from Virginia, forced out of my home. Furthermore, I am betrothed to a British nobleman who will be coming for me."

"That might put a different light on your situation. Maybe you could plead your case before the general." Agan encouraged.

"You mean I will have to go to Marietta?"

"I'm afraid so. But I will take you to the colonel, and perhaps he will dispense leniency toward you."

"Colonel----?"

"Turner."

The momentary hope Elizabeth had experienced plummeted. By this time the good colonel probably had figured out their ruse and was none too pleased. Also, he would be pressing her for Rachel's location. Her friend must have made him furious when she refused to cooperate with him.

"Well, well, well," came the familiar voice of Colonel Turner. "What have we here, sergeant? Yesterday when we were here, I thought the rats had abandoned the sinking ship, but I see that I was wrong. So Mrs. Meredith has decided to cooperate has she? By the way, where is she?"

"There's no one here, sir, except Miss Donahue," Agan responded with a salute.

Colonel Turner's eyes slid over Elizabeth from top to bottom. She lifted her chin, her head erect and her eyes daggers.

Turner turned toward Elizabeth and snarled, "Where is she and that 'sick' young woman? Where is the soldier you were hiding under the bed?"

Elizabeth quirked a brow at him. "What soldier?"

"The wounded officer. That was quite a performance you put on. But it will only get you in deeper trouble if you don't cooperate with me."

With a wry chuckle Elizabeth retorted, derision in her voice, "Cooperate with you?"

Turner's face flushed crimson, and he stepped toward her, grabbing her arm. "If you don't, I shall not be responsible for what may happen to you."

"If I cooperate, then you will be my protector?"

Suddenly his hand holding her arm, loosened his grip. His fingers trailed down to her elbow, and he crooned, "you might call me that. Depends entirely on how well you cooperate."

Elizabeth jerked her arm away and stepped away from him as Agan watched the scene play out through half closed eyes. "I don't think I have the stomach for that. Besides the kind of protection and cooperation you are talking about is revolting to me."

Agan winced. He knew the Colonel's temper and had heard of his reputation in the treatment of women. Miss Elizabeth was only endangering herself further.

"Then you will suffer the consequences, Miss. I have been sent here under orders of General Stoneman who received his orders from General Sherman. You are under arrest for treason and will be marched to Marietta where you will be incarcerated until you can be sent north. I suggest that you tell me where the rest of your family is so I can offer you at least some modicum of leniency."

"I have no family. They have all predeceased me," Elizabeth whispered.

"Then Mrs. Meredith is not your family?"

"No. Only a dear friend. Laura and I were here because your great General Milroy exiled me from my home in Winchester, Virginia. So why you are arresting me for treason proves a great mystery."

"My orders were to arrest all owners and operators of the mill and to destroy by fire the mill and housing of all the participants."

"Those orders wouldn't include me, surely."

"You may or may not be directly involved with the mill, but if you withhold information as to the location of these fugitives, then you are guilty of withholding evidence. I know that Meredith owned the mill. I also know that he arrived just before we did, confiscating all the fabric and uniforms. He transported it to the enemy and probably returned for his family. I and the general want to know where he is and you are going to tell me." Turner's tone softened as a deadly intimidation threaded through it.

"They have left and should be safely away by now."

"You wouldn't be here if they had escaped." he responded with a malicious snicker. "A Southern gentlemen would never abandon a lady in distress. He'll be back. When he comes, we'll hang him."

A shiver ran down Elizabeth's spine, even as she attempted to appear unafraid and calm, "He didn't abandon me. I chose to return over his objections. He has more important considerations than my safety."

"Oh?"

"Yes, his wife and his niece. His wife is expecting a baby."

"That still leaves an unanswered question as to why you chose to come back."

"I had a very good reason that I see no point in discussing with you."

"Even if I arrest you and send you north?" Turner sneered.

"I would take care before you do that. I am betrothed to Sir Philip Duval, who is an important English lord. He is coming for me. If anything should happen to me, I guarantee you that it will cause an international event that will not be pleasant for you, your general or your president. Do I make my self clear?"

Turner laughed derisively, "So that's why you returned, so lover boy could rescue you? Well let me assure you, my good lady, all your refined airs don't impress me nor does the status of your intended. Anyway, how is it that a southern woman connects with a British lord?" He sneered.

"He is a friend of both Rachel and Andrew."

"So he has been cooperating with the Rebels." Turner nodded his head, an evil smile parting his thin lips. "The general will be very interested to hear this. Let your intended come. He might not find the welcome and influence that he expects."

"He is not assisting the Confederacy. He was a friend of the Meredith family before this horrible invasion began. Rachel met him in France, and they extended their hospitality to him when he came over here."

"General Sherman won't look favorable toward a traitor, whether he is an American or a foreigner."

"Traitor? How can you call an Englishman a traitor?"

"You would have to convince me and the general that he hadn't been aiding the enemy. Besides maybe it is he who has aided in their escape." Turner raised a questioning brow.

"I guess your commander doesn't mind provoking another international crisis." Elizabeth answered with a bravado she didn't feel.

"No, quite the contrary. His intent is to end this war anyway he can. And the best way to do that is to make the people suffer. If others who are not rebels get in the way or impede the progress, then so be it. They will suffer. It really angers him when someone hinders his objective and as you already know, his fury is not to be taken lightly."

"I have heard what a monster he is."

"I think you had better watch your tongue, young lady. I will not tolerate your disrespect of my commander nor of me," Turner threatened.

"A person earns respect, Colonel. So far General Sherman nor you have done anything to warrant a modicum of respect."

"He is a winning general."

"Winning? He hardly stops to fight troops that are armed. His brave army flanks and forces his will on unarmed civilians, mostly women and children. The few times when he has confronted our army, he has been soundly defeated. I consider his tactics barbarous and cowardly."

Turner's face flushed and his eyes narrowed. "Don't you dare speak of my general like that! And as for your fiancée, don't pin your hopes on his help. You might consider what happened at the Roswell Mills. When General Garrard arrested the operators of the Roswell Mills, he found a Frenchman running it. We even heard that there was some British investment in the mill. Maybe your Lord Duval is invested in Sweetwater Mills. If so, he will share the same fate as you, maybe even worse."

Elizabeth frowned at Turner without saying a word.

He gloated, "That's right. General Sherman informed General Garrard to burn the mill and it would suit him fine if he executed the Frenchman. It seems this Frenchie hoisted a French flag when the troops arrived. I suppose he hoped, like you, to claim neutrality. So as you can see foreign connections don't impress my generals or me."

"You better reconsider because when Sir Philip arrives here and doesn't find me, heads will roll. Starting in Washington. Did I mention my fiancée has the ear of the President? He has a ship building operation in Boston, and the President has issued him a free pass to travel anywhere in the country. When Sir Philip came for me in Winchester, General Milroy certainly took notice of the President's involvement and let me go. So you see, he will be coming here," Elizabeth exclaimed with far more bravado than she felt.

"I doubt seriously he will find you." Turner chuckled. "He may never find you. Our orders are simply to incarcerate you and send you north, so no telling where you will be or how he can find you."

The truth of Turner's remarks settled into Elizabeth's very bones. A sense of desperation threatened her composure, and she responded, "We'll see."

Turner's eyes left Elizabeth for a moment sensing his victory and swept the room, almost licking his lips at the treasure trove the library offered for his taking. As the highest-ranking officer in command of this project, he had his pick. That was why he had told Colonel Silas Adams that he would take care of this mill, and Adams' men could take care of the New Manchester Mill and Factory Town. Even now Major Thompkins was arresting the operatives and burning the mill and town. But they would find slim pickings there. The owners of that mill lived in Marietta with all their finery while the Merediths lived near the mill with their wealth surrounding them...wealth and provisions that were solely at his disposal. Suddenly his eyes lingered over the fireplace, and he jerked his head toward Elizabeth, "What did you do with it?"

Her eyes widened and she crooned, "With what, Major?"

"Colonel!" He shouted, his gaunt face crimson.

"Oh, yes, pardon me. It is Colonel. Rank makes little impression on me."

"What did you do with the painting?"

"I have done nothing with any of the paintings. The wall seems loaded with good artwork. Of course you will have to have quite a large wagon to carry them in, and that might be a problem. You know some of your superiors might want you to share them or maybe take all for themselves. What a pity. Did you have any particular one in mind?"

"You know very well what I mean!"

"Is something missing?"

"The portrait."

Elizabeth walked over to the fireplace and looked up. "Oh, the portrait of Rachel. Did you like that, Colonel Turner? I thought it rather unusual, rather sensual. I'm sure her husband wouldn't have wanted her to leave that behind or for you to have it."

"She did leave it behind. It was here last evening... right there on that wall. The servants all ran off so they wouldn't have taken it. I warned them to leave everything as it was. I scared those darkies enough, they would never have defied me. I know her husband does not have it unless he came in with you and is hiding somewhere. But then you are good at hiding people!" Anger pitched his voice.

"I can assure you I'm not hiding Andrew. Gracious, he's too big and strong to hide. Much too brave, too. Don't you think he would have taken it before he left?"

"So he was here?"

A triumphant grin parted Elizabeth's face, and for a moment mischief sparkled in her eyes, "Oh, yes, he was here. He rescued his wife and niece right under your nose."

"And the wounded soldier," Turner growled.

Elizabeth smiled again, enjoying Turner's discomfort. "Oh, yes, let's don't forget Josh. Wonder how your general is going to feel when he finds out you let both of them slip through your fingers!"

Ignoring her dig, he shouted, "I asked you what have you done with the portrait. It was mine. I claimed it, and I am going to have it! "

Elizabeth sighed as if he were a petulant child, "I told you Colonel Turner, I have not taken that portrait. Perhaps you dreamed it was still here."

Turner turned toward Agan and bellowed, "March this woman down to where the others are waiting. It will do her good to walk to town in that fine dress. Then we will see how she looks. You come back in and assist me, Sergeant. We are searching this house from top to bottom. I mean to have that portrait. Meanwhile we will box the others up. I will take them framed as the frames alone are worth a fortune. Also be sure to get the whole library of books and any produce left in the larder. Hurry up now. We have a house to burn." Turner commanded.

Elizabeth paused and looked around. Her memory took her up the elegant staircase and into each room above, remembering the exquisite furnishings. Something akin to hate teased her soul as she thought of the incredible waste of such beauty. Suddenly sorrow engulfed her as she thought of Rachel and her love for this home. Her dream had become a reality. Now it would be reduced to rubble. How many people ever experienced their dreams develop into a reality only to lose them in a moment? She looked at Turner, and suddenly hate turned to pity toward this instrument of destruction.

"May I get the rest of my belongings?"

"No, you may not. Not cooperating with me has a price to pay." Once again his eyes slid over her, before adding, "And just be glad I will be too busy tonight or it could be higher."

He abruptly turned his back on her and bounded up the stairs to begin his search. Agan remained fixed where he was, then smiled at Elizabeth and reached behind the couch and retrieved the painting. "Come along with me, Miss Elizabeth, I'm afraid you have a long journey before you."

Elizabeth nodded her head. "The longest of my life."

Chapter Twenty

The hot sun beat down on Elizabeth, and rocks pierced her foot through her boots, boots made for riding, not for walking. The journey to Marietta had just begun. It would be long after nightfall before they could possibly arrive. And then where would they be housed? She looked at the long line behind her of women and children waiting for the wagons to arrive. Some would have to walk. Sherman had ordered the arrest of all the people, female and male, connected with the mills and let them foot it to Marietta under guard. He had anticipated the women would howl. But what did he care? War was war and the end justified the means. Or did it?

The women had been told to go to their houses and to retrieve only the bare necessities they should need for their journey. They were to get no more than what they could carry in their arms. There must be at least two hundred of them with a few men too old or too young to fight scattered among them. The wail of babies and young children filled the air, hot and thirsty from their wait in the relentless July heat. They had waited since six o'clock the evening before. Some of the women bore young children on their hips. All would not find room in the wagons that were to come.

Suddenly Colonel Turner arrived on horseback; disgust snarled his face as he surveyed the waiting throng. His eyes spotted Elizabeth, and he motioned her to him. Pointing to his saddle, he commanded, "Sergeant, assist Miss Donahue up here." Turner pointed to the place behind his saddle.

"No, thank you. I will wait for the wagons," Elizabeth declined.

"I have no intention of assisting you to Marietta. I have something I want you to witness; so do as you are told."

The breeze generated by the fast cantor proved a welcome relief to Elizabeth despite her revulsion of her seat situated behind the colonel. They passed the smoking ruins of the mills and she wondered what the vile man was up to now. She trembled at the thought of what might be awaiting her at the end of the ride.

Shortly they were turning up the driveway, and the elegant lines of Sweetwater manor came into view. Her heart constricted. What did he have in mind taking her back to the deserted house?

When they galloped up to the front porch, Turner swung out of the saddle and reached up for Elizabeth.

"I will stay here, thank you, Colonel, and I insist that you take me back to the other waiting prisoners."

He gave a derisive chuckle. "You are in no position to make demands. You need not worry for I have no plans to do you any bodily harm. I just wanted you to see what the penalty for not cooperating with us can be. Rachel Meredith was offered protection and the survival of her property if she would cooperate. Because she refused and because they supported the rebellion, they will pay with all that they have. If you ever see them again, I want you to describe to them

347

as an eye witness what happened to their wealth."

"If I ever see them again?" Elizabeth asked.

"That's right. You are going north. Since you only carry the clothes on your back, I hardly believe you will be able to return here or that your fiancée will find you. But just in case, I want you to be an eye witness of the destruction of all that they had."

"Not quite all, Colonel. I believe you have lined your pockets sufficiently from what you had time to retrieve."

His Cheshire grin told her that many of the treasures, which belonged to Sweetwater, were now Colonel Turner's. "As with the mills, my men have saturated the buildings with flammable material soaked in oil. I reserved the pleasure of putting the torch to it for myself."

Soon flumes of black smoke boiled up from the lovely old mansion as flames belched out the roof and windows. Before long the entire structure was ablaze, and tears coursed down Elizabeth's cheeks.

Elizabeth's eyes were not the only ones to weep. Andrew and Rachel watched from their vantage on the banks of the Chattahoochee. Smoke rose like a like a dense black cloud from their home. Even from this distance the scent of burning timbers permeated the air and attached itself to them. He could smell it in her hair as she buried her head on his shoulder, her tears turning to sobs.

He held her, but no words of comfort sprang from him. How could he comfort her when his own heart was breaking? A sense of failure inundated him as he admitted to himself that once again he had encountered an area in life that was out of his control. The hopes and aspirations of all their dreams now drifted above them like a black veil wafted by a sweltering July breeze. He had tried to provide her with everything her heart desired and now it was gone. He proved helpless to protect and defend the one thing that meant more to her than anything else in the world. In a few hours the world that she knew and loved would be in ashes.

He held her more tightly, but said nothing. He shook his head at the enormity of the sorrow she must be feeling. What would this loss do to her, to their relationship, the future of their marriage?

Would she resent him, blame him for not being there; consider him a coward for not facing the enemy, attempting to intervene? He shuddered.

Rachel felt him shudder and raised her head. Her eyes, red from crying, questioned him.

He looked at her, and all he could do was shake his head. He didn't have an answer. He didn't have a solution. He began, his voice broke, "I am so sorry, Darling. If I had stayed..."

Rachel placed a finger on his lips. "Hush. If you had stayed, then it would have been you that I lost. Sweetwater Manor is only wood, brick and mortar."

"But you loved it. It was your dream."

"Esteemed it, valued it, but love it? I did once, but I have changed." Rachel shook her head, and fastened her eyes, brilliant as emeralds on him. "You are my love, my life, my other half. As long as I have you, nothing else really matters."

"And the baby," he reminded.

She smiled through her tears and patted her stomach. "Yes, and the baby."

"But your sobs, your tears..."

" I am crying mostly for you, Drew. I know how much Sweetwater and the dreams for us meant to you. Now your dreams are ashes."

Andrew drew her to him in a tender embrace. "But beauty can come from even these ashes, my darling; together we can make a new beginning. As long as I have you, I have everything"

In the distance, the sound of approaching horses broke through their sorrow. "Elizabeth must be back. If so, we can be on our way."

Andrew nodded. "We must leave immediately if we are to make an escape. Sweetwater is not that far down the river, and enemy patrols might appear at any moment."

"And then you would be arrested and sent from me."

"Don't fret, Darling. We will make it, if we can leave soon. Our men are across the river."

Josh and Laura's horses galloped out of the dense forest into view. Agatha had secured Josh's arm to his body to stabilize his shoulder, forcing him to manage his horse with one hand. His cavalry days proved beneficial in his ability to cope with this handicap, and he handled the situation with apparent ease. Even so pain made his mahogany eyes appear big and dark in his pale face. Laura looked uneasy with the situation as she kept watchful eyes on her charge.

Rachel peered into the brush behind them, but Elizabeth failed to emerge.

Josh shook his head at the question in Andrew's eyes. "Jon arrived back at the camp and said that Elizabeth had been taken prisoner. She had instructed him that if anything should happen to her that he was to tell us to go on without her. She assured him that Philip would find her. Jon said that he hid in the woods for two days to make sure and when he saw that mean Colonel bring her back on his horse and set fire to the house, he knew he'd better tell us. Agatha said that it was imperative that we leave now. She said that the Yankees were already crossing the Chattahoochee north of here. If we are to get away, it is now or never."

Andrew helped Rachel to mount, then hoisted himself into the saddle, "I'll go back to see what I can do."

Josh shook his head, "Agatha said to tell you not to even think about it. It will get you nothing but arrested and maybe even hanged and 'you tell that white man, he better be lookin' after my baby.' Those were her exact orders, and I agree. I can do little to protect these women with only a left arm free, and we do have to think about Rachel's condition. Besides were you given an order by General Johnston?"

Andrew sighed. "To tell you the truth, current circumstances had completely wiped it out of my mind. Ok, Josh, let's get moving. Do you think you can make it?"

"If I can't, leave me behind. We must get Laura and Rachel out of here."

Laura reached out and touched his shoulder gently. "Never. I will never leave you behind! If I have to fight the whole Yankee army!"

"That's my girl!" Josh chuckled. "With you to look after me, what do I have to fear?"

And in the midst of sorrow and destruction, humor had its way.

In the distance the sound of hoof beats reverberated through the woods, and Andrew slowly drew his pistol from his holster, "Josh, you and the ladies go on down river, I'll cover you."

"Drew, come with us. Surely we can get across before any one can apprehend us."

Andrew shook his head. "To cross here is not an option. You would be sitting ducks because the other side offers no concealment. You will have to take your chances that there is another place shallow enough to cross. Meanwhile I will hold them off until you get away. Now GO!"

He hit Rachel's mount, and the horse galloped off followed by Laura and a reluctant Josh.

Andrew waited as the intruder neared. Relief spread through him. It sounded as if it was a single rider. Maybe he would be able to join Rachel after all. He concealed himself behind a thicket of muscadine vines just as the rider came into view. The rider wore a blue sergeant's uniform and paused at the ford and dismounted. He knelt and examined the hoof prints on the ground.

"Drop your weapon, Sergeant and state your business." Andrew commanded as he stepped from his hiding place.

The young soldier whose back was turned to Andrew did as he was commanded. He unbuckled his belt, and his side arm dropped to the ground.

"Now turn around slowly with your hands in the air."

"Agan!" Andrew shouted, his gun still leveled at the blue clad soldier.

A broad grin parted Agan's golden face. "The one and the same."

Then Andrew frowned. "Have you come to extract your revenge? Obviously you were looking for us."

"Not revenge, help."

"And what kind of help could, you, a Yankee, have for me, a Confederate?"

"None for a Confederate, but I hope much for my family." A soft smile illuminated Agan's eyes.

"You could be court-martialed for this. Sherman would hang you."

"I am well aware of that. Believe me, it was not an easy decision, but my temporary commander made it easier."

"Temporary commander?"

"Yes, I was reassigned to Colonel Turner's regiment. After what he did at Sweetwater and to Miss Elizabeth, I knew I had no choice."

Andrew's heart lurched. "What has he done to Elizabeth?"

"He has arrested all the women and children associated with the mills and sent them to Marietta to be transported North. Miss Elizabeth is with them. He has charged you and Mz Rachel with treason. He can hang you if he catches you."

"Elizabeth is not part of our family but a refugee from Winchester."

"She explained that to him, but he would not listen. She hopes to see General Sherman and make her plea to him."

"So why are you here, Agan?"

"First to give you this." he said as he reached into his saddlebag and pulled a protruding role of canvas from it. "The colonel had his heart set on this. For obvious reasons I didn't want him to have it and I couldn't conceal it from him for very long. The other reason is to lead you to a better fording place on the river. One that will put you nearer your lines, and the river is not as swift or deep."

"How did you know about where we were and where another crossing is?"

"Remember Daphne and I spent several days in those woods beyond the river. I saw Elijah before he left, and he told me about Agatha. I realized that you would try to get across at this ford and hoped I could find you before you crossed. I knew that you would be waiting for your friend so I could get to you and to tell you that there was nothing you could do and to go on. This is not a good place to cross because soon our forces will be on the other side of the river. They are already across at Roswell. You need to get across quickly and go south of Atlanta. You still have some time if you choose your route carefully."

"How can I thank you, Agan?" Andrew asked.

"You already have. I owe who and what I am to your generosity. The young boy you set free, educated, mentored, and trusted to run your plantation owes you a lifetime of gratitude. I could do no less. Now, be on your way; you don't have much time."

Andrew swung into the saddle and then gave Agan a smart salute, "Until we meet again."

Agan returned the salute and galloped away in the opposite direction, wondering if he would ever see his benefactor again.

The sultry July heat pressed down on Elizabeth, packed in with a mass of other women and children in abandoned classrooms at the Georgia Military Institute. Situated on a hill overlooking Marietta, the stately quarters no longer garrisoned young cadets. They had left to fight in West Point, Georgia on the Alabama line ready to defend their state. The Institute now housed the headquarters of General Thomas and the Army of the Cumberland. His Union troops were housed in the comfortable ten men barracks adjacent to the parade grounds. The women and children arrested for treason remained huddled together inside until they overflowed to the outside where they were quartered under the spreading trees. Already the beautiful rose gardens and manicured lawn had been trampled underfoot, first by soldiers and then by the mass of bedraggled prisoners.

It had been a long and uncomfortable ride from Sweetwater to Marietta in rough army wagons, but she had been one of the more fortunate ones. She had not had to walk as some of the women had. Agan had seen to that. He had found her a place in the first wagon and helped her aboard. Shortly after, he vanished from the scene to appear in Marietta with the troops that went along to "guard" these "ferocious" enemies. Elizabeth's heart broke as she looked around her at the women from Andrew's mill and the New Manchester Mills.

She met Lizzie Stewart from the New Manchester Mills who had her daughter, Cynthia Catherine, and three of her other children with her. When they rode into town, the young girl stood up in the wagon and pointed to a soldier, identifying him as the man who had taken her Bible from her. Elizabeth cringed. What monster could do that to a child?

Lizzie pointed out another friend who had her nine children with her and another with five by her side. She cried. What were they to do? Were they going to be imprisoned wherever they were to be sent? Would they be released in a strange and alien land without any hope of sustenance or a way to feed and clothe their children? And what about her husband? If he survived the war and returned, would he know what happened? Could he find them? How would he have the money to bring them back? He would have no job. With the mills destroyed there would be no job to return to. Who made the monstrous decision to bring down such punishment on women and children who were simply trying to earn enough to eat?

Elizabeth's stomach churned, her gentle spirit boiling with anger. Her own situation remained dire. She had nothing of value but the ring hidden beneath her only dress. The wealth that she possessed remained out of reach. It would do her no good in her present circumstances, but compared to the state these women and children found themselves in, she had little to complain about. She was young and strong. If by necessity she had to find a job, she could work. She clung to the hope that somehow she could get the ear of a general and make him understand that Philip would be coming for her. But then how would Philip know? And when? When he came would it be too late?

She must get to General Thomas if she couldn't see Sherman. But all access was denied to her. The only acts of kindness Elizabeth witnessed in the Union army were from Agan and Major General Dodge who had arrived from the field and noted the plight of these women. He instructed Assistant Surgeon John Ashton to hire as many of the girls as he could and gave a hundred dollars out of his own pocket to defray the cost. Despite the absence of Sherman's consent to release any of the prisoners, a few of the younger women found employment and escaped the uncertain future that loomed for the rest of the captives.

Elizabeth clamored to see a general or anyone with the authority to act on her request, but it proved futile. Each man in charge relayed the same message. The generals were too busy to see her. General Sherman had given his orders that they were to be transported north, and that was what would happen.

She thought of the few girls that General Dodge had rescued and had hoped she could get to him. But that was not to be. His visit to wounded soldiers proved too brief for her to get an appointment. That left only General Thomas or General Sherman to hear her plea, neither of whom would exhibit a sympathetic ear. They both considered the mill operatives as traitors. And she acknowledged that if they investigated, they would find that she had filled in for Rachel on occasion when she had needed her. But it was all done as one friend helping another. There was never any pay involved. Her name would not appear on the payrolls, but if the workers were pressed they might be willing to tell of her involvement in a bid for leniency.

On July 9, she found herself crammed in a cattle car on her way north to Nashville. The stench of unwashed bodies stifled in the oppressive heat of the car, making it hard to breathe. But the physical discomfort paled beside the anguish she felt inside. With each strike of wheel hitting rail, Elizabeth's heart beat harder as her promising future slipped away mile by mile. How could Philip find her? Turner had laughed and said that he would never find her. Would he even want her now? She looked down at her only dress, stained with perspiration and filth. Bedraggled and unwashed, her hair stringy and nails broken she shuddered at the sight she must be. And she wouldn't even have the luxury of a change. Colonel Turner saw to that when he refused her time to gather any of her belongings. She had no money to buy anything, clothes or food. Without it and only nine days menial rations how could she survive?

Elizabeth was not the only one who listened to the rhythmic click-clack of a moving train. Andrew and Rachel along with Josh and Laura in an easier than expected journey through forest and roads arrived just south of Atlanta. As expected, the train station was a mass of refugees trying to evacuate Atlanta before the battle began. When Andrew presented his credentials as part owner of the railroad and General Johnston's orders to go to Savannah, they were ushered aboard the first train available, which proved to be immediate. Now they were approaching the lovely port city.

It had been a hot and tiring journey. They had not enjoyed their usual accommodations. A private car was no longer available to them so they shared the coach with all shapes and forms of fleeing humanity.

Andrew's brown eyes were somber as he caught her attention. He was standing at the window, stretching his leg as the train chugged along the last miles before pulling in to the Savannah station. She smiled a tremulous smile, hoping to reassure him. "I'm fine."

"The baby?"

"The baby's fine. We are both strong, don't you worry about us." Rachel winced.

Immediately, Andrew was at her side, concern wrinkling his brow. "What's wrong?"

Rachel gave him a radiant smile. She took his hand and placed it on her protruding abdomen, and asked, "Do you feel that?"

Alarm deepened Andrew's frown. "Yes, what's wrong?"

Rachel laughed and caressed his face. "Not one thing but your son showing his strength. He just kicked his mother."

Relief smoothed the lines in Andrew's brow and he smiled, relieved, "A disrespectful little rascal! But it might be a girl!"

"I doubt that. He is strong and active, just like his father."

"I wouldn't mind a little girl, you know," Andrew mused. "I would want one with emerald eyes and magnificent hair just like her mother."

"And I wouldn't mind if she had dark eyes like muscadines and flowing black hair like her father."

"If not this one, then maybe the next." He grinned.

"There will be a next?"

"Oh, yes. If I have any say in it, we'll fill up the house with our offspring."

Rachel's eyes brightened as tears threatened. "Our house? We no longer have one."

"But we will, my darling." Andrew comforted.

"Where?" Rachel asked.

"I don't know. We will have to get this war over. It might be Savannah or it might be Sweetwater. Wherever it is, it will be a bright new beginning for us. One without the threat of war hanging over us."

Rachel smiled. "A new beginning without a threat hanging over us and a passel of children. I can't think of a more glorious future to wish for. It doesn't matter where, just as long as we are together."

Andrew sat down beside her and pulled her into his arms, her head resting on his chest. "We will be there soon. I only wish Philip would be there so he could go fetch Elizabeth and bring her home to Balmara."

"What if she is not in Marietta?" Rachel put words to the doubts that had been bombarding Andrew for hours.

***

Lights blazed from the elegant mansion as the entourage made its way up the moss draped lane in the rented less than stylish carriage. But no one complained. They realized how blessed they were simply to have found one. Even then Andrew had to apply pressure and line some man's pocket with a gold coin. As soon as they had arrived in the mid afternoon, Andrew sent a wire to General Johnston affirming to him that so far the railway was in good condition all the way from Macon to Savannah.

Rachel had feared that Johnston would order Andrew to return immediately. The good general relieved her mind by ordering Andrew to stay in Savannah and requisition food and grain for the horses to send north to supply the troops gearing up to defend Atlanta. A broad grin plastered on Andrew's face as he crawled up in the carriage beside her. "It looks as if you will have to put up with me a while longer. I may even be here when the baby arrives."

"What happens if Johnston can't stop Sherman in Atlanta, and he comes here?"

"We will cross that bridge when we get to it. Meanwhile let's treasure each moment that we have together." Andrew encouraged just as they pulled up to the front steps of Balmara.

The large ornate door swung open and a large familiar figure stepped out to greet them.

"It's Philip!" Rachel exclaimed.

Andrew was out of the carriage and up the steps, forgetting Rachel and the rest of the occupants in the carriage. Eager to see his friend, he grabbed Philip's hand. "Am I glad to see you, dear friend. I thought you were still in England. It has happened just like you said, and we followed the plans we made."

"So you have the ladies with you, I presume."

Pain darkened Andrew's eyes. "Only Laura and Rachel."

"But I see three people in the carriage," Philip protested.

Andrew shook his head. "She's not there, Philip, I'm so sorry," Andrew began.

"Where is Elizabeth? Wouldn't she come? Has she gone back to Virginia? Has something happened to her? She gave me her word. I came back to marry her. To take her back to England with me." Emotion raced Philip's words.

"We don't know exactly where she is. I hope she is in Marietta," Andrew said and then related to Philip what had happened.

"Why did you let her go back to the house? I thought better of you than that, Andrew. I thought you would look after her." Anger and fear raised Philip's voice.

"I could not dissuade her. It seems that she had hidden your ring for safe keeping, and when we left in such a hurry, she forgot to retrieve it."

"That ring is of no value next to her life. Didn't she know that?"

"I told her you would feel like that, but she insisted that the ring was irreplaceable, and she could never face you if something happened to it."

Philip dropped his head and moaned, "Foolish girl, she means more to me than a world full of sapphires and diamonds."

Andrew patted Philip's shoulder. "Philip, I feel sure she was able to present her case to one of the generals, and she is probably waiting for you in Marietta. If I know Elizabeth, she is at one of the field hospitals right now helping the wounded be they northern or southern boys. That's just the kind of lady she is."

Philip moaned, "Don't I know it. How I love that woman. My world needs her to be complete. I thought after Rachel there would be no other, but what I feel for Elizabeth far surpasses anything I've ever felt. She is my soul-mate."

"That's because God sent you the one meant for you, just like he did for me."

"We are blessed," Philip whispered, shaking his head as if to clear it, then barked, "That is if I can find her. When I do, I might just wring her pretty neck. Thinking a ring is that important to me. "

Andrew chuckled. "There are times when a man just can't comprehend the thinking of a woman."

"This is one of those times. I will leave on the first train out of here.

I still have my pass to get across the lines." Philip's voice strengthened, determination threaded through it.

Andrew nodded just as Rachel, Laura and Josh made their way up the steps to where the two men stood. "I will arrange immediate travel for you, and I trust that you and Elizabeth will be together shortly."

Early the next morning Andrew drove Philip to the station. He had managed to schedule a train to leave for the journey to Macon and then on to Atlanta on the basis of the army's need for supplies. Although it proved a difficult task, he finally secured grain and food as well as a few cattle overnight. Even now they were being loaded into boxcars for the journey north. After that it became a simple matter to procure Philip comfortable accommodations in the one passenger car that would make the trip. He would not experience the same crowded conditions that the four of them had. No one wanted to go north.

"When I find Elizabeth, Andrew, we won't be coming back here. I will travel to Boston and then back to England."

Andrew frowned, a question in his warm, brown eyes.

"My father died, and I must return. I have duties that I cannot shirk. But first I will find Elizabeth and make her my bride; then we will make the journey home."

"Then this will be goodbye."

"I'm afraid so, my friend. Wish me Godspeed and His blessings. If I can't find her, I don't know what I shall do. A future without her is no life at all. I can't contemplate not spending the rest of my life with her. I will find her, if I have to search to the ends of the earth."

"My prayer is that your search will end in Marietta. But be prepared for an unpleasant confrontation. Sherman is anything but a gentleman. He is determined to win this war, no matter the cost. Charging women and children with treason for making a living is beyond reason and the action of an irrational man."

Chapter
Twenty-One

A weary Philip rode into Marietta and headed toward the Fletcher House. When the trained pulled into Atlanta, he had to wait for his horse to be unloaded. Andrew had insisted that he carry one for he knew that he would have a hard time getting to Marietta otherwise. Of course train service had been interrupted and horses, except for the army's, were non-existent.

Arriving in the lobby, Philip noted a makeshift hospital in the room beyond and he looked around, expecting to see officers in residence. He asked the clerk if General Sherman was in residence there. Disappointment flooded over him upon hearing that the general had already left the area.

"Do you know anything about the operatives of the mills that were brought to town?" He asked the gum-chewing clerk, dressed in a slovenly blue private's uniform.

"Yeah, I saw them girls. Rough looking bunch." He laughed, "I heard General Sherman wanted to get rid of 'em fast as he could.

Can't say as I blame him."

Philip reached across the counter and grabbed the man by the front of his shirt, and in his clipped British accent demanded, "Watch your tongue man. My fiancée was in that group. Now you tell me exactly where they are."

"Sorry, mister, you don't exactly look like someone who would be courting one of those women. Must have been some I didn't see."

"Never mind that, tell me where they are!"

"They ain't here."

"What do you mean they are not here?" Philip shouted, fatigue and worry taking its toll.

"That's just what I mean. The general shipped them all outa here. You're too late."

Philip's heart fell, "Where were they shipped to?"

"North is all I know."

"Who could tell me where?"

"All the officers in charge of those women have left town. Gearing up for a battle south of here, I reckon. They were housed down at the Georgia Military Institute until they were put on trains. Guess you could go there to see if anybody is left who could give you some information. Some of the troops are still here. They left me here to man the desk because of the hospital and all."

Philip took the steps to the Military Institute two at a time his heart pounding. The door creaked on its hinges as he entered the large empty hall. Bits of trash littered the floor and the building appeared deserted. His shoulders slumped in defeat. "Too late," he muttered aloud. "What am I to do?"

Just then footsteps sounded down the hallway and paused just out of view. A raspy voice shouted out the window, "Private, you make sure you place those items on the train bound for Boston with my name on them. If I am missing one item when I get home, I personally will have your hide. Do I make myself clear?"

Philip heard rather than saw the soldier respond, "Yes, sir, Colonel Turner. I shall make certain these items arrive safely."

Philip turned the corner and almost collided with the colonel.

The officer looked up at Philip with a scowl. "Can I help you? What are you doing here anyway? These buildings are off limits to all rebel civilians."

"Except for innocent women and children who have been charged with treason?"

Turner's eyes widened. Then an evil smirked parted his thin lips. "By your accent I perceive you're not a rebel civilian."

"That's correct, and I demand some answer," Philip all but shouted, fatigue and the heat taking its toll on him.

Turner turned toward the door and said over his shoulder in dismissal, "I'd be very careful with your accusations, Mister. As far as demanding answers, I don't think your accent will garner you any special favors this time. Now, I'm busy and will be on my way."

"Oh, yes, I heard. You must oversee the contraband you have stolen."

Turner halted and turned toward Philip. "And you are?"

"I am Lord Philip Duval , and I am looking for my fiancée."

Turner gave a derisive laugh. "Would that be a Miss Elizabeth Donahue?"

Hope ignited. "The very same. Where is she? I have come for her."

Turner looked him up and down remaining silent for a moment, a malicious light in his eyes, and then sighed in triumph. "Well, Lord Phillip Duval, you are about two days too late. That little lady is on her way north, and I'm not at liberty to tell you where, even if I knew."

Anger glinted in Philip's eyes as he took a step forward. "You will tell me."

Turner retreated a step, the smile wiped from his face as he encountered the look on the golden giant's face. Dwarfed by the young British lord, Turner realized a fight with this angry Goliath would not end in his favor, and there was no one to call for help. The building stood empty except for the two of them. "I don't know where they went. Only that General Sherman sent them north."

Philip stepped closer. "You know, or you will find out."

"As you can see we are moving out. I must join my men. Anyway you had best be careful. General Sherman is not in any mood to put up with Rebel sympathizers who masquerade as loyal British subjects. The young woman in question had ample opportunity to avoid arrest but would not."

"With what is she charged?"

"Treason and harboring fugitives. You better be glad that she is traveling north instead of dangling at the end of a rope. I must warn you that if you continue this harassment and falsely accusing our army, then you will experience grave consequences. We have already arrested a Frenchman, and he barely escaped a noose. So being a foreigner will offer you small protection. Now I will be on my way."

"Not so fast, colonel. Which train was she on, and what was its destination?"

"I do not know. She told me you would be coming for her."

"And you arrested her anyway?" Philip shouted.

"As I have already told you, titles of foreigners mean little to me. You best go on back to England. By the time that little lady reaches her destination, I doubt seriously that you will want her."

Philip took a step toward him, smoldering anger threatened to erupt and ruin any chance he might have to find Elizabeth. Who did this popinjay think he was? He drew himself up to full height, towered over the vile officer. The warm blue light in his eyes turned to icy daggers as he said quietly, "I will find her and you, Colonel, will not escape retribution for the barbaric deed that you have done."

"I was under orders," Turner responded, his voice less confident.

"Orders or not. The deed is indefensible. And one way or another you will pay for this."

"I would be careful how I spoke to an occupying officer, if I were you."

"You disgrace the very word officer," Philip ground between clinched teeth.

A malevolent smile parted Turner's thin lips. "War is war and is not meant to be a genteel garden party."

"These women and children had nothing to do with the war except to try to survive."

"I beg your pardon. Their husbands were fighting in the rebellion, and they were supplying the troops."

"They were trying to earn enough money to feed their children and as for Elizabeth, she was a bona fide refugee who was exiled from her home. I find it hard to believe that General Sherman considered the consequences his order would put into play. Where is he?"

"He has moved out and understood completely what he was ordering. I followed his orders explicitly."

"Including stealing to line your own pockets? I think he would be highly interested in what is in those wagons."

Fear flashed in Turner's eyes for a moment, then he turned to leave and said over his shoulder, "Like I said before, spoils of war go to the conqueror. I have nothing to tell you about the whereabouts of your fiancée. My suggestion is that you catch the first train north if you really want to find her."

"North? Which train?"

"How would I know? Just north!"

"Were all the detainees scheduled for the same destination?"

"How many times do I have to tell you? I have no idea and could care less." Turner shouted as he pushed through the door.

Philip reached him in two strides and grabbed his arm. "This is not the end of this conversation. This war won't last forever, and you will be held accountable."

"Are you threatening me, an officer of the United States Army? You are skating on thin ice, mister. I could call my men and have you arrested on the spot and hanged if I so choose."

"We both know you won't do that. You have too much to hide to allow me to go to court."

Turner placed a hand on his side arm. "Yes, well, maybe a bullet would be the better choice."

"And cause an international incident? I have here a letter from the President of the United States giving me complete immunity. Do you really want to take on your President?"

Turner turned his back on Philip without replying and stomped down the steps and out into the dusty street.

The train chugged out of the station, its destination Nashville, Tennessee. Philip settled in for the long ride, his heart pumping. "Would she be there? Would he find her in time?"

After his conversation with Turner, Philip had visited the many hospitals in town hoping that somehow Elizabeth had managed to escape the long journey north and was ministering to the wounded.

Each makeshift hospital he visited met with disappointment. No Elizabeth and no knowledge of what had happened to her or the other captives. Finally, after he had almost given up hope, he wandered into a larger home now converted into an infirmary and spotted Tim Hutson.

Bone weary, Tim was making his last rounds before he could get a break. He had heard that the battle for Atlanta was on the verge of starting. If he were to get any rest, he would have to take it soon. He collapsed in a chair just beside the open door, hoping to get an errant breeze to cool his flushed cheeks. The humidity clung like a hot wet blanket and the reek of torn and wounded flesh made it difficult to breathe. He bent forward, dropping his head in his hands. The July's blistering heat combined with the body heat of the wounded made his job almost unbearable. He often wondered what had possessed him to stay in North Georgia and not return to Boston. He knew. She had hair of spun gold and eyes like a summer sky. Her hands were like a ministering angel and her voice like a melody of the morning. And she belonged to another. Even now in the midst of the heat and labor, her vision would not leave him. He sighed and shook his head. His heart as well as his body ached from fatigue, one from the work, the other from longing for something that was denied him.

A hand touched his shoulder rousing him from his brooding. He looked up into blue eyes that mirrored the pain in his own. Philip stood above him anguish burning in his eyes.

"Philip, what are you doing here?" then fear gripped Tim, "What has happened? Is there anything I can do?"

Philip sighed and plopped down in the chair beside him, "I hope so."

"Tell me." Tim encouraged.

"Have you seen Elizabeth?"

Tim shook his head, a puzzled look in his eyes, "No, is she in Marietta?"

"I don't know where she might be. I've looked everywhere. No one has any information on her. I thought she might be helping in the hospital."

"She did assist me earlier, but she and Laura left before the Union forces occupied Marietta. I assume she is at Sweetwater," the doctor explained.

Philip shook his head. Disappointment overwhelmed him. "Then you didn't know."

"Know what?" Tim asked.

"Sweetwater has been burned. All the operatives of the mill have been arrested and sent north."

"Surely not Elizabeth and where is Laura, er the family?"

"In Savannah. They evacuated before the troops arrested the people and burned everything."

Relief warred with disappointment in Tim as he heard the news. He was glad that Laura was safe, but the distance between them proved a finality that he was still unable to accept. He shook himself and asked, suddenly attentive to Philip's anguish, "And Elizabeth was not with them?"

"No. She went back for something she had forgotten, and while she was there, they arrested her."

"Surely they would let her go. She is a fugitive in exile, not a mill operative."

"I had hoped that was the case, but I had a confrontation with the officer in charge, and he insisted that she was sent away, but claims to have no information as to where. I was hoping beyond hope that she might have been released and would be working, but she isn't." Philip dropped his head, his erect posture stooped with defeat.

"Let me see what I can find out. I had only heard snatches about the arrests. As you can see I have been very busy. There were a few young women who were among the operatives, and they have been doing laundry for the hospitals. They may know something. Let me call them in," Tim said.

In only a brief while, Tim returned with two women following him. "These women were arrested also but by the generosity and compassion of General Dodge escaped the exile north."

Philip turned toward them, lifting an inquisitive brow, his eyes intent, "Have you seen Elizabeth?"

"We saw a very beautiful woman whom Colonel Turner treated especially cruel. She was in our wagon and lodged at the Military Institute. I heard that she left in the first trainload sent north. I don't know how she will fair. We were told that the horrible man refused to let her bring even a change of clothes. At least the rest of us were allowed to bring what we could carry in our arms. I don't know what the lady will do, no clothes, no money." Both ladies shook their heads, sorrow darkening their ebony eyes.

Philip grit his teeth trying to bring his emotions under control. "Do you possibly know where the train was going?"

"We heard it was Nashville, but that was only a rumor."

Philip dropped his head, defeat outlined in the droop of his broad shoulders.

Timothy touched him on the arm, bringing him back to the moment. "Philip, I believe there is an afternoon train for Chattanooga. Perhaps you should take it. She is not here. Maybe you can find her there or maybe north in Nashville."

The train lurched forward on its slow trip to Chattanooga, and Elizabeth braced herself as best she could on the wooden bench fashioned from a single board. Her back hurt and her clothes clung to her in the unbearable heat. She tried to lift her head to catch a breeze from one of the two narrow windows in the car. But it was no use; her seat was too far back. At least she had a seat. Many were seated on the straw covering the floor. The stench of animal droppings beneath the hay combined with the odor of unwashed bodies fouled the air until nausea boiled up in Elizabeth's throat. She buried her nose against her shoulder as best she could, but nothing helped.

She raised her head and looked around her. For a moment she forgot her own discomfort as she watched the mothers imprisoned in this car trying to comfort their children. Some whimpered, others wailed. Their little faces were flushed from the intolerable heat. How could she, or anyone, survive this torturous trip? The heat, the smells, no privacy, and hunger gnawed at her insides, but the very thought of food in this environment churned her stomach even more. If she were hungry, the little ones must be ravenous.

After a brief rest stop in Chattanooga where the detainees were given time to eat their meager rations in the open air, they were herded into another train headed for Nashville. The conditions proved no better than the last, but physical exhaustion found Elizabeth nodding off to sleep.

This time she had managed to get a seat in the back of the car, and she leaned back against the hard metal wall. Although located further from the window, darkness and traveling north brought a welcome coolness to the air. Most of her fellow occupants this time were younger women without small children. This journey provided a quieter ride with only the grumble of adults disturbing the rhythmic strike of wheel against rail, which finally lured an exhausted Elizabeth into an uneasy sleep.

Finally, the tortuous trip ended, and once again like mindless animals, soldiers steered them out of the boxcars into a cavernous room. With only a few benches to accommodate up to four hundred women along with their children and a few male passengers, most found seats on the floor as they waited to find out what their fate might be.

After hours of waiting a young officer along with one aide strode into the room. Despite his youth, his face bore the strain of war, and his rumpled clothing bespoke a hectic night that denied his sleep. He took off his dark blue wool cap with two leather braids signifying he had already attained the rank of captain. The gold insignia of crossed sabers marked him as a cavalryman. No wonder he appeared distressed. A horseman on foot and having to deal with women and children! It had to be the ultimate frustration for a man who was accustomed to battle. Despite his blue uniform Elizabeth felt a brief pity for the young man. Clearly someone assigned him a role he felt great reluctance in carrying out.

"May I have your attention, please?" His pleasant baritone commanded.

The room responded with the exception of a baby here and there who would wail briefly before being silenced. Over four hundred faces looked up at the captain with hopeful eyes. Maybe this could be the end of the nightmare. Maybe they were to be released. Nashville was a long way from home but not an impossible distance.

Elizabeth took heart. When Philip heard what had happened, he could catch a train and find her. She looked down at her filthy attire and shuddered. How could she meet him in this condition? Would he even want her now?

She shook her head. No money, no clothes, and soon to be no food. Perhaps she could find work until he came. Her hand went to her throat and rested on the ring beneath her bodice. She could sell it and buy both food and clothing. How could she face him if the ring were gone? That was the very reason she remained corralled here in this place with all these other unfortunate people. Would he understand? How could he? One would have to experience this nightmare to understand it.

A groan rippled across the room, bringing Elizabeth back to the present. "What did he say?" She whispered to the young girl on her right.

"We are being shipped to Louisville and maybe across the river to Indiana."

Elizabeth's heart fell, "All of us? Why?"

"General Sherman's orders are to ship us north where we can do no more harm. As if we were doing harm!" Disgust and anger distorted her face. "This captain said they have no room for us in Nashville prisons, and the city is already filled with more refugees than they can accommodate."

"What shall they do with us up there?"

"He claims that if we pledge an oath of loyalty to the union, we can go to work in factories up there."

"Why not here?"

"They don't need any more factory workers here. How do we know there would be any up north even if we pledged an oath of loyalty? You know and I know, we pose a problem here that they just want to get rid of. If they turn us loose, we will die of hunger. If they imprison us they have to provide for us. What a dumb thing Sherman did when he arrested all of us. All I can hope is that it all comes back to haunt him."

"Oh, dear, will our loved ones ever be able to find us?"

"Be a lot harder because I doubt they are keeping records. Of course someone like me wont' be having anyone look for them," she sighed.

"You are one of the women from Roswell, aren't you?" Elizabeth asked.

"Right. My name is Annie. Me and my two sisters were left alone. Our pa and ma worked in the mill. When the war came, Pa got conscripted; and after he had gone Ma died of consumption. That just left me and my sisters to work in the mill."

"And where is your father now?"

"He got kilt in one of them battles."

"I am so sorry. Where are your sisters?"

"They ran away in the woods and hid. I went back to the house to get this locket that was my Ma's and that's when they nabbed me," the young woman explained.

Elizabeth nodded. "Same thing happened to me."

"Do you reckon we put too much stock in things?"

"I don't think it was the article but the person it stood for."

"I reckon you are right. Only now I wish I had high tailed it out of there like my sisters."

"Perhaps they will look for you."

"No, they ain't got the money or the way to even if the war was over. If'n I survive and can find a job or get married, I might can find my way back home," she sighed, " But right now the predicament we are in wipes out all my concern for the future. Do you think you can stand another train ride like the last two?"

"It will be very hard. But just think of the hardship of those women who have little children."

"I know that's the truth. We could try to escape!"

"Then what would we do? I hate to mention it, but we don't look our best! Who would hire us?"

Annie giggled. "You got a point, don't smell like rose blossoms either. I guess we will have to endure this journey and hope that at the end of it we find a bath and some food and clothes. Uh oh! He's lining them up. Looks as if we are going to be at the last of the line. No choice of a better place to sit for the likes of us."

The crowd moved out, three abreast and crowded into the boxcars awaiting them. The procession slowed and finally came to a halt twenty women in front of Elizabeth and her new friend. "What you reckon is going on now? I'm ready to get on with it. The sooner we leave the sooner we will know what's gonna happen."

The young officer marched over to the last car and climbed into the doorway, "What's going on in here? We still have a score of women who stand outside. Can't you make room for them?"

Suddenly he turned and jumped down as his aide closed the door behind him. He motioned toward Elizabeth and the group waiting.

"You people come with me."

Hope ignited in Elizabeth. Maybe something could be worked out after all. Maybe they could stay in Nashville. "What are your plans for us, officer?" Elizabeth asked.

"I plan to tell my general we have a problem. That's all the plan I have."

"Could we wait where we could get a bath and maybe a change of clothing?" Elizabeth pressed her hands against her soiled skirt.

The young captain looked at her a moment then burst out laughing, "Lady, you must be jesting. I don't even have a crumb of bread to give you. My main concern is how I am going to dispose of you and carry out General Sherman's orders."

"I was not jesting. I am under arrest by mistake."

"Sure you are. All four hundred of you are! Or that's what I have been hearing over and over. Now please return to the group while I report to my commander."

Night turned into day as Elizabeth, Annie and the other women waited, huddled on the floor wondering what was to be their fate and measuring out and eating the measly rations of the food given to them days before. They didn't know how long they would be detained or if they would be fed.

Three days later the young captain returned, the harried expression on his face unchanged. This time two burly men not in uniform followed him. "Since we lacked the space to place you on the trains going to Louisville, and the following trains were needed by our troops, some of you will be transported by water to Louisville and others of you to Indiana."

"Which of us will go where?" Annie asked.

"I have no idea nor do I care. All I know is that you will be transported by water. Our boats have already left the dock, but when we contacted them, they agreed to wait mid river to take you onboard. However, it will mean transporting you by dinghy five at a time to the waiting boat. These men will be manning the dinghies.

Elizabeth shuddered at the thought of being in a small dinghy in such close contact with either of the evil looking men. She watched as they took in each woman, leering at them and felt their eyes on her even as she dropped hers. She feared that they were in for an unpleasant ride. She hoped it would be a short one.

There was no pushing and shoving to load into the dinghy. In fact the reluctance of the women provoked the tallest of the men to curse them as he jerked their arms forcing them forward. Finally he had his allotted five aboard a craft made for four at the most. He made way to shove off when he spotted Elizabeth and shouted to her, "Hey, you! Get aboard."

She shook her head, protesting, "You already have more than your limit. Do you want to sink her and drown all aboard?"

"Tis a good craft and you best get aboard right now. I would hate to have to come after you."

"There is nowhere to sit."

"There's plenty of room in my lap." He laughed.

"I'll not be sitting in your lap or any other," Elizabeth objected.

"You will be doing as I bid or find yourself at the bottom of this river, maid," he threatened.

Her new friend who had been the last to load, whispered, "Come on, Elizabeth. It's just a short distance. I will move over. You can sit by me."

The mammoth of a man grabbed Elizabeth by the waist and plunked her into the boat, setting it to rocking fiercely. The ale on his breath revealed the source of his careless actions.

She nestled in next to Annie who took her hand. Elizabeth noticed that hers trembled. Would they even make it mid stream and down the few hundred yards where the converted steamboat waited? There was nothing she could do now. Her safety and the safety of the others rested in God's hands.

The small boat rode low in the water from its overload and progressed slowly as the drunken man rowed them down stream and then across the current. With each splash of the oars, the water that drenched Elizabeth landed in the boat, making it all the more hazardous. Finally the dinghy reached its destination, and the waiting vessel dropped a rope ladder for them to climb aboard. One by one the women took hold of the bottom rung and clambered to the top where sailors gave the soaked women a hand up. Finally Elizabeth's turn arrived, and just as she stood up to reach for the ladder, the beefy oarsman lost his balance. Grabbing for Elizabeth, he turned the small craft over, dumping both into the swirling dark waters of the Cumberland River.

The murky water closed over her head as her skirts wrapped around her legs. Down, down she went. Her chest felt as if it would explode. It was no use. She had learned to swim as a youngster, but the current was too strong, the river too deep, and she was too tired. How easy it would be not to fight, just give in... open her mouth and take in the water, give up the struggle. Then she felt the ribbon around her neck move, and a metallic article hit her nose. She grabbed it just as her feet touched bottom. With all the strength she had left, she shoved upwards, ring secured in one hand, her other fighting for the surface. Finally the waters parted, and her head broke through. Air, she gulped in a fresh breath filling her tortured lungs, and for a brief moment, she glimpsed the large hulk of the boat upstream from her. What was she to do? She had not the strength to swim against the current. Even if she made it to the boat, how would they know she was there?

While she pondered her predicament, the current swept her further downstream as she treaded water. Her long skirts threatened to pull her under again, and she was rapidly losing strength. Just as she was about to go beneath the surface again, a journey she knew would be her last, something solid nudged her shoulder. She grasped a wide plank, probably the remains of some ill-fated craft. With her last ounce of strength she pulled part of her body up out of the water and rested on the makeshift raft. She clung to it as the waters swept her further and further downstream and away from any hope of rescue.

Chapter
Twenty-Two

"What do you mean there is no train to Nashville tonight? My fiancée has been taken by mistake and is on her way to Nashville with a group that Sherman had arrested."

"I'm truly sorry, sir, but all civilian transportation tonight has been suspended. The Army needs the cars because of precisely what you are talking about. The transporting of all those mill employees has impeded the supplies our forces need and also we have troops that we need to move. The next train available leaves tomorrow afternoon."

Phillip shrugged, his usual sunny disposition dark and threatening. "If anything happens to my fiancée because of this senseless arrest, somebody's head will fall. I will personally see to that if I have to go all the way to the President."

"May I remind you, sir, the President is in favor of whatever will bring this war to a satisfactory conclusion."

"I hardly think that arresting and torturing innocent women and children would qualify as a satisfactory conclusion to anyone but that demented Sherman."

The young officer looked around nervously and whispered, "Sir, those words could get you arrested. I can understand how upset you must be, but kindly consider the position you are putting me in. I would be expected to arrest you for a disloyal statement like that."

Phillip let his breath out slowly in an attempt to calm himself. "I have been without sleep for thirty hours, I fear for my fiancée's life, and I am a bit fractious."

"A bit! Why don't you get you a nice hotel room if you can find anything available and get a good night's rest."

"I will not rest until I have my Elizabeth back with me under my protection. I should never have left her. But how did I know that some..."

"Careful sir."

"That she would truly be in harm's way," Phillip amended, gritting his teeth.

The next afternoon came and went without passage to Nashville being available. When he did arrive in Nashville three days later, he found no Elizabeth and no information about her except that all had been shipped north to Louisville. After another three days delay, Philip found himself on a train headed for Louisville and what he hoped would be the last leg of his journey. Hope bubbled up in him as he neared the train station in Louisville. Surely before nightfall, he would have her in his arms, never to let her go again.

"I don't know what it is, suh. But something has washed up on shore down yonder. I don't spec' you be wantin' to go down there with me to see what it might be."

"Why, Evan, you're not afraid are you?" Adam Sinclair asked his employee as they paused on a bluff overlooking a secluded sandy beach below them. Sandbars in the Cumberland River slowed its tempo as it flowed by his large estate and marked its southern most boundary.

"No, Suh, but you can't never be too careful. I've heard of them 'river haints.' "

"River haints?"

"Yas, suh. They bees the haints of all them peoples who done drown in that river."

Sinclair's green eyes sparkled with vitality as he threw back his head and laughed. "I wouldn't miss this for the world. Let's go meet one of your 'river haints,' Evan."

"Now you no need to dismiss my warnings, Mr. Adam. I hear tell of those 'river haints' a killin' and a robbin' good folks like you."

"Well if they are 'haints,' why would they rob people? Seems to me they wouldn't have much need for money," Adam teased.

"I don't know, Mr. Adam. I jest been hearing sech tales fer a long time now."

"Maybe I shouldn't go down there, Evan. I might just get hurt, and we wouldn't want that," Adam observed, struggling to control his amusement at such absurd nonsense.

"Naw, Suh. I didn't mean you shouldn't go down there with me. Just mean you, I mean we, need to be careful."

Adam nodded his head, mischief lighting the amber lights in his eyes. "Oh, I see. As long as you are there to protect me, then everything should be alright."

"I was more thinking if the both'n us went together, it would be heap more safe."

His employer nodded his head as he headed his powerful black stallion down the treacherous pathway leading to the river. Evan stayed a good distance behind, his eyes so wide, the whites formed a vivid frame around the ebony in them.

"Oh, my, Mister Adam. That ain't no haint. That be a dead girl."

"I think you may be right, Evan. Wonder what in the world a girl was doing in the river?"

Adam dismounted and approached the form lying partially on a wide waterlogged plank. He bent down to turn the girl over, and she groaned.

Evan, who had also dismounted and followed Adam, screeched, "You hear that, Mr. Adam? Sho nuff, she ain't jest dead she is a haint."

"Hush, Evan," Adam commanded as he leaned over Elizabeth and touched his hand to her mouth. "She's alive, but barely. I feel her breath, she is only unconscious. I don't know how badly she is injured, but she needs assistance. We'll have to carry her up by horseback since we can't get the carriage or a wagon down here."

"I'll strap her on my horse and lead it back, Mr. Adam," Evan offered.

"No, I will hold her in front of me, and we will ride back to the house."

"You gonna get mighty dirty, Mr. Adam. She be covered in mud," Evan observed without volunteering his services.

"Nothing that won't wash," Adam muttered as he picked up her hand.

"What's this?" He asked as he prized her cold fingers open to reveal a sapphire ring encrusted with diamonds. "Oh, oh, we must have a little thief here. Probably she was trying to get away with it and fell into the river. I have heard of some pretty rough goings on in Nashville. Perhaps she is one of those 'women of the street' that I have been hearing about. You know the government is issuing them a license?"

"Sho nuff?" Evan asked, his eyes still wide with wonder, still not convinced that the body was not a 'haint.'

"Sho nuff," Sinclair mocked gently. He had been trying to help Evan with his diction, but in all the excitement old habits surfaced. "They claim they had to do that so that they could force them to have a doctor's certificate in order to protect the soldiers."

"I do declare, Mr. Adam. What in the world is this country coming too?"

"I know, Evan, it's bad business from which nothing good can come only heartache. How many of those men who consort with these women have wives and sweethearts at home whom they expect to wait faithfully for them?" Adam shook his head; sadness touched his warm green eyes. "Now as to our visitor, when she comes to, we'll try to get to the bottom of this and return this beautiful piece to its rightful owner. For the moment I'll take care of it, " Sinclair said as he put the ring in his pocket. "We may have to call the sheriff. Meanwhile, let's get her back to the house, get Aunt Lucy to oversee cleaning her up and perhaps call Dr. Bannister just in case. Maybe after a bath and some warm clothes she will answer some questions. Although she probably won't tell us the truth."

"Nah suh. You can't expect the truth from them kind of wimmen." Evan agreed.

"There, there, my pet," the woman crooned softly. "It's time to wake up."

Elizabeth opened one eye and then the other. She reclined in the center of a large poster bed dressed with exquisite linens. Gossamer curtains covering the wall of windows opposite the bed rippled in a cool and refreshing breeze laced with the fragrance of lilacs. Surrounding the massive bed, carved furnishings of walnut bespoke of wealth and elegance. She gingerly turned her head toward a slender, silver haired lady who sat by her side holding her hand. The woman, probably in her early seventies, had the kindest countenance she had ever encountered. "Where am I?" Elizabeth croaked with a voice strange to her ears.

"Welcome back!" the silver haired lady exclaimed. "You are a miracle lady!"

"What happened?"

"You are at my nephew, Adam Sinclair's estate. You washed up on shore sometime yesterday. He found you on the sandy beach unconscious, and you've been unconscious until now. Who are you, and where did you come from?"

Fear darkened Elizabeth's eyes as the memory of incarceration and accusations of treason flooded her mind. What should she tell her benefactor? She was an escaped prisoner. If she told her, would they send her back? Finally she said, "I am a refugee."

"Refugee from where?"

How should she answer that? It was obvious this lady was not Southern by birth. If she admitted she had arrived from Georgia would they know she was a prisoner, not a refugee? "Originally I came from Virginia."

"Virginia? How did you get in the Cumberland River?"

A rue smile lifted one side of Elizabeth's mouth, as she croaked, licking her swollen lips, "The dinghy capsized, and I nearly drowned. In fact I thought I had! To open my eyes in this place almost seemed as if I were in Heaven. Clean clothes, warm bedding, how can this be?"

"Oh my dear! How long were you in the water?"

"I have no idea. The last thing I remember was floating with a plank supporting me. I was so hungry, and I thought that I was dying, then just nothing."

"And you very nearly did. I'm sure the good Lord guided that board onto that beach in just the nick of time."

"It had to be Him as I had no resources left."

"You didn't say how you got here from Virginia."

"It's a long story."

The lovely lady nodded her head as if understanding and stood up. "And we will hear it at a more convenient time. Meanwhile my name is Lucy Sinclair, Aunt Lucy to most, and I want you to concentrate on getting well. We will sort out the rest when you are stronger. I think I hear May Beth bringing up your dinner."

Elizabeth nodded. "That, too, sounds heavenly. Food. A privilege never considered before this horrible war disrupted our lives. I will never take it for granted again."

Lucy Sinclair frowned, as she thought of her nephew's assumption concerning this young woman's identity. As astute as he was, she believed with all her heart this time he had made a mistake in his evaluation. In every aspect, the young woman appeared to be a well-bred lady. But then there was the ring to be considered. A jewel of great value clutched in her hand could not be taken lightly. But she knew Adam and had the greatest confidence that he would get to the

388

bottom of this diligently and fairly.

After two days of bed rest and proper food, Elizabeth regained strength and was able to dress and venture out from the room that had been her abode for the past few days. Lucy suggested that she take a short stroll around the rose garden to test her stamina. She warned her not to try too much the first day.

So for the next few days, Elizabeth's morning ritual was a stroll around the rose garden, increasing her walking time each day until she almost felt back to normal. She asked Aunt Lucy where her nephew was because she wanted to thank him for rescuing her.

Lucy Sinclair frowned, then laughed and told her that he was away on business. She wasn't sure exactly when he would return, but there would be ample opportunity for her to thank him.

She looked forward to meeting the master of the house. Lucy had stirred her curiosity about this stranger who appeared something between Sir Galahad and Solomon in his aunt's eyes.

It would be well into two weeks before Elizabeth would meet her benefactor. In the meantime she had regained not only her strength but some of her weight back. Somehow Lucy had found a couple of lovely dresses that one of the servants had altered to fit her. What a glorious feeling to be clean, well dressed and well fed.

She pulled her dark hair, now full and lovely again, up into a nest of ringlets that escaped and framed her face. Her pastel gown enhanced her brown eyes bringing out amber lights with only the hint of sadness dulling their sparkle. For even though she rejoiced in her miraculous rescue, her future remained unsure. Where could she go from here? Would her future reside in the hands of a stranger, this Adam Sinclair? Would he dictate her fate? Lucy Sinclair assured her that she had no worries because Sinclair was a good man and would take care of her. But would he send her back to prison if he knew the truth? Assisting rebels carried a severe penalty.

And where was Phillip? Could he ever find her? If he did locate her, how could she tell him that somewhere in the swirling waters of the Cumberland River lay his ring? How could she ever face him now? Had her hope for lasting happiness been lost somewhere between Sweetwater and this magnificent estate on the Cumberland River? She shuddered and turned from the fragrant roses toward the palatial home. Inside quite possibly her whole future would be decided.

"Elizabeth, Adam has arrived and wants to see you in the drawing room." Lucy Sinclair announced. Her usual effervescence marred by a frown.

"Is there something amiss, Miss Sinclair?" Elizabeth asked, her heart racing.

Lucy's attempt at a reassuring smile fell flat. "Nothing that can't be sorted out. Just tell Adam the truth, dear. He is a generous and kind man who will do the right thing by you. You must be open and truthful with him. The one thing he has no patience with is prevarication."

Elizabeth frowned. "I have no intention of lying to your nephew."

Lucy nodded her head. "I'm sure, my dear. I just wish we had taken the time to sort things out when it was just the two of us. Then I could have been more assistance to both you and Adam."

Elizabeth followed the tall, willowy woman into the drawing room, her heart in her throat. What had happened to disturb this kind lady who had befriended her? Lucy abruptly stepped to the side, leaving Elizabeth to face a handsome giant with large green eyes and copper hair.

Their eyes locked, and for a moment silence reigned. Then Sinclair took a deep breath and remarked, "My, my, my, you do clean up well."

Elizabeth stepped forward and offered her hand. "Mr. Adam Sinclair, I presume? I am Elizabeth Donahue from Winchester, Virginia."

Sinclair stepped back. A frown wrinkled the wide space between his intense green eyes, "That was quite a trip astride a wide board all the way from Virginia."

"Of course that is not how I arrived from Virginia."

He cocked his head and gave her a grave look. "And just how did you arrive from Virginia?"

"By train. How else?"

He gave a mirthless chuckle, "Let's quit playing games, Miss Donahue or whatever your real name is. I know your business, and I am compelled by law to see that you are apprehended."

Elizabeth's face paled, her hand went to her throat, "You may think you know, Mr. Sinclair, but if you think that I have done anything wrong you have reached a mistaken conclusion. I am a refugee from the war in Virginia, and any other conclusion at which you may have arrived is completely false."

"In the first place, Miss, we have no refugees from Virginia in Nashville, Tennessee. Why in the world would one leave the battlefields of Virginia for the battlefields of Tennessee? But be that as it may, I have evidence right here of the nature of your character," Sinclair remarked as he pulled her ring from his pocket.

"Oh!" Elizabeth shouted. "You have found my ring."

"Oh, yes, little miss. I have found someone's ring."

"It is my ring."

"If it were not such a valuable ring, I might believe you received it for services rendered, but I hardly think that even your services, as beautiful as you are, could garner this as payment." Sinclair snarled, her beauty suddenly tantalizing him, making him uneasy.

Elizabeth grabbed for the ring. "It is my ring. It was given to me, and I thought it was in the Cumberland River. My hopes and dreams are wrapped up in that ring."

He jerked it away from her. "I can believe that. Steal it, leave Nashville and your dubious occupation behind, go to a strange town, and sell it for a healthy sum. You would have a nice nest egg for a new life."

"Dubious occupation?" Elizabeth frowned.

"Even though our fair city is issuing permits for the likes of you, that doesn't elevate it to an honorable occupation in my mind."

"I don't know what you mean. That is my ring, given to me by my fiancée."

"Really? And who might that be?"

"Philip ."

"You mean Sir Philip Duval?" Sinclair laughed. "And I'm the Prince of Wales."

"Do you know Sir Philip?" she asked, ignoring his sarcasm.

"I know of him. He is a British duke who has extensive land holdings in Britain and Ireland."

"That's his father. My Philip is an entrepreneur with holdings in Massachusetts and a plantation in Savannah."

"My Philip?"

"Well he would have been my Philip if this war had not interfered. Now I would appreciate it if you would return my property."

"I'm not convinced that this is your property. I think I shall call for the sheriff. He might be very interested in a ring of this value being in the possession of a girl like you."

"I wish you would quit referring to me like that."

"So how should I refer to you?"

"As the lady that I am."

Adam squinted his eyes and gave her a long look, then threw back his head and roared. When he finally regained his composure, he commented, "Someone trained you well. You could almost make me believe there is truth to what you say. I'll bet you do demand a high price but surely not this high! We are back to the ring and the sheriff. Shall I send for him? Or are you going to tell me the truth and to whom this ring belongs? If you will tell me, and I return it to him, perhaps he won't press charges. If he has a missus, I doubt seriously he would want to make this public. If so, I will return you to what you were doing before, and perhaps you will be wiser this time."

Elizabeth eyes widened. If the sheriff were called in he would discover who she was. He surely knew of the women prisoners and the accident. If so, for her it would mean prison and her ring would be lost anyway.

"Please don't call the sheriff. I have told you the truth. The ring is the family ring. Inside you can see their crest engraved on the band. The son gave it too me. Please return it to him."

"Easier said than done. But if you are telling me the truth, then I shall endeavor to return it to him. I don't know what the circumstances were which found him here and involved with you, but that remains his affair, not mine. I doubt seriously that he would bring charges if he gets his property back. It would not be publicity that he would want for a man in his position. The next question is what am I to do with you? There is no reason not to send you back where you came from."

"Where I came from?"

"Oh, yes. I know how you came to be in the river."

Elizabeth's eyes widened, fear trembled her lips, a reaction that Sinclair didn't miss. "What did you hear?"

"It seems that for some reason the boat headed for Louisville with a few troops aboard was delayed mid river, and some ruffians ferried you and your friends out for the pleasure of the troops aboard. One of the boats capsized dumping you and one of the hooligans into the river. Neither of which was ever found...until now."

A relieved flush tinted Elizabeth's face. He only thought he knew the truth. Then reality rushed in, and her hand went to her throat. Would he send her back to Nashville to the unspeakable life he thought she was a part of?

Sinclair continued, "Now the big question is what am I to do with you? Obviously our esteemed government considers yours a lawful occupation since they licensed it, but I, for one, have a problem supporting it. I look at you and my question is could you be rehabilitated? Obviously you wanted out, or you wouldn't have risked your very life to steal something of this great value." Sinclair rubbed his chin, his large eyes squinting.

Lucy Sinclair who had remained silent throughout the conversation now spoke, "Adam, don't send her back to that kind of life. Who knows what precipitated her decision? When a person is hungry and cold without resources, they can make grave mistakes just trying to survive."

Hope flared in Elizabeth's eyes, "Please don't send me back. I will work for you in any capacity. I will pay you back for your kindness."

"There is the issue of your thievery," Sinclair reminded.

"I have stolen nothing." Elizabeth's eyes were wide and pleading.

Sinclair shook his head, "You are a convincing little minx. If I didn't have the evidence in my hand, you might con even me into believing you."

"Oh, my prayer is that someday you will. But even if you can't, let me stay here, work for you and prove my innocence."

Sinclair looked at his aunt, a brow raised in question.

"Adam, I will take full responsibility for her."

Philip strode the streets of Louisville, stretching his legs as he tried to let the morning air clear his thinking. The walk was anything but pleasant. The largest city in Kentucky was a dirty metropolis on the banks of the Ohio. The atmosphere lay heavy with the stench of hogs running freely through the streets and throngs of refugees clogging the walkways, many of them being forced to beg. His heart pounded with anxiety. Elizabeth had no money, no change of clothes and from what he had been told possessed only nine days of ration when she left Marietta. That would have been consumed long ago. Where was she? How could she survive? He only hoped that she would sell his ring, then perhaps she could purchase her way out. But would she? The protection of his ring resulted in her being in this predicament. Would that he had never sent it!

Now she remained lost to him because of it. Where would he begin his search? All the minor officers with whom he had metso far had little information about the mill women. Although Sherman had ordered the arrest of the women, no formal charges were issued against them so no formal records could be found of their transporting or confinement. Some would say they were one place and then another. But to his dismay, he nor anyone he talked with could find a list of the women and their whereabouts. It was as if they had disappeared, as if they were of so little value no one cared if they survived. After the fact, Philip found out that some of the women were still in Marietta and had never left. The rampant misinformation that he received could have sent him on a wild goose chase, and she might still be in Georgia. If that were true then he had wasted valuable time, and time was not what he had.

As much as he had come to love America, hate for the war and the inhumane decisions that had brought him on this journey rankled his gentle soul. And then there was the urgency of completing his business in Massachusetts and returning home. His father's death had set a whole new set of priorities in place for him. He had to find Elizabeth as quickly as possible. The thought of returning without her seemed intolerable to him; yet, he had other pressing business to attend. On and on his thoughts clambered as he walked the streets of Louisville.

When Laura had been imprisoned, Lincoln had been sympathetic and helped him then. But according to all he had heard recently, the president supported Sherman, condoning all his actions. His goal and Sherman's objective seemed to coincide which was ending the war by whatever means it took. He could count on no help from Washington as long as the war was going Sherman's way.

On and on the unsettling thoughts thrashed within him. After he had been in Louisville for the most part of a week, a young officer with a soft-spoken dialect identifying him as one from Tennessee encouraged him by telling him he had heard that a large group of women which had recently arrived were housed in a newly built hospital building on Broadway Street. Hope aroused, and Philip rushed down

Tenth Street toward the corner of Broadway. If most of the women were transported to a new building, then the conditions must be tolerable. Surely he would find Elizabeth at long last.

What he found was a group of women imprisoned in a new building without water or gas and a large enclosure surrounding it where they could not go in or out. The conditions proved wretched. Small children with faces flushed with fever whimpered in their mother's laps. Without help life expectancy in the dismal conditions was low indeed.

In each long hall and rectangle room, he searched for Elizabeth. Some remembered her, others did not. None saw her board the train in Nashville. Day after day Philip returned to the make shift prison, and questioned women about Elizabeth. Finally one day a woman remembered seeing her standing in line at the station with a girl named Annie. She told him that they were at the last of the line, and they never boarded the train. When he asked her if Annie was in Louisville, she said that she had heard that she was in Evansville, Indiana.

Relieved to leave the squalor of Louisville behind, Philip reached Evansville the following day. Now the search was on to find Annie and maybe Elizabeth. His heart thudded with renewed hope. Maybe today was the day.

Arriving in Evansville, Philip was directed to a refugee camp where tents had been set up to house the refugees temporarily. The conditions mirrored those in Louisville only much worse as most of those confined were too ill to speak with Philip. He turned to leave when a young woman with bright red hair stopped him, "I heard you were looking for Annie. I am Annie. Can you help me?"

Philip's heart broke as he looked at the emaciated young woman.

"I'll do what I can, ma'am. Can you help me?"

"How?"

"I was told that you were with a young woman named Elizabeth in Nashville."

Annie nodded her head as her eyes filled with tears. "Yes, sir. Miss Elizabeth was a kind and beautiful woman who made my stay in Nashville more tolerable."

"Was?" Philip croaked.

"She drowned in the Cumberland River."

"Drowned? How was that possible?"

"They didn't have enough room on the train for all of us so they sent us by the river. They carried us in small boats to the big boat, and the one Miss Elizabeth was on capsized just as she reached the ladder. Both she and the ruffian who carried us out to the middle of the river were lost. No way they could find them in the fast moving river."

Philip's face paled, and he sagged to the ground, placing his head in his hands. Grief growled from his inner most being as the brightest hope of his tomorrows died in the filth of a refugee tent.

Sherman invaded Atlanta southeast of the city on July 22, 1864. After capturing the railroads in order to disrupt supplies to the Southern army, he began a five-week siege of Atlanta. On September 1, General Hood evacuated the city. Jefferson Davis had made what many deemed an unwise decision to sack General Johnston and replace him with Hood. The Confederate president and Johnston had been at odds all through the war. When he deemed Johnston too passive in thwarting Sherman's march through Georgia he made his decision, a common scenario when politicians direct desktop battles and allow their conflicting personalities to influence their judgment and decisions.

Summer floated into fall as Elizabeth settled into her new environment with ease. Despite the harsh realities of the battles raging north in Virginia and south in Georgia, she remained cocooned against what was going on outside her immediate world.

Her accommodations were comfortable, sustenance more than adequate, but it was the warm friendship of Lucy Sinclair that nurtured her spirit. Despite what her nephew believed, Lucy had faith in Elizabeth's character. At every opportunity the kind gentlewoman gave her more and trusted responsibility in running the large household.

At first she worked as a housemaid, taking her meals in the kitchen with the rest of the staff. Elizabeth never complained but continued with a sweet spirit and an efficiency with which even Adam had trouble finding fault. Not many weeks had passed before it was almost as if he had dismissed how she had gotten there and no longer held it against her. Often he complimented her work with a warm friendliness. Sometimes Elizabeth felt his inquisitive green eyes on her, as if he were evaluating more than just her work. He never mentioned the ring again, and she was left to ponder whether or not he had been able to contact Philip.

As week followed week, Elizabeth's hope dimmed that Philip would come for her. At first she hoped that as soon as he received the message, he would come immediately and the whole mess would be cleared up. When he didn't come, all sorts of scenarios filled her mind. What if something had happened to him? What if his father objected so strongly to their marriage that he had given up the idea? Lastly, what if he believed Adam Sinclair's story that she had turned to prostitution as a way to survive? The very thought became so abhorrent to her that she cried out in agony during the night. "Philip, Philip where are you? I have waited and kept my love pure for you. Don't believe a stranger's misjudgment."

By night she sobbed into her pillow. Daylight found her performing her duties with a thankful heart that she wasn't resting at the bottom of the wide river, which flowed just beyond the palatial home that now imprisoned her.

Her respite was her daily walk in the rose garden and the path beyond that led to the bluff overlooking the river. With her duties finished, each day she would stroll in the garden to a bench overlooking the river. Sometimes she would just sit, gazing at the water, while troubling thoughts raced through her mind concerning what might have been. At other more pleasant times she would take a book that she had borrowed out of Sinclair's library with Lucy's permission. Those times proved more productive to her mindset, and she set a goal of reading a book each week to broaden her mind and to guard it against the morass of fear that clamored to claim her spirit.

It was there that Adam found her in late September. He had been going over the estate accounts when restlessness propelled him out of the house and into the garden for a brisk walk. When he discovered Elizabeth perched on one of the benches with book in hand, he came to an abrupt halt, a frown wrinkling his forehead and almost shouted, "Elizabeth! What are you doing here?"

She had been so absorbed in her reading that she had failed to notice him until he spoke. His voice startled her, and she jumped up. "Oh, Mr. Sinclair, I have finished my chores, and Miss Sinclair gave me permission to borrow a book from your library. I hope you don't mind."

Adam cleared his throat, embarrassment at his sharp tone flushed his face. "Of course I don't mind. You just surprised me, that's all."

Elizabeth breathed a sigh of relief and tried to hide a smile as she asked pertly, "Surprised that I was here or that I can read?"

A sheepish grin replaced the frown, and he answered, "Both I guess."

"To answer your question, I find a wonderful quiet respite in coming to this beautiful place, and I can read quite well. My parents insisted on a good education. at least the kind women are supposed to get these days," and pausing she added, "or before the war, that is."

"And what kind of education is that?" Sinclair asked her, his curiosity suddenly aroused.

Elizabeth grinned as one who understood she had suddenly gained the upper hand in the conversation. "How to run an elegant household and to fulfill the role of a proper wife and hostess."

"So that explains it."

Elizabeth cocked her head, not understanding. "Explains what?"

"Your expertise in all matters concerning the management of a home. I've watched you. You do far more than a regular maid. I've observed you setting the table. Never a question of what goes where. I know that you have arranged all the flowers that are picked daily and that you have even planned the meals. In fact, you have taken over most of Aunt Lucy's duties and with finesse I might add."

"Thank you."

"However that leaves a greater puzzle."

"And that would be?"

"Your former occupation and the theft of that ring."

"Why must you insist on believing that lie!" Elizabeth all but shouted.

"Because I investigated and found the answers. I found out how and why you were in that river. Also, I have yet to hear from Philip . His failure to respond is an indictment in itself. I can only assume that the loss of that ring is preferable to admitting his sordid relationship with you."

Tears stung Elizabeth's eyes at his harsh words as she dropped her head. "Believe what you will, Mr. Sinclair, but the ring is mine, and the relationship with Philip was anything but sordid."

"I can see we will never come to common ground on this issue, so on the basis of the present and the assistance you have been to my aunt, I have a proposition for you."

"And what might that be?" Elizabeth's usual sweet tones dripped acid.

"That's no way to begin a discussion on your future. I'll have to admit, I was reluctant to keep you here, but my conscience wouldn't allow me to send you back to your former life. I doubted the wisdom of trying to rehabilitate you. But I was wrong, and my aunt was right. The experiment has turned out quite nicely."

Elizabeth's ebony eyes turned to steel. "Well, pat yourself on the back, Mr. Sinclair."

Shock dropped Sinclair's chin. "Why you ungrateful little wench!"

Elizabeth's eyes widened, and she mocked, "Sharper than a serpent's tooth to have a thankless child."

"But you are not my child," Adam objected, stunned that she could quote Shakespeare to him.

"That's right! I'm an experiment! Or am I an additional accolade of goodness to crown your achievements!"

"Woman!" Adam shouted. "Can I never get through to you? I was about to offer you the position as companion to my aunt, to sit at our table, to join our functions as a member of our household. In short you have gained my trust. Now if you would just admit the truth all issues would be settled."

Elizabeth dropped her head in a mock bow. "Thank you, your lordship. This undeserving maid is grateful for your kind beneficence."

Adam ran his hand through his thick hair, then lifted both hands in defeat. With his voice quieter, now under control he responded, "Elizabeth, I can see that we are far apart on some issues."

"There is truth to that as long as you want me to confess to a lie. I was not a prostitute, and I did not steal that ring."

"Then explain the information I found when I investigated."

"You received wrong information."

"It was verified by three people, one of them the sheriff. And then there is the issue of a non-response from Philip ."

Pain brightened Elizabeth's eyes as she raised her chin with defiance, and spoke through clinched teeth, "I can't answer why you received wrong information or why you have not heard from Philip. But this one thing I do know. I am not the woman you think I am."

A strange light brightened Adam's eyes, and he said nothing for a long while. His intense gaze caused Elizabeth to drop her head, all defiance suddenly draining from her. She turned from him, her small shoulders drooping in defeat and missed the momentary longing that touched the eyes fastened on her.

With October's arrival the iridescent orange, reds and gold of fall denied the fierce battles raging in Virginia. The month proved a respite for both Elizabeth and Georgia. While Sherman secured his bases and prepared for his tortuous slash and burn journey through

Georgia, Elizabeth settled seamlessly into her new role as companion to the older Sinclair. She ate at the dining room table with Adam and Lucy as well as when guests were present. By a force of her will she put aside her animosity toward Sinclair and came to appreciate what he had done for her despite what he believed about her. Although she knew Lucy's affection for her motivated Adam's largesse, she had to acknowledge that he was an honorable man in every way. In his treatment of her, he proved the perfect gentlemen.

As her rancor decreased, a warm give and take developed between the two, and soon Adam depended on her more and more. He astounded her when he suggested she take over the household accounts. It was obvious at this point that he had put aside his distrust of her, which amazed her since he thought she had stolen a valuable piece of jewelry.

Finally one night when Lucy had left the dinner table early and only the two of them remained, she asked him, "Mr. Sinclair..."

He gave her a heartwarming smile and interrupted, "Don't you think it is time to call me Adam?"

"I, er, I don't know about that."

"Well, I do. I'm much more comfortable being referred to as Adam in the intimacy of my own table."

"Exactly what does this entail?" Elizabeth asked, wariness at this new development.

He paused before answering. "Nothing except one friend addressing another. It means nothing beyond that, Elizabeth. I believe my actions thus far have been honorable, and I promise that they will be in the future."

"Thank you, Adam. That eases my mind, and, with all that has gone on before, I consider it an honor that you think of me as a friend rather than foe." Elizabeth responded, relieved as well as touched by his answer.

"You had a question for me?"

"Yes. It has been a mystery to me why you have placed so much responsibility on me, especially administering the household accounts if you think I am a thief."

Adam leaned back in his chair and, placing his fingertips together, remained quiet for several moments as if searching for the right words. Then he answered, "If I say I believe you have been completely rehabilitated that would offend you or make you angry, and I don't want that. Neither do I believe that would be the whole truth."

"You still believe I stole the ring?"

"I have come to believe that to say you 'stole' the ring is too harsh. I would rather say you 'took' the ring."

Elizabeth rolled her eyes, amber sparks igniting, "What is the difference between 'stole' and 'took?'"

"To steal something is to take an item that isn't yours or you have no right to. To take something that doesn't belong to you without permission is wrong also, but sometimes a person will do that when they feel entitled to it. It still doesn't make it right, but there is a logical explanation for why it happened."

"So that's what you've come to believe?" Elizabeth asked, steel threading her voice, her lip in a tight line.

"Yes. You must have been made some promises that proved to be lies. When you found out, you took the ring because you felt entitled to it and needed it for a better life. It was wrong, but I can understand how you must have felt."

"So how have you come to that conclusion?" Only the flexing of her jaw revealed the effort to control her temper.

"Being around you, getting to know you. In short, Elizabeth, my judgment of you was insensitive. You have won my trust. It's like Aunt Lucy said, how can we know what circumstances may have brought you to that point? What we know of you is decent and honorable. You have been a positive addition to our household. Does that answer your question?"

She nodded her head and rose from the table before he could see her tears. When this war ended and she was no longer at risk of imprisonment, this man would hear her story completely. Then he would understand and perhaps regret. As for why Philip made no response, perhaps part of what Adam said was true. The ring was payment for promises broken.

Meanwhile Adam watched her retreating figure, a strange sensation gripping his heart.

On November 16 when Sherman began his march through Georgia to the sea, he believed that the Confederacy's economic and psychological capability could be irrevocably broken. As a result, his scorched earth plan required his troops to burn crops, kill livestock and to live off the land. He planned the route his march would take place by studying the livestock and crop production information from the 1860 census. He would march through areas where he could send out "bummers" to forage most effectively. What they didn't need they would destroy. He ordered the destruction of all cotton gins and storage bins because Southerners used cotton to barter for guns and other supplies. His men tore up the railroad and heated the rails. The rails they twisted and left wrapped around trees became known as Sherman's neckties. It was the first time a commander had left his supply lines behind and set out to live on the land only. His plan caused consternation in Washington.

On December 21 when Sherman occupied Savannah, he wired the president "I beg to present you as a Christmas gift, the city of Savannah with one hundred and fifty guns, plenty of ammunition, and twenty-five thousand bales of cotton."

To which Lincoln replied on the day after Christmas, "Many, many thanks for your Christmas gift, the capture of Savannah. When you were leaving Atlanta for the Atlantic coast, I was anxious, if not fearful; but feeling that you were the better judge, and remembering that 'nothing risked, nothing gained', I did not interfere. Now the undertaking being a success, the honor is all yours."

While Sherman had moved his devastation through Georgia, Hood turned his attention toward Tennessee, hoping to lure the Northern general from his destructive march. Sherman sent Thomas to counter Hood and once again the battle lines reached Tennessee. Hood suffered severe losses in Franklin but remained determined to attempt capturing Nashville. The battle of Nashville took place on December 15 and 16 where Gen Hood was soundly defeated. He then retreated to Tupelo where he resigned his commission.

As the war moved toward its inevitable end, Sherman continued his scorched earth march into South Carolina while business as usual continued in Tennessee which remained firmly in the North's control.

When the frigid winds of November arrived, Elizabeth had buried her hope that Philip would come. She prayed that somehow, some way that Balmara had been out of the line of fire and that her dear friends had safely wintered there. She prayed that somehow Andrew remained with Rachel. Thinking of them brought back unwarranted memories of Philip and the sweet times they shared at Sweetwater. Reminiscences she tried to push aside because unanswered questions of 'why' flooded her mind, threatening her newly found serenity.

While concern for her Georgia friends and heartache over Philip lay heavy in Elizabeth's heart, she reveled in the distraction of the approaching Christmas season. On the heels of Hood's defeat, Adam decided that Christmas would be a festive celebration. He announced at dinner one night that he would like to invite some friends in for the holidays and perhaps have a dinner party or two. Lucy looked at her young friend and lifted a surprised brow.

Afterwards when the two had a chance to talk, Elizabeth asked her friend why she was so surprised by her nephew's announcement. Lucy chuckled. "Have you noticed any visitors in this home?"

"Come to think of it, no. I've never thought about it much, but you are right. Why is it? Does Adam not have any friends?"

"He used to. He and Rose had many friends. In the past each holiday would find the house filled with guests. Everyone coveted an invitation."

"Rose?"

Aunt Lucy frowned. "I suppose it is time that I told you Adam's story."

Elizabeth nodded. "Beginning with Rose."

"Rose was Adam's wife. Beautiful beyond measure, and they were so much in love. It was like being in sunlight just to be near them;

then tragedy struck."

"What happened?"

"Rose was expecting a baby. They were ecstatic about it. She was an excellent horsewoman and refused to give up her rides. Adam was against it, but because he loved her so, he always gave in to her. He insisted that she not ride alone but to wait for him. He had to be away on business for several weeks, and she became restless and decided to ride anyway. It was a brisk fall day and the horses were full of vigor. It was just the way she liked them so she let her mount have his head. They were running like the wind out across a field in which she normally avoided. Her horse stepped in a hole and fell, throwing her off. Her head hit a rock, and she never regained consciousness. Of course the baby was lost as well. All these years he has blamed himself for allowing her to ride. I have tried to convince him that it was not his fault. Rose rode that day in direct opposition to his wishes. The fault was hers, not Adam's."

Sorrow for her benefactor gripped her heart. "And all the social functions stopped?"

Lucy nodded. "He said without her, he wouldn't know where to begin."

"But now he has made a beginning."

"Yes, now he has you." Lucy remarked a strange look in her eyes.

Christmas and New Year's festivities ran smoothly, thanks to Elizabeth's efficient and gracious planning. The guests enjoyed themselves and clamored for more of the same. They thanked Elizabeth for the hospitality, even while they seemed puzzled by the beautiful woman in an exquisite blue gown, who neither danced nor visited with the guests. One who seemed content to remain in the background directing every servant, assuring that every part of the festivities was a success.

Meanwhile, more than one inquisitive male asked Adam about the mysterious brunette who directed the festivities but took no part in them. To which he replied, "A dear and trusted friend who is a companion for my aunt."

"But she doesn't dance?" they would ask.

"She declares she is too busy," came his curt reply.

Many went away shaking their heads. From the way Lucy Sinclair whirled around the floor with one partner after another, it seemed she hardly needed a companion. Perhaps it was Adam who needed a companion. After all it had been five years, and he was still in his prime. Perhaps he was having second thoughts about his vow to never marry again. How sad to grow old alone, not to have children to carry on his name to inherit his fortune.

Following her success as hostess during the holidays, Elizabeth and Adam enjoyed many evenings during the cold winter nights of January and February sipping hot chocolate before a roaring fire where they discussed a book that one of them had recently enjoyed. Even Elizabeth found it hard to deny the enjoyment of those evenings and to admit the companionship nurtured her soul. For brief moments she would forget the reason she was there or the false ideas that Adam had of her. When she did, the camaraderie proved even more pleasant.

As March approached, Adam suggested a Saint Patrick's Day ball. Elizabeth shot him a puzzled look. Then her gaze shifted from his eyes to his hair and back again.

He chuckled, "Now you know my secret."

She showered a brilliant smile on him. "What a dunce I am, never put that copper hair and green eyes in context."

"Now that you know, what are you going to do about it?" he teased.

"Throw you the biggest party you've ever seen!"

"On one condition."

She smiled. "You name it."

"That you order yourself a ball gown, give me a dance and enjoy this party."

"But I need to...."

"Delegate some of your responsibility. I had quite a few questions during the holidays concerning your not dancing."

"Oh, you just want to waylay any considerations of just what my role is here,"she said in jest. "How 'bout I make an announcement that I am not a slave nor am I held here against my will, nor any other untoward circumstances."

Suddenly Adam grew serious and picked up her small hand, placing it between his two large ones. "But sometimes I fear you are."

"Are what?" Elizabeth asked, discomfort growing at the path their conversation took.

"A slave, here against your will."

Elizabeth pulled her hand from his and sighed, "Adam, there are still unresolved issues between us. I know they will be resolved someday but until then, I remain here because I want to. Besides I have no other place to go."

"But you work so hard, much harder than anyone in my employ. By the way, have I told you lately that you are doing a superb job?"

"Work has a therapeutic effect. It can help to keep heartache at bay. I believe you can understand that."

"Aunt Lucy told you about Rose."

"Yes, and I'm so sorry. I know what it means to lose someone you love. But I can hardly imagine the loss you must have felt losing both wife and baby." Elizabeth shook her head as if the thought were too painful to consider.

"The first three years were hellish. Then as you say, I threw myself into work, but all the fortune I've amassed could not fill that empty void that Rose left. I said I would never marry again because I could never find anyone else I could love like I did her. It wouldn't be fair."

"You are young. Maybe someday ....'

"Yes, maybe someday. I've been thinking more about it of late. I am still a fairly young man, and at times I have been very lonely. By the way, the evenings we have spent together have been very enjoyable to me. I hope they were to you."

An impudent sparkle flickered in Elizabeth's eyes, "Extremely so after we put our differences to rest!"

Adam laughed. "Well, yes. We don't want to tread those waters anytime soon."

Elizabeth's eyes grew somber, "Soon, Adam, we will revisit the issues between us. Then I will prove to you that what you have believed about me has no foundation."

"Perhaps now?" Adam asked.

Elizabeth shook her head. "This is not the time, but very soon all this misunderstanding will be resolved."

The day of the ball dawned clear and glorious. For once spring visited early, and the birds chirped in the cherry trees whose tight buds promised a fruitful harvest. North of Nashville, the South was in its final agony as the nine-month siege of Petersburg drew to a close. No one attending the gala that night thought of the bloody battlefield or the young lives being snuffed out defending a cause that was lost before it ever began.

The ballroom glowed with shimmering lights, the ladies decked out in their finest ball gowns and the banquet table set with a feast that defied there had ever been shortages. Elizabeth took her final peek around the rooms, making certain everything was in order before she took her leave to get dressed in the new ball gown fashioned to accent her lovely figure. The emerald green silk organza gown enhanced the rich tones in her dark hair, and excitement flushed her cheeks. She looked in the mirror and was satisfied. Hard work and healthy habits had returned the vitality to her skin which looked smooth and creamy. Her hair, pulled up in a cascade of brunette curls, revealed a slender perfectly shaped neck that begged for adornment.

Just as she finished dressing, Mable, the upstairs maid, knocked on her door, then opened it and entered holding a jeweler's box. "Mr. Adam say he wants me to put these on you."

Elizabeth frowned and opened the box. There nestled against the burgundy velvet rested a perfectly matched string of pearls and a pair of diamond and pearl earrings. She gasped, "I can't wear these."

"Oh, yez, ma'am, you can. Mr. Adam done tolt me, and I be in a heap big trouble if'n you don't," Mable protested.

"Where is Mr. Sinclair? Give them to me."

"He be in his study."

Grabbing the box, Elizabeth ran down the hall to Adam's upstairs study that connected to his bedroom suite. She knocked on the door and called his name.

He walked out of his bedroom into his study and stopped, mesmerized at what he saw. Beauty beyond description greeted him, and Adam Sinclair stood there in danger of losing his heart for the sec-

413

ond time in his life.

He pursed his lips, then commented, "A vision of loveliness if I ever saw one. The dress was a perfect selection. There is no doubt who will be belle of the ball tonight. Remember to save at least one dance for me."

His admiration startled Elizabeth. For a moment she paused speechless, then remembered her errand and responded, "Why thank you Adam. The dress is lovely."

"No, my dear. It is you who are lovely; the dress is merely an adornment. Now did you need something?"

"Oh, yes. I can't possibly wear this jewelry."

He frowned. "Why not?"

"They are much too valuable, and they must have been your wife's."

He sighed, "Oh, I see."

"No, you don't see. I feel that I would be somehow treading on her memory."

Adam smiled, "Not at all, my dear. Those were my Grandmother's. They belong to Lucy, and she wants you to have them."

"I couldn't possibly take them. They are far too valuable, and I'm sure they need to be passed down in your family."

"To Aunt Lucy, you are family. It would mean a great deal to her if you would accept them and wear them."

"What about you?"

"It would please me very much if you would," he replied simply.

"But if I remember correctly, it is a piece of jewelry that stands between us."

"Not anymore. I've satisfied myself as to why you took the ring. You felt that you were in the right, that it was payment for broken promises. Since we never heard from Duval , I have to agree. There will be no more talk of it."

A half-smile teased Elizabeth's full lips as she corrected quietly, "Oh, yes there will, Adam. There will be one more conversation about it, and then it will be over."

She turned from him, pearls in hand and made her way down the hall leaving a puzzled Adam in her wake.

When the music began, Adam's prediction came true. Nashville had a new belle of the ball. Every young swain invited stood in line to sign her card. Finally when the last song began, Adam broke to the front of the line and whisked her out onto the floor. His eyes devoured her beauty; a new awakening fired his green eyes.

The following weeks went by in a whirl. Adam invited Elizabeth to ride with him each evening, delighted that she was an accomplished horsewoman. A fact that puzzled him even more when he considered her background. They spent each night together in the library and enjoyed a roaring fire on cold March evenings while discussing every subject imaginable except her past and the war.

On a bright spring day the last week in March, Adam ordered a picnic lunch and invited Elizabeth for a ride and a picnic down by the river. He had chosen a spot far away from the treacherous trail and sandy beach where he found her, but rather a grassy knoll overlooking the slow moving water. He had taken her to the far reaches of his estate, explaining his business endeavors and his plan to turn his stables into award winning stock.

Elizabeth thoroughly enjoyed the day. She could scarcely remember a day since the war began that she had relaxed and enjoyed a day packed with simple pleasures. The food superb, the ride stimulating, and Adam's company satisfying. He had planned it all.

Despite the conflict that lay between them, her affection for Adam and respect for the man he was grew with each passing week. She had come to realize that his core values dictated his personhood, and those values were the reason he had chosen to rehabilitate her from what he thought was her former life. That he could try to assist her, knowing what he believed about her, spoke to a depth of character that she had to admire.

They dismounted and sat down beside a babbling brook to consume the last crumbs of their lunch. Both laughed as they scrapped every last morsel from the basket. The ride, the conversation, the companionship had proved a respite for both Adam and Elizabeth. The sun sank low in the horizon before they had finished. Adam remarked that night would fall shortly, and they needed to go. He stood up and offered Elizabeth a hand. He pulled her to her feet, and then drew her into the circle of his arms. She offered no resistance, just looked up into his eyes, hers questioning. A struggle raged in his.

He bowed his head, his face in her hair, the fragrance of lavender filling his nostrils. His breath was ragged, and finally he spoke.

"Elizabeth, when Rose died I vowed I would never love another, never marry again. But lately I realized that I am lonely. I need a wife. These weeks with you have been wonderful, and I have come to have great affection, maybe even love, for you."

Elizabeth stepped back, leaning against his embrace. He raised his head, and she gazed into his eyes. "Do you realize what you are saying, Adam?"

"Certainly. I want you to be my wife."

"Even with what you believe is my less than honorable past?"

"I don't care about your past anymore. I know there is some good explanation for it. In my eyes you are a lady in every way and trustworthy beyond fault."

"You trust me?"

"With my life."

"You do me a great honor Adam to ask me to be your wife, but I fear your perception of my past would be too great a barrier. And then there is Rose," she reminded quietly.

"When God forgives us our past, those sins are gone, my sweet. As far as I am concerned, your past has been wiped clean. And the issue with Rose... I will always love her, but my heart is big enough to love another. Have you never loved anyone, Elizabeth?"

Tears filled her eyes and spilled over as she whispered, "Oh, yes. I loved Philip, with all my heart."

"Do you still love him?"

"I have tried to quit loving him, but I can't."

"Would that keep you from loving me?"

"That's not the problem. You see, Philip has betrayed me and because of that a wall of protection encircles my heart. I don't know if I can ever love, ever trust again."

"I will wait. I will chip away at that wall until you can love me with all your heart."

Elizabeth placed a tender caress on Adam's cheek and whispered, "You are a noble man, Adam Sinclair, and I am honored that you have offered me your love and protection this day."

Adam took her hand and kissed it. "I can wait until you are ready."

Meanwhile the war marched on relentlessly to its conclusion. On April fifth, Richmond was evacuated and on April ninth, Lee surrendered what was left of his rag tag army. Although throughout the month and the months to follow small areas of resistance would surrender, for all practical purposes the hostilities had ended. Tired and hungry troops dispersed to return to a splintered and broken South that would take decades to recover. With the war's end, Elizabeth's fear of imprisonment ended.

When the news of Lee's surrender reached Nashville and the palatial home on the Cumberland River, Elizabeth was seated in the library pouring over the household accounts. When Adam returned from Nashville with the news, he took the steps two at a time calling her name as he strode through the house.

"Elizabeth, this god-forsaken war is over. At last, the killing will stop."

She stood up, her face aglow, and turned toward him. Whisking her off the floor, he whirled her around like a small doll and then planted a lingering kiss on her upturned lips."

Stunned by his passion, she became very still. When he released her, his eyes danced with merriment, "I've been wanting to do that for a very long while. Today was a good excuse. Here, let me try it again!"

She stepped back and pushed him away, a merry laugh caught in her throat, "Behave yourself, Adam Sinclair, before I call your aunt."

He threw back his head and laughed. "She would encourage me on."

"Oh she would, would she? We'll just see about that."

He started toward Elizabeth again, and she sidestepped him, her arms outstretched in defense, "Now let me soak this all in. Times will go back to normal. I can return to Winchester."

Adam stopped, all merriment drained from his face. "What are you talking about?"

"Did you not remember that I said I am from Virginia?"

"I remember your tale," he responded. "Don't you understand, my love? You no longer have to stick to that story. I have wiped your past away. If you will become Mrs. Adam Sinclair, you will only have a present and a future. Past times will be forgotten."

Elizabeth took Adam's hand and led him over to the ample love-seat built for two. "Adam, we need to talk. I told you that someday we would settle the issue between us. It is true I am from Winchester, Virginia. I was exiled from my home by a cruel general by the name of Milroy."

"So that's why you did what you did. To survive."

"No. Some women chose to resort to that, but I didn't. I have friends who rescued me and took me to a home in North Georgia. The man who rescued me was Philip ."

Adam got very quiet, a thunderous expression on his face.

"Because Philip was a British citizen and neutral, he was able to get us out of there and take us to my friend's family near Marietta."

"And I guess he exacted payment from you."

"Absolutely not. He was the kindest, most considerate man that I had ever met. Which is why I am at a loss as to his recent behavior. After many weeks at my friend's home, we fell in love, and I agreed to marry him. He wanted to marry me right away, but I insisted that he get his father's blessing before I would marry him. So he went away. Not long after he left, I received that ring you hold in the mail. That's the last I heard from him. Since you have had no response, I can only assume that he could not get his father' blessing and as you said, I should consider the ring as payment for broken promises. Of course I wouldn't. I shall return it to him at first opportunity."

"That explains the ring, but what about the river? What were you doing in the river?"

"The first thing you need to know is that the women who were rowed out to that boat in the middle of the river were not prostitutes but innocent women who were taken prisoner by General Sherman and charged with treason. I don't know what might have happened to those poor women when they dumped them in that ship full of men, but beforehand, they were innocents unduly imprisoned."

Adam's ruddy complexion turned ashen as Elizabeth relayed the rest of her story to him. "My dear, will you ever forgive me? Why didn't you tell me the whole story?"

"Because I thought you would send me back to the authorities. I couldn't stand the thought of prison. You were kind and provided for me well here. I had a chance to work for my keep, and I hope I earned my way."

Adam took both of her hands in his and raised them to his lips, "Can you ever forgive me?"

"There is nothing to forgive. You have a kind heart, a gentle spirit and strong principles. If you hadn't, I would be in a worse place than prison. But there is the question of what to do with the ring. Of course I don't want to keep it. We must find some way to return it to the family. It is an heirloom."

"Marry me, and we will return it when we take our honeymoon."

"That is quite a tempting order, but I do have some loose ends to tie up."

"Like what?"

"I need to see if my home in Winchester survived the war. Most of all, I want to find out about my friends who evacuated to Savannah. How did they fair during Sherman's march? Rachel's baby, did Josh and Andrew survive the war? I know they had to report back. They needed every man they could muster."

Adam nodded sympathy softened the light in his green eyes. "Yes,

I heard that even young boys from the academy were opposing Sherman's forces. I understand your concern for your friends."

"They were so gracious and kind to me, but, beyond that, I love Rachel and Laura as if they were my sisters by birth."

"I will find out about them. I will start right away."

"Beyond that there is a question of my resources and how to access them."

"Mine are at your disposal."

"It might surprise you to know that I am quite wealthy in my own right."

"That's hard to believe when I have seen how hard and diligent you labor. No spoiled rich woman works like you."

Elizabeth laughed with abandon. "I have not always been wealthy. I am a wealthy widow whom my parents married off to an abusive older man because of his affluence. They never realized what a beast of a man he was. They only looked at his outward trappings."

"No wonder your heart is encased in protection."

She nodded. "I thought that Philip was different so I let my guard down, and now look at what's happened."

Pain flared in Adam's eyes, "Don't fret, my pet. I never want to hear that man's name again and if I ever see him…. Well I just won't be responsible for my actions."

"Something must have happened to him. I can't believe he would treat me like that. Abandoned without a word. That's a coward's way, and I could have sworn that Philip is no coward."

"Perhaps it was a case of family approval. The British are a stickler for class distinction."

"I can understand, but not to respond to your inquiries makes no sense." Elizabeth mulled.

"Cowardice is the only answer."

Elizabeth laughed, brittle, not from the heart, "Be careful that you don't jump to another wrong conclusion."

"Perhaps I have an ulterior motive this time." Adam observed.

"That being what? "

"To prove to you that I'm more worthy of your love than he," he confessed.

Elizabeth patted his hand. "Adam, you are worthy of any woman's love. You have everything a woman wants in a husband."

He smiled. "And that is?"

"Handsome, considerate, strong moral values, compassionate, courageous and might I add, very wealthy." She smiled, giving him an impish grin.

He smiled and patted her hand, "After those loose ends are tied up, how about marrying me?"

"Let's tie them up first."

"It will be a while before you can travel. I could make some inquiries about your home."

"Would you? It might save me a long tedious journey."

"It would not be possible for you to go up there for at least a few months, now what other 'loose ends' are dangling?"

"My money is safe in England so that's not a pressing need."

"In England?" Adam inquired.

"Yes. When the war looked inevitable I transferred most of my assets to a bank in England, just in case."

A broad grin spread Adam's lips, "Not only is she beautiful and accomplished in all the social graces but also she is a wise business woman."

"However, what I didn't transfer was lost, so at the moment my wealth is not available to me.

I do need something to live on and to pay you back for a beautiful ball gown and my upkeep for all these months."

"The dresses were a gift, and your upkeep was earned by your work. Consider any liability more than satisfied. And as for future needs, let me provide for you as your husband."

"It's too early to even think along those terms. Please be patient with me, Adam."

"I'm willing to wait as long as it takes."

"What if I continue to work for you as I have been doing to earn my keep until I can return to Virginia?"

"You can work for me until the cows come home!!!!! What a difference you have made in my household, both with the master, his staff and his belongings."

"Thanks, Adam. I look forward to those evenings of conversation and companionship we have grown to enjoy."

"You mean those wonderful moments when I realized I was falling in love with you."

"Please, no pressure."

Adam threw up his hands in surrender, "Your timing, my Darling."

April drifted into mid May before Adam was able to garner any information about Elizabeth's home. When word did arrive, it was good news. Her home had been spared. It had suffered some damage from the multiple battles that took place in Winchester, but it stood. However, when he received word from Savannah, the news proved disturbing. He told her that somehow Sherman's sweep had missed Balmara. It had suffered no damage, but her friends were not there. In fact, the plantation was deserted. Elizabeth's heart fell. What could have happened? She never considered that they had not made the safety of Balmara. Where could they be? Were they even alive? Had they been imprisoned also? Disturbing visions of what might have happened clamored her mind, and she shook her head as she wept for her friends.

Adam took her in his arms to comfort her, and her tears soaked his jacket. He gently patted her back and promised that one way or another, he would find her friends or at least what had happened to them.

It took the full month of May before all pockets of hostility ceased. Adam refused to let Elizabeth go until he was certain that adequate rail service had been established and her safety secured. He implored her to allow him to go with her, but she adamantly refused. It was a journey she must take alone. When he insisted she take a maid with her, she finally acquiesced, and they made plans for her return the last week in June.

Elizabeth placed the final garment into the reticule. Her steamer trunk stood in the corner, packed with the new garments that Adam had insisted she acquire before returning home. Of course he was right. It would be quite a while before circumstances evened out, and normalcy returned. She had no idea what she would face when she arrived in Winchester.

She opened the door to her room to encourage the cool breeze that drifted in from the bank of windows. She heard the wheels of a carriage crunching in the drive and pondered what business Adam had to attend to this morning. Maybe it was someone with word about Andrew and Rachel. Her heart ached with the thought she would be leaving tomorrow without any assurance that they had survived and were well. With only one more day here, perhaps today would be that day.

She knew that even after she left, Adam would continue his search. He had made a commitment to her, and he would fulfill it. He was just that kind of man...a man of his word. A soft smile illumined her face. She could do much worse. A future alone did not appeal to her. She was young and Adam was a man of integrity and kindness. She felt that she could come to love him someday. Perhaps not with the same intensity or passion she had felt for Philip, but it would be a good match. She would find no problem in devoting the rest of her life to making him happy. But was that enough? She pushed the thought away.

The doorbell chimed sending its pleasant sounds throughout the hall and drifting up to her room. She smiled. Adam would answer it. He always did when he was expecting a business associate. She turned to the mirror to smooth her hair. He might want his guest to stay for dinner and more often than not she, rather than Lucy, officiated as hostess. She paused, then frowned as angry shouting rose from the hall below.

Adam had stridden from his study toward the door. He was expecting Aaron Burton from Nashville, but it was a bit early for Burton' arrival. He hoped instead that it would be news about Elizabeth's friends. He so wanted to give her good news before she left tomorrow. He had spent a small fortune trying to locate them. Maybe today it would pay off.

When he reached the door to open it, he came face to face with a tall handsome stranger. Puzzled Adam asked, "What can I do for you, sir? "

"I am Philip Duval, and I have come to collect what is mine."

Anger flushed Adam Sinclair's face, "You mean you have come for your ring?"

"Yes. And some answers as to how it came into your possession."

"You are a rascal if I've ever met one. First you make her wild promises that you fail to keep. Then you break her heart by abandoning her. Now you want your ring. What kind of man are you?" Adam shouted.

"Failed to keep promises?"

"Yes, you go off to England, forsake her to a fate worse than death, send her a ring and never another word from you. Then demand your ring back. What happened? Did your father think you were marrying too far beneath you? It will take years before her heart heals."

"Mister, I don't know what you are talking about. What I do want to know is how and where you obtained my ring," Philip demanded, then shook his head as if something Adam said just connected. Narrowing his eyes, he grabbed the front of Adam's coat and murmured with clinched teeth, "What do you mean take years for her heart to heal?"

Suddenly Philip's eyes widened as he glimpsed a movement behind Sinclair. He shouted, "Elizabeth!"

Pushing Adam aside, he held out his arms, and she ran into his crushing embrace. "Oh, my Darling, they told me you were dead," he whispered as he kissed her forehead, her eyes, her cheeks and then her lips.

Tears streamed down both their cheeks as the truth dawned ... they were together at last.

Adam Sinclair quietly retreated, his heart contracted within him. He would know the story soon enough. What his eyes had observed, his heart recognized. Memories of the love he had once known flooded his being. He knew where Elizabeth belonged, and it was not with him.

Hours later he and Lucy heard the story of how Philip had searched and searched for her. The young Lord described the excruciating pain he had endured after Annie told him that Elizabeth had drowned.

Elizabeth interrupted, "Do you have any idea what has happened to Annie?"

Philip smiled and took her hand. "I secured her a place to live and gave her enough money to sustain her for several years or see her back home."

"Thank you, my dear. She had endured so much tragedy."

"Indeed she has, but I checked on her on the way here and found out that she has married a young man in Indiana and will make her home there. I met her young man and was very impressed. In fact, I'm afraid I rather envied their happiness."

"A happy ending to a tragic story."

"As ours will be."

"Perhaps, but why did you wait so long to respond to Adam's message? Surely you wanted your ring back."

"I didn't come right away because I wasn't sure I could endure having the ring back with all the memories it represented. In fact, I resented it. I blamed the ring for loosing you. Regret for having sent it to you tortured my soul."

"What changed your mind about responding?"

"I had to return to America to close my business interests here and I thought perhaps I could bring closure if the woman who had taken it would have some information about your last days. I never realized that the woman to which Sinclair referred was my very own love."

Philip also relayed to Elizabeth the good news that Andrew and Rachel were safe and the proud parents of a healthy baby boy. By some miraculous turn of events, Balmara lay outside the scope of Sherman's march and remained untouched except for the desertion of all the slaves.

Andrew had fought with General Hardee in the defense of Savannah. Josh had rejoined Wheeler's cavalry. They had continued the fight into the Carolinas where Andrew joined his old commander, Joe Johnston. He and Josh both escaped injury. When Johnston surrendered on April 26, both men were allowed to return home.

"But Adam checked. There is no one at Balmara," Elizabeth exclaimed.

A broad grin spread across Philip's face. "That's because they are in Boston. As soon as I arrived from England, I sent a steamer down to Savannah for them. All five of them are with Daphne."

Elizabeth frowned, "They are going to live in Boston?"

"No, I just wanted to see them. Because I thought I had lost you, I needed the comfort of my friends so I sent for them. It was Rachel who suggested that Adam might have some information that might help me."

"So what are their plans? Will they stay at Balmara?"

"Andrew gave Rachel the choice of returning to Sweetwater and building it again or Balmara. Can you guess what she said?"

Elizabeth rolled her eyes and chuckled. " Is there any doubt? Sweetwater of course."

"As a matter of fact, she didn't."

"What? I can't believe that."

"She told Andrew that she wanted to stay at Balmara. She wanted a new beginning for their lives together."

"So what are they going to do with Sweetwater?"

"I haven't told you the biggest news. Laura and Josh were married when he came back in May. They will return to Sweetwater to rebuild it and start a new life together. They seem perfectly happy to inhabit the overseer's cottage until Sweetwater can be rebuilt. Probably not on its formally grand scale but it will have their hopes and dreams invested in it."

"And what are your plans?" Elizabeth asked.

"To return to England and sort out the mess father had let our estates get into the last few years. Since I needed the extra funds to rehabilitate my estates, I sold Balmara back to Andrew. As for the ship building factory, I will retain it under the able management of Agan until he is able to purchase it."

Elizabeth's face fell, and she remarked, "Sounds like you have a full schedule ahead of you."

"I do. But first and foremost on my list is to make you my bride."

Pleasure flushed Elizabeth's cheeks, "You haven't changed your mind?"

"Never in a million years!"

"You think a Southern girl like me can execute the duties of a duchess?"

"With ease and grace." Philip smiled, his heart in his eyes.

A shadow dulled the light in Elizabeth's eyes and she looked down, not willing to meet his eyes, "And your father? Did you garner his approval before he died?"

"As a matter of fact, I did. And you were right, when I assured him that you had wealth of your own and weren't after our family fortune, he gave us his blessing and said that it would be an asset to introduce some new blood into our family tree."

"Then I take it, you reconciled with him before his death."

Philip nodded. "My return proved a sweet reunion. Too bad he didn't live long enough for us to enjoy our renewed relationship, but I feel that it was his illness that brought about the change in him. I am thankful he removed the obstacle to our marriage that you put in our way; so my love, let's call a preacher. I've waited much too long."

Sinclair and Lucy had sat quietly, mesmerized by the story and emotions playing out before them. Now Adam stirred and asked, "What about a Nashville wedding? That's the least I can do."

"How soon can you get the minister? This time I will not risk her getting a way."

"As soon as you want one."

"Tomorrow?"

Elizabeth laughed, "At least give me a week."

"Two days at the most."

"What about a dress?"

"Who cares about that? I'll buy you a ton of them later."

"I think I have a solution," Lucy spoke up. "And it won't take a week."

Elizabeth eyes brightened, "How so?"

"Our mother's wedding dress. She was about your size, and the dress is lovely."

"Are you sure you don't mind?"

"She would be honored to contribute to such a wonderful love story."

Adam tucked Elizabeth's hand in the curve of his arm. "Are you ready, my dear?"

She looked up at him, her eyes luminous and whispered,"More than ready."

Sorrow touched Adam's eyes for a moment bringing a tear to Elizabeth's. "Adam, I'm sorry."

He patted her hand, "I know, but it would have never worked for us."

"Perhaps."

He shook his head.

"Why do you think that?"

"Would you ever look at me the way you looked at him?"

Elizabeth couldn't speak. She patted his arm in understanding.

Adam continued, "Don't feel sad for me, Elizabeth. What you did for me was to point out a need in my life and the possibilities that I had denied. You made me realize that holding on to the past too tightly destroys the future. I thank you for that and everything else you have taught me. Now, I hear the organ and someone is waiting downstairs to claim you for his own. He has waited far too long."

Philip looked up from where he stood with the minister just as she appeared. Glowing, she was a vision wrapped in ivory lace and silk. His heart skipped a beat. In a few moments the minister would pronounce that she was his. God would approve, and tonight he would make her, his own for a lifetime. All the pain and heartache that he had endured paled in the joy of this moment. He was about to make his Beth the Lady Elizabeth. Indeed two would become a glorious one, and life would have a new beginning for both of them.

The End

Epilogue

While the characters, Sweetwater Plantation, and even Sweetwater Mill were figments of my imagination, the historical occurrences are accurate. The arrest and deportation of over 400 mill workers (with their children) from the New Manchester Mills on Sweetwater Creek and the Roswell Mills in Roswell, Georgia resulted from a little known, inhumane order issued by General Sherman in his quest to win the war at any cost. Transported in a cattle car in the stifling July heat, the hardship these women endured as they were sent north was intolerable and inexcusable. Their plight is well documented in the beautiful Sweetwater Park in Lithia Springs, GA.

While Col. Turner is also a fictitious character, the other generals and officers mentioned are historical figures their attitudes and actions verified by historical research.

General Milroy's ill treatment of the female residents of Winchester, VA during his occupation there is a historical fact. Although his conversation with Laura Meredith is fictitious, it properly reflects the historical records of his attitude and hatred of "Secesh" women as he called them.

War as it ushers in the loss of life and property is always tragic, but the war that divided our nation and pitted brother against brother proved the most deadly. The death toll reached 2% of the nation's population; the total deaths of 620,000 exceeded the casualties in both World Wars combined.

The tragedy of this war is documented when unreasonable men refuse to be reasonable.

MILITARY DEATHS IN AMERICAN WARS

Civil War:	620,000
World War II:	405,000
World War I:	116,516

CPSIA information can be obtained
at www.ICGtesting.com
Printed in the USA
BVHW030805160720
583605BV00004B/4